THE KING'S COMMANDER

By

John F. Schork

For Phil Jennings,

A Marine, a mentor, and a friend.

PROLOGUE

Oxford University
Oxford, England
August 1936

Two men walked down a narrow cobblestone street between the pale, yellow-brick buildings of one of the most famous universities in the world. The older man was in his 50s, tall with a full head of shortly cropped grey hair. He wore a sport coat and bowtie identifying him as a member of the local academic community. His companion was a young man casually dressed in slacks and a short-sleeved shirt. They were almost alone in the street, the academic year currently in summer recess. A quiet summer day for some, the two men were engaged in a lively conversation.

"We're going to miss you, Jack. You're sure you won't reconsider?" the older man asked.

"Ian, it's been a great year. Honestly, I don't think I had any idea what I was really getting into when I was selected for the program." They reached the set of steps leading into a large hall and stopped to face each other.

"Jack, you're one of the best science students I've ever known. If there's such a thing as a natural physicist, you're it. You'd be the perfect candidate to move forward for your doctorate and then into research." The professor set his briefcase on the ground, shoving both hands in his pockets and leaning back against the stair rail.

"As much as I may want to pursue that goal eventually,

I've got an obligation to repay my country for my education. I've gotta see how I can do as an aviator."

Ian Thompson was one of the senior lecturers in physics at Trinity College and had been Jack Stewart's faculty advisor for the last year. The young man had become an honorary member of the Thompson household and Ian didn't want to see him leave. "Ah yes, join the Navy, see the world and all that?" There was a hint of condescension in his voice.

"That's not totally fair, but I do want to see the world. This last year has made me even surer of that. You can appreciate that, can't you?"

"Of course I can, Jack. Believe it or not I was young once. I see such tremendous potential if you apply yourself to school. And I'll tell you, I'm not looking forward to dealing with Pamela when you leave."

Jack looked down at the ground. Ian had touched on the one real obstacle to his departure. He had met the professor's daughter on the day of his arrival. Over the ensuing year their relationship had deepened.

"Pam and I talked about this. I'm a Naval Officer now. I've got a set of orders that tell me to report to flight training next month. There's nothing I can do about that, but she knows it as well as I do. I don't know what's in my future. I could turn out to be a terrible pilot and get washed out. I'm not ready to go into flight training with a new wife. It wouldn't be fair to Pam, either."

"I suppose that's it then. Certainly I know you two have talked it over. I guess I'm just a bit selfish. You're entitled to that as you get older you know." The older man's shoulders sagged. "What time do you leave?"

"I'm on the 4 o'clock train. Pam's driving me to the station." said Jack, sounding both hesitant and excited.

"Did you get a chance to say good bye to Dicky?" Ian's son and Jack had become fast friends over the last year. Both of the young men shared a talent in physics, a love of rugby and many rounds in the local pubs.

2

Jack smiled. "I was able to catch him before he left for his match in Coventry. Wished him luck in the game and at the pub after the match. Not that he'll need it."

Ian offered a firm handshake. "You've got that right." His expression changed and there was a sad look in his eyes. "God speed, Jack. Safe journey and please stay in touch."

He picked up his case, squeezed Jack's shoulder and walked up the steps into the building.

Jack walked back down the street, dreading the idea of saying goodbye to Pam. He couldn't see any other options. As a young officer he needed to start flight training. He'd already accepted a one-year delay in his aviation career when he was selected for the Rhodes Scholar Program, so it was past time to get his naval career moving. His contemporaries were already wearing their aviator wings and building up flight hours.

Typically, he'd worked out everything besides a beautiful English girl entering the picture.

CHAPTER ONE

Alameda Naval Air Station
Oakland, California
November, 1942

The bartender walked down to the deserted end of the dimly lit bar and greeted the khaki-clad officer as he eased into a perch atop a high-backed wooden chair.

"What can I get you, Lieutenant?"

"A hot shower and 24 hours of uninterrupted rack time would be great, but a bourbon and water's gonna have to do."

"Beam okay?"

"More than. Make it a double while you're at it."

Grabbing a glass from a row of tumblers, the bartender put it on the bar in front of his customer. "Kitchen opens in 15 if you're looking for chow."

"Thanks. Do I look that bad?"

The bartender topped the ice cubes with several inches of the whisky. "We get lots of transients through here waitin' for flights. Food seems to come in a distant second request, right after a stiff belt." The heavy set man smiled as he set the drink on the bar.

"Guess the mileage's starting to show."

"Let me know if you want some food. Believe it or not, the burgers here are actually pretty edible," the bartender said as he headed to the other end of the bar.

Jack thanked him with more of a nod and grunt than a

full sentence and gulped half of the drink, looking at himself in the large mirror behind the bar. *Yeah, it's starting to show.*

He mentally reread the orders packed away in his bag, having committed them to memory days ago.

Stewart, Jack.

Lieutenant, United States Navy, 81854.

Detach and proceed on or about 15 November, 1942 from Tripler Army   Hospital to the Bureau of Aeronautics, Department of the Navy,   Washington, D.C. for duty.

He'd been able to arrange for a seat on an eastbound MARS flying boat of Navy Transport Squadron Two from Honolulu to San Francisco, or more specifically, to Alameda. Normally, an officer on travel orders to a new duty station would've been consigned to riding an Army transport ship for the weeklong drift from the islands to the states. But Jack had run into a roommate from the Annapolis, Mike Malone. Mike was an Aircraft Commander for Transport Squadron Two and regularly flew the San Francisco to Honolulu logistics run. When Jack mentioned he was getting ready to execute his orders, Mike told him he could get him a ride in the cockpit if he kept schtumm. Dreading the slow boat, Jack jumped at the chance to go by air.

After two days of waiting around a sweltering hangar for engine problems and weather-bound acts of God to subside, Jack couldn't help but wonder if his dwindling stores of youthful enthusiasm had cheated him out of a soft bunk. Funny how the tropics tend to lose their exotic sheen when the humidity hits a rusty building that already smelled like axle grease and stale tobacco.

The initial takeoff was an incident of professional interest to Jack. He'd been a Naval Aviator for nearly five years, but he'd never actually been aboard a flying boat. His world had consisted of single engine aircraft, most recently the Grumman F4F Wildcat. The brutal rhythm of the waves and the sheer size of the boat convinced him it was due to come apart at any moment. Just when Jack thought he was about to see a shower of rivets pop out of the airframe, Mike pulled back on the yoke and they were airborne. Over the next 11 hours he dozed, chatted with Mike, and wondered about his future with the itinerant lack of power over the proceedings that feels unique to life in the service.

Five months ago he'd been in the thick of the war. On the fast track professionally, he'd been spot promoted to Lieutenant. In a lucky chain of events he'd been assigned as the Operations Officer of Fighter Squadron 42 aboard the U.S.S. *Yorktown* (CV-5).

For a Naval Aviator, Jack was in the right spot at the right time. He'd joined 42 as a "fleet-experienced" aviator having spent his first sea tour in the Fighting 2, flying off the U.S.S *Lexington* (CV-2). It was harder work than he'd ever known, but two years of operational flying convinced him there was no better job in the world. He was flying the best fighter in the Navy, had a ready room full of friends who'd all kill and be killed for one another, and was seeing the world. The very real danger attendant to the job was something he learned to put out of his mind.

He'd adopted one of the core philosophies of aviation:

"it's always going to happen to the other guy".

Jack had been a company commander at the U.S. Naval Academy in Annapolis and his natural leadership abilities blossomed during his first tour. He quickly qualified as the skipper's wingman and within a year he, was a section leader. Then on to a division lead; which allowed him to command a four-aircraft division on operational missions.

When his tour of duty was ending with VF-2, the commanding officer approached him about going "sea duty to sea duty". VF-42, one of the fighter squadrons on the *Yorktown*, was getting ready to start workups. Their squadron operations officer had been medically grounded, and the skipper was looking for a pilot who was current in the Wildcat, had a good operational background and was a solid stick. The job included a "spot" promotion to Lieutenant, not a bad thing for his career. Jack didn't hesitate. Originally, he was under orders to be a flight instructor at Pensacola, but he hadn't been looking forward to spending his days trying to keep student aviators in the air.

Jack's transition from the Fighting Two couldn't have gone better. He was working for Jim McKenzie, one of the best officers and aviators he'd ever met. The skipper made being in the squadron a special experience. He trained his pilots hard, and they partied just as hard to compensate. Mckenzie emphasized air-to-air gunnery, division tactics and did as much night flying as possible. The result was a group of young aviators that were confident, combat ready, and not about to shrink from any challenge thrown their way.

Originally attached to the U.S.S. Ranger (CV-4), the squadron was based at the N.A.S. Norfolk in Virginia. Jack was in heaven. He had spent a lot of time nearby in Tidewater when he was at the Academy. Malone was from Norfolk and the two of them would spend weekends at Mike's parents' house on Summers Street.

As the clouds of war gathered in Europe, it became pretty obvious to the Atlantic Fleet aviators that it was not a matter of if there was going to be a war, but when. Despite the neutral rhetoric of the press and politicians, the military saw the inevitable and was doing everything they could to prepare. The war in the Atlantic was becoming more and more violent but the Navy was to maintain strict neutrality.

Fighter Squadron 42 was initially assigned to Yorktown for a routine patrol in September 1941. Their green-tailed Wildcat fighters were hoisted aboard the ship, which was destined to become their new permanent home. The F4F-3 was the newest fighter to roll off the Grumman assembly line in

Long Island and it'd become one of Jack's personal favorites. They were operating on the fringe of the war in the Atlantic, but he always wondered if there was a German U-boat watching the Yorktown through its periscope. They weren't destined to stay in the Atlantic, though. On the completion of that fall patrol, the decision was made to transfer Yorktown to the Pacific Fleet.

The whisky was doing its job and the aches and pains had dulled slightly, but noticeably. Despite the fact it was now happy hour, the bar was still deserted. Jack thought it might be a good time to get an order into the kitchen.

"Think I can get a hamburger out of your cook?" he asked the bartender. A burger had always been a great way to calm his stomach. It was his patented hangover cure in flight training when he'd overdone it the night before. No better way to get back on track for a flight than a burger, a Coke and a cigarette.

"Sure thing, how do you want it cooked?"

"Medium and if they could find some fries that'd be great."

"You bet," the barman said over his shoulder as he walked into the kitchen.

As Jack returned to contemplate his drink he noticed an army colonel looking around at the far end of the bar.

"Have you seen the bartender?"

"Yes, sir. He'll be right back. He's taking my order into the kitchen."

"How's the food here?"

"Depends on how much you trust bartenders, sir."

The colonel sat down with one stool separating them, draping his raincoat over the chair next to him. "Didn't I see you get off the Honolulu flight that just landed?"

"Yes, sir," he replied.

"You know, I didn't see you back in the cabin during the

flight. Were you flying the plane?"

"I wasn't the pilot in command," Jack replied.

"Name's Bob Miller." The Colonel extended his hand. "Where you headed?"

"Jack Stewart. Nice to meet you, sir. I'm on my way to D.C."

"Makes two of us. Bartender, could you bring me a scotch and water?"

Jack's food arrived and the Colonel ordered a club sandwich. They exchanged the usual banter about the drudgery of travel and the desire to finish their journeys.

Jack liked the manner of the older man. He seemed straightforward and pleasant. And he didn't seem overly impressed with the fact he was ranked considerably senior to Jack. His campaign ribbons told of active duty in the First World War.

"So what do they have you doing in Washington, Jack?"

"Not a clue, Colonel. I'm going to a large organization where I will occupy a small desk and move a lot of paper from one box to another." Sarcasm did not escape Bob Miller.

"Sounds like a staff job is not quite the dizzying heights you aspired to. Am I correct?"

"That, Colonel, would be an understatement," he said, shaking his head back and forth.

The Colonel smiled. "I think I know how you feel. I expect the greatest danger I'll face in this war'll be falling off a barstool, but all we can do is what they tell us to do and hope it makes a difference."

The Colonel asked for a refill and ordered Jack another drink. "I'm on the 2100 Union Pacific out of Oakland but there's always time for one more."

"I'm on the same train and I couldn't agree more."

The two newly cemented companions clinked glasses.

"Glad to be traveling with you, Jack."

The Union Pacific Flyer
Transiting Colorado

Colonel Bob Miller and Lieutenant Jack Stewart were just two of thousands of servicemen on the move as the United States accelerated to wartime footing. Their departure from Oakland had been noisy and hectic. A quick check with a conductor and they were able to get in the same sleeper car. The Pullman coach was on the male end of the train, a tactic adopted by the railways craving expediency while trying to move an ocean of men and a relatively scant few women. There were shower facilities at each end of the train and sleeper cars for each sex. The common ground was the double dining car, which was situated a third of the way back from the hulking, cacophonous diesel engines propelling them east.

Jack heard a knock on his door and opened it to find Miller, who he hadn't seen since they both headed for their compartments the night before.

"Morning, Jack. Catch up on your sleep?" the Colonel asked.

Jack did feel good, considering he didn't have a hangover and he'd been able to get a hot shower. "Come in, Colonel. I was thinking about how I was going to put up with two more days of scenery until we get to Chicago."

The older man moved to the unoccupied bunk and sat down. "I've found passing rail time most effectively is best served by a carefully calculated ratio of good books to better scotch."

"Your seniority knows no bounds, Sir."

Jack liked Miller. He was a lot more relaxed than the senior Naval officers he'd encountered. Most of them were more concerned with buttressing the trappings of bureaucracy and their own ascensions than really getting to know their men. His squadron commanding officers were the exception. They'd been lieutenant commanders, the Navy's equivalent of major. In addition, they were aviators. There was a big difference between the officers who served aboard the Navy's surface ships, the "black shoes" and the small group of officers that made up Naval Aviation. He was a "brown shoe" and was proud of the brown boots he wore with his aviation working green uniform. Aviators didn't sweat the small stuff.

"Jack, I'm sure it's no different in the Navy. One of the principal responsibilities of an officer is the care and training of his troops." There was a twinkle in his eye. "And as the senior officer present I feel I must do my best to demonstrate the correct procedure for spending a quiet afternoon on the Union Pacific Flyer en route to Chicago." Miller stood up. "Lt. Stewart, put on your uniform blouse and stand ready to sortie with me to locate that bottle of scotch. I'll conduct the first training lesson."

Twenty minutes later they were in Miller's room with two tumblers of scotch and water on the table between them. They gazed out the window at the stands of pine trees passing the window in the late afternoon sunshine. They filled the ensuing two hours with easy conversation.

Robert Randolph Miller was not your typical army colonel. He'd been recalled to active duty in 1940 from his law practice in San Diego. An infantry officer in the Great War, he'd seen heavy combat on the Western Front. As a graduate of San Diego State University he knew it would have been futile to contemplate a career in the Army following the war. He left running the peacetime army to the West Point types and returned to sunny California. Miller got married and began a successful practice as an attorney.

In 1940, he received a letter from a friend and fellow attorney he'd met during his time in Europe. Miller thought the world was headed into another war, but he assumed he'd be standing on the sidelines this time. After all, he was 47. Too old to be a serving infantry officer. But things have a way of working out. His friend had also been called to government service and needed help. That was how Bob Miller, a respected attorney in San Diego, became the Deputy Director for Operations of the Office of Strategic Services under his old friend, Major General William "Wild Bill" Donovan.

Jack intrigued Miller. Perhaps it was his new job, or maybe it was just his unshakeable sense of attorney's curiosity. Either way, he was going to get to know him better during this trip. Miller glossed over his own specific job and organization by telling Jack he worked in"public relations", which was true to a useful degree. The rest of his background was the truth, though. He referenced his time on the Western Front at the end of the last war. He talked about law school and starting his own practice, but Miller wanted to learn more about Jack. A question volleyed Jack's way here and there kept him filling in the details of how he came to be sitting on a train in the middle of Colorado.

Jack was unmarried, a graduate of the Naval Academy, class of 1935 and a qualified Naval Aviator. He' grown up in Seattle and Annapolis was his first time away from home. He'd apparently done well academically, and was selected as a Rhodes Scholar; the only one in his class. The program delayed the start of flight school but he'd been able to travel to England and Europe. Quite an adventure for a young man from Seattle. He studied physics and thought he might be able to use that in industry if his naval career didn't pan out.

It took a fair amount of scotch before Miller got him to talk about more recent events in his life.

"Jack, it seems unusual for a qualified Naval Aviator to be heading back to a desk job with a war in the Pacific that's being fought by carrier task forces. You said you'd been grounded by a medical board in Hawaii?"

Jack had been reluctant to talk about his time flying off the *Yorktown*. He wasn't sure why, most aviators are notorious for telling war stories. But he felt empty when he thought about what had happened and how it changed his life. "Colonel, I'm officially 'NPQ.' Not physically qualified for duty. So, for the foreseeable future I'm gonna be a paper pusher, not a fighter pilot."

"What happened, if you don't mind me asking?" Miller said quietly.

"I had to jump out of an F4F at Midway. I hit the empennage, or tail, as you'd call it. I was lucky enough to be picked up by a destroyer. Between my back and head I was sent to Hawaii for treatment and evaluation." Jack stopped for a moment, remembering the time in the hospital, alone and trying to come to grips with the battle. He took another long drink of scotch and continued.

"After three months I went before a board of flight surgeons. They decided I wasn't medically able to fly as a pilot in command. Simple as that, a bunch of ground pounders clipped my wings. Not much room for an appeal with a medical board so they reassigned me to the Bureau of Aeronautics." What he didn't tell the Colonel, what he could never tell anyone was he was shot down, along with his wingman because he was pressing for a last kill. A victory which would have made him an "ace". He survived, but Terry Simpson didn't. Terry was one ghost Jack was having trouble living with.

Miller said nothing, waiting for Jack to continue.

This was the time to let the client talk.

"In the great scheme of things, my situation isn't a big deal. I lost a lot of good friends at Coral Sea and Midway. I just thought I could make a contribution to this war flying airplanes, not as a rear echelon paper pusher. This country is in the biggest war in its history. I was trained to be a Navy fighter pilot and I think I'm pretty good at it. But now it looks like I'm gonna spend it flying a desk in D.C. while my squadron mates are out there taking the fight to the Japs." Jack knew he should shut up and let it drop, but the scotch and the company had loosened his posture and his tongue. He'd been looking straight ahead and turned to Miller, "Sorry, I'm still pissed about the medical board. I know my job is to follow orders and I'll do that. It's just something I have to get used to. At least I'm here."

Miller wasn't sure what to make of Jack's outburst. "I can't put myself in your place. This war's already changed so many lives and before it's over, the world will be a very different place. I just hope those of us that fit into the 'old or broken' category can make a difference. I'll tell you something else. I wouldn't be in a uniform if I didn't feel I could make a difference. I probably won't get back on a battlefield, a little old for that. But there's so much that has to happen if we're going to beat those sons of bitches. I think we all do whatever we can."

Jack gave a slow, languid nod, but didn't reply. He listened to the sound of the train as it made its way east. He couldn't help but wonder what it meant, being a man at war indifferent to his own mortality. He'd never admit to as much, but he couldn't truly decide if he was a fool or an asset.

CHAPTER TWO

The White House
Office of the President
November 1942

As many times as he'd been there over the years, he never failed to get a sense of the power and history associated with the men who walked these halls. Major General William "Wild Bill" Donovan was scheduled to meet the President and his Chief of Staff, Admiral Bill Leahy at 1000 for their regular intelligence update. Franklin Roosevelt had pulled Donovan back from the public sector as his Coordinator of Information in 1941. By executive order in June 1942 Donovan transitioned COI to what was now called the Office of Strategic Services. He was faced with the formidable task of gathering information from around the world. That would've been hard enough, but it was just as difficult analyzing that information and making recommendations to the President.

When he arrived in D.C. he'd set about building an organization which would be able to provide the intelligence support the nation would need in the event of a full-scale war, which he felt was coming. He'd been exploring every avenue in his search for talented people who could rise to the task. So far there had been some success but his organization was still in its infancy and had a long way to go.

He walked through the west wing on his standard path to the President's outer office. There was the normal level of simmering intensity radiating from the offices as he passed down the corridor. While he might have attracted attention in many offices in the capital, one more senior officer transiting the White House was not unusual. He was tall, in good condition and his uniform was impeccable. Extreme heroism in combat in the First World War had resulted in Donovan being awarded the nation's two highest decorations for bravery, the Congressional Medal of Honor and the Distinguished Service Cross.

"Good morning, General Donovan. The President and Chief of Staff are ready for you." Grace Tully was the President's personal Executive Secretary and the gatekeeper to the Oval Office.

"Thank you, Grace." Donovan smiled as he moved past the desk and into the open doorway into the office.

Roosevelt was sitting at the massive mahogany desk which, as always, was always covered with folders and briefing jackets. "Top of the morning, Bill. Please sit down. Coffee?"

As he moved to the straight-backed chair in front of the desk he nodded to the Chief of Staff, "Good morning, Admiral. No thank you, Mr. President. I'm fine."

Roosevelt keyed the intercom, "Grace, we're all set here. Please make sure we aren't disturbed."

He heard the metallic acknowledgement from the secretary and the heavy wooden door closed quietly. Leahy walked over and sat in the companion chair. Donovan began the standard weekly briefing with a quick overview of each major geographic area of the world and the significant intelligence items associated with each. He then summarized the Strategic Projection Report. Each week his analysts produced the report for the President. It allowed Roosevelt to compare the passels of information he received from the War Department and Navy Department objectively. Roosevelt and Leahy would make an occasional comment and sometimes request additional information or a follow up briefing folder on a specific subject.

"Bill, thank you for a superb briefing as usual. I'm very impressed with the expansion of capabilities you've orchestrated in the OSS in such a short time. It will become more and more critical to stay ahead of the Axis powers in the future. On the issue of combining our intelligence effort with the British, I've had a series of communications with the Prime Minister and I think we've struck a deal." Leahy said nothing, and didn't betray whether or not he'd been informed of this new development.

FDR continued, "Winston has agreed to take one of our fellows into the inner sanctum of their Special Operations Executive, Section D. That's the easy part. But as they say, nothing is that easy. They are putting a most unusual condition on this assignment."

"Mr. President," Donovan interrupted. "For us to be able to go beyond our current liaison relationship with Section D there are few things we shouldn't be willing to do. The Brits have too many critical links into the continent. They've been at it much longer than we have."

"What exactly do they want?" Leahy interjected.

"They want to be able to hold our fellow totally under the provisions of their Official Secrets Act. It would allow them to exercise full control over his actions and operations." Roosevelt shifted in his chair as he continued. "They're requiring our man accept dual citizenship. If he's military he must accept a commission in their armed forces. Total control, I'm afraid."

"Jesus. I thought I'd heard everything. This makes no sense," Donovan said. "What does our man do if it comes down to us or the Brits?"

Leahy got up from his chair and moved slowly over to the window clasping his hands behind him. "I'm sure that's just what they want to control. Frankly, I don't blame them. Not that I expect it would ever be a problem. We're on the same side after all."

The President looked Donovan straight in the eye. "Bill,

I want to do this. Find the right man for the job. Take any steps you feel necessary. I've already told the Prime Minister we would comply with their requirements. He made their Defense Attaché, Major General Highcombe, our contact point, initially. Have you ever met him?"

Donovan remembered a reception last summer at the British Embassy. "Yes, sir. I met him once about six months ago, seemed like a pretty solid fellow."

"Good. Then it's settled. I want you to move quickly on this. As unusual as it sounds I want to meet whomever you select. This is so far outside the bounds of anything that could be considered standard procedure, I want to make personally certain he understands everything that's at stake."

OSS Headquarters
2320 N Street
Washington, DC

There was dead silence around the conference table after Donovan went over the project with his four senior directors. These men were in charge of the four main areas which comprised the Office of Strategic Services. "I've arranged a meeting with General Highcombe. At that time I'll find out the details and what kind of timeline they envision. What I need from you is a candidate. I'm not sure what we want for qualifications but figuring that out is a starting point. The bottom line is the President wants this to happen. It's a tremendous opportunity for this organization and the country. Meet back here at 0900 tomorrow morning. Bring the qualifications you feel are important to support your group."

The four men—two men in uniforms and two in suits —rose and walked toward the closed door of the conference room.

"Bob, stick around for a minute. I want to go over a couple things."

Colonel Bob Miller, the Deputy Director for Operations, turned back toward Donovan and stood at the edge of the table. "Yes, sir."

"What do you think about this one?" Donovan smiled. Twenty years of camaraderie and mutual respect were difficult to suppress.

Miller knew Donovan wanted his full candor and he was used to providing it on a daily basis. The General was one of those open-minded individuals who liked to hear every viewpoint. He looked at all sides of an issue to make a decision based on 'what's best for the outfit.'

"I'm already scratching my head. How do we grab some young man and tell him he's about to become a British citizen and probably a member of the British Army?" The problems were racing around in Miller's mind as he pulled back the chair and sat down across from Donovan.

"It'll be an interesting conversation. I do think we want to limit our search to serving officers. They're more inclined to react well to orders, and military discipline will be a crucial key to making this successful."

"Makes sense to me," Miller agreed.

"I want everyone's thoughts on qualifications. But I suspect whomever we choose will come from your department. It's important to have someone who's used to action."

"Yes, sir."

The next morning's meeting lasted two hours. Over several carafes of coffee, the five men discussed criteria for selecting the new operative. Donovan, true to his style, had listened intently to the discussion adding points and elaborating on other's comments.

"Okay, let me summarize what we think are the main selection criteria."

He looked down at the pad of paper in front of him and made tick marks as he worked his way down the page.

"Active duty military, non-service specific. Marital status, prefer single. Operational experience is very desirable. Educational expertise, graduate degree desired with good base in scientific disciplines. Foreign language is a plus but not a requirement. Candidate must be fit and ready for active service."

The men around the table all nodded.

Miller was the first to speak. "I think I have the largest pool to screen, but we should leave it open for each of us to take a look at our own departments for promising candidates."

"I agree with Bob." Larry Hitchcox was the Director of Intelligence and the second most senior Director after Miller.

"The toughest hurdle we've set for ourselves is the combination of operational experience with a solid academic background. But I'll look at my folks. When do you want the names?"

Donovan, always known for his predilection towards swift efficiency, replied "Sorry for the press, but I need names by the close of business tomorrow. I told General Highcombe we'd have our candidate ready to meet with him by next Friday. That gives us very little time. Also, I want this low-key. Don't make a big production with your own staffs."

A chorus of "Yes, sir's" ended the meeting.

Miller was walking slowly back to his office on the third floor doing an early mental run-through of his available personnel when he stopped dead in the middle of the hall, turned his head slightly and said, to no one in particular, "Damn..."

CHAPTER THREE

Constitution Avenue
Washington, D.C.
November 17, 1942

Jack sat in the back of a taxi as it worked its way through a blustery winter morning in northwest Washington. It was not a long trip to the Navy annex, but it was raining and he wanted to look presentable for whatever lie ahead of him.

His experience as a fledgling bureaucrat had not been as bad as anticipated. A Marine captain who seemed like a decent sort shared his office. He was to be Jack's Marine counterpart in the liaison with the Grumman factory in Long Island. Understandable, the Marines were just as anxious as the Navy to get new fighters in the air over the Pacific.

He'd been a week into trying to navigate the strange waters of the new job when he received a call from the head of his division, a Navy Captain named Flynn. Jack had gone through the normal check in brief with Flynn earlier in the week and didn't think there were any problems.

When Jack reported to the senior officer, Flynn said, "You must have some pretty heavy connections, Stewart," and handed him message sheet.

Lieutenant Jack Stewart, USN is directed to report to the Office of the Director, Office of Strategic Services, 2430 E Street NW at 1030 hours, Tuesday the 17th of November, 1942.

He couldn't fathom what could lead to him receiving a summons from an entirely different organization, particularly one that he'd not even known about before that morning. All he knew was the OSS was a follow-on to the Office of Coordination of Information.

He entered the outer office which simply said "Director" and saw a nameplate on the large desk. It read, "Mrs. Eloise Page," and bore no warning for the very stern-looking woman that sat behind it. "I hope I'm in the right place."

She took the telex from his hand, read it, looked directly at him, suddenly warmed, and said, "You certainly are, Lieutenant. Have a seat and I'll see if they're ready for you."

She got up, opened the inner office door and closed it behind her. The only sound in the office was the hissing of a radiator on the wall and nothing he could see was doing anything to allay his confusion.

"The General will see you now," Mrs. Page announced as she opened the door, motioning for Jack to proceed into the inner office.

An imposing man in an Army service dress uniform came from behind the desk to greet him. "Lieutenant, my name is Donovan." The older man extended his hand. The nameplate on his desk said, "William J. Donovan, Major General, USA."

After shaking hands with the General, Jack turned to see Miller standing by the window.

"Please, sit down," the General said, motioning to one of three chairs around a low table. "I believe you know Colonel Miller?"

"Yes, sir." He sat down and looked at Miller who smiled.

"Good to see you again, Jack."

Miller came over and sat in the chair next to Jack.

Donovan went over to a credenza on the far wall and poured a cup of steaming coffee from a ceramic pitcher.

"Coffee, Lieutenant Stewart?"

"No, thank you, sir. I'm fine."

The General moved over to the two seated officers, but remained standing. "I'm sure you're wondering why you were summoned here this morning, Jack."

"Yes, sir. That would be an extreme understatement."

"Jack, you're here because we think you might be the person we've been looking for to undertake a mission that's very important to this war. We've screened a lot of young men and we think you're the best qualified on paper." Donovan set his coffee down behind him and leaned in closer to Jack.

"That being said, it's a very unusual assignment. Strictly voluntary. It'd take you out of the country for an extended period of time. That's all I can say at this point. Interested?"

Jack knew he was interested. He was genetically incapable of being anything other than completely, hopelessly interested in the face of an offer like that.

"Yes, sir, General. I'm interested. Is there anything else you can tell me?"

"Bob." The General motioned to Miller who opened a folder on the table and produced a pen, which he handed to Jack. "The nature of this assignment requires that you sign a document which allows us to lock you up and throw away the key if you divulge anything that's said here. I make light of it, Jack, but this is deadly serious. By signing this non-disclosure document you'll be read into this project and your life will change."

"Where do I sign, sir?"

Donovan came over and sat down at the table. He opened another folder which had a wide red stripe diagonally across the manila cover. "Jack, I'm going to brief you into Operation Colonial. I'll go over the key issues. Then I'll ask you if you're willing to continue. If you decide at that time it's not for you we'll end the discussion. You'll leave the room and never, I mean never, mention the project or your meeting with us to anyone. Got it?"

Jack nodded. "Yes, sir."

"Jack, this war can't be won with just tanks, planes and ships. We may be on the right side of history and have the bravest soldiers in our ranks, but if we don't win the intelligence battle, the ultimate outcome of the war can't be predicted. This is a more sophisticated war than we've waged before, and the side that wins the battle for more lethal and effective weapons may be the side which triumphs, regardless of all other factors. We're relative latecomers. We're still building our organizations—including our networks for intelligence gathering. The British are a world ahead of us, and we need to be part of their effort to penetrate Germany."

Donovan got up, went over to the credenza and poured another cup of coffee.

He continued, "We've been trying to get hooked up with the most secret of their sections in British Intelligence. They've been fine at providing liaison and help on the normal levels, but when it came to one area—Section D to be precise —their lips were sealed. The President approached Churchill and made a personal request. Churchill needs us for a number of things, and this was a chance for him to repay FDR for his ongoing support—particularly for the tanks and artillery we sent to Egypt after the fall of Tobruk."

Donovan smirked, softening a hair at the thought of the Brits owing America one.

"The Prime Minister's inclined to grant whatever request he received from Roosevelt. So far so good, but the kicker is the British want to have ultimate control over whomever we send. There are provisions of their security rules, the 'Official Secrets Act,' which allows only British subjects access to material of the highest classification. They've agreed to have an American member of section D, but he must accept dual citizenship making him a subject of the King and a commission in the armed forces of Great Britain. In your case, the Royal Navy."

"What?" Jack blurted out.

"That's right, Jack. You'd be commissioned in the Royal

Navy."

Miller spoke up, "We know this is an unusual condition, Jack. But it is what it is. It's their turf, so we have to play by their rules."

Donovan set his coffee cup down. "Jack, Colonel Miller and I are going to leave you alone to think about this. We need an answer before you leave the building, yes or no. Take your time. If you reach a decision before we get back, let Mrs. Page know and she'll contact us. This is a total commitment. Don't say yes unless you're ready to take on all the responsibilities this will entail. You'll have to be able to divide your loyalties. This isn't a magic show. You'll be a true subject of the King. As a serving officer in the Royal Navy you'll be obliged to comply with all rules, regulations and customs. We realize this is asking a lot, so take your time."

Jack was stunned.

Pamela Thompson immediately entered his mind. He felt bad about how they'd drifted apart over time, but he'd been in his world and she was back in England. They tried to write, but that didn't work out. There'd been the occasional note from Ian or Dicky, which became less frequent over time. The idea of going back to England was like a lightning bolt arcing through his chest.

He never thought he would see Oxford again. Or Pam.

No matter what lie on the other side of the ocean, it had to be better than counting airplanes at a desk in D.C.

If Miller and General Donovan think it's that important, and I'm the best person for the job, so be it, he thought.

He got up and opened the door to the outer office. "Mrs. Page, I have an answer for the General. He said to let you know."

"Thank you, Lieutenant. If you'd go back in and take a seat, the General will be right here."

Jack was standing by the window when Donovan and Miller entered the office and closed the door. "Well, Jack. What's your decision?"

Stepping toward the two men, Jack smiled and said, "General, I'm game."

Donovan and Miller both offered their hands to Jack.

The General said, "You're in for quite an adventure if my hunch is correct. Let's get started." Donovan motioned for Jack and Miller to sit down. He went on, "Jack, there are several things that made you a natural choice for this job. I'll remind you what we're about to discuss is classified 'Top Secret', as is much of what you'll be seeing going forward."

Jack tried to focus on what the General was saying.

Donovan went on, "You have two key qualities that were very important to us. You have a master's degree in physics and you speak French and German. What do you know about the concept of atomic power?"

Jack was taken back to the late night discussions with Ian Thompson at Trinity. "I know there are a number of theories which hold it's possible to create a cascading chain reaction in material at the atomic level. Theoretically, it would create a potential energy discharge beyond anything mankind's ever seen."

The General shifted forward in his chair and continued. "Over the last few years, there've been a lot of smart men who've theorized that it's possible to create an atomic bomb. This weapon could destroy entire fleets or cities in one detonation. Unfortunately, there are smart men in Germany who have the same theories. That's why I said new weapons could bring victory to the side that develops those weapons first. Section D, where you're headed, is the heart of the British effort to discover Germany's plans to develop new weapons."

Miller spoke up, "This effort is so important that we want to be able to support the British in any way possible. At the same time, we want to be developing our own capabilities to build a deep-penetration platform like they have right now. By having you right in the thick of the battle, you'll be able to help facilitate any American support. You'll also be building experience that we would eventually be able to use when you come back to us."

"I'd return to the U.S. and the Navy?" Jack thought this was sounding more reasonable. "How long's this supposed to last?"

Donovan said, "There's no set time. We're doing something we've never done before, so this is very much an experiment in action. We'll make sure the time you serve with the Brits will count for longevity, pay, promotions and the like."

"Jack, the other reason you're our top candidate is that you have combat experience. That checks a few boxes. First of all, the Brits have been in the thick of this war since 1939. They look at us as the new guys. Your combat in the Pacific allows you to face them with some credibility. The other side of your combat experience is obvious to us, but it may not be to you. We have lots of people in training, but you've already proven yourself in combat. You can function under pressure and take care of yourself. We don't know how the Brits will want to use you, but it seems to us you have a set of talents that will hold you in good stead no matter what happens. Your year at Oxford is another plus for us. You've lived there, experienced the culture and have a better feel for how they look at things."

Jack felt overwhelmed, but excited.

His exit was taken care of by Miller, who said, "Plan on being back here tomorrow at 1000 hours in your best service dress uniform. We have one meeting tomorrow, then you'll be cut loose to start wrapping up your personal affairs. Expect to leave the country within a month for a long time, could be years. The next appointment will be Friday morning at 0800. Bring a small bag with the basics. The Brits will billet you until your departure. Don't worry about returning to BuAir, we'll take care of that. You have lots to do in the interim. Any questions?"

"No, sir," Jack said.

Donovan rose and headed toward the door, a clear signal for Jack to get moving. He extended his hand. "Lieutenant, thank you."

Jack said, "Yes, sir." and walked his first steps towards the unknown.

The next morning when Jack entered Donovan's outer office his head was still swimming with all of the things he'd been trying to wrap up. He'd been in D.C. less than a month. It still took most of yesterday afternoon to wrap up his affairs, arrange for storage of his gear and give notice at the Bachelor Officer Quarters at Anacostia Naval Air Station.

Donovan met him in full uniform, cover in place and heading out the door. "Perfect timing, Jack. Right on schedule, but no time to tarry." The big man didn't break stride as he moved past Jack and out the door.

A quick about face and Jack fell in tow. The General headed for the waiting staff car, parked at the entrance steps. The Army driver had the door open. The General put his hand on Jack's back and said, "Hop in."

As they pulled away, Jack glanced to the right and tried not to show his surprise when he noticed Donovan's decorations. He'd never actually met anyone who'd been awarded the Medal of Honor. The decoration under the small blue ribbon with five white stars was the Distinguished Service Cross. It takes something special to get either one of those and he had both of them. It's not unusual to get those two awards posthumously, Donovan was there to wear them.

"Jack, I normally don't like to surprise people. I knew that if you knew where we were going this morning you'd have spent a very sleepless night. To emphasize the importance of what you're doing, the man who was instrumental in setting it up wanted to meet you. We're going to the White House and you're going to meet President Roosevelt."

Sitting in the sedan, Jack Stewart now understood the importance of the decision he had made. He was about to meet the President and embark on a mission that might be important to the outcome of the war. It wasn't fear Jack felt, he knew that too well. More than anything else, he felt concern that he was out of his league. All he could do was his best.

"Is there anything special I should know about meeting the President, sir? I've never been in a situation like this."

"He's your Commander in Chief. Act like you would with the most senior officer you've ever met. There're no secret tricks. I think you'll find he's not intimidating at all. He'll make you feel at home. Just don't get too at home, if you know what I mean. He'll be sitting at his desk and I'll help with the introduction. Expect to shake hands across the desk."

"Yes, sir."

They spent the remainder of the ride in silence.

The next hour was a blur for Jack. He tried to take it all in but there was so much. He'd driven by the White House many times while a midshipman at Annapolis, but he'd never been inside. They were cleared through the gate quickly and Donovan knew the way to the Oval Office well. Outside the President's door, Jack tried to look calm. He thought to himself, *it's just like your first carrier landing, do your best, keep your brain engaged and don't do anything stupid.*

"You may go in, General," Grace Tully said.

Jack followed Donovan into the most famous office in America. The President was at his desk, wearing a white shirt and bow tie, looking at some papers. Roosevelt looked up, and Jack saw the smile he had seen so many times in the newsreels.

"Please, come in, gentlemen," FDR said closing the folder he'd been reading.

"Mr. President, I would like you to meet Lieutenant Jack Stewart."

The President smiled again and extended his hand across the desk, which Jack grasped firmly.

"I'm pleased to meet you, Lieutenant. Please have a seat." He and Donovan sat down as the President moved smoothly into what may have been a prepared speech.

"You've been entrusted with a very critical mission for

your country. I've received a full briefing from General Donovan and feel you're a superb choice for what may be one of the most unique and significant missions ever given a serving officer."

Jack said nothing knowing full well the dizzying degree to which he was in over his head.

"Lieutenant Stewart, this assignment will be carried out in the full spirit of the conditions the Prime Minister has conveyed to us. As your Commander in Chief I am acknowledging that you'll be required to tender you full loyalty and obedience to the British crown for the duration of your assignment. I hope that doesn't put you in any difficult situations, but we can't know what the future holds. You're a graduate of Annapolis and as such, you fully understand honor and integrity. We put ours on the line with Mr. Churchill and the British Government when we agreed to your dual citizenship and commissioning in the Royal Navy. You must throw yourself fully into this arrangement. There's no middle ground. Your country is counting on you, and more importantly, I'm counting on you."

"Understood, Mr. President."

Roosevelt relaxed his serious demeanor and smiled again. "That's all I needed to hear, son. You have the full support of your President and your country. In a very short time you'll be on new ground, but I still have the ability to provide perhaps a little assistance. General, would you lend me a hand?"

Donovan got up and took the blue folder the President had in his hand. He opened it and set it in front of Jack.

The President went on, "You were on the list for selection to the rank of Lieutenant Commander which was to be released on January 1st. We're going to accelerate that. By signing this acceptance of office, you are hereby promoted to the rank of Lieutenant Commander, effective immediately. This ought to give you a little more horsepower with our Allies."

Jack managed to get out a quiet, "Yes, sir." He signed the sheet of White House correspondence, directly under Roosevelt's own signature.

"I have one further action for you to perform on your arrival in England. To come full circle on this arrangement, I'll make sure you meet the Prime Minister. He's a champion in this cause and when he meets you, one more link will have been built in what's becoming an historical collaboration between our countries. For you, it will soon be both of your countries."

CHAPTER FOUR

The British Embassy

3100 Massachusetts Ave
Washington, D.C.

Jack was reminded how he felt little when his father had taken him down to King Street Station in Seattle in the summer of 1931. He'd boarded the train for Annapolis a cauldron of excitement and firing nerves. He was as keen and bewildered then as he was now, flung once again headlong into the thick fog of the unknown.

Donovan and Miller accompanied him in the staff car for the short trip from OSS headquarters to the embassy. He would be meeting the British Defense Attaché, Major General Geoffrey Highcombe.

A Royal Navy Lieutenant met the trio when the staff car pulled up to the main entrance of the embassy on Massachusetts Avenue. A starch-stiff salute greeted them as the car stopped. The Lieutenant remained at attention as they got out.

"Good morning, gentlemen. I am Lieutenant Sharpe. General Highcombe is expecting you. Please follow me." He led them through the double doors and down a long corridor. They walked past a reception area where a young lady sat at a round desk. Proceeding up a circular set of stairs, they stopped on the second floor. The young officer had not said anything since his greeting and kept a brisk pace. The group arrived at an outer office with two large desks, one of which was occupied by a young lady in uniform. She rose as the group entered.

"Good morning, sir," she said, looking at Donovan. "General Highcombe is expecting you."

The Lieutenant opened the door and ushered them into the inner office. Major General Geoffrey Highcombe, DSO, rose and walked around his desk to meet them. "General Donovan, so good to see you again." He smiled and shook hands with Donovan.

"Good morning, General. May I present Colonel Miller and Lieutenant Commander Stewart," Donovan said.

Highcombe smiled and shook hands with Bob Miller. "Delighted to meet you, Colonel." He extended his hand to Jack and looked him directly in the eye, pausing a split second. "Welcome to the embassy, Commander."

"Thank you, sir," Jack replied. He was still adjusting to being called "Commander." By custom, both Lieutenant Commanders and full Commanders were accorded that salutation.

"Please, sit down." Highcombe gestured to a circle of chairs next to his desk. "Can I offer you coffee, or tea, perhaps?"

With the coffee delivered and the expected pleasantries exchanged, the discussion turned to the first steps of Operation Colonial. Highcombe outlined his proposed transition plan for Jack. "We're all on rather new ground here I'm afraid. I've put together a plan which I trust will help Commander Stewart assume his position in the most rapid manner possible." He went on to describe in detail the training and indoctrination program. Most of Jack's time would be spent at the embassy. Highcombe also projected that Jack would be in England by Christmas.

Donovan and Miller expressed their appreciation for the embassy reacting to this tasking in such a rapid manner.

"Gentlemen, the PM has directed that we put Operation Colonial at the top of our activities list. Mr. Churchill was very specific that he was taking a personal interest in our progress. I daresay it would behoove us all not to disappoint the man."

Donovan put his coffee down on the table and rose, Miller followed suit. "General, we don't want to take anymore of your time. I'm sure the sooner you get started, the better." They moved toward the door.

Jack stood up, still trying to digest the changes that were about to take place in his life. The arrangement between Donovan and Highcombe had put the ball strictly in the British court. The only contact Jack might have with the OSS for the foreseeable future was a possible contact in England. Other than agreed upon meetings with whomever that might be, Jack's connection with the United States government was about to be severed.

"Commander, good luck and take care of yourself." Bill Donovan nodded to Jack, and stepped through the door.

"Good luck, Jack," Bob Miller said. He smiled at Jack and followed Donovan.

General Highcombe walked back over to Jack. "Commander, I have assigned Lieutenant Sharpe to be your 'running mate' as it were while you're here with us. He can make sure you get with each of the people assigned for your briefing series and as well as help you with the many details you'll need to master in a very short time."

"Thank you, sir. The assistance is quite welcome."

Jack tried to act calm and collected while being painfully aware of his nerves as he stood alone with Highcombe.

"We'll get into the very cut-and-dried tasks straight away. After those mundane tasks, we can concentrate on the more important aspects of this rather unusual indoctrination."

Highcombe was true to his word. Lieutenant Sharpe had taken him in tow. He spent the next three hours being photographed and measured, filling out form after form covering all of the significant information pertaining to his life since he arrived in Annapolis in 1931. He was required to list all addresses where he'd lived, all trips outside the United States, his training in its entirety and all pertinent data on his immediate family. Jack was finishing up the last set of forms as the door opened.

Sharpe stepped into the office and asked, "Are you hungry, Commander?" It was the first time Sharpe had relaxed from his role as Jack's very formal and official escort all morning.

"Lieutenant Sharpe, what do your friends call you?" Jack said as he stood up and stretched his sore back.

"Les to my friends, sir." Sharpe replied, with a surprised look.

"Les, my name is Jack, and I'm starving. So please, lead on."

The young officer smiled and said, "My pleasure."

It turned out Les had been on active service since 1939. His most recent assignment was on a destroyer operating on convoy duty in the North Atlantic. He was on a short 'non-related' tour, which should see him return to the Atlantic as an Executive Officer of a destroyer or perhaps skipper of one of the large patrol boats being used in the approaches to the British Isles. They stopped in the general dining room and sat down to a lunch of boiled cod and potatoes.

"We'll get you up to your quarters after lunch and give you some time to relax. The only other meeting we have today is with the General at 1800 hours. After that meeting you're on for dinner with him in the formal dining room at 1900 hours."

Jack sat in his spartan bedroom on the third floor of the embassy. There had been a pile of briefing papers sitting on the desk when Les dropped him off after lunch. He'd been encouraged to start working his way through the stack of bound folders, pamphlets and several London newspapers. The material amounted to a primer on Great Britain and the Commonwealth. During his time at Oxford he did learn about the country and people but primarily he had been learning physics. This information was a lot to absorb in a short time. The briefing papers covered many aspects of modern England which he'd never given a second thought. There was a series on the structure of government and the supporting evolution of the government over the last several centuries. He found briefing papers on the current British armed forces and their command structure. He learned a great deal about the monarchy and how it fit into the Commonwealth, the government and the fiber of English life.

It was interesting to Jack as he read the most recent newspapers. He had not seen the Times since he left Oxford in '36. The total impact of the war on the country and people was evident as he read through the pages. There were notices and warnings on subjects like air raid procedures and to what to do if you encounter an unexploded bomb. Jack had followed the "blitz" in the newspapers but hadn't made the connection it had on everyday life. It was sobering when he opened to the page which listed the most recent casualties. He ran down the lists of names realizing the British had been taking it for over three years.

The afternoon flew by as he worked his way through the material. It was almost 1800 when there was a knock at the door. He opened it to find Les in his service blue uniform asking if he was ready. He put on his blouse with the newly added Lieutenant Commander's two and a half stripes, and followed him downstairs to Highcombe's office.

Les entered the General's office with Jack following. The Lieutenant led them over to Highcombe's desk.

"Reporting as requested, sir."

"Thank you. Do be seated, gentlemen." Highcombe paused. "Commander Stewart, I have the honor of informing you that your commission as a Lieutenant Commander on the active list of the regular Royal Navy has been approved. You will date your rank from today for reporting purposes."

Highcombe paused again then continued.

"As you are being commissioned into the Royal Navy, no

oath of allegiance is required. Your acceptance of the royal commission assumes your allegiance to the crown. I have here a number of documents."

He began to lay articles on the desk from left to right.

"Your naval identification card, your identity disk, which I believe you call 'dog tags', your British passport, your medical and dental folder and finally your service record."

He got up and walked behind his desk to a small coat closet. "Lieutenant Sharpe if you would assist me by helping the Commander with his blouse."

Highcombe removed a dark blue uniform blouse from the closet and walked over to Jack who was now standing in his blue uniform trousers, white shirt and black tie. The General held the blouse out inviting Jack to insert his left arm. As he slipped the blouse on Jack noticed the two and a half stripes of a LCDR and the extra circle on the upper stripe which was customary of British Commonwealth naval officer's uniforms.

"Congratulations, Commander. You are now officially accepted into the King's service. Welcome aboard."

Les produced the Royal Naval combination cover with the large embroidered crest on the bill.

"Thank you, sir," Jack said.

"Take a look at yourself in the mirror and see what you think. Our uniform folks did the best they could with only one set of measurements."

Feeling self-conscious, Jack moved over to the half mirror over the small wall table. He was surprised when he looked at himself in the mirror. On the left breast of the blouse was an embroidered set of gold wings with a crown inset. Beneath the wings was one ribbon. It had purple and white diagonal stripes.

"I'm..." Jack stammered.

"Our people and your people have been busy, Commander Stewart."

What Highcombe didn't describe to Jack was the direct involvement of General Donovan and the President of the

United States. FDR in turn cabled the Prime Minister of the United Kingdom who contacted the First Lord of the Admiralty. In very short order there were a series of trans-Atlantic cables to the embassy with specific direction and authorization in the case of newly commissioned Lieutenant Commander Jack Stewart.

"You have been awarded the British equivalent of your Naval Aviator wings. They are the wings worn by our pilots in the Fleet Air Arm. You are a fully qualified carrier pilot and your qualifications merit the award of the wings. You will also see that you wear the Distinguished Flying Cross. Your actions in downing four Japanese aircraft, two in direct defense of Australia, have been recognized by the King with the award of the DFC. It is my honor to bestow this award on behalf of his Majesty in grateful appreciation for heroic service."

Highcombe produced a small presentation box lined with velvet and within lay the actual medal.

"The accompanying citation has been made part of your official service record."

Jack was at a loss for words. He'd been overwhelmed by emotion since learning of the plan for Operation Colonial. The emotional rollercoaster which began in the skies over the Pacific with Terry's death and his crash seemed to have reached a crescendo when he saw the wings and the ribbon.

"Sir, I'll wear this uniform with all the pride anyone could ever have in their Navy and country."

In the space of only a few hours, something had happened in Jack Stewart. His memories of England flooded back. The last three years of the war in Europe now seemed very personal. He felt in his heart that he could truly pledge his loyalty and honor to the King and to England. He was now an officer of the King in all respects.

"Jack, I think those who chose you knew that before you did," said Highcombe, as he went over to the alcove behind his desk and came back with a tray.

"I think this calls for a toast."

He poured an inch of whisky in each of three small tumblers, handing one to Les and one to Jack. The General lifted his glass, "Gentlemen, to England, and to her victory."

"To England."

CHAPTER FIVE

Southeastern England
December 1942

Major Tommy Hudson of the British Army stared out the window of the nondescript government car as it made its way out of downtown London in the customary gray gloom of winter. The day was cold and the wind had cut through his overcoat when he left Baker Street on his way to RAF Biggin Hill. He was to meet an American B-17 which was making the trans-Atlantic ferry flight from Dover, Delaware in the States, with one stop in Gander, Newfoundland. There was a growing U.S. presence in England and it was the Eighth Air Force of the United States Army Air Corps. However their aircraft normally flew directly to their future home bases which were located farther north. Biggin Hill was one of the RAF Fighter Command's bases dedicated to the air defense of London and the cities of the southeast.

Hudson had been dispatched following a short briefing from Colonel Greene, the head of Section D of the Special Operations Executive, MI-6. Major Hudson was the Operations Head of Section D, a special group tasked with the primary intelligence and espionage effort into occupied Europe. Originally an infantry officer, Hudson missed service in the first war. He subsequently spent most of his operational time in the Middle East dealing with the aftermath of the war. He was slowly pulled into the world of military intelligence. The British Empire was trying to mandate a working governmental system across the entire region. Hudson found he had a talent for ferreting out information. Following his return to England in 1934, he transferred to Army Intelligence and remained there until the war broke out. As MI-6 rapidly expanded, he'd been recruited for his experience with operational intelligence matters. A no-nonsense type, he was renowned in Section D for his dry sense of humor. To Hudson, there was a mission to accomplish. Everything else came in a distant second.

Hudson checked with the Operations Duty Officer in the two-story brick building which served as the flight operations command center for Biggin Hill. The flight lieutenant told Hudson they had received a radio transmission from the aircraft, "Army 186 Bravo," about 15 minutes earlier, estimating arrival almost on the hour. He checked his watch and saw he had twenty minutes to wait. Despite his heavy overcoat the damp chill seemed to sink right down into his bones.

"Army 186 Bravo"
10,000 Feet
50 Miles NW of RAF Biggin Hill

Jack leaned forward, resting his elbow on a knee as he crouched between the seats of the pilot and co-pilot. There were several air navigation charts open on the lap of the co-pilot in the right seat as he went over their progress.

"I have us tracking inbound on the Biggin Hill beacon, 310 degree radial. We're at the correct altitude for the approach according to the chart." 1st Lieutenant Sean Mills was glad their navigator had done a great job on the crossing. Now it was up to him to provide the navigational direction to the aircraft commander, Captain Robbie Warren.

"See if you can get Biggin Approach or Biggin Tower on the horn." Warren was a big believer in the rule, "when in doubt, get on the radio and talk to someone." Tired after the long over-water flight, the young aircraft commander was in unfamiliar territory. The last thing he needed was to screw something up on his first day in England. Looking down he was able to make out the green countryside through a very thin layer of clouds 1,000 feet below.

Sean dialed in the frequency and keyed the radio, "Biggin Approach, this is Army 186 Bravo. Estimating our position at Marsden intersection at 10,000 feet, over."

The response was immediate. "Army 186 Bravo, this is Biggin Approach, no other reported traffic, you are cleared to descend to 6,000, over."

"This is Army 186 Bravo, roger, leaving 10,000 for 6,000."

Jack watched the crew go through the descent and pre-landing checklists. He was happy to be in the cockpit and not stuck in back. It was comforting to be back in a familiar world and watching the crew go through procedure. Any shred of familiarity was something he treasured very deeply these days.

After the last two weeks at the Embassy, he needed a little quiet time. He felt like he was drinking out of a firehose each day as he went over briefing books and met with the subject matter experts in particular subjects. He had covered in excruciating detail all aspects of the government, the military, the war, civilian institutions, the structure of law, currency, banking, media, daily life, and wartime restrictions in England. His different briefing officers filled in the smaller details and he was able to get a sense of the temper of the country. They continued to drill him on customs and traditions to prevent any problems when he got to England. His hosts continued to produce additions to his uniform kit and by the time he left the states, he owned most of the working uniforms of the King's Navy.

He'd been fortunate to get manifested on one of the bombers heading over to England as part of the buildup of the Army Air Corps. Military Air Transport Command flew Jack to Delaware from D.C. on a Navy R-4, the military version of the DC-3. His American accent coupled with a Royal Navy uniform had produced a few strange looks. Most people probably thought he was Canadian. On arrival in Delaware, the scheduler assigned him to this particular crew for the flight. The co-pilot had been very helpful getting him a flight suit and thick flight jacket for the long and cold flight across the Atlantic.

He remembered his last trip to England. Six days on the S.S. Eden Isle, New York to Southampton. What a great time as a young unattached naval officer off to see the world. At least this trip had been uneventful despite the winter weather and for that he was thankful.

The big bomber broken out of the clouds and below stretched the English countryside he remembered. Green and lush, in the distance he could just make out the city of London in the morning light.

"Should be on deck in about ten minutes if my map's correct," Sean said. "Switching to tower." He rotated the dials of the VHF radio and made the transmission, "Biggin Hill Tower, Army 186 Bravo, a single B-17, ten miles west for landing."

"Hullo Army 186," was the crackling response. "Winds are currently 070 at 10 knots, gusting to 15. You will be cleared to make a visual straight in approach to runway nine. Report a visual."

"Wilco, tower."

"Co-pilot to crew, prepare for landing. Skipper, I think I see the field at 11 o'clock."

Warren had been busy checking his switches and going down his pre-landing checklist. He looked up. "Rog, I got it. Standby on the flaps." He banked the big bomber slightly left as he pulled the throttle levers back an inch. As he leveled the wings, he called out, "Half flaps."

Sean said, "Flaps, half." He moved the lever out of its detent.

"Gear coming down," was Robbie's next call. Followed by "Three down and locked." He keyed the radio, "Biggin, Army 186, three down and locked at 3 miles for runway niner."

"Army 186, you are alone in the circuit, you are cleared

to land runway nine, wind 080 at 15."

Major Hudson had been alerted to the arrival of the B-17 in time to watch it touch down smoothly. The olive drab bomber decelerated to a fast taxi as it cleared the runway. The RAF ground crew trotted out from the flight line hut with wheel chocks and a handcart. The B-17 had already shut down both inboard engines as it approached the parking area. Hudson could hear the brakes squeak over the subdued rumble of the radial engines. The ground crew leader raised his hand over his head to signal where the aircraft should park. As the bomber turned toward him, he began to move his arms in rhythm with standard taxi signals. The taxi director raised his hands in a cross in front of him to signal 'stop' and signaled his men to chock the wheels. Once the chocks were in place he crossed his hand across his throat signaling to cut power to the engines.

The last two engines wound down and the hatch opened under the cockpit. Men started swinging down from the hatch as other crew members exited the fuselage door at the rear. Five men emerged from the nose and four of them walked toward the operations building. The RAF ground crew was talking to the fifth man as a fuel truck approached the aircraft.

The crew members approaching Hudson were all wearing the same dark green flight suits, heavy leather flight jackets and combination caps. Three of those caps were the dark green covers worn by the U.S. Army Air Corps while the other cap was the white cover that went with the Royal Navy's service blue uniform.

Hudson walked purposefully toward the group. When he was within several feet he called "Commander Stewart?" The man in the white cap cover detached himself from the group and walked over.

"Hello, Major, I'm Jack Stewart." Jack was thankful the embassy had drilled him on the rank insignia for all of British forces.

44

They shook hands as Hudson greeted him, "Welcome to England, Commander. I'm Tommy Hudson. I've been sent to gather you up and get you back to Baker Street."

In short order they retrieved Jack's bags from the line crew, said farewell to the B-17 crew and were on their way back into London.

Jack sat back in the seat and tried to get comfortable. "How long will it take to get into the city?"

"No more than an hour, depends on detours. Lots of repair work going on downtown," Hudson answered. "How was your trip?"

"Not bad. The crew and the weather were both quite cooperative, thankfully."

Jack was enjoying seeing the countryside go by. It reminded him how much he liked the area around London.

"Glad it went well. I guess it can be a tough trip this time of year," he replied. "Too bad you had to be away from home for Christmas."

Jack had thought about that. He couldn't have gotten home to Seattle, anyways.

"Major, in my mind, I am home."

Hudson turned to Jack, smiled and said, "Please call me Tommy."

"Agreed. Call me Jack."

MI-6 Headquarters
64 Baker Street
London

After dropping Jack's bags off at the Connaught Hotel, they arrived at the building which was the counterpart of the OSS headquarters on N Street in D.C. From Baker Street, the activities of all overseas, non-military intelligence efforts were controlled. That included both espionage and sabotage by the operatives of MI-6. Much like the OSS, MI-6 had gone through a rapid evolution and expansion but had done so several years ago in response to the crisis in Europe. The expansion was still very much ongoing and each day was a challenge for the men and women that lined those clandestine halls.

The two officers had to show their identity cards to the sentry at the front security station. Jack was surprised to see he was already on the access list.

"Colonel Greene is going to see us at 1400 hours," Hudson said. "Until then, let's work on getting some of the administrative work done for your arrival. We'll need your service record to make the endorsements. We can also get you signed in at the officer's mess. I'll give you a quick tour of the building. We can meet some of the key people so you can start learning names."

Hudson led him down a hallway to an office labeled "Administrative Services."

Jack noted how this check-in process was similar to all his previous experiences. In short order, he was on the rolls, endorsed, his mess bill was paid and he was memorizing names and faces. He liked Hudson's easy manner. The Major was quiet but everyone they met seemed to defer to him, not out of fear but a clear respect. He was extremely polite and soft spoken, something that normally would have irritated Jack, but he wasn't alone in it endearing Tommy to him.

They were on time for their meeting with Colonel Noel Greene, head of Section D. An Army Sergeant ushered them into his large office on the third floor. The room had the polished wood smell Jack remembered from the library at Trinity College.

Greene was one of the most experienced officers in British Intelligence. He'd been commissioned out of Sandhurst in 1914 and survived the horrors of the Western Front as an artillery officer in the Royal Lancaster Guards. His postwar experiences were primarily in India and the Far East, where his regiment was posted to several garrison tours. On his return from Singapore in 1924, he requested a transfer to intelligence and had been there ever since. Greene was now one of the key officers driving the expansion of the British intelligence service as the war continued.

"Come in, Tommy. This must be Commander Stewart," he said as he looked at Jack and smiled. "Welcome to Baker Street, Commander."

Tommy had told him the 'old man' was a superb boss. But he did have a terrible hearing problem from the last war.

"I'm very glad to be here, Colonel. Your people have given me a great welcome. Major Hudson has helped me get squared away."

"Splendid," Greene said. "We're happy to have you with us. Whatever we can do to make your move go smoothly just let us know. Now, into the swing of things. Major Hudson and I have given some thought to the best way to get you settled into the section." He sat back in his chair and crossed his legs. "Please, do sit down."

Hudson took the chair closest to the door and Jack took the one next to it. Greene pulled a pipe from the desk drawer and began the ritual of filling and lighting it. "We think the best way to bring you up to speed, as it were, is to put together a program of work and learn. The work part will begin straight away. We're assigning you as the Assistant Operations Officer for D Section working directly for Tommy."

Jack liked what he was hearing. Working for the right man made a world of difference to him. Greene went on to explain the Operations Staff was expanding as operations picked up, not only on the continent, but also around the world. This assignment would also be the best way for Jack to learn the mechanics of intelligence gathering and dissemination.

"You'll have a full agenda working the operational issues with Tommy. But we also think it is imperative you understand the training and education of the field operatives. We'll have you up to our training facility at Arisaig. You can observe and even participate in that training, if you'd like. There are several crack officers up there who will show you the ropes in short order. There really isn't a better way to meet the people you'll be sending on missions. You will also get a feel for what they have to deal with and the tools they have in their possession."

"Another issue," Greene continued. "You've been granted an 'Ultra Secret' security clearance, with 'compartmentalization authorized'. Which means you will be read into compartmented security programs. Compartmentalization is how we ensure the smallest number of people are aware of our activities. It's important to remember that by the virtue of having the clearance and the knowledge which will come with the clearance you'll become a target for enemy intelligence."

The proximity of the European theatre of operations hit Jack. The reality of the war was back with him, something he last left floating in a raft in the middle of the Pacific. He was finally back in the action.

"We're all in that situation, Commander. For that reason we try to maintain a very low profile. You're authorized to tell the appropriate people that you are assigned to MI-6, but that's it. Your connection with SOE or Section D is strictly close-hold."

"Yes, sir. I understand."

"What we do is take the fight to Jerry. Close and personal. The agents are in extreme danger and a number have not come back from missions. We'll continue to do everything we can to protect our operatives. Maintaining anonymity is crucial for us."

Greene stood up and took a drag on his pipe. "Now, I'll let you two get busy. Commander, you have a great deal of work in front of you. Let me know if there's anything I can do."

In the next week, two things became glaringly obvious to Jack. He was a novice in the world of intelligence, and Tommy was a pro. The two spent hours going over procedures, networks, training, personnel acquisition and ongoing ops. Tommy was patient and Jack worked hard to absorb the many details effecting the Operations Section. By the end of the week he was getting familiar with the people and the routine within Section D. He'd actually been able to start taking care of some of Tommy's more mundane tasks, freeing the Ops Boss to concentrate on the big issues.

After several nights at the Connaught, Tommy suggested Jack take the second bedroom at his flat. Jack jumped at the offer. The flat was only a ten minute walk from Baker Street and certainly large enough for two. Tommy was divorced, a victim of marrying young and going overseas. He had family in the north of England, but right now the SOE was his family and took all his time.

Late Friday night, they were having a nightcap at the flat going over the plan for next week.

"Jack, I think it's time to get you up to Arisaig. We're finishing up one class and the work load is down a bit. Several of our top training officers would be available to give you a good overview of the program. They could lay out a schedule for you to come back for portions of the course."

"Sounds like a plan. I'm getting comfortable enough here that I might actually sound like I know what I'm talking about up there." Jack laughed and took a drink.

"I like a good scotch but I just can't get used to not having ice in it."

Hudson said, "Most of the places we established our empire, it was damn difficult to get ice. India, Burma, Singapore, they had to learn to get by without."

He poured another short shot of scotch in his glass. "Do you have any plans for Christmas?"

"You know I do have something I've been thinking about. How hard is it to get to Oxford by train these days?"

"Oxford?" Tommy asked.

Oxford, England
Christmas Day
1942

The trip from London was over familiar ground but the mood was different. There was predictably light traffic on Christmas Day and Jack enjoyed the trip. What intrigued him was the tone of the people around him at the station and on the train. Perhaps he hadn't been tuned in when he first got to England, after all. The people he'd met at Section D were upbeat and full of energy. Here he could sense a weariness which he had missed before. This was the third year of a war which had been brought right into the heart of their world. There had been great loss of life both overseas and at home during the air raids of 1940. Rationing and the privations of wartime life had taken a toll on the British. But he also sensed that strong resolve he remembered from the rugby fields. Everyone was carrying on with their lives, Hitler and the Germans be damned.

"That'll be two pounds three," the ticket seller told him from behind a glass window at Paddington station. "Train will leave at 2:35 from platform 6."

She handed him his change and a ticket stub.

Jack had great misgivings about going to Oxford today. He didn't know what he would find when he got there. His last contact with the Thompsons was in late 1939. At that time, Dicky was in pilot training with the Royal Air Force, Ian was still lecturing at Trinity and Pam was working on her master's degree in literature. At one time he'd felt that if there was such a thing as love, he felt it for Pam. They'd even talked about a future together. He knew that she felt the same way about him but it didn't make sense at the time. He'd always taken the sensible route and to try to add a wife to his life as he tried to launch his naval career wasn't reasonable. They parted with promises to write and a vague commitment to something in the future. As their correspondence became less frequent, they both got on with their lives.

Sitting on the train, Jack wondered what would've happened if they had stayed together when he finished at Oxford. How would it have affected his performance in flight school or when he got to the fleet and started real operational flying? Would he have held back when he needed to push himself? Would he have taken the 'safe' missions and worried about getting home every night? He wasn't sure now.

He remembered the first time he'd been truly scared in an aircraft. There had been the normal nerves in flight training and the sick feeling when there was an accident among the students, but all in all, he had a pretty uneventful course of training.

He possessed a solid ability in the air and over time, he became an accomplished aviator. His confidence was well founded and he slowly learned how far to go without getting in trouble. His first taste of true fear came off the coast of New York. It was the winter of 1938 and the ship had sailed north from Norfolk as part of the final fleet war problem of the year. His squadron was supposed to provide air cover against Army Air Corps bombers operating from ashore. The weather was marginal and the seas extremely rough. The carrier deck was pitching 15 to 20 feet in the ground swells with a 30-40 knot wind whipping the sea into whitecaps.

His section of aircraft was flying combat air patrol about 80 miles from the ship when he noticed he was losing oil pressure. He turned for the ship and declared an emergency with his engine starting to run rough. He was losing oil pressure and oil quantity. The normal result of oil problems in the R1830 Pratt and Whitney radial engine was for it to seize in a short period of time. Losing your engine was the one thing every carrier aviator tried to put out of his mind. You have two options when the motor quits: bailing out or ditching the aircraft. Over land, while neither option is ideal, they're both acceptable. When operating at sea over 55-degree water and 15 foot waves with no destroyer close by to fish you out, neither choice was good. With 60 miles to the ship, he was sure the engine would not make it. To complicate his situation, the ship was getting ready for the next launch.

A dozen aircraft occupied the landing area. That was when Jack first felt truly scared. If the motor held out, if they could clear the deck, if he could find the ship, and if they would let him try to land, he could do it. But so much was out of his control. He'd started to shudder involuntarily, his feet shaking on the rudder pedals. It didn't last long, though. He reached inside, told himself that he was either going to make it or he wasn't.

When he finally shut down the engine on the flight deck, his flight suit was soaked through with sweat, but he'd crossed the line which all combat aviators have to cross to be effective, a combination of courage and fatalism. It was that attitude which allowed him to attack and win in aerial combat in the Pacific, but he still wondered , what if he had a wife and kids? Could he still handle it?

35 West Bridge Street
Oxford

December had even drearier than usual for Pamela Thompson. She'd been working twelve hour shifts for most of the month. The only way she could describe how she felt was totally and completely worn out. The personnel shortages from earlier in the year had abated somewhat. However, as one of the most senior floor coordinators at Fighter Command Headquarters, Flight Officer Thompson was still in demand for both training and operational shifts. While the pace was nothing like the nightmare of 1940, the units of Fighter Command, especially 11 Group, were actively engaging the

Luftwaffe every day. The Hurricanes and Spitfires now were primarily flying convoy escort, reconnaissance and cover for the daytime bomber missions. Although the blitz was behind them, lives still depended on accurate reporting and appraisal of the airborne situation over Southern England.

Pamela worked to ensure the flow of information was accurately received and plotted for the flight direction teams. She then had to make sure the fighter direction instructions were relayed to the sector controllers for further transfer to the airborne aircraft. Knowing everything you did might decide the fate of many people would wear anyone down over time. It was a piece of sheer good fortune she was authorized a leave over the three-day Christmas weekend.

Her father was back from his many trips to London and she'd be able to finally spend some time with him. Ian Thompson never remarried after the death of his wife in 1934 and Pamela became the woman of the house at age 17. She'd done a superb job running the household for Ian and her brother Dicky, but having been away, Pam was enjoying being back in familiar surroundings, especially at Christmas.

Pam called up the stairs, "Dad, do you want me to make some holiday punch?" Ian had been working tryingly long hours running back and forth between Trinity and London. She could see the toll it was taking on him and she was determined to pamper him over the short holiday.

"Marvelous idea, Pam. I'll be down in a few minutes."

It was a Thompson family tradition to drink their Special Pimm's Punch on Christmas Day. She had fond memories of the times they'd spent laughing and talking by the hearth. Her Mum would make a version without any spirits for her and Dicky. After she passed away, the two Thompson children graduated to the genuine version. Pam assembled the ingredients in the small kitchen and began to mix the punch.

"Just in time," Ian said as he walked into the kitchen. "My inner being felt an overwhelming need for the kind of solace that can only be found in a good mug of Pimm's."

"You're terrible. I don't know why I humor you like I do."

She finished stirring the punch and was getting two mugs down from the cabinet when they both heard the front door knocker clank three times.

"I'll get it," he said as he walked down the hall. Ian expected some paperwork from the office but hadn't thought they would deliver it today. He walked into the entryway and opened the door. It was twilight, and in the fading light he saw a Royal Navy Lieutenant Commander standing on the steps. "Can I help you?"

"Yes, sir. Could you provide shelter for a poor yank standing out in the cold?"

Ian leaned forward a bit, wrinkled his brow and tentatively said, "Jack? Jack Stewart?"

"Hello, Ian. Long time."

"Jack, come in, come in! I'm afraid you have me a bit turned around."

Jack removed his cover and stepped into the hallway. It was just as he remembered from six years ago. Being back here rekindled wonderful memories.

"Here, let me take your coat." Ian took the heavy overcoat from Jack and hung in on the coat rack. "I'm at a total loss, Jack...."

Pam called, "Dad, who's here?" She turned into the hallway from the kitchen. There was a dishtowel in her hand and a look of expectancy on her face. Her dark brown hair was disheveled from her kitchen work and she smoothed it into place with her hand.

"An old friend, my dear," was all Ian offered.

Pam walked down the dimly lit hall. She first saw the uniform and wasn't sure what her Dad meant. She looked at the visitor's face. A little older, a bit more weathered, but she realized it was Jack. Her heart literally skipped a beat as she walked up to him.

"Jack?" She put her hands on his elbows, looking into his eyes. "It *is* you."

"Hi, Pam."

She immediately wrapped her arms around him and squeezed him as tight as he'd ever been squeezed. He put his arms around her and returned the hug. They stood together for a few moments and then both stood back to look at each other.

For his own good, Jack had hidden her beauty away in one of the deeper recesses of his mind. Now it flooded back, her big brown eyes and smooth skin, that warm smile. She'd matured from the 19-year-old student to the 25-year-old woman and it became her. Did her reaction tell him something? Was it just the surprise of seeing an old friend or was there still something there? All of a sudden, his mind and heart were racing. Could she still be unattached? He never imagined after all this time she wouldn't have found someone.

Ian moved back a bit toward the kitchen.

"I would say this calls for a drink!"

CHAPTER SIX

Gestapo Headquarters
The Lutetia Hotel
45 Boulevard Raspail
Paris

Sergeant Klaus Oberiter slowly climbed the stairs to the third floor. A large and powerful man, he wore the uniform of the Schutzstaffel. The SS. Stationed in Paris since the fall of the city in 1940, the big man considered himself lucky. He could be in Russia freezing or maybe in a North African prisoner of war camp. This was a good assignment. There were enough women who didn't mind being seen with German soldiers, the wine was plentiful and he was doing what he liked best. Klaus intended to keep his superiors happy. That meant doing what he was told and keeping his mouth shut.

From the headquarters in Paris, the Gestapo Regional Director was responsible for all aspects of Reich internal security matters. This area covered almost two thirds of France and was a critical security zone. Utilizing a combined force of Gestapo agents and designated SS units, the Germans kept the security of the region under tight control.

There were a number of resistance groups and cells operating in the region, but momentum was currently on the Germans' side. The eventual resolution of the war seemed very much to favor the Axis powers, which brought collaborators out of the woodwork. Using sophisticated techniques developed in the late thirties, the Gestapo had been able to co-opt a large number of French citizens.

These traitors became the Gestapo's informant network, keeping them apprised of the pulse of the populace. Efforts by the British to penetrate the continent had been sporadic at best. The lightning conquest of the low-countries and France decimated their established intelligence networks. Developing new networks and procedures took time. With the Gestapo web in place, it was very difficult to get a group too big before they made the mistake of including a member of the informant network. After that, it was a simple matter of surveillance to flush out the resistance agents and deal with them.

On the third floor, the Sergeant walked down the corridor to the door marked "Section 3 – Authorized Personnel Only". He knocked twice and opened the door.

"Sergeant Oberiter reporting as ordered, Herr Standartenfuhrer." The big man came to a rigid position of attention in front of a large wooden desk. His huge hands held tightly against the seams of his dark uniform trousers.

Standartenfuhrer Gunther Schmidt opened a file on his desk. "Stand at ease, Sergeant. I have a prisoner arrival report. Denis Masur arrived this morning from Nancy. Our agents in Rouen arrested the prisoner three days ago in a raid. We have reason to believe he has extensive information on the resistance ring which is operating in and around Rouen." Schmidt's tone was very professional and to the point. "It is very important we find out everything Masur knows."

Oberiter remained looking straight ahead but he knew what was coming and felt good. He feared Schmidt. The senior agent's reputation was one of total ruthlessness in pursuit of information. Several of Oberiter's comrades fell short of Schmidt's expectations and found themselves with orders to a decidedly more dangerous combat unit.

In a voice that completely lacked any emotion, he said,

"I'll interrogate Masur in 72 hours. By the time I see him, I want him ready to talk. You're authorized to take all necessary action to accomplish this. Do not impair his ability to pass information to us when the time is right. Do you understand?"

"Yes, sir. I understand."

"You'll find him in cell block III. This is your sole duty for the next three days. Let the duty officer know you're working for me. I want progress reports every twelve hours or anytime there's a significant event. Dismissed."

He returned to reading papers on his desk.

Schmidt didn't care for the burly Sergeant but he knew the man could get information from anyone given enough time.

Gunther Schmidt was a former policeman from Munich. Drawn into the political battles of the late 1920's and early 1930's, he'd thrown in with the hardline Nazis and become a steady and dependable member of the party. As the Weimar Republic slowly died, he gave up his police job and committed himself full time to the SD, Hitler's select security service. He rose forcefully in the organization, and when it transitioned to the SS/Gestapo he was rewarded with a commission. Schmidt was the perfect Gestapo officer. He neither had nor wanted a family and was totally dedicated to the SS. He was ruthless and ready to take whatever steps were needed to accomplish his mission. He looked at his watch, noticing it was time for his noon meal at the Café Montrache.

Oberiter knew he could make the man talk given three days. But he must make sure the Frenchman survived to be able to talk. The Sergeant felt he was a master of subtle interrogation. No sleep, very little water, no food and enough pain to break the spirit of the prisoner mentally. He smiled to himself as he descended the stone steps to the basement cell blocks.

He found Masur in cellblock III, leaning against the wall of a 10 by 10-foot concrete and brick cell. The man was wearing the grey prisoner's garb common in French jails. Originally locked up in the Rouen Prefecture of Police, he'd been under control of the French Police. Operating with a memorandum of understanding, the French police turned him over to the Gestapo.

Oberiter's French wasn't great, but he knew enough to do his job. He looked through the small opening in the steel door and felt the excitement he always felt when he was going to hurt someone. Opening the door, he went inside followed by his assistant, Corporal Papen. The Frenchman had a pair of manacles around his ankles and his feet were bare. His hands were handcuffed behind him and he had a look of total fear in his eyes. Papen was carrying a long piece of manila rope in his left hand. Oberiter walked slowly up to Masur, who didn't back up. The large man stared in his eyes for a moment and then viciously brought his right fist up sharply hitting the man in the stomach. The blow knocked Masur backward. Oberiter followed up with another blow to the stomach, which doubled Masur over. Two more hard blows to the man's midsection and he collapsed on the floor.

"Tie the rope," the Sergeant ordered quietly. The Corporal tied one end of the rope to the handcuffs and passed the other end through a large steel ring anchored to the ceiling. Both of the Germans pulled hard on the rope, lifting the Frenchman's arms up behind him. Masur was on his feet with his arms pulled tightly up over his back. This forced his head and torso horizontal to the concrete floor. He was breathing heavily and clearly in severe pain.

"Let's go." They left the room to the sounds of Masur groaning in pain.

35 West Bridge Street

Oxford

There was an awkward moment of silence. Ian grabbed Jack by his arm and led him down the hall. "Come in the kitchen. Your timing is perfect. We're just getting ready to have our Christmas punch."

"I remember those... They've got a way of sneaking up on you." Jack remembered a very crazy Christmas Eve in 1935. Four of them drank a lot of Pimm's and sang every Christmas carol they could remember. Jack recalled adding a few American songs to the British medleys.

Pam had not let go of Jack's other arm as they entered the kitchen. She got a third mug down from the cupboard and filled the three. She handed a mug to Ian and then one to Jack.

Ian raised his mug. "To our very best Christmas surprise."

He beamed and took a long drink. Pam and Jack also raised their mugs and drank, looking directly into one another's eyes.

"Let's go into the sitting room and you can tell us by what miracle you've appeared on our doorstep."

The three settled down around the small, round table that still had Mary Thompson's picture on it. Jack unbuttoned his blouse but kept it on.

"Jack, I do think I can recognize the uniform of His Majesty's Navy. I'm at a bit of a loss to see you in that uniform."

"And wearing a DFC," Pam added.

"To say it's a long story would be an understatement," Jack started. Not sure exactly how to describe his situation he decided to be very general.

"I'm on active service, duly commissioned in the Navy and only recently back in England."

"Sorry, Jack. This is a lot to take in at one time. Are you here on duty or passing through? And where have you been?"

Ian leaned forward in his chair and took another long drink of holiday punch.

Jack looked at Pam who was also expecting a full explanation. "I'm here, assigned to duty in London. It's a long trip from the South Pacific to Oxford, but I'm glad to be back." He looked directly at Pam. There was something in her look. Something invisible but significant. It felt like a bridge being rebuilt after a storm.

"But enough about me. How have you been? What are you two doing? How's Dicky?"

Over the next three hours they caught up on the many activities of the Thompson family. Pam had been with the Woman's Auxiliary Air Force since the fall of 1939, spending the entire time with Fighter Command, most at RAF Stanmore. Dicky received his wings and commission in 1940 with an assignment to Bomber Command. He was flying Bristol Blenheims and stationed at RAF Wattisham. Ian still lectured part time at Trinity and was involved in a research project in the city, spending about half his time each month in London.

"So where do they have you posted, Jack?"

It was like it was in 1935, this family felt like his own. He decided to share what little information Greene would allow.

"Actually I'm with a group in MI-6, a data gathering outfit."

Jack thought he was vague enough.

Ian flashed his eyes briefly at Jack, "Oh, I see. There are so many different agencies and the like. Hard to keep track of them all, eh?" He got up and looked at the large wall clock.

"Jack, you'll stay with us tonight? It's too late to catch a train, and we have Dicky's room."

Although he hadn't expected to stay, Jack now hoped it might be possible. "Only if it's no imposition. And, of course, if the lady of the house doesn't object..."

"Commander, there's no way I'm going to let you out of my sight," Pam said.

She was genuinely happy for the first time in a long time.

Later, when Ian went to bed, the two of them were putting away dishes in the kitchen and making small talk. Pam closed the cupboard door and turned to see Jack staring at her.

She walked over until she was very close to him looking up into his eyes. He leaned down and they kissed, wrapping their arms around each other.

"Pam, it's my fault for not staying in touch. I just thought you would've found someone else. With the war it just seemed too hard." Jack's voice trailed off as he realized how weak is excuse sounded.

She pulled back and looked at him, "Did you find anyone else?"

"No, I never did. It would seem the universe saw fit to confirm my suspicions that you were irreplaceable."

She smiled. "And what made you think I could find anyone to replace you?"

"Guess I didn't think I was anything special."

They stood with their arms loosely around each other's waists.

"I thought I'd never see you again and after five years you walk in my front door. Jack, I never stopped loving you."

She pulled him close and for the first time in along time Jack Stewart felt at home. Peace during wartime.

Gestapo Headquarters
Paris

Over the next three days, Denis Masur descended into a waking nightmare. Oberiter made sure a number of his ribs were broken, ensuring additional hot needles of pain each time the two guards hoisted him up and administered beatings, not to mention through the simple and unfortunately unavoidable act of breathing. He'd been stripped of his clothes to endure the ordeal totally naked in barren, already frigid cell. Alternating shifts, Oberiter and Papen made sure he didn't enjoy the pyrrhic refuge of sleep, either.

Allowed to lay in his own filth, by the fourth day he was covered with smeared feces and smelled of urine. Large ugly bruises covered his body but his face was unblemished. Oberiter considered it a matter of professional ability that he could do his job without disfiguring the face. It also made it much easier for the prisoner to communicate. A prisoner with broken teeth, split lips or a swollen tongue had difficulty confessing. He'd learned the hard way that head trauma could also have adverse effects on prisoner coherence.

In preparation for the interrogation Oberiter and Papen hosed Masur down with cold water, cleaning off most of the filth and leaving him shivering over the drain in the middle of the cell's floor. Returning his pants and shirt, they let him drink a small cup of water. After dressing, they moved him to an interrogation room. For the first time in three days Masur was allowed to sit. He squatted on a small stool in front of a desk at the far side of the room. The two guards removed the ankle manacles and refastened his handcuffs in front of him. Masur sat quietly, but his face reflected shock and confusion.

Schmidt was punctual, as always, arriving at 0900. He possessed a very good working knowledge of French and required no translator. "My name is Schmidt. I'm here to ask you some questions. Do you understand?"

Masur nodded. His hair was matted and wet. There were dark circles under his eyes.

"It's very important you understand that we will get the answers to our questions one way or the other. You've just spent three days with the sergeant. If you don't answer my questions correctly I will be happy to let you spend the next week with him. Unlike you, we have all the time we need. Do you understand?"

Again Masur nodded.

"All I need from you is a list of names. It's that simple. You worked with a resistance group in Rouen. I want their names. If you're smart and tell me what I want to know, there's some hope for your future. You will certainly be sent to a concentration camp. I wouldn't try to fool you. But when this war is over you'll have a chance to return to your home and family. Do you understand me?"

When Masur nodded, Schmidt shouted, "Tell me you understand!"

"…I understand."

"We can do this with pain or without. It's entirely your choice. If you don't provide the names, you'll spend more time with the sergeant. He won't be as gentle this time. You'll tell me in time. And we'll check and verify what you tell us. If it's wrong I'll have every member of your family in Rouen arrested and they'll go through the same process. Do you understand?"

Masur looked at Schmidt and said nothing, his face an expression of hopeless bewilderment. The German got up and walked over to Denis and put his hand under the wretched man's chin, lifting his face upward.

"I want an answer now. Trust me, your life and the lives of your family depend on what you are about to say."

Schmidt backed up and put his hands behind his back.

"Will you provide the names?"

Denis knew he had no choice. If he had no family perhaps he might have the courage to resist this man, but he knew he couldn't risk his wife and children. Quietly, almost in a whisper, the defeated man said, "I will tell you what you want to know."

CHAPTER SEVEN

Prefecture of Police
Rouen, France
January 15, 1943

Schmidt lit a cigarette and stared out the office window of the senior Gestapo agent in Rouen. This entire operation had been almost flawless. When Masur identified the six people in his immediate network, Reich security forces went into a well-practiced routine. The papers and background of the six members of the network were screened for family members who were immediate family, living outside the local area. Two of them met those criteria.

A man, Phillipe Wiegand, had a son who was working in Orleans for the local government. There was also the sister of Marie Chapuis, who was a teacher in Caen. The closest Gestapo offices arrested the relatives and they were transported to Paris. Once in Paris, they'd were put in solitary confinement and photographs were taken of them. Schmidt was now into phase two.

Following a well laid surveillance plan, Phillipe Wiegand and Marie Chapuis were picked up as quietly as possible. Both of them lived in remote parts of town. Schmidt's men were able to arrest each one in the early evening hours without the knowledge of their families. The two had been put in separate interrogation rooms, under guard, but not mistreated in any way.

Schmidt knew time was critical and put out his cigarette, heading downstairs to the detention wing. He anticipated the first confrontation, the terror on their faces, the ultimatum and then the final surrender. He decided on Wiegand first. It was always better to test your wits on the men. Breaking a woman was too easy.

As he entered the room, he saw Wiegand was an unremarkable type, about 40, thinning hair, small mustache, and medium build. Strange he thought, the ones with the guts to join the resistance generally don't look the part. Wiegand was standing in front of the desk with a uniformed guard directly behind. Schmidt took a seat at the table and pretended to read the papers. His routine was set in his mind. There was nothing in the papers he needed to read.

Trying to look officious and detached the German leafed through the papers and offhandedly asked several questions.

"You are Phillipe Wiegand?"

The Frenchman barely whispered, "Yes, I am."

"Do you know Denis Masur of Rouen?"

"I think… I may have met him."

The man's hesitation continued.

Schmidt was enjoying playing with him.

"I too have met Masur. Do you know where?"

"No, sir I don't."

Wiegand had the look of a cornered animal.

The German got up slowly and came over to the man. In a tone which was deadly and threatening he quietly said, "It was in the Gestapo Headquarters in Paris. He was our guest for several days. You know, he didn't look very good when I last saw him. Apparently our hospitality was not to his liking."

Schmidt walked behind him and continued. "He was very forthcoming with information after my men spent some time with him. And interestingly your name came up. What do you think of that?"

The man's legs were shaking slightly. "I don't know about that."

"He gave you up, Phillipe. As well as the others in your group. So don't insult me and try to deny it. I have the authority to have you summarily executed based on his confession." Schmidt walked back to the desk and reached for photographs in the folder. He held up a large black and white photograph and asked, "Do you know who this is?"

Wiegand opened his eyes fully and focused in disbelief, "Charles?"

"Correct. Your son Charles. He is also our guest. It's now time for you to make a decision, Phillipe."

He accented the man's name.

"Does your son live or die? Or does he spend time at Romainville under reasonable conditions? Or do we let him experience what Masur went through and then hang him? It's your choice. I need a decision. And be quick about it. I don't have all day."

Schmidt knew it was checkmate. Only the weakest of men would let their son die to protect themselves. He didn't think the Frenchman was that weak. Schmidt would soon start Wiegand down the path of forced collaboration which was so effective in infiltrating the French resistance.

The girl was easier. Schmidt laid out, in great detail, her future as a prostitute on the Eastern Front if she failed to cooperate. Within two hours, both were on their way home with specific instructions for the third phase. The next step would consist of setting up communication procedures and conducting several loyalty tests. The ultimate goal was not to silence this small group but to penetrate the larger organization. Schmidt looked at the process like a chess game. He would, move by move, discover more cells. He could then identify more individuals and break into their communication channels. It had been a good night's work. He would head back to Paris in the morning after a good meal tonight. According to the local Gestapo agent there was a magnificent local beef and wine stew.

Arisaig House
Invernesshire, Scotland
March 1943

As the weeks passed, Jack's "new guy" label was starting to wear off. Slowly he was beginning to become a productive member of Section D. Every day brought more knowledge of a side of the war he never knew existed. He was learning the entire support organization for the intelligence assault on Europe. Every facet of intelligence gathering was demonstrated to Jack. He learned the communication systems, equipment and training procedures. Some of his most interesting time was spent in the special material support area. These different shops found, stole or fabricated all of the material operatives might need on missions into Europe. Another area he visited was the document and forgery group. They researched actual document requirements and produced replicas which could pass the closest scrutiny. Jack was also able to visit a group simply called the "dirty tricks" gang. They devised clandestine items an agent might need to gather information, defend himself or destroy a target. However the most enlightening part of his training had been his trip north to Arisaig.

Upon arriving in Scotland, Jack realized he was going to be treated as one of those square front office types who came to sniff around, take notes and go back to their cushy chairs in Baker Street. He decided to quickly set the school straight. He told the staff he wanted to be treated like any student and he wanted to learn what they learned. There were times when Jack wondered if that had been such a smart thing to do.

He jumped into the full syllabus: hand-to-hand combat, radio operations, covert movements, enemy organization, local customs, and weapons training. He found it was not only interesting and challenging, but it turned out he had something of a knack for it.

He was in a strange situation at Arisaig. The Military Training Officers worked for him. However he was also there as a student. In that role he was supposed to be getting a good understanding of the training all prospective agents would receive. The senior MTO was a crusty old Scot named McClaren. He'd seen action at the end of the last war and been in the organization before it formally made the transition to MI-6. Jack enjoyed his view on the world, which was very irreverent and often colored by a bit of scotch whisky. But Major Billy McClaren took his job very seriously. He knew what he taught the agents at Arisaig would be critical to the war effort and to their personal survival. Some of the people they trained wouldn't come back and McClaren never forgot that. But he was intent on making sure they had the best possible chance to complete their missions and survive.

"That's right, sir. Block the upward knife thrust by crossing your forearms and catching the opponent's blade arm. Then quickly bring the palm of your hand smartly up into his nose and upper teeth. That will break some teeth, and drive the nose cartilage into the sinus cavities. At that point, assess your ability to either commandeer his knife or resort to a flipper kick to the genitals." Jack was in the middle of the self-defense class. The class was going over a scenario when the agent has no weapon and the opponent is armed with a knife.

"Commander, if I might have a word?" It was McClaren, standing on the edge of the training mat.

"Good morning, Major McClaren." Jack wiped his sweaty forehead.

"I think I'm getting the hang of this."

"Taking to it like a duck to water, if you ask me. I think we need to get you a commando knife, a parachute and turn you loose on Jerry."

Jack laughed.

"Billy, I'm a rookie and I know it. But I *am* getting a better feel every day for what our folks have to be able to do."

He arched his back. Jack had been pleasantly surprised his back was holding up under significant physical punishment. Maybe someday he could take on the medical board again, he thought.

"That's the whole idea, Jack, my boy. By the way, had a call from the boss. They want to wrap up this phase and bring you back to Baker Street."

Jack was disappointed to be leaving this group of students. He'd gotten to know some of them well. But he had to admit there were times he felt a little guilty to be out here knowing Tommy was carrying the load back at Baker Street.

"I'm sorry to have to leave, but if you'll have me, I'd like to stop out again and learn more."

McClaren smiled, he was one of the few people who had ribbed him about his "Canadian" accent. The older man had genuinely enjoyed getting to know the American.

"You're always welcome at Arisaig. The light'll be in the window and the scotch'll be poured."

Billy patted Jack on the back as they walked over to the billet area. "Besides, we can probably learn a wee bit from you!"

Jack thought he'd be able to spend some time with Pam this weekend. Maybe she could come into the city.

64 Baker Street
London

"Tommy, Stewart is on his way back," Noel Greene said. "Let's decide what direction we want to go with him."

Colonel Greene and Tommy Hudson were going over a number of items at their normal daily meeting. Hudson knew they were going to get into Jack's future. He didn't have an answer for Greene because he had no answer for himself.

Greene continued, "You're stretched thin enough as it is. Don't you agree?"

"I'm not going to try and deny it. The pace of operations and expansion is keeping me on my toes." Hudson knew he was stretched thin and something should be done for the sake of the section.

"First of all, what's your opinion of our young Commander? Does he have what it takes to be a full member of the team? What's his attitude toward this rather unusual situation?" Greene knew Tommy had been in very close contact with Stewart, and he trusted Hudson's judgment.

"Colonel, you may find this hard to believe. I sense Jack Stewart is as comfortable in his current situation as either you or I. Since he arrived I've seen nothing but full effort, great attitude and a genuine desire to be part of Section D. He's hit it off very well with all of the shops. They seem to connect with him."

Hudson surprised himself with the tone of his endorsement but it was accurate. Tommy also sensed Jack was carrying some burden from earlier in the war. But it hadn't affected his work and he was inclined to give him the benefit of the doubt.

"Tommy, you know how far Billy McClaren and I go back. He told me Stewart is one of the most natural agents he's ever seen. To get a seal of approval from that crusty old git is rather remarkable." Greene sighed and went on, "It appears we have an opportunity here which neither of us would have ever anticipated. We've talked about the possibility of a special section for the last year. Who would've thought Jack Stewart might make it possible."

Beside the ongoing intelligence gathering effort and occasional sabotage, Greene and Hudson knew there were two very critical intelligence areas which must receive extra attention. The Germans were developing two weapons systems that could be crucial to the eventual outcome of the war. The first was their effort to create an atomic weapon. Much of the intelligence gathering and effort to thwart those plans were under way and aimed at occupied Norway. However Greene also knew they must deal with the new advances in German radar technology.

The British had taken the technological lead and also pioneered the tactical employment of defensive radar systems in 1938. Green was convinced it was the skill and bravery of the RAF pilots which ultimately made the difference in the Battle of Britain. However without the radar systems directing the right number of fighters to the right spot, time after time, bravery might not have been enough. Now Greene was getting indications the Germans were moving past British technology and might deploy a much improved radar in their twin-engine fighters. The Luftwaffe night fighter squadrons had already taken a heavy toll on Bomber Command. Operational reports showed bomber losses to the enemy were due to anti-aircraft fire and night fighters in equal proportion. If Jerry was ready to deploy a more effective radar system for their fighters, it could be disastrous for the RAF.

"Do you think it's time to stand up a special section for the radar project?" Greene asked.

Hudson didn't hesitate, "I do, sir. And Stewart should be the section lead." Tommy would miss Jack's help with the workload, but mucking up the Germans' airborne radar effort was critical.

"I think they should be tasked with both the technical intelligence effort and also look into any interdiction efforts which might be feasible. I say we let Jack build his team, then we give ourselves the option of using them against radar or any other key project as events unfold."

Greene nodded, "I totally agree. But if the reports are accurate the new air intercept radar is imminent. Let's have him focus on that issue straight away and get his section operational."

Cambridge

Jack had seen Pam as often as he could that first month

after their reunion. This last month in Scotland had made him realize how much he missed her. He couldn't wait to get off the train and make his way to the Thompsons'. Ian wasn't going to be able to get out of London this weekend and Pam traded her weekend shift on the operations floor. Seeing her had become very important to him. As a combat aviator, he'd always told himself a long-term relationship would be out of the question. He simply couldn't afford any distractions. But that part of his life was over for now. He wouldn't be strapping in any cockpits for a long time. Maybe this was what fate had in store for him. For now, Jack Stewart was going to let things go where they might.

Her eyes lit up as she opened the door. She smiled at him and moved into his arms. "Hi, Yank." She pulled away only enough to kiss him softly. "Before you get carried away, I have to warn you we have someone in the sitting room. So please behave yourself."

She took him by the hand and led him down the hallway.

Dicky Thompson lounged on the sofa, reading the *Times*. He hadn't been home to Oxford for several months due to operational schedules and a training course.

"Who's there, love?" he asked without even lowering the paper.

Pam brought Jack into the sitting room with her finger on her lips signaling quiet.

Jack thought he recognized the voice and hoped it was her brother.

"Just one of those lonely Royal Navy types," her voice betrayed her mischievousness.

Dicky lowered the paper and frowned for a moment, looking more at the uniform than the face.

"Got a pint for a poor sailor?" Jack laughed.

He came over to the sofa as Dicky stood up dropping the paper in a heap.

"I'll be damned. What in the world is going on here?" He paused for a moment and then extended his hand.

"Jack, what in the world are you doing here?"

"Long story, but let me assure you there's no other place I'd rather be."

The three decided to walk down to the pub and celebrate their reunion. Dicky had been completely surprised. Pamela and her father conspired to keep Jack's arrival a secret with the hope they might arrange a surprise reunion. Pam was only sorry her dad couldn't make it. She would enjoy relating the story when they saw each other again.

Dicky was caught briefly in between duty stations. He'd finished his flying tour in Blenheims and was looking at a stint as an instructor in one of the many training squadrons which were churning out new pilots. However there'd been a request for operationally experienced pilots in a new squadron standing up at Tangmere. He'd volunteered and recently finished his transition training in the Westland Lysander.

"I wasn't really ready for a break from ops, but I was ready for a break from Jerry's flak and the damned night fighters," Dicky said. They started on their second round of ale in the local pub, "Castaways".

"Dicky, I don't know how you guys do it. For every hour of night time I logged, there were 20 to 30 hours of day flying. But I guess it makes too much sense if you have to fly into the teeth of the Luftwaffe and are out of range of your Spits and Hurricanes."

Jack felt completely at ease with Dicky despite the years of almost no contact. He guessed it was a combination of their old friendship and a common bond as combat aviators.

"So what'll you be doing in the Lysander?"

"A bit of everything I guess. Logistic and courier flights... could also see the odd flight into the continent."

Dicky put down his half-full glass and smiled, "But at least I don't have to fly formation or put up with any more bloody night flights with all those evil bastards trying to kill me."

As he finished his ale he said, "If you two will excuse me I'm planning to drop by the Millers. See if Francis would like to go out for dinner." He had a long-term friendship with Francis Miller, the daughter of one of Ian's Trinity faculty mates. There was nothing very serious at this point but they did try to see each other when the opportunity arose. He stood up and said, "Don't wait up. I could be on the town til' the wee hours."

Smiling, he put his hand on Jack's shoulder.

"Good to have you back, old boy."

After dinner, Jack and Pam walked slowly back to the Thompsons'. Pam broke the silence.

"I'm glad you were able to see Dicky."

"It seems the years just melted away. Tonight could've been 1936 and we could have just finished beating Swindon. He's quite a guy."

"You two always seemed to hit it off. I was glad of it then, and I'm glad now. With so many things in our lives turned upside down, family is even more important."

64 Baker Street
London

Monday morning, Tommy told Jack of the scheduled meeting with Greene. A meeting sounded ominous, especially after being recalled from Arisaig. When he asked Tommy if he was in trouble, the Englishman only laughed. "Not just yet, but the day *is* young."

The meeting flew by. Greene was enthusiastic as he outlined the big picture. Jack was to form a section within Section D, designated Section F. Jack would have administrative and operational control. Section D would function as the parent command and F would receive operational tasking from Tommy. It was up to Jack to bring together assets and operational planning to accomplish their assignments. Greene's general guideline was a team consisting of ten operatives and ten more support staff.

It took Jack several days to lay out his game plan. He talked at length with Tommy and bounced ideas off him. Jack decided he needed an experienced intelligence officer who could be an anchor for the section. He also needed a couple of key players for supply, admin, research and operations. It was almost like a small aircraft squadron and that was something he understood. His most difficult task was trying to find talent that could do the job in the field. A trip to Arisaig and a chat with Billy McClaren seemed like the best way to attack that challenge. Tommy provided Jack a recommended list, but the final decision was up to him. It took several days, but Jack put together a group which looked balanced and experienced.

Terry McGinty already had the nickname "Bags" when he came into SOE from the Royal Highlanders. A hard-nosed Scot from Glasgow, he was famous for being able to find or steal anything his regiment needed without ever arousing suspicions. An ugly incident with the Royal Air Force made it advantageous for him to take a transfer to the SOE in the fall of 1941. Since then, he'd been working special projects for Tommy and finding scarce items in a war-rationed England. SOE had a much lower supply priority than the Navy or Air Force. McGinty always seemed to find a way to make sure the SOE came out on top of any supply issue. When Tommy told McGinty that his roommate needed the "best scrounger in England," he agreed to take the job.

When Jack asked the Scotsman to join Section F, he went straight to the point.

"Sergeant Major McGinty, I've been told you're the best procurer in England."

"Aye, sir. I've 'ad some luck putting me hands on the odd item now and then. But there's one condition before I agree to join your little band."

"Which is?"

Jack liked the stocky man's no nonsense attitude.

"Sir, you must never ask where anything might've come from. It's better for me that way... and for you."

Jack laughed. "You've got a deal. And a job."

Hiram Baker was selected as the section intelligence officer and administrator. His talent for intelligence analysis was matched only by his ability to take care of anything associated with official channels. He was a whiz at arranging personnel transfers, disbursing payouts, security clearances and official orders. He'd been a special assistant to the senior director of Lloyd's before the war. Jack knew his own attention to administrative items wasn't his strength and he was pleased he had Hiram on board.

Tommy had suggested Jack drive down to Section IX to talk with some of the scientists who were working the research issues. Section IX was located in a remote country house on the outskirts of the city where MI-6 had assembled some of the smartest minds in the country. The group did everything from dreaming up exotic gadgets for use in the field to analysis of all intelligence reports from a scientific viewpoint. Jack needed someone who could join the section and be the conduit for information and analysis on these new German weapons.

Jack decided to take Baker with him. He wanted to get to know the young officer better and decide how they would lash this new organization together in such a short period of time. Tall and thin, Baker didn't look like a combat veteran who had won the Military Cross. He'd been a Captain in the infantry whose unit had been decimated in France in 1940. Severely wounded just before Dunkirk, he transferred to MI-6 after his recovery on the recommendation of his Colonel, an old friend of Noel Greene.

Jack liked the quiet young man. During the drive, Baker outlined how it would be very easy for Jack to recruit section members if they were already part of SOE. If Jack went outside of MI-6 it wasn't difficult, but it would take time and the vetting process for security clearances would be more cumbersome. The real challenge would come if Jack recruited any foreign nationals as agents. Because they could never rule out a German plant, foreign nationals were kept very compartmentalized when it came to classified material. So far Jack was in good shape. Every member of Section F had come from within the organization. Today would be no exception. Everyone at Section IX was fully vetted and cleared for the most sensitive material.

As they pulled into the country estate, originally called The Frythe, Jack felt he was assembling a solid group of people. He knew he was in new territory, but if he listened to the experienced types and let his experts do their jobs, he'd be okay. They were going to meet Geoffrey Matthews the section head at Frythe. Matthews had been given their requirements and today Jack and Hiram would be meeting Matthew's nominee for research lead of the section. After showing their identity cards to the guards, they were taken to his office.

Geoffrey Mathews sat in a second floor corner office overlooking a neglected rose garden. A career educator, he'd been recruited by Hugh Dalton, SOE's first director. He'd been handling the "dirty tricks boys" ever since.

"Delighted to meet you, Commander Stewart."

They shook hands. He was a large man with a flushed complexion and large bushy mustache.

"Mr. Matthews, Captain Baker, my intelligence officer."

"Hello, Captain. Please have a seat."

The two sat down, as did Matthews.

"Noel Greene gave me a quick idea of the areas you'll be concentrating on with the section. I looked at our folks and I think I have the perfect choice for a researcher who can cover either area of your interest."

"The team objectives are going to be demanding from a

technical aspect. We'd benefit from someone who knows the technology and how the intelligence gathering and reporting system covers those areas." Jack had thought this through at length. The team must have someone who can identify the key and critical elements of an assignment from a technological standpoint. They didn't have time or assets to waste.

There was a knock on the door.

"That must be him now."

Ian Thompson walked into the office as the others stood up.

Jack and Ian looked at each other but said nothing as Matthews did the introductions.

As they shook hands, Jack said, "Ian, it's good to see you again."

"Do you know each other, Commander?" Matthews asked.

Ian interjected, "Commander Stewart and I have known each other since he read physics for me at Trinity."

"Is this going to be a problem, Commander Stewart?"

Matthews was clearly taken by surprise at the turn of events.

Jack smiled at Matthews.

"I should say not. I can't think of anyone more qualified from a scientific standpoint. I look forward to working with you, Ian. If you still want the job."

"Oh, I wouldn't miss it for the world," Ian laughed.

"Not for the world."

Hiram waited in the car while Ian and Jack stood talking in the driveway.

"When you left Oxford back in '36 I very much wanted you to return and resume your studies at some point."

The older man had a bemused look on his face.

"Never would I have envisioned the situation we have right now."

"I guess I'm still the student and you're still the teacher."

Jack leaned back against the car.

"Ian, I think we have a chance here to make a real impact on the war effort. Your technical expertise is crucial if we're going to throw the right wrench into their gears at the right point. Take a look at everything we have on the new radar. We'll meet at Baker Street the day after tomorrow. Can you make that?"

"Two days. Baker Street. I'll be there."

Jack had one final interview for the team. The team was solid but still needed someone with actual experience in penetration operations. Jack pressed Hudson pretty hard and Tommy came through for him.

Phillip Hatcher had been a London policeman before the war. One of the youngest inspectors in the history of Scotland Yard. Hatcher was Jack's age.

He had backed into the intelligence world after Dunkirk. Pressed into service conducting debriefs of newly arrived Frenchmen, he'd gotten to know a number of the MI-6 interrogation specialists. They were impressed with Phillip and after a series of phone calls, Phillip was seconded to MI-6. He'd been involved in putting three operational teams into France and one into Germany. He'd been on the ground in France during a quick raid, or and "in-and-out".

Jack had arranged to meet Hatcher in the new Section F offices on the 4th floor of 64 Baker Street. The former cop was on time and Baker brought him into Jack's small office. He wasn't what Jack expected. Stocky like a wrestler, he had a ruddy complexion and curly blond hair.

"Hi, I'm Jack Stewart. Please come in."

"Phil Hatcher. Nice to meet you, sir."

The two sat and Jack got right to the point.

"We've got an interesting startup here. I need someone with solid operational experience to handle the ops lead."

Jack watched Hatcher, but there was no reaction.

"I think we have some good chaps here already. We'll be focusing on a couple of high priority projects for Colonel Greene."

"Sounds interesting. Where exactly would I fit in?"

He remained reserved and cautious.

"I need someone who can run the agents we'll be sending into Europe. According to Tommy Hudson you're the man for the job."

Still no reaction.

Hatcher asked, "Would I have complete authority over the operational decisions for these missions?"

Jack felt he was being interviewed.

"That's the same question I asked Colonel Greene. He assured me we would have complete administrative and operational control of anything the section does."

"We see things the same way, Commander."

Hatcher smiled for the first time since he'd come in the office.

"If I'm going to have to make decisions involving people's lives, I want the authority to make the right decisions."

Jack liked his straightforward attitude.

"I think we're in agreement there. We want to go operational next week if you're ready."

"Fair enough," he said.

"Let's get this thing started. But I have to warn you. I don't have anything to prove to anyone. If I don't like how it's shaping up, I'm out."

"As you say, fair enough."

Jack extended his hand and they shook on the new arrangement.

CHAPTER EIGHT

Tourny, France
May 4, 1943

Gunther Schmidt made it a policy to always conduct face-to-face meetings with collaborators, far from their home turf. It was one more procedure, which he felt would assure the greatest chance of success for his plans. So far, he wasn't unhappy with the progress with Wiegand and Chapuis. Both had proved responsive to his requests. Consequently he'd been able to put together a much more extensive map of the resistance organization in Northern France and arrest several lower-tier agents. However, true success would be uncovering the communication network linking the main groups in Rouen, Le Mans, Amiens and Lille.

In recent months the Gestapo noted an increased effort by British intelligence to penetrate that area with agents. The resistance often provided the initial contact and support while these groups of agents set up their operations. There was talk the allies were already planning for the invasion of Europe and these teams of agents were one indication it was more than a rumor. Schmidt hadn't seen many cases of sabotage during the last six months. It appeared the enemy was more concerned with gathering intelligence and sending information back to England.

"There he is now," Schmidt said to Hans Priller, one of the agents assigned to his office. "Follow him. When he turns up the street we can pick him up."

Priller put the Citroën into gear and slowly drove up the wide street. Schmidt hated the French car but he gave up his Daimler to be as inconspicuous as possible. As Wiegand turned into the side street, Priller followed and pulled alongside.

"Get in the front seat, Phillipe." Schmidt told him. The senior agent sat in the back seat. He had his hand on his pistol in case Wiegand had some misguided ideas to end his treachery. The man complied and got into the front seat by Priller. "Let's get out of town and head for Vernon."

Priller pulled on the main road and accelerated south out of Tourny.

"Phillipe, I wanted to have this meeting for two reasons. First, you've provided excellent information, so I thought you should be rewarded. Here's a card written by your son last week. You'll see he's well. We've upheld our end of this arrangement." He handed a small envelope to Wiegand and continued, "Second, we're interested in the agents the British continue to infiltrate. How does your group find out when an agent is going to be arriving?"

"Marcel listens to the evening broadcast of the BBC. There are certain phrases telling us our group has a mission. We then tune into a specific frequency on our radio for a short transmission with the details."

"Then I need two things from you, the frequency of your radio and a warning the next time you're alerted for a mission." Wiegand didn't reply and Schmidt continued, "Don't fail on this. I have other sources of information. If I find you didn't notify us of the next operation you'll have signed your son's death warrant. Do you understand?"

"I understand. I'll pass the information in the normal way." Wiegand was referring to the contact method he used: a drop and pickup system in a park in Rouen.

The two Germans dropped Wiegand on the outskirts of Vernon and headed back to Paris. Schmidt was pleased at the progress of this phase and felt it was time to clean up loose ends. Denis Masur remained in solitary confinement at the Paris Headquarters. For the last four months, he had served as insurance for Schmidt. The Gestapo agent never liked to leave anything to chance. He wanted to be sure his work with Wiegand and Chapuis worked out as expected. Both collaborators had met his expectations. Now it was time to get rid of Masur. He couldn't risk the prisoner getting word outside to the resistance about possible collaborators.

"Contact Sergeant Oberiter when we get back. It seems Denis Masur is going to die of a massive heart attack tomorrow." He rolled the window down a crack and lit a cigarette.

"God, I hate these shitty French cigarettes."

Priller grunted an agreement and concentrated on driving.

64 Baker Street
9 May, 1943

Jack, Hatcher, Baker and Ian Thompson attended the first meeting of Section F with two additional attendees: Noel Greene and Tommy Hudson.

Jack introduced Greene, who reinforced the need to beat the Nazis' attempt to field new weapons. Greene then turned it over to Hudson.

"Gentlemen, as they say, timing is everything. We've been concerned Jerry was ready to field an improved version of their Lichtenstein airborne radar. German night fighters are already taking a heavy toll on our bombers. We estimate fully half of our losses in Bomber Command are due to Jerry night fighters, and they're getting ready to put a more effective radar into service. Our attrition rate right now is just above the breaking point. If we start losing more aircraft, our strategic bombing mission is over, and this war will drag on much longer. Your mission is to gather intel and to try and find an opportunity get your hands on the new radar. We know we can't stop production. But if we can get a head start on some type of countermeasure device it'll save a lot of lives."

He turned to Ian.

"Dr. Thompson, could you brief the group on the latest development."

"This morning, by way of an aircrew defection, we apparently have our hands on a JU-88 night fighter with the older Lichtenstein SN-2 radar installed. We also have the crew. We hope they'll provide valuable information for our project. This couldn't have come at a better time. Someone must be on our side."

"Gentlemen, there's one more fact I think you will find most interesting," Noel Greene said. "This is most secret. There are lives depending on this fact remaining very close-hold. A crew member of the German night fighter at Norwich is one of our boys."

Norwich Constabulary
Norfolk

Hauptmann Karl Mann sat on the small cot with his back

against the masonry wall. He was smoking a cigarette and wondering again if he'd made the right decision. The British had separated him from his crew, Rolf Buenner and Gerhard Sommer, as soon as they landed.

Mann had thought about defecting for over a year. However with a three man crew it seemed impossible. He'd been crewed with Rolf and Gerhard for 8 months. During the time there were many opportunities to gauge each man's loyalty. The more they talked, the more it became evident to Mann the three of them did not like the war or the Nazi Party. He remembered the day Rolf was particularly frustrated with operational scheduling and muttered something about "they ought to fly to England and check out of this war."

It was soon clear they all felt the same way. The big question in Karl's mind was if they'd take that last step and actually agree to defect. There were questions about what would happen to their families. What would be their treatment in England? What would happen if Germany won the war? There were no answers to any of these questions. Six weeks ago they agreed to take the final step. Fate works in strange ways. A month ago the squadron was forward deployed to the Luftwaffe field at Abbeville, France. They were now less than 30 minutes flying time from England. In addition the air controllers in that area were using the rail-mounted version of the large Wurzburg radar. The rail-mounted version was not as accurate and often had large areas of poor coverage. This was a key part of their plan. They would try to fly into one of these areas during a combat engagement. They would then transmit they'd received battle damage and cut off radio transmissions. If the aircraft was near the Channel it would appear they had crashed into the water. A little confusion would make their flight to England easier and hopefully free of German pursuit. If the British were smart, the Luftwaffe would not even be aware of their defection.

Last night Mann's aircraft was one of several night fighters vectored toward an RAF formation over the North Sea. As the fighters headed north, Karl knew they would be at the edge of the Wurzburg coverage and over water. During the first engagement Karl took advantage of the normal confusion of aerial combat to make a short transmission and head for England.

At the operations center at Abbeville, the Commanding Officer of Mann's squadron was talking with the Group Operations Officer. "So your last radar paint of Mann was right here," he said, pointing to a spot in the North Sea off the Dutch coast.

"That was at about 0335. Three minutes later we received a cut off radio transmission using his call sign. It was garbled, but it sounded like they were hit and bailing out."

The Major sounded tired and resigned to bad news.

"We've notified the Kriegsmarine. They'll divert a patrol boat to the area to search for them. We need to get with the day fighters to provide cover for the search. That water is cold. If they didn't get into their rafts, it doesn't look good."

The CO turned and shook his head in agreement.

"I think you're right. It's too bad. They were a good crew."

He walked out.

We need to run our damned intercepts over land where we have better radar coverage. He'd push to revise their rules of engagement, but he wasn't hopeful the sector commander would agree.

Norwich Airfield
9 May, 1943

At 1445, two RAF Hudson bombers touched down at the Norwich airport. Half of the deplaned group went directly to the hangar, while the other group got into three waiting police cars and sped off the airfield.

When the night fighter crew was originally brought in, Constable Chief Ryan O'Neal put each of the Germans in separate cells. Not really sure what to do he offered them food, water and cigarettes. The Germans all seemed to be taking events easily. O'Neal decided to leave them alone while he waited for the RAF. When it came to police work O'Neal knew his business but this was something out of his experience. Best thing to do was put the Germans in lock up and wait for the experts.

This was a day he wouldn't soon forget. The phone call from the airport had come in at 4:40 am. Not really sure what to do, he called out the home guard section like they had practiced back in '40 in case of attack by paratroopers. Racing out to the field he couldn't have been more surprised to find out the airmen were defecting.

As he waited for the RAF, O'Neal went over every detail in his mind to make sure he didn't overlook anything. It made sense to have the aircraft towed into a hangar and out of sight. To make sure security was tight, the hangar was now sealed off by police and the home guard. A few of the soldiers did a cursory exam of the aircraft for explosive devices. Nothing was found, but no one was an expert, so it was assumed there might still be dangerous items aboard. O'Neal had told both his policemen and the people at the airfield this was to be kept under wraps until the military arrived. The senior constable recorded the names, ranks and service numbers of the Germans. He couldn't think of anything else to do, except perhaps a chat with the pilot.

Mann wasn't sure what he'd expected. He was getting bored sitting in a cell with nothing to do. After asking his name and number the British brought him some food, tea and cigarettes. He'd been alone for the last four hours. The outer cell door to the cellblock opened and he heard someone coming. He saw a middle-aged policeman in company with a younger man arrive at his barred cell door.

"I'm Chief Constable O'Neal," the older man said.

"My name is Hauptmann Karl Mann."

Funny, O'Neal thought, he looks just like one of our boys in that flying suit. He asked, "Is there anything you need?"

Mann had practiced English since his decision to defect.

"What will happen to us?"

"There are some people from the Air Force coming to take you back to London."

O'Neal decided there was no harm in telling him that piece of information.

"My people will be with me?" Mann asked, realizing he was very rusty with the language.

"I suspect so. Although once the military arrives it's their show. I do have one question you could help me with if you don't mind."

"Yes?"

"Your aircraft. Does it have explosives aboard?" he asked. Why not ask the man, he thought. He wouldn't want anyone to get hurt.

It took Mann a few seconds to figure out the question.

"No bombs. There are bullets in the guns but can't fire on the ground."

He had secured the gun circuits for the forward firing guns and Rolf would have engaged the safety on the MG 50 before landing, it was procedure.

"Would I be able to see my people?"

"We must wait for the Air Force, I'm afraid. They'll let you see your chaps soon enough." O'Neal had the answer to his question. It was a matter of waiting.

A third policeman came down the corridor.

"Chief O'Neal, the military people are here from London. I put them in your office."

O'Neal found six men waiting in his office, four were in uniform and two were wearing civilian clothes. He learned the senior man was an Army Major named Hudson. The Chief Constable was introduced around and the visitors immediately wanted all of the details of the morning's events. He gave them a chronological report starting with the call from the airfield. There was the occasional question from the group. When the Chief Constable finished, it was the Major who spoke first.

"Thank you, Chief Constable. We'd like to head back to the airfield straight away. Please put Mann and Sommer in one car and Buenner in another car. I don't want handcuffs on any of them. I'd like a third escort car with your people to lead the way back to the airfield."

"Right, Major. I'll have my men bring them out to the cars. They're parked by the jail entrance. That's on the opposite side from where you entered. I'll have one of my lads take you down there."

Hudson divided the group. He would drive the second car with Jack, Ian and Buenner. The other two Germans were riding with Hatcher, Baker and an RAF Major named Whitney who had joined them at Biggin Hill. The Germans came out one at a time with a policeman walking on either side. All three were still wearing their dark green flying suits. Once in the cars the procession moved out toward the airfield.

As Tommy pulled the car onto the main road he said, "Gentlemen, I'd like you to meet Flight Lieutenant Brian Collins, Royal Air Force. Recently returned from extended duty with the Luftwaffe. Welcome home, Brian."

The young man smiled as only a free man could.

"Good to be home, Major. It's good to be home."

"Brian, we're going to get on a Hudson and head for Biggin Hill. I want to hold any debriefing until we get to London. Right now, relax. One question. What's the condition of your aircraft? Is it flyable?"

"Other than needing petrol and oil there weren't any significant discrepancies when we landed," Collins replied.

That fit into Hudson's plan. Major Jack Whitney was one of the most experienced Mosquito pilots in the RAF. Tommy wanted to get the aircraft back to Biggin Hill. His two options were to have Whitney get a brief from the pilot and fly it himself, or, if Brian felt it made sense, have Karl Mann fly it to Biggin Hill with two RAF crewmembers on board. For security reasons, Tommy wanted the flight to be at night. Because of that he was inclined to go with the German. Whitney was a superb pilot. But making your first flight in a strange aircraft with only a few hours to become familiar with it was a challenge. Once they could discuss it, he'd make a final decision.

With Brian bound for London, Tommy and Jack gathered in the hangar with the rest of the group. Jack and Tommy asked the German pilot to step over where Major Whitney stood looking at the aircraft.

Tommy offered his hand to the German, "Hauptmann Mann, I am Major Hudson. This is Major Whitney and Lieutenant Commander Stewart. I understand you speak some English. I would like to conduct this discussion in English but I speak German also."

"Yes, Major. I should like to work my English," Mann replied.

"First, let me say you showed great courage in what you did. I want to clarify your status as a defecting member of a hostile armed force." Tommy thought he could put some of the German's fears to rest right away which would make the rest of the discussion much easier. "Because you voluntarily defected we do not consider you a prisoner of war. I hope you understand your time spent in a cell here was because the local authorities don't deal with situations like this often."

Mann was concentrating hard on Hudson's words. He waited a moment after Hudson finished. "I will not be a prisoner?"

Hudson continued, "No. In fact, after you sign a pledge of loyalty, you'll be considered a private citizen. Of course we'll want to spend some time with you debriefing a number of subjects. But I assure you that's voluntary on your part. You'll be free to remain within the United Kingdom or we can facilitate your travel to another country."

Mann looked surprised and relieved. "Thank you," he said.

"We do have one thing we want to ask of you." Brian had told Tommy he had no qualms about having Mann fly the aircraft to Biggin Hill. Brian even volunteered to go, something Tommy immediately ruled out. With Mann airborne, he wanted his Luftwaffe crew with their feet firmly on the ground. "In order to keep this event as quiet as possible for both your protection and our advantage we want to get the aircraft to an RAF base. Would you be willing to fly the aircraft to Biggin Hill with two of our chaps as your crewmembers?"

Although he understood the question, Mann was almost speechless. He'd never imagined the reception would be anything like this. He was happy to be of whatever assistance they wanted. "Yes, I can fly it for you. Could I go with my crew?"

Jack interjected, "One of your crew is already on his way to London. We want our people with you for navigation and to talk on the radios. You've come too far to be shot at by our side."

Mann agreed with him. When he found out Major Whitney was a Mosquito pilot and would be going as his engineer, he seemed pleased. Within an hour Jack and Tommy were airborne following the first Hudson with Collins, Ian and Phil on the way to London.

At 0400, there was a single takeoff from Norwich airfield. The twin-engine night fighter rose into the night sky and banked gentyl, turning toward London.

64 Baker Street
Section F Offices

Brian Collins turned out to be a wealth of information about the new Luftwaffe radar system. As a JU-88 flight engineer, he'd been sent to a week long course on the new equipment. He worked with Ian Thompson and the radar technicians at Section IX to try and put together a best estimate of the system's capability. Potentially the most devastating improvement was the transition from the current single operating frequency to a multiple frequency capability. Because radar countermeasures are dependent on the frequency involved, knowing what frequency your enemy is using is critical. The exact frequencies hadn't been disclosed at Collins' school but there were going to be six selectable frequencies. The choice was up to the crew based on weather or squadron doctrine. Bomber Command recently started using "window," a type of metallic foil cut specifically to counteract a specific frequency. Against the new radars, this type of window would be ineffective. The attacking aircraft would only switch to a different frequency if the bombers were using the foil. Jack's section had to find out the six new frequencies for the Lichtenstein radar.

Jack met with Hatcher and Baker and tried to sketch out a plan to accomplish the tasking. The more he worked with Hatcher, the more he liked the hard nosed ex-cop. Diplomacy was not his strong suit, but he seemed to have a natural ability to come up with options and courses of action. His prior experience on missions into Europe helped the process. There were long hours looking at maps and discussing how they could approach the problem. Jack discovered Hatcher was one of those people who could totally focus on a problem. As they began to craft together a plan, it was clear to Jack he'd made a superb choice for his ops boss. Phil took each step of the plan and filled in the details. At that point Hiram would gather all pertinent intelligence data, sort it, analyze it and present the team with the best information available.

Following several days of discussions within Section F, Jack felt they had a plan which was workable, had a good chance of success and could go operational in short order. But Jack had to convince Tommy Hudson, who wasn't going to be a pushover. There were too many lessons learned in blood over the last year.

"Okay, Tommy. We've got a plan to go after those frequencies." Jack had dropped by to see Tommy after his regular morning meeting with Noel Greene. He put a folder on Tommy's desk and kept one in his lap.

"Let me hear the plan, then I've got something for you."

Tommy sat back with the folder in his lap.

Jack launched into the plan. "We don't know for sure when they'll field the system, so the sooner we go after it, the more time we might have if things don't work out. There'll also be a backup plan shortly. Phil's putting the last details in place. Brian thinks Jerry'll have the radar operational within the month. The whole purpose in transferring his squadron to Abbeville was to be able to hit our bombers earlier in their missions and prevent as many as possible from making it to the Hinterland."

Jack opened his folder and Tommy did the same.

"Why don't you give me the overview," Tommy said. "Then we can work our way down to the details."

He started to page through his folder.

"The first challenge is to determine when the new aircraft arrive at Abbeville. I'm comfortable our radio interception folks, combined with a physical watch by resistance forces near the field, can determine when they are on station."

The team knew there were several resistance units within reasonable distance of Abbeville. It would be feasible to have them watch the parking areas to see when aircraft with new side markings and or new antennas arrived. The Germans were very methodical about aircraft markings. The new series aircraft would be marked distinctly different from those now at the station. The British communication intercept people were probably the best in the world. Monitoring call signs of the aircraft operating at Abbeville would be an independent indicator of new aircraft arriving.

"Sounds good, go on."

"When we know the new aircraft are at Abbeville we send in a small insertion group. The team will make its way to the field with the help of the locals. Using information from Brian, we know exactly where they perform radar maintenance and keep the spare systems. The building is located on the perimeter in an area we think we can penetrate with a high probability of success. You can see it marked on the large photo. Once in the facility, we'll have several options. We can steal manuals, take measurements or actually grab some of the key pieces of equipment from the spares."

"And Jerry will conveniently vacate the premises while your boys do their dirty work?" Hudson asked.

"We have Bomber Command conduct a nuisance raid while we're penetrating the building. According to Brian, Luftwaffe procedure is for all personnel except anti-aircraft crews to go to the air raid bunkers during attacks. And we know how Germans follow orders."

Jack knew the plan was aggressive but a lot depended on getting those frequencies.

"Tommy, you know as well as I do this plan might risk a team of three people. But if we're successful we may save hundreds of lives and aircraft. I've looked at every option and this is the best plan to handle your tasking."

"At first look, I tend to agree. Let me read through it all again and I'll take it to Greene this afternoon."

He closed his folder.

"Tommy, one more thing. I intend to go as one of the team members."

"Come again?"

Tommy was looking at him, not smiling. He sat back and joined his hands at the fingertips in front of his chest.

"You told me I'd have complete operational and administrative control of my section. That includes selection of personnel for missions."

Jack knew this wasn't going to be easy, but he'd learned leadership came from the front, and that's where he planned to be. Maybe he had something to prove to himself, but he wasn't going to sit while other people went in harm's way.

"We also told you from the very beginning that by virtue of your knowledge you were considered a target for enemy intelligence. What sense do you think it makes to put yourself in extreme danger? Are you trying to prove something to someone? Because we don't have time for bloody heroics."

"Tommy, I have the technical knowledge. I have the language capability. I understand aviation equipment. And I've been through McClaren's course." Jack knew he was right and he felt Tommy did, too. "This mission has a better chance of success if I'm on it."

Tommy shook his head.

"You've also been summoned to the War Office to meet the Churchill. Your timing's impeccable, old boy. That was the other matter I had to discuss. How do we explain to Franklin Roosevelt and Winston Churchill that their joint project's been killed in action or captured by the bloody Gestapo?"

"You tell them he was doing what they told him to do. Helping the war effort by penetrating the German hold on Europe. And tell them he's no more special than any of the other men and women who are going into Europe every day," Jack said, trying to conceal his growing frustration.

"Damn it, Tommy, I never asked for anything except to be able to do a job. This's how I want to do it. Now let me have a shot."

Tommy shook his head.

"Greene's going to go 'round the bend on this one!"

Pam had been able to get a two-day leave and planned to meet Jack at the Connaught at 4:00. Jack had already reserved a room for them. She knew Jack was working and was going to visit several of her school chums when she couldn't spend time with him. The last several months had been exhilarating. The terrible dark days of 1940, which changed to an on-going grind at headquarters, had now become a period filled with a renewal of her love of life and of one man in particular. Her several romances after Jack left England never matured past infatuations coupled with the urgency of a country at war. While she hadn't been waiting for Jack, she never stopped thinking about him. When he did return she suddenly realized what had been missing in her life. Their relationship, which began in a very innocent and relaxed manner many years ago, was now a mature love with all of the joys and potential pain. She was gloriously happy and couldn't wait to see him.

She was sitting by the large stone fireplace in the lobby reading the Times, but she couldn't keep her mind on the paper. Her eyes kept straying to the main entrance. Part way through the second section she saw him walk in the door.

Jack didn't see Pam and walked across the lobby to the dark wood reception desk. "Good afternoon," he said to the desk clerk. "I have a reservation." He put a small suitcase on the floor and placed his cap on the counter.

"Name, sir?"

"Stewart. Leftenant Commander Stewart."

"Yes, here it is. I have you in room 404. Will you be alone?"

"No, my wife will be joining me. There she is by the fireplace." Jack made a small wave and smiled as Pam walked up to the desk.

"Commander, would you like help with your luggage?" He was motioning for a bellhop.

"No thanks, we'll be fine. I'll need a second key, though."

She waited until they were in the room to take his cap off and pull his head down for a long kiss. "I've missed you terribly."

Jack smiled, trailing her into the bed.

As he lay there in the semi-darkness of the curtained room he thought about his remarkable cosmic luck, finding Pam again after all these years. So much could have happened to either of them: Coral Sea, Midway, the Blitz, or just finding other people. But here they were, deeper in love than ever. What if I hadn't been sitting in that bar in Alameda? What if Colonel Miller hadn't wanted a second scotch?

Pam was stirring from a light sleep. The sheet lay across her stomach with her head over on his pillow. She rolled on her side. "Hey, Yank. You let me fall asleep."

He rolled to face her and put his hand on her bare back.

"I thought you needed it after all the hard work." He smiled.

"You seemed to enjoy yourself, Commander."

He loved how she said, "Commander."

She rolled off the bed and walked to the bathroom.

"I'll be in the shower, if you feel like getting wet."

They had a quiet, secluded dinner in the main dining room on the first floor. They were enjoying each other's company, sitting quietly, looking at their wine glasses.

"You're on your own for most of tomorrow. I've got two meetings I can't miss in the morning and one appointment at 1400. I'd guess I'll be back here by 1600 at the latest."

"Perfect. I'll sleep in, meet Jeannie for lunch and then do a bit of shopping." It'd be a wonderful break from the ops floor. She was supremely happy, she was on a mini-holiday in London, and she was with Jack.

There was a note waiting on his desk at Baker Street when Jack arrived at 0700. Colonel Greene would meet with him at 0900. There were several details for him to work on for the next two hours. The section was putting the final touches on a detailed timeline for the raid. It was to commence at touchdown in France. The touchdown point was unknown at present. Although they could request a desired site, the final call was from the resistance. A veto by the French might be due to anything from a change in the condition of the field to enemy activity. Timing the raid became an open-ended exercise. Once they were at the objective, it was easy to construct a timeline.

The key planning factor for Jack was to have the RAF bombing raid commence at the correct time and last at least 55 minutes. The Germans would need time to get to the shelters. Jack and the team would then have time to move into the building, do their business and get out. Jack wanted at least 10 minutes before the all-clear was sounded in case they ran into problems. It was also very important the team was in place on the perimeter of Abbeville at least an hour before the raid. This would allow a final reconnaissance. Everything depended on the final approval of their landing field.

The raid had been given the codename "Quarry." After looking at many factors, the final team assignments would be Jack, as the team leader and Hatcher who would go as the operational coordinator. The two of them had selected, on McClaren's recommendation, a former army commando, Warrant Officer Terry Howe, as the primary weapons coordinator. Jack would be the onsite expert to assess the material in the facility and what action to take. Phil would coordinate all communication and travel issues. Terry Howe would be the most lethal member of the team. He would be carrying heavier weapons and was an expert in close in combat. The plan was to be on the ground in France only on the one night of the raid. Staying any longer significantly increased the odds of problems with locals or discovery by the Germans.

Sergeant Major McGinty kitted them out well for the mission. Jack and Phillip would be carrying silenced Colt .45s, silenced MKII Sten sub machine guns, and Sykes-Fairbairn commando knives for quiet work. Each would have two hand grenades, one a stun and one high explosive. Howe would be carrying the Thompson sub machine gun, which had a higher rate of fire and heavier bullets.

By the time Jack got to Noel Greene's office he'd reviewed the plan from beginning to end five more times.

"Good afternoon, Jack. Do come in and have a seat." Greene was sitting at his desk and Tommy was on the sofa by the far wall. "Tommy's given me an overview of your proposal, Jack. Let's take a closer look and see what we have, shall we?"

Jack went over the plan for the Colonel like he had so many times in his mind. The briefing took twenty minutes. When Jack finished he asked Greene if there were any questions.

The Colonel hesitated for a moment and said, "No Jack, I think you've covered the plan thoroughly. It seems like a plan we can approve from a feasibility standpoint. It clearly fulfills the tasking we provided. The real issue, of course, is your participation on the mission. We have concerns on several levels. The most obvious is your importance as the section head. You're responsible for the planning and execution of future missions. We're not in a hurry to lose you. Also your security knowledge would be extremely detrimental to SOE in the event of your capture. And finally there's your original medical problem from the Pacific. If you're disqualified from flying how can you be fully fit for a mission such as this?"

Jack calmly and methodically went through his logic.

"Colonel, both at Annapolis and when I was in aircraft squadron I was taught to lead from the front. This is no different. I picked the people for the team who have the best chance of successfully completing the mission. I understand my knowledge is very sensitive. I don't have any effective way of wiping out my memory, but I think I only have a few small pieces of a very large puzzle. In my mind the risk is reasonable. That's your call, of course. Finally, I'm happy to submit to a physical exam to show you that I'm able to handle whatever the mission might require."

Jack knew he was on thin ice, but it was what it was.

"Commander, it started to become obvious this situation might arise during your first trip to Arisaig. Tommy and I made a decision at that point to narrow your access to compartmentalized information. You're right; you do hold several pieces to the puzzle. But there are many more we withheld in case we needed you on the continent. I do want Dr. Morton to take a good look at you so we don't have any problems in France, but barring any fuss from him, Operation Quarry is approved. I want you on a 72-hour alert. We don't know when the new aircraft will arrive at Abbeville, but when they do we want your team there straight away. Now you need to get on your way. The Prime Minister is not someone to keep waiting."

Hudson and Greene remained seated after Jack left for his appointment.

"We're taking a large risk, Colonel," Tommy said.

"In this business, everything is a risk," Greene replied.

"But this feels good to me, Tommy. I think we've have found someone who can spearhead our toughest projects. This mission will tell us a lot."

"Yes. Yes it will."

Sitting in the staff car on the way to his drop off point near Parliament, Jack was exhilarated and surprised. He didn't think they would sign off on the plan so easily. Nor did he think Greene would've approved his participation with only mild protest. Were they so experienced or so smart they saw something he didn't? *Am I missing something here?* In any case, Quarry was on. Even though he was nervous about meeting Churchill, the mission was what concerned him now.

The Cabinet War Rooms
London

Jack arrived at the reception point near Parliament a few minutes early. A Royal Air Force Squadron Leader met him at the steel doors. The two men wound their way down through several security checkpoints and additional blast-proof doors. His escort, Hugh Wylie, gave him some protocol hints. "You'll find the Prime Minister is a very direct individual. He prefers direct answers and will be very blunt with you as well. Don't sit unless he does or he tells you to sit down. He may smoke. You may not. We never know how long these meetings will last. Sometimes it may be ten minutes. Other times he'll talk for two hours. He doesn't have anything on his schedule today until 1700."

The area they were entering had been constructed as a result of the bombings of 1940 and Churchill's complete refusal to leave London. The War Room complex was a work in progress as it expanded to include more members of the Prime Minister's immediate staff. Wylie led him into a large conference room with maps of all theatres of operations for British forces around the world. There was a bank of large clocks on the wall set to local times in Moscow, Tokyo, Washington D.C. and New Delhi. In addition to the large conference table, there were several desks manned by RAF and army personnel, typing and organizing messages. Wylie asked Jack to stand by for a moment while he checked with the PM. Jack paused for a moment to look around, literally standing in the heart of the British Empire.

Wylie came out of the unmarked door.

"The Prime Minister will see you now."

Jack entered a sparse office and saw Churchill getting up from behind a modest wooden desk. The PM came around the desk and greeted Jack with a large grin.

"Commander Stewart. I've been looking forward to meeting you." He was wearing a white shirt and bow tie, his coat was nowhere in sight. Jack was surprised. Churchill was actually taller than his pictures indicated. His complexion was ruddy and his manner very collegial.

"Please, sit down."

He motioned to a group of two chairs near the desk.

"It's a pleasure to see the final result of the pact I struck with President Roosevelt."

"Sir, it's an honor to be here." Jack felt very comfortable sitting with one of the most famous men in the world.

"As I check the time, the sun is certainly over the yardarm somewhere. I think a sherry would be appropriate. Can I offer you one?"

Wylie hadn't briefed him on this, but if Winston Churchill wanted a drink, he wasn't about to let him drink alone.

"Yes, sir. I'd like that very much."

"This is one of my favorites, a Spanish Amontillado. I trust you'll like it." He poured a generous amount into two sherry glasses.

"I read a summary of your career prior to your arrival in England. How did you find the capabilities of the Japanese carrier pilots?"

He handed Jack a glass.

"They're good, sir. The Zero is a hell of a dogfighter. I saw a lot of very aggressive flying from their pilots. We took some losses until we adapted our tactics to counter their strengths."

He didn't expect talking to Churchill to feel this easy.

"The victory at Midway will go down in history as one

of the most significant naval battles of all time. If your chaps hadn't stopped Yamamoto and the Imperial Fleet, this war could've been lengthened for years."

"There was a good deal of luck involved, sir. Everyone knew what was at stake, and we lost a lot of good men out there."

Jack looked down at his drink, his thoughts flashing to Brian Simpson. He wasn't sure what else to say.

"Too true, sadly. So tell me, Commander, how have you found your time here in the SOE?"

"I've been extremely impressed by the people I've met, Prime Minister. There's a drive and dedication among the people that's something quite special."

"It seems that you've jumped right into the fray. I read the report following the defection of the Junkers 88. My understanding is you'll be involved in exploiting the information."

Churchill was looking at him as he took a drink from his sherry.

Jack wondered how much Churchill knew about their plan. He was certainly cleared to know any and every detail of SOE operations. Jack didn't know if it was appropriate to go into it here.

"Yes, sir. My section has taken it for action."

For the next forty minutes they talked about the war, England, Franklin Roosevelt and Jamaican rum, which they both had enjoyed on trips to the Caribbean. After another sherry, Jack talked about Pam and their renewed relationship which Churchill found very interesting. The Prime Minister finished his second sherry, glanced at the clock and said, "Jack, it has been a pleasure to get to know you. I think it's delightful you have found one of our English ladies. They tend to stick with you through thick and thin as I know quite well."

Jack got up. "Thank you for seeing me, Prime Minister."

They shook hands and Churchill made one last comment.

"Jack, do be careful in France. I wouldn't want to explain to Franklin that something had happened to you." He winked at Jack.

Caught off guard by the familiarity, Jack could only say, "Aye, aye sir."

CHAPTER NINE

Abbeville, France

June 23rd, 1943

Phillipe Wiegand hid his bicycle under a clump of brush well off the narrow country road that ran from Abbevillle north toward Buigny. There was a knoll which couldn't be seen from the road but did provide a good view of the German airfield. His group had been given the job of keeping the airfield under surveillance. Each day they wrote down the large numbers and letters which were painted on the side of the twin engine Junkers JU-88's at the field. He didn't know the reason, but that was very normal in the resistance. The less each person knew, the better. Each day they'd compare the day's side markings with previous observations. If there was a significant change or addition of new numbers they must communicate with London.

Phillip was glad to be on his own today. His day-to-day terror at being found out by his group was taking a toll. He continued to feed information to Schmidt in return for the life of his son. *Trapped* was the only way to accurately describe his life now. He'd tried to think of how he could get out of the situation but there was no way. Even killing himself wouldn't save his son. Schmidt told him his death for any reason, even at the hand of Germans, would seal Charles' fate. He knew he couldn't tell the resistance. That would immediately stop the flow of information to Schmidt, dooming Charles. He knew the resistance too well. They would look at Charles as expendable. He must continue to work for the Germans and hope something happens to free him from this hell.

From the knoll, he could easily see the field. The markings on the aircraft were so large he was able to see them without using the small set of glasses he carried. He spent four hours in position, well hidden in a small group of bushes. At four o'clock he decided to head back to town. He took his list and carefully folded it. Next he put the thin strip of paper into a hollowed out piece of cheese in his saddlebag. It was unusual to be stopped by the police, but he couldn't take chances. If he were to be picked up, it would be hard to explain the list. If he was detained, there would be questions from his group, which was something he had to avoid.

It took two hours for Phillipe to make the trip back to the small safe house in the western part of Abbeville. The house belonged to a cousin of Henri, their leader. The cousin had escaped south to Vichy during the months after the fall of France in 1940. It was a good location with few neighbors and several ways in and out of the area.

When he got back, only Henri was at the house. He put his bicycle in the small shed behind the main cottage. Looking around he didn't see any activity. There was still a small candleholder sitting in the back kitchen window, the signal everything was okay inside the house.

"How did it go today?" Henri asked, as Phillipe entered the back door of the cottage. The leader, Henri, was sitting at the kitchen table eating an apple.

"It went well. I didn't see a single German on the road, going or coming." Weigand sat down at the table after grabbing a wine bottle from the counter and a glass from the shelf. He poured himself a large glass.

Henri Broussard had been a lawyer before the war with a good practice in Rouen. Married, with one child, he hadn't gone into the army when the war started. His two younger brothers both joined the infantry in the patriotic frenzy of

1939. The blitzkrieg offensive of 1940 had stunned everyone with its ferocity. A German victory looked inevitable as the British Expeditionary Force and the remnants of the French Army retreated to the coast. Some of the toughest fighting in the Battle of France took place around Dunkirk. It was during that final phase of the battle both of the Broussard brothers died.

When Henri found out about their deaths he realized he couldn't hide from the war. He grew to hate Germany and their troops for what they had done to his country and his family. It was an easy transition into the resistance. Several of his lifelong friends started the first group in Rouen. Those friends asked him to take over a splinter group in the northern part of the city. The resistance tried to keep their networks small for security purposes and over time, the new group became an effective part of the effort. The name Orange-2 was given to them by their parent group.

"Here, have some apple," Henri said, as he cut off several slices. "I'll check the numbers against our old lists and see what we have."

Phillipe reached in his bag for the block of cheese, opening it up and handing the paper to Henri. Picking up a slice of apple he munched it slowly with his wine.

Henri opened a wood panel under the cupboard and withdrew a small packet of papers. Laying them on the table next to today's papers he began methodically checking the numbers.

"Phillipe, it looks like there are four new aircraft at Abbeville that haven't been there before. We'll need to make a radio call tonight at the normal time."

Whitchurch Training Area
Hampshire

Warrant Officer Terry Howe had finished cleaning and

was now reassembling his Colt .45 after a 100-round target practice session on the combat training range. He enjoyed the quiet and methodical ritual of cleaning and assembling the weapon. The time on the training range was a nice break from the intensive team training of the last three weeks. The training officers had really put them through their paces. Terry felt they had come together as an effective team. He liked the team leader Stewart. Bit of a strange lash up, a Yank in the Royal Navy he thought. But he knows his job and lets me do mine.

The war had turned Terry Howe's very predictable world in the peacetime military upside down. The tall Welshman had grown up as a farmer's son just outside Shrewsbury. Generations of Howes before him worked the land, first as tenant farmers and then on their own land, which they acquired bit by bit when they could. Terry never took to the farmer's lifestyle and at 17 told his father that his brothers could work the land, but he was off to see the world. In 1933, a farmer's boy from Shrewsbury had two ways to see the world: the Army or the Navy. His limited experience on the water—which was limited to several ferry rides to the islands —convinced him his destiny was on dry land. He enlisted in the Welsh Guards and found he was actually quite attuned to military life. By the beginning of the war he'd risen to Company Sergeant Major, establishing a solid reputation within the regiment.

There had been a call for volunteers in 1940 as the Army began to stand up the new commando forces. Terry decided to see what this new mission was all about. He spent the next two years in the deserts of North Africa. His talent in special operations and steadiness in combat was quickly recognized and he was promoted to Warrant Officer. It was the lure of the unknown which attracted him back to England when they solicited experienced commando operatives for the expanding SOE. He made a very good impression on Major McClaren when he went through training at Arisaig and was assigned to Section F and then Quarry in rapid succession. The youngest member of the team at 27, he was getting along well with both of his more senior team mates. Once past the initial introduction, all three soon became very comfortable with each other.

Stewart stuck his head into the weapons shack. "Terry, we just received an alert order from Colonel Greene. We're going to assemble our gear at 1800. Then go by lorry to Tangmere. We'll get our final briefing from our chaps down there."

"1800 it is, Jack," he replied.

It was still difficult to address Stewart by his first name, but Jack insisted the team be on a first name basis, for brevity of communications and security once on the ground in France.

Jack walked up to the billeting area. He found Phil Hatcher in the canteen having a cup of tea.

"Time to saddle up, Phil. We just got our alert order from Greene. Let's get our gear ready. There'll be a lorry here at 1800 for the run to Tangmere. We'll meet Tommy and Hiram there."

"I guess that's it then."

He left his mug on the table as he and Jack headed for their rooms.

Two hours later, the three of them were on the road for Tangmere. The trip would take two hours. Terry was driving the staff car. The small ½ ton lorry driven by McGinty was directly behind them. They were fully outfitted with all of the material laid out in the operational plan. Because they'd be working with the resistance, including traveling on public roads, they'd be wearing civilian clothes. Specially prepared, these clothes were designed to blend in with what would be worn in the French countryside. McGinty also had several wooden ammunition boxes which contained the live rounds and grenades for each man. The weapons were stored in a separate storage crate. There was the occasional comment as they made the drive in the fading light, but each man was lost in his own thoughts.

Tommy arrived at Tangmere Cottage at 1640 and immediately began to set up a final briefing. He'd brought Brian Collins along with him in the event there were any last questions on the airfield or procedures. There had also been a final photo pass by a Mosquito that morning allowing him to show them the latest airfield configuration.

The radio transmission from Henri Broussard was actually secondary confirmation of a new group of JU-88's at the field. A special section of the SOE radio-monitoring group had picked up radio transmissions, which included a number of new radio call signs. The photographs from this morning showed four JU-88's on the parking ramp, which looked in much better condition than the others. Many of those had been in combat for over a year. These appeared to be new production models directly out of the factory and freshly painted. But the resolution on the photographs wasn't sufficient to tell if the antenna arrays were different from the other night fighters already at Abbeville.

Tommy and Brian had everything laid out by 1730 awaiting the Quarry team driving down from Hampshire. There was plenty of time. Hudson notified 161 Squadron a 2100 takeoff would put them right on the timeline.

Jack stared out the window of the staff car. He found himself wondering why he was sitting here on the way to a very dangerous mission. He knew he didn't have to do this, but several months of combat in the Pacific had taught him that he could perform when the shit hit the fan. He wasn't kidding himself. He'd been scared at Coral Sea and Midway, but he'd been able to keep his head and complete the mission. No matter how tough it might be, there was an unwritten code "you just hung in there."

They even had a wisecrack phrase for it,
"...better to die than look bad...."

It didn't make a lot of sense if he really thought about it. Why do men risk death or injury? Simply because it's expected? He thought about the thousands of British troops that went "over the top" during World War One only to die by the thousands. Duty, honor or country? Why do men keep doing it? At what point do people say no?

Jack remembered his first air-to-air kill. He was the section lead of a two plane section escorting four Dauntless dive-bombers on a strike against the Japanese carrier Zuikaku. Brian Simpson had been his wing man. He saw three Jap Zeros setting up for a beam attack a little forward and above the bombers. He didn't stop to think as he jammed his throttle to full power and set up an intercept on the Japs. The biggest thought in the back of his mind was not his own safety or survival, but "Don't let me screw this up." The Jap fighter pilots were so intent on the bombers they didn't see the American fighters until it was too late. He was 150 yards at 7:00 o'clock from the left wingman when he fired his four .50 caliber machine guns.

He'd always been a natural in air-to-air gunnery. The rounds impacted the enemy aircraft's cockpit and engine compartment. Before he knew he was under attack, the Jap pilot was dead. His leader, realizing he was in trouble, commenced a barrel roll to the right, pitching away from the U.S. bombers. Jack had the sun on his side and pitched up to slow down his closure on the Jap leader. Brian latched on the third Zero and was pumping rounds into him. Jack had been able to get his nose back down as the Jap scooped out from his roll. Within ten seconds, his four .50's had the lead fighter in flames. When it was over, his heart was pounding but he felt in control. With no time to gloat over three victories, he and Brian sped to catch up with the bombers. It seems like that happened in a different world, another lifetime.

Hatcher sat in the back seat, staring out his window. The

small talk had gradually died away and they were all left with their own thoughts in this calm before a potential storm. He was the old hand when it came to this kind of mission, taking part in an "in and out" about 8 months ago. The mission was a kidnap and return to England of a suspected French double agent. He hadn't seen a single German on that mission and it seemed anticlimactic. He did remember the tension and fear when the Lysander landed on French soil that night. It was the same dark feeling he used to get as a young rookie policeman on evening patrol in the west end of London. The fear of the unknown is the worst fear of all. It had taken Phil a long time to learn to only worry about what he could do something about.

Terry Howe was thinking how different this was from his time in the desert. A nice staff car, everyone clean and well rested, and there's an airplane waiting to take us to our objective. He remembered the mind-numbing extremes of the desert, the heat and cold, dirt and sweat. There always seemed to be another wadi to cross. This was different but the nerves are still there, some things never change. In many ways this mission was more like his patrols in the desert. They were going to try to quietly penetrate the enemy's location. He knew what it was like to lay waiting, knowing in a few moments you'd quietly move out of cover and creep closer to the enemy. He remembered the first time he dealt with an enemy soldier one on one. It was during the second big push toward Tobruk. He had been on a reconnaissance patrol trying to locate a major fuel distribution station for the Afrika Corps.

As they made their way toward what intelligence thought was the marshalling area, he was on the point. He'd seen the German sentry sitting on a rock cupping a cigarette in his hands. It was cold, quiet and this German was right in their path. He'd taken his commando knife and silently moved up behind the man. It was over in a flash. Hatcher quickly pulled his head back with one hand and slashed the knife from right to left, under his chin with the other. The man slumped down without a sound. Only then did Terry realize his hands were shaking. There were more times after that, but his hands never shook again.

It was 1810 when they passed through the gate at RAF Tangmere. They asked for directions to Tangmere Cottage, the unusual name given to the operations building. Tangmere was a perfect location for flights into the continent. Located only seven miles from the coast, a Lysander could leave Tangmere, hug the waves to stay below any German radar and be over France in less than 30 minutes.

They found the cottage and Tommy was waiting for them in one of the briefing rooms.

Prefecture of Police
Rouen, France

Herman Walck was the local Gestapo agent in Rouen. One of his duties was to conduct the communication drop system between the Paris office and the local collaborators. He had notified Standartenfuhrer Schmidt when he didn't receive a response to their last drop. After talking with Schmidt, it was decided that Schmidt would drive up to Rouen. Walck had never worked directly with Weigand and Schmidt thought it might be time for a little reinforcement. Both of them found it puzzling that Wiegand had been very reliable until about two weeks ago. There had been one further communication from Wiegand and then nothing. He wondered if the group had discovered they had a traitor in their midst or he just couldn't get back to town?

Schmidt had been running collaborators for two years and he didn't like the way this felt. In going over possible reasons for the break in communication with Wiegand he only came up with two, which made sense. Either Phillipe had been discovered, in which case he was already dead. Or he hadn't been able to get back to Rouen to service the drop.

He hoped it was the later but he needed to know for sure and quickly. In his last contact Wiegand said he had been asked to watch the airfield at Abbeville, but he didn't know why.

Schmidt had decided not to notify Abbeville. No reason to overreact to what may simply be general intelligence gathering. And he wasn't aware of anything significant going on at the airfield.

Priller stopped the car at the main entrance of the prefecture where the Gestapo maintained a suite of offices. Schmidt knew the way and went up the stairs to Walck's second floor office.

He didn't knock as he entered the office. "Herman, do you have any new information for me?"

Aware he was giving the wrong answer, he said, "No, sir. We've made one more check of the drop. Nothing. We made a few discreet inquires. No one admits seeing Wiegand for the past several weeks."

Schmidt was frustrated.

"Did you check with the Chapuis woman?"

"Yes, sir. She said she knew there was something happening. She's been ill and the section leader told her she wasn't needed."

"Damn!" His backup plan for a situation like this had failed. He was in the dark.

Abbeville, France

Phillipe Wiegand was close to panic. He'd been unable to find a reason to get away to Rouen. If something happened and Schmidt found out he hadn't told them in advance he was terrified of what might happen. His problem became worse when they received the sequenced radio message from the BBC. London told them to prepare to receive a Lysander with an insertion team.

The intended landing field was north of the village of Oisemont, identified simply as "Lima 23." It was located in an area of orchards and pastures. The anticipated arrival time was 2200. London told them to be prepared to provide transportation for a team of three to the Abbeville airfield. The recognition code was "Abby – Church".

Phillipe knew he was in trouble. There was no way he could get word to Rouen tonight. Although they'd made him memorize an emergency phone number, he had no access to a phone. If he tried to make up an excuse to go into town it would look suspicious. He was out of ideas.

The Operations Cottage
RAF Tangmere

The final briefing lasted one hour. The group went over photos of the airfield, expected weather and for the first time, looked at the landing field. Several specific resistance procedures were covered at the time. These included the airfield recognition sign, a confirmation code to be used when they made first contact with the resistance and several safe areas to use if the plan ran into problems. There was also a safe house noted in Amiens for medical help. If all went as planned they would proceed to another field designated "Foxtrot 2" for the extraction. Fox-2 was well north of their landing field and west of the German airfield.

At 1900, the pilot from 161 Squadron came in to meet the team and go over flight procedures. Flight Lieutenant Keith Standish was wearing his flying coveralls and carrying a map case.

Dicky Thompson walked in behind him carrying a brief-case.

Tommy saw them coming down the hall and said, "Here's your pilot now."

"Hello, gents. Anyone need a lift to France tonight? My name's Keith Standish, 161 Squadron. This is Dicky Thompson, my backup pilot. Let's go over the timeline and navigation. Then I'll go over our procedures."

The pilot opened his map case which contained a detailed chart of the area from the coast inland to Amiens. Jack and Dicky looked at each other, but both turned to the briefing by Standish.

"I've made a number of these flights. The only thing I'm sure about a Lysander trip to the continent is every single one is different. However, I can guarantee it beats arriving by parachute."

He covered his route of flight, altitude, timing and procedures in the aircraft. "When I get to Lima 23 I'll pass over the area at 500 feet. Then climb to 1000 feet, starting a wide turn. I expect the ground party will have the recognition light on and we'll turn in on short final for landing when we're abeam the lights. Once on deck I'll reverse course and stop. We'll be waiting for the ground crew to approach the aircraft. There are two signals which are critical. I'll have my cabin window open and I expect to see three short flashes from their torch, followed by two more. If I see that, fine. No flashes and I'll go to full power. Mission abort. Assuming we get the signal I'll tell you to hop out. You should exchange your own recognition code. Once you've done that, offload your gear as quick as you can. The engine will never stop. As soon as I see you close the panel, I'm going to roll. Any questions?"

For the first time, Jack felt that pre-mission excitement he knew from flying combat. It was time to get the operation rolling. There were no questions for Standish. Jack walked over to Dicky and they shook hands.

"So this is what you Lysander drivers do on a nice, quiet

English evening?"

"Jack, what the bloody hell are you doing here? You said you were in an information-gathering outfit. Pam never told me any more that that, either. Said she really didn't know what you were doing."

Dicky was keeping his voice down but Terry, Tommy and Phil were looking at them.

"Pam doesn't know what I'm doing. And I *am* in an information gathering outfit. Sometimes we just have to go to France to get it. Don't say anything about this to Pam. I don't want her to worry. This is a pretty straightforward op."

"I've made several of these trips into France, Jack. There's nothing straightforward about any of them," he said.

"Dicky, wish me luck. If all goes well, we can have breakfast together tomorrow morning. Now I've got to go."

Jack turned and walked over to the Quarry group.

Dicky stood looking at his old friend.

In a moment, Standish walked up. The two pilots left the room heading for the flight line.

Tommy asked, "What was that all about?"

"That's Pam's brother, Dicky. We were mates when I was at Oxford and yes, he's Ian's son. This is getting very complicated."

He sat down at the table and started to review the mission plan.

Hudson sat down next to him. "You going to be all right?"

"It just caught me by surprise. I'm fine. Let's go over the airfield procedures one more time and then I think we'd better head for the aircraft."

Rouen

France

Gunther Schmidt felt it was time to take action and regain control of whatever situation was developing. The three Gestapo agents left the Prefecture and drove to Wiegand's house. It was already dark and they arrived unobserved. Schmidt thought the mousy woman was going to faint when they forced their way into her living room. They told her the visit was a matter of Reich security. If she didn't provide information she would be arrested. Schmidt couldn't tell if she knew the husband was in the resistance but he assumed she did. He told her they must know Phillipe's whereabouts. She broke down sobbing. Phillipe had been at the house a week ago, she told them. At that time he told her he was staying at the cottage of a cousin of Henri Broussard on the outskirts of Abbeville.

She did provide the name of Broussard's cousin and the approximate location of the house. After telling her she must not tell anyone of their visit, the agents left for Abbeville.

They'd been on the road for thirty minutes and Schmidt was still not sure he was doing the right thing. If Wiegand had been found out by the resistance, Schmidt wouldn't find him. His body would be rotting in some shallow grave in the woods. If Weigand were still alive, what good would it do to find him? It might do more harm in revealing their knowledge of the unit. Schmidt was lost in thought as the car sped northeast.

CHAPTER TEN

Line Operations Hut
RAF Tangmere

It was a short walk from Tangmere Cottage to the flight line. The team found Keith Standish going over last minute details with his plane captain. They gathered around Standish as he signed a maintenance form and handed it to the technician.

"We're all set. We'll be in the new Mark Four Lysander, which has been specially modified for these kinds of trips. The forward edge flaps and new twin tail allow for very low landing speeds. The cockpit is a bit of a tight fit, but the trip is short. Your gear is located right behind the passenger seats, but is accessed through a hatch on the right side. Once you're all up, the boarding ladder the cockpit slides forward to lock it in place. There's no intercom but you can hear well enough over the engine noise. Once we get out to the aircraft, check your gear to see it's secured. Then in you go. The safety belts fasten across your waist. Whoever sits behind me will need to lock the canopy slide. I'll show you how. Any questions so far?" He took a moment to pull a cigarette from his flight suit pocket.

Jack looked at the others, "Guess we're set. Any other questions?" The other two shook their heads.

Twenty minutes later, the team was strapped in place with the engine running. Standish was going over his post-start checks. The tight fit in the cockpit surprised Jack. Originally a two place aircraft, this new arrangement allowed more efficient transportation and, in a pinch, a litter could be fitted in the passenger compartment. The engine began to wind down. He saw Standish remove his flying cap and turn to the team.

"We have an oil leak. A quick fix, I hope. The mechanics will know shortly. Just stay strapped in for now." He turned back to his instrument panel and began moving several switches.

No comments came from the team. Each man was alone with his own thoughts. This was the toughest part, the wait prior to getting in action. Each man had learned that for himself long before tonight.

For Jack it was an especially tough wait. The appearance of Dicky brought his personal life into the middle of the mission. He'd been doing a good job of fooling himself this mission was just like Coral Sea or Midway. All he had to do was go out and complete the mission. But his thoughts kept returning to the shoot down and Brian. If he had only checked for Jap aircraft one more time. Jack had pressed for the perfect sight picture and didn't see the section of Zeros moving in behind Brian. He remembered the frantic radio call from Brian to "Break left."

It had been too late for both of them. The nightmare surged back into his mind. The sickening thuds as the Zero's cannon shells impacted his aircraft, the smoke pouring from his engine, acrid fumes filling his cockpit, then the terrible realization that the aircraft was coming apart around him. Somehow he pulled the canopy open, unstrapped, and threw himself out of the stricken fighter. Later, in the hospital, he made a vow. He wouldn't let anyone down ever again, regardless of the consequences. And now with Pam in the picture, he was torn between his duty and his love for her. How could he justify going on a mission knowing what it would do to her if he didn't come back? He'd made the decision not to tell Pam anything was up. He wouldn't be able to tell her anything specific, anyway and she'd worry for no reason. At least that's what he kept telling himself. It's funny, he thought, Ian and Dicky know I'm going on a dangerous mission but not Pam. Ian helped put the mission together. It's conceivable Dicky could actually become part of the mission. It was just as well. Maybe in five or ten years, I'll let her know. Maybe twenty or thirty.

They heard Keith talking with the ground crew. Slowly the engine began to turn over. Several cranks and the big radial roared to life. Following his instrument checks Keith turned back to the team. "All set now. We're on our way."

An uneventful takeoff with a southerly departure put the Lysander, call sign "Tiger 44," over the English Channel at 1000 feet. As an aviator, Jack's senses tuned in to the aircraft, but his conscious thoughts were now on the landing in France. The plan called for a team from the resistance to meet them at the field and provide transportation to the German aerodrome at Abbeville. The trip to the airfield was the most unpredictable part of the mission. They'd have to travel on the roads and there was no guarantee they wouldn't run into Germans. Each team member had documents, which were the best forgeries the SOE could produce. Every possible effort would be made to avoid any confrontations or incidents. Intelligence had told them there was not a significant troop presence in and around Abbeville. The Luftwaffe personnel at the field were the only real ground forces in the area. The German civilian administration was located in Rouen so they shouldn't be a problem. If they could make the trip without incident to the airfield perimeter he felt they had a good chance for success.

"Okay, gents, we're about 10 miles off the coast. External lights are off. We're descending to 500 feet." Standish called over the engine noise.

Hidden in the trees at the north side of the field, Henri Broussard waited with Phillipe and Louis. Three cars were parked behind them on the dirt path which ran into the trees from the main road a mile away. One car was Henri's cousin's old Citroën. Louis had a Peugeot which he borrowed from a friend in Abbeville. Wiegand drove his neighbor's newer model Citroën.

Henri was nervous. Normally when they met agents it was simply a matter of getting them on their way and then going home. Tonight they would transport these men to the German airfield, let them do their work and then try to get them to their pickup point. Any time they spent on the roads was dangerous, although there hadn't been much police activity in the area recently. If they met the German police, there was no doubt they'd be in danger. On the other hand, the French police were always an unknown. Some were willing to look the other way. But there was a percentage which supported the Nazis and would turn you in to the Gestapo. He was snapped out of his thoughts by the sound of an aircraft engine approaching from the northwest.

As Standish brought the Lysander overhead Lima 23, Gunther Schmidt was at the Prefecture of Police in Abbeville. Walck had met their car and quickly briefed them on recent activity in the area. According to the agent, it had been very quiet for the last two weeks. Schmidt brought up the information they had received from Weigand's wife and asked more about this cottage. Walck relied on the local police for that kind of information and told him they needed to talk with the local police chief.

Schmidt knew he was taking a chance bringing the French authorities into any investigation, but he needed information and using the local police should at least get them started. He would be careful to protect Phillipe Wiegand. If he was still alive, Schmidt was not done with his services.

The Lysander flew overhead low and slow. The pilot must have seen the signal because he climbed slightly and reversed his course turning back toward the field.

"Phillipe, be ready with the flashlight. I'll tell you when to send the signal." Henri continued to watch the aircraft as it lost height and rotated to a slightly nose-high attitude for landing. The engine power was at idle and there was very little noise. Henri found himself holding his breath waiting for the touchdown.

The aircraft landed and began to decelerate. Suddenly the Lysander twisted violently to the right. The left wing and propeller dug into the ground and the engine stopped abruptly. There was a dust cloud hanging over the aircraft as it came to rest with its nose on the ground and right wing angling toward the sky.

"Let's go, let's go!"

Henri began running toward the downed aircraft.

Jack knew they were in trouble. He'd been thrown hard against the left side of the fuselage and his ears were ringing. He tried to get up and realized his lap belt was still fastened. Tripping the quick release lever, he reached forward and put his hand on the pilot's left arm.

Standish jerked back in pain and let out a groan.

Jack turned to check the team. There was a sharp pain in his back. He knew that pain from before.

"Jack, what happened?" Phil asked.

"I don't know. You okay?"

"Yeah, I think so. Terry?"

"I'm alright." He unstrapped.

Jack reached up and flipped the canopy latch, hoping they could slide it back after the accident. He felt it start to slide.

"Help me pull this back."

As the canopy slid aft, Jack climbed over the cockpit edge and started down the ladder. He had to jump the last three feet to the ground and a shooting pain jabbed his lower back as he crumpled to the ground.

He realized there were three men right behind him. As he twisted to face them the pain again shot through him.

One man reached down and took his arm.

"Easy, monsieur. Easy."

"Help get my men out of the aircraft."

Phil was already over the canopy rail and the other two men were helping him down the ladder.

Jack looked up as Terry's head appeared. "Terry, check on Standish."

The stranger helped Jack to his feet.

"My name is Henri."

"Jack, I think he's got a broken arm or shoulder," Terry called down to Jack.

Stewart ignored the Frenchman. "If he's conscious, tell him to switch off the fuel and mags." The last thing they needed right now was a fire.

"Done. I'll need some help to get him out."

Jack turned to Henri. "Can your men help us get the pilot out of the front cockpit?"

"Yes, of course."

Jack saw the Lysander's right main landing gear was twisted severely. The port main gear had collapsed completely. Every blade of the big prop was bent back and there was oil streaming from under the engine cowling. He watched the men carefully help Standish out of the wrecked aircraft. The young pilot knelt on the ground.

"What happened?" Jack asked Keith.

Standish was taking deep breaths and was obviously in pain. "Normal landing. Then we hit something. Must have been a ditch."

"Where're you hurt?" Phil asked.

Hatcher knelt down to face him.

"I think my arm's broken."

He was cradling it with his right hand.

Jack knelt down closer. "Can you walk?"

The pilot nodded his head. "Think so."

Jack stood up. "Terry, let's get the gear unloaded. We need to get out of here."

Ten minutes later they were loading their weapons into the two cars. Jack and Henri stood apart from the others and discussed their options.

"How long will it take to get to the airfield?"

Jack asked the man, who looked about 40 with a wiry build, wearing a plain coat and cap.

Henri Broussard was relieved the stranger named Jack spoke good French, it would make his job easier. Henri explained they should be able to get to the field in about an hour. But it was a big airfield, where exactly was the team headed?

Jack knelt down slowly, feeling the pain in his back. He pulled out a large-scale map of the field and his torch.

"Here's the building we need to get near."

He indicated the JU-88 radar building.

Henri looked at the map and traced several roads to get his bearings.

"I know the building. It's on the southeast edge of the perimeter. Our observation spot is about 400 meters south of it."

Jack looked at his watch, it was 2225. Bomber Command's attack would commence in two and a half hours "We're still on schedule. Assuming the aircraft doesn't catch on fire, how soon before we could expect it to be discovered?"

Broussard took off his cap and ran his fingers through his hair. He said, "This is a remote site. We're almost four miles from the main road between Rouen and Abbeville. If no one reports it, they may not discover it for days."

Phil walked up and said, "Jack, Standish is in the car. He's hurt pretty bad. His arm is swollen, so there must be some internal bleeding. There isn't much we can do but try to immobilize it and give him some painkillers. I'm concerned about the swelling, though. The bone may have done damage to the blood vessels."

"Henri, is there anyone we can trust for medical help?"

"Not in Abbeville. If we were in Rouen, maybe."

Jack went over the options. Standish's best chance was to get back to England. There were medical supplies in their gear including morphine. "Phil, splint the arm the best you can. Then give him a vial of morphine. Henri, can we have one of your men take him directly to the pickup spot and wait until we get there?"

Henri thought about the area around the pickup spot. It was not as secluded as this spot. Trying to hide a car until early morning might be dangerous. "Yes, we can do that. But I think it would be dangerous to wait that long in the area. We have a safe house on the outskirts of Abbeville where he could rest for a couple of hours. Then we could take him to the field."

"Alright. Let's get going as soon as Phil finishes the splint."

Prefecture of Police
Abbeville

It had taken twenty-five minutes for Jean Paul Fabien to arrive at police headquarters. The heavyset police officer had no love for the Germans, but it was wise not to meet a call from the Gestapo with questions. The local German authorities normally left him alone to take care of routine civil matters and Fabien was loathe to jeopardize the current arrangement.

As he walked into the building he recognized Herman Walck, who he knew was Gestapo. Walck was standing by a table where two other men were sitting. Judging by their clothes Fabien thought they must be Gestapo, too.

"Fabien, this is Standartenfuhrer Schmidt from Gestapo headquarters in Paris."

Walck moved back so Fabien could approach the table.

"Jean Paul Fabien, Herr Standartenfuhrer."

The policeman nodded to Schmidt, but didn't offer his hand.

Schmidt had no time for formalities. "We're conducting an investigation of importance to Reich Security. We need your assistance."

This was new territory for Fabien. A Gestapo colonel out in the middle of the night could only mean trouble. He'd do his best to make sure the trouble didn't effect him or his men.

"We're at your disposal."

"I need to locate an address. All I know is the name of the person who lived there some time ago." He pulled a notebook from his inner coat pocket. "Gabriel Broussard. The house was located on the outskirts of Abbeville."

The name meant nothing to Fabien, but he didn't know everyone in Abbeville. "I'll ask my men. Then we'll check the town registry."

Fabien walked over to his two policemen and talked briefly. He walked back over to Schmidt. "Sergeant Villenueve knows this house. It's in the southwest part of town. The owner is in Vichy as far as we know."

Maurice Aleron sat in the bedroom of the safe house on radio watch. The radio was set to the correct frequency and his only instructions were to listen. Under no circumstance was he to transmit on the frequency. His orders were to carry any messages to Henri using the old Citroën parked under the trees on the far side of the road. He'd been listening for almost five hours without anything coming over the frequency and he'd bored. Getting up to stretch his legs, he heard the radio crackle to life.

"Normandy, Normandy this is Dover. Requesting any information you may have on Tiger 44."

Normandy was their call sign, which changed about once a month. Dover was the call sign of the British command section. He didn't recognize Tiger 44. But he knew if the British were transmitting he needed to get the message to Henri. He turned the radio off, disconnected the antenna and hid it in a wall panel behind the mirror in the bathroom. Grabbing his coat, he hurried to the car. Henri should have been at the airfield by now.

As Maurice got in the car he saw headlights coming down the far road on the other side of the tall poplar trees. He thought it was strange to see a car on the road this time of night, so he decided to wait a few moments. His heart froze when the car stopped fifty meters from the house. Four men got out of the car and began to walk slowly toward the cottage. Maurice sat quietly, hesitating even to breathe. He couldn't be sure, but the car looked like a big Daimler sedan. German. The four shadowy figures approached the house very carefully and were so intent on the house they hadn't noticed his little Citroën.

The urge to flee was overwhelming, but Maurice stayed put. They would hear the engine, anyways. As he watched the men enter the house he had an idea. He slowly opened the door and put the car in neutral. Pushing with all his strength, the car slowly began to roll on its own as the road gradually sloped downhill.

Schmidt was convinced they were on to something. The house was partially furnished and the lack of belongings and the general state of disarray told him this was a temporary hide out. Methodically, the men swept each room. There was some food in the kitchen: a little fruit, some cheese, and several bottles of wine. Yes, he thought, this could be the base of operations for Wiegand's little group. But there was nothing he could find to outright confirm Phillipe's presence.

Phillipe Wiegand didn't know what to do. He had an injured, sedated British pilot in his back seat and his orders were to take him to the safe house and then on to the pickup spot. Now was his chance to try and alert Schmidt. But there wasn't a phone at the cottage. He decided to stop at a small inn near the cottage that would be open.

Lost in thought, he pulled up to the cottage. Turning over options in his mind, he didn't see the big Daimler parked behind the trees. Phillipe was getting out of the car when the door to the cottage opened. His heart stopped when he saw Schmidt.

The senior agent turned to Priller and said, "Keep everyone in here until I come back." As he stepped off the porch he could see that Wiegand was alone.

The trip to the airfield had given Jack time to assess the situation. The team was intact and with the exception of his back, all were in good shape. Standish should be back in England in six hours or so if all went as scheduled. That was the best they could do for him, he told himself, we have to concentrate on the mission.

Henri drove for another twenty minutes, passing only one small truck going the opposite way. So far Jack hadn't seen any indication of Germans. The car slowed and Henri turned off the main highway onto a hard dirt road. They followed the road for half a kilometer before it disappeared around a bend. In another ten minutes they were driving through a forested area and climbing a slight grade. Broussard pulled off the dirt road and into a wooded area. He swerved hard to the left, put the car in reverse and backed behind a copse of five or six small trees.

"The observation point is a ten minute walk from here," Henri said. He opened the door and got out.

They grabbed their gear and followed Henri up the trail. The terrain was hilly, covered with clumps of small trees and knee length grass. As the group crested a rise, Jack could see lights in the distance.

They stopped and Henri pointed out some of the landmarks for Jack to get his bearings.

Taking binoculars from his haversack, Jack surveyed the field. He'd studied both pictures and diagrams so many times it was easy to locate the electronic maintenance building. There were several streetlights on power poles providing illumination around the building. Phil and Terry walked up next to Jack.

"I make it 500 yards from here to the perimeter fence, and maybe 30 more from the fence to the electronics building. I don't see any sentries around the building, but let's keep an eye out for roving patrols. Brian said the Luftwaffe security troops conduct patrols around the entire perimeter."

Phil checked his watch.

"Jack, it looks like we've got about twenty minutes before we need to push off."

"Right. It looks like the grass and trees will give us plenty of cover."

He handed his binoculars to Phil.

"Take a look about 75 yards due south of the building. There's a clump of trees I think we can use."

Phil looked at Jack's suggested spot. "Looks like it'll do the job. Let's hope the Bomber Command isn't too far off target. Be a damned shame to get done in by our own chaps."

Terry looked over the target area. "We won't need any wire cutters. The perimeter fence looks like a simple three strand barbed wire setup. We can squeeze between the strands."

"Concur. We'll stick with our original plan. Through the fence and in the back door if possible. Phil, you'll work the lock while Terry checks the interior through the rear windows. My biggest concern is the German technician who decides not to head for the shelter. Be careful with your light. We don't want to alert anyone who may have stayed behind. There should be lots of noise and confusion to cover our entry. Once inside we need one more quick survey to make sure we don't get surprised."

Terry handed Jack the binoculars. "I'll cover the front door in case any krauts come back early."

Jack stuck the glasses back in his pack. "Let's hope

they don't," he said wryly.

"Hello, Phillipe. We've been looking for you." Schmidt pulled his Walther P-38 from its shoulder holster and pointed it directly at Wiegand.

"I... I...haven't been able to get away to call you. There was no way. You must believe me." Wiegand felt sick. "Wait. I can help you now. I have a British pilot in the back seat."

Schmidt backed up two steps and pointed the weapon toward the rear of the car.

Phillipe quickly said, "He's drugged. He was hurt in the landing and they gave him sedatives."

"Tell me what's happening and you may actually live to see the sun come up."

In ten minutes Phillipe told Schmidt everything, including his orders about Standish.

The German thought for a moment. He told Wiegand to get in the car and find a secluded area to wait until it was time to drive to the pickup point. Schmidt didn't know what the British agents were up to at the airfield but if he could capture them and possibly destroy another aircraft, he'd be able to find out the purpose of the mission. Conceivably he could even keep Wiegand operating. He told Phillipe to be ready to escape into the woods at the first sign of the Germans.

After pointing out the pickup point on Schmidt's map, Phillipe was on his way with the still-sedated pilot in his back seat.

Schmidt went back into the house.

"Let's go. I need to get to a phone."

Leaving Henri and Louis at the observation spot, the team moved slowly toward the small clump of trees that would serve as their jumping off point. Constantly watching the perimeter fence, the team was looking for any patrol activity by Luftwaffe security troops. They arrived at the spot with ten minutes to spare before the RAF attack.

A siren began to wail from the far side of the field. Right on time. As the siren continued, Jack could see activity among the buildings as people moved toward the north end of the complex. The light went out in the electronic maintenance building. The main entrance was on the opposite side and they couldn't see if anyone left the building. Street lamps across the base went out simultaneously, plunging the area into darkness.

"Let's go," Jack whispered.

Moving toward the fence, the team was in single file with Jack in the lead. In five minutes they'd closed the distance to the fence. While watching for activity, they helped each other through the barbed wire.

"Come on," Jack said, heading for the back of the facility.

Arriving at the wooden clapboard building they could hear the sound of aircraft engines from the north.

Terry moved down the line of windows, peering in each one while Phil pulled a lock pick from his back pocket and started working on the door.

"Got it," Phil said. The door swung open. He pulled his pistol out of the holster and moved into the building in a crouch.

"Terry, come on," Jack said quickly.

He moved slowly, listening for any indication they were not alone. The lens on his lamp was partially blacked out, but there was enough light to see up the corridor to main radar maintenance area.

Terry tapped Jack on the shoulder, pointed to himself and then toward the main entrance.

Jack nodded. He saw Phil enter the maintenance room and followed behind him. Quietly closing the door, he turned to survey the room. It was large, with two workbenches running the length of the room. There were electronic boxes on each of the benches with power cables attached. Jack could also see several electronic meters and one large cabinet with some type of glass screen located directly in the center. Turning on his light, he told Phil to look for any manuals while he examined the equipment.

Peering out the small window by the main entrance, Terry could see a string of explosions erupt near the aircraft parking area. Heavy tracer fire from Luftwaffe anti-aircraft sites pierced the dark skies above in search of attackers.

Henri saw the ugly, reddish-yellow flashes as the first bombs made impact. Over the field, the engines from the British bombers roared as they made their runs from north to south. He'd never seen anything like this. The concussion from the explosions rolled across the empty fields.

Louis was also watching the explosions when he suddenly turned and raised his rifle.

"Someone's coming."

Broussard picked up his weapon and slid on his stomach behind a bush. His eyes strained in the darkness and he saw a lone figure walking up the trail.

"Henri... Henri, it's Maurice," came a voice out of the dark.

Standing up, he moved to meet the new arrival.

"Maurice, what's wrong?" he asked urgently.

"We have trouble. They discovered the house."

"What do you mean?"

"I received a message from control asking if we knew anything about Tiger 44. I didn't know what they meant, but I knew I had to come and tell you."

"You did the right thing."

"As I was leaving," he interrupted, "I saw a German car pull up and four men got out. They went up to the house and went inside. I was able to push the car far enough to start it out of earshot and come here. No one followed me." Maurice was excited and scared at the same time.

"Somehow the Germans found out about the house. I

don't know how." Henri was thinking aloud. "We can't go back there. If they find the radio you can bet they'll start searching the area."

His mind raced. What led them to the house? Would they connect his cousin to him? He was at least two hours from his house once they got these men on their airplane. He must get word to his wife and to Marie. He had to let them know they'd been found out. The waves of explosions on the airfield continued, as did the anti-aircraft fire. Henri looked at his watch and saw it was 0115. The British must hurry!

Jack checked both workbenches, examining the equipment at each workstation. There were two units on the bench closest to the window. From the diagrams Brian had provided, those units looked like the older model transmitter modulators. They also looked like they'd been in service for some time. There were small scratches and grease on the outer housings. On the other bench, there was a partially disassembled transmitter array, which looked like it had just come from the factory. The markings and placards were all in place and clean. The assembly was a little larger than the other models and had several extra fittings and attachments.

"Phil, I think this is what we're looking for," he whispered loudly. Jack took off his haversack and began to put pieces from the bench into it.

Phil quietly crept over to Jack. "Judging by the condition and dates on these manuals, they're the ones for the new radar."

Jack realized he no longer heard either bombs or anti-aircraft fire. "Go get Terry. I need his pack for this last piece."

"Right." Phil moved to the closed door. As he was opening it a siren began to wail. The street lamps throughout the building complex came on with a brutal glare. Phil looked at Jack and their eyes widened.

"Get Terry!"

Jack pulled his own pack on and picked up the second box. Maybe they didn't need this specific part, he thought, but better to get more than not enough.

Terry came through the workroom door before Phil could leave. "They're coming down the street from the shelter," Terry said. The light in the main corridor had come back on with the power, but it was still dark in the maintenance room.

"Quick, give me your pack." Jack said, reaching toward Terry. "Listen at the door. Phil, see if you can open that window."

Phil moved over to the center window and began working on the locking latch.

"Someone's coming!" Terry hissed.

Jack dropped Terry's pack and pulled his .45, kneeling down behind the maintenance bench.

Phil moved from the window, drawing his pistol and moving behind the second bench.

Terry moved behind a desk, which sat to the right of the door.

The door swung open flooding the room with light from the corridor. A German technician wearing coveralls came through the door. The man reached for the light switch on the wall and snapped on the overhead lights. His eyes opened in horrified surprise as Terry surged forward with his commando knife in his right hand. He thrust the knife viciously upward and it entered the German's chest just under the breastbone. Terry drove the blade toward the man's left shoulder as hard as he could, aiming for the man's heart. The man was thrown backward, his mouth open wide with terror, but not uttering a sound. Terry moved forward, catching him by the back of the neck and laid him on the ground. The German was dead before he reached the floor.

The door swung shut as both Jack and Phil leveled their weapons at the door. They all froze, listening for any reaction.

Jack broke the silence, "Get that light out. Phil, get the window open. Terry, get that body hidden." Jack came around the bench and grabbed a rag off the table to wipe up the small pool of blood on the floor. He moved down to help Terry who'd found an equipment cover tarp and put it over the body.

"Okay, that's good enough. Now let's get the hell out of here."

Once out the window they stayed in shadows as much as possible and made their way to a darkened section of the fence. Ten minutes after leaving the building, they were back at the clump of trees and kneeling down to catch their breath. Jack looked at his watch and saw it was 0140.

"We need to keep moving. No telling what the raid stirred up in the area. The farther we get from here the better." Jack didn't wait for a response but moved out toward the observation point.

As the team returned to the knoll, Jack couldn't see anyone.

"Spread out and be careful."

They moved forward with deliberate slowness, peering into the trees and bushes.

Henri moved from behind two small trees and walked to Jack. Two other men appeared and they all converged. "Jack, this is Maurice. Dover called asking about Tiger 44. Your airplane, I presume?"

"Right. He was overdue. Did your man tell them anything?"

"He didn't know what happened. He left to come and tell me. As he was leaving he saw Germans arrive and go into the house. This isn't good. Phillipe should've been getting to the house about that time."

Jack was angry now. "The Germans might have Keith by now. Let's get out of here."

Henri paused for a moment. "I know of a place, very close to here."

Without further discussion the six men started back down the trail toward the cars.

Prefecture of Police
Abbeville

Schmidt sat back in the high backed chair in Fabien's office. He was talking into the phone, a lit cigarette resting in an ashtray in front of him. The senior agent was furious. He'd been trying to talk with a Luftwaffe security officer at the airfield for over an hour. The air raid closed the switchboard and they couldn't locate the major. Finally, he'd been connected with the security service.

"Tell the major I want to talk to him right now. I don't care if there has been an air raid." He picked up his cigarette, took a drag and said sarcastically to Priller, "Apparently, the Luftwaffe can only do one thing at a time. And they already have a problem at the airfield."

Priller shook his head.

"Major, this is Standartenfuhrer Schmidt, Gestapo, Paris. I have an urgent matter of Reich security and it affects you. Do I have your attention?"

He didn't wait for a reply.

"Very well. Listen to me and listen carefully. We're searching for a group of enemy agents who landed near Abbeville tonight. I need twenty men from your security troops and vehicles to apprehend these men immediately." Schmidt was quiet for a moment as he smoked and listened to the phone. "Does it not occur to you that the two incidents might be connected? I want your men at the following location as soon as you can possible. Eight kilometers west of Chambron on the Treport Road is the intersection with the road running north from Moyenneville."

Schmidt replaced the phone on the receiver, and turned to Priller. "A maintenance technician was found dead following the air raid. The initial investigation showed there are parts and documents from their newest radar system missing near the scene of the murder," he said, angrily stubbing out his cigarette.

"Let's go."

CHAPTER ELEVEN

Tangmere Cottage
0200

When Keith Standish had been overdue by thirty minutes, Tangmere initiated a search of standard frequencies and then called the RAF stations in the immediate area.

With no indication of what had happened, Hudson contacted Noel Greene. It was obvious by midnight that something was very wrong and also out of their control. He had a great deal of faith in Jack Stewart, but he knew all too well that sometimes events are out of the control of anyone. He hoped this was not one of those times.

All they could do was launch the recovery aircraft and attempt the 0400 pickup at Foxtrot-2. To complicate what had become a very sticky problem, the backup pilot was Dicky Thompson, Jack Stewart's good friend. It was too late to change pilots. Dicky was briefed and set to fly the mission. Hudson walked to the briefing area. As he entered the room, he saw Dicky and the base Operations Officer standing over a chart on the briefing table.

"There's been no word from Keith," Tommy said. We don't know what's happening over there but we want to stick with the original pick up plan."

"Right," Dicky replied. "Any chance they'll get to a radio over there?"

"We did send an inquiry, but there's been no response.

The group they're working with does have radio capability, but may not be near the radio. Sorry we aren't giving you much to work with on this."

"We'll give it a go. That's what they're expecting."

Dicky lit a cigarette and stared at the chart.

"I'll get a weather update and to preflight the aircraft." He picked up the chart, put on his cover and walked to the door.

Tommy fell in behind him. "I'll walk along if you don't mind."

After a quick stop at the meteorological office, they headed down the bricked path to the flight line. Dicky lit another cigarette.

"I remember Jack in a pub in Swindon after a match we won. There were some locals who took exception the final score. Jack was ever the gentleman, but when you push him too far, watch out. He took several of the locals on at once, and they came out much the worse."

"You've known him longer than I have," Tommy said.

"But in the time I've known him he's shown me he's one of those people that will do what they have to. I'm not worried about Jack. What does worry me are the things Jack can't control, no matter how good he is."

Tommy hung in the background as Dicky went over the maintenance logbook and talked with the plane captain. He followed him out to the Lysander parked on the ramp and watched as the young pilot pre-flighted the aircraft.

When Dicky finished, he walked over to Tommy. He looked at his watch. "I'll start in a minute. I want to give them time to work any post start problems and still be airborne by 0300. That'll give me twenty minutes of buffer time for the trip. Never know when you might have to make a detour. Better get on with it."

The older man offered his hand. "Good luck."

"Piece of cake," Dicky said as he walked away toward the parked aircraft.

Occupied France

Henri Broussard was torn between the mission at hand and the ultimate survival of his group. It was agreed Maurice would immediately head for Rouen to alert several key people including Broussard's wife. Those people were in immediate danger and must flee the area. Each group member always had an escape plan ready. Normally it involved quickly leaving the immediate area and going to ground with a close friend. Relatives, unless they were very distant, were too easy for the Germans to track down. Once the initial move was made, several days would be spent in deep cover. Only then would they travel to their destination. Henri wanted to start those first moves tonight. Any delay might prove fatal.

The two cars carrying the team sped down the dark country road heading west in the direction of Rouen. Henri planned to turn off the road past Chambron and follow country roads to an abandoned farm south of Boismont. They could wait there for thirty minutes and then make the short drive to Foxtrot 2. That would put them at the landing field about 0330, plenty of time to scout the area and get the signal ready.

"What will you do if your group's been discovered?" Jack asked. He was concerned about these men who had risked their lives and were now in grave danger.

Henri was trying to concentrate on the road, but he sensed the foreigner was concerned. "We have planned for this problem, but I might not be able to get the word to Rouen in time for my people to move." He glanced in the rear view mirror to make sure Louis was still in sight.

He turned off the main road, slowing slightly as the car hit the dirt road.

"Henri, as soon as we get to the field, just drop us off," Jack said quietly. "Then get on your way. We don't want to hold you up," he said, sensing the man's anxiety.

Fifteen minutes later, the two cars pulled up to a small cottage with a barn twenty yards from the house. Henri kept the engine running while he got out and opened the door to the barn. He got back in and drove inside.

Louis parked the Peugeot next to the Citroën.

"Louis, close the door. I'll check out the house and make sure we don't have any new tenants."

There was a regular door at the opposite end of the barn but no windows. The place smelled of animals and damp. Louis closed the main door. He produced two candles from his car and lit each one placing them on a raised workbench.

For the first time since the briefing at Tangmere, the team was able to sit down and rest a moment. Phil and Terry were sitting on the ground with their backs against the wall. Kneeling down next to them, Jack stretched his back. "Are you doing alright?"

Phil grinned. "I'm thinking it's time for cold gin and a hot shower."

Terry was more subdued. He looked tired.

"I'm doing fine. How's the back?"

Jack smiled. "Needs cold gin and a hot shower."

Jack walked to the small door in the back. Opening it, he stepped outside into the darkness. There was still some moonlight and he could see Henri walking back from the house. "Henri, over here."

The Frenchman walked over to Jack.

"The house is clear. No sign anyone has been here."

The two of them stepped back into the barn. Louis had produced a package, which lay on the bench by the candles.

"Anyone hungry?"

Opening the wrapping paper, he held up a large sausage and a big piece of some type of cheese.

Henri reached into his bag and pulled out a bottle of wine, which he uncorked and set on the bench.

"Please, help yourself," Henri offered.

"We have about twenty minutes before we have to leave."

Schmidt checked his watch and saw it was 0305. He'd been at the intersection waiting for the Luftwaffe security troops for over twenty minutes. "Where in the hell are those people?" he asked.

Priller and Walck sat in the front seat smoking cigarettes with the windows rolled down.

There was no sound of approaching trucks and Schmidt knew the night was slipping away. They'd been able to get a good map of the area Wiegand had indicated as the landing field. It showed two roads leading into the valley. One ran in from the south to the east side of the large field and another came in from the northwest and ran down the west side. His plan was to have the security troops flank both directions while he came in from the south, but he couldn't do anything if the troops didn't show up.

Driving down the darkened road, Jack thought about the mission so far. With the exception of the loss of Standish, things were on track. He was certain they had the right material to determine the frequency capability of the night fighter radar. Now they just needed to get it home to the scientists in Section IX.

"We're almost there," Henri said. "You can see the southern part of the field and the road that runs around those trees and parallels the field running north. There's a place we can park about a kilometer from here."

Jack could see the field clearly. More accurately described as a pasture, it must have been used for farming at some point. There were remnants of a fence running along the road, with an occasional pile of stones which must have been part of the fence at one time. The ground ran downhill from the road but the grade couldn't have been more than five degrees. He looked at the trees, noting there was almost no wind.

A scattered layer of clouds hung at what he estimated was 3000 feet. Those clouds wouldn't be a problem for the Lysander pilot.

Henri stopped the car and peered into the darkness. "There's a car parked up there in the trees. I don't like this." He killed the lights and pulled the car off the side of the road under some large bushes. As he killed he engine he said, "Wait here."

"We'll back you up. Let's go, Phil."

Jack got out of the car and followed Henri about ten paces back. Louis parked directly behind the Citroën and Jack saw Phil move back to talk to them. Looking down the road past Henri, who was hugging the brush on the side of the road, Jack could make out a vehicle.

Broussard looked closely and was confused by what he saw. The car looked like the Citroën Phillipe had been driving earlier that night, but that couldn't be possible. He crouched down and pulled out his revolver. Slowly he approached the car. A man was visible in the driver's seat and Henri carefully moved up the side of the car. Moving quickly next to the window he aimed his pistol at the head of the driver who turned to face Henri.

"Phillipe!"

A dark green Kubelwagen followed by two larger trucks rumbled to a stop at the intersection. An officer got out of the small car as Schmidt and the others exited their car.

Raising his hand in a salute, the officer introduced himself. "Standartenfuhrer Schmidt, I am Major Helmut Lenz of the Abbeville security detachment."

Not in the mood for pleasantries, Schmidt snapped.

"How many men did you bring?"

"We have twenty men. Ten in each truck. Each man is armed with either a Mauser or machine pistol. Each truck is also carrying an MG-34 machine gun."

"Very well. We're in pursuit of a team of enemy agents

we believe are trying to rendezvous with an aircraft within the next hour. The field is located about nine kilometers north. Priller."

The junior agent turned on his light and opened the local map on the hood of their car.

"I've marked the field with a circle," Schmidt said.

"Yes, sir." The major leaned down and examined Priller's map.

Pointing with his finger, Schmidt outlined his plan.

"I want one truck to follow me and another to follow you. I'll proceed up this road from the south. I want you to follow the main road and take the turnoff right here. You can intercept this road running in from the northwest. Do you see it?"

"Yes, sir." The Major was not going to do anything to antagonize a senior Gestapo agent, but he knew how these roads could get confusing at night.

"I want road blocks on the two roads, here and here. Use the machine guns and park the trucks in the road as physical blocks. Then deploy the troops in your group on a line across the northwest side of the field. I'll put my group here. Tell them to be quiet. We're expecting a plane at 0400. Stay as concealed as possible. Our goal is to capture the people on the ground and also disable the aircraft. Wherever the people are waiting, they must break cover. When they do that's our signal to open fire. Be very aware we're setting up crossfire. Brief your troops. I want to capture these agents, but the priority is they don't escape. Understand?"

Lenz nodded his head. "Yes, sir."

"Phillipe!"

Henri lowered his pistol as Wiegand got out of the car.

"And just who would it be, Henri?"

He saw Jack approaching the car and turned back to Broussard. "Did all go well at the field?"

Henri was still surprised at seeing Wiegand after what Maurice had said. "Yes, it went well. Where's the pilot?"

"In the back seat. The morphine began to wear off a while ago. He's in pain."

Jack was near the rear door and opened it. He saw Standish with his back against the side of the car and his legs stretching across the back seat.

"How're you doing?"

Jack couldn't see much in the darkened car.

"Still here. Arm's hurting a bit." His voice was strained.

"We'll have you on your way home in no time."

He leaned back out of the car and walked up to Henri and Phillipe.

"How'd it go at the house?" Broussard asked Phillipe.

"Just like you planned. The pilot was still out. So I made him comfortable in the car and waited at the house until it was time to go. It was quiet."

Phillipe lit a cigarette and exhaled.

"So, you saw no one at the house?" Henri asked.

"No. Maurice was gone. Don't know where he went."

He took another drag on his cigarette.

Henri took a step back from Phillipe and coldly said "He was watching the police that were at the house when you arrived. You lied to me." He raised his pistol and pointed it at his friend. Without taking his eyes off Wiegand he said, "Jack, we have to get out of here. This could be a trap. Phillipe, if you want to live for more than ten seconds, you better tell me the truth. All of the truth."

Raising both hands slowly Phillipe pleaded, "I'm sorry, Henri, I'm sorry. I never meant to do this. I had no choice, I...."

"Shut up and tell me what's happening. Now!" He raised the pistol and pulled the hammer to the full cocked position.

"The Germans know about the pickup tonight.

They're probably on their way here now." He hung his head.

"I'm sorry, Henri. They have my son. I had no choice."

"Give me your gun. Carefully."

The collaborator slowly reached down to his waist and removed a small pistol from his waistband. "Now get in the trunk." Phillipe opened the trunk and crawled inside. Henri slammed the lid and turned to Jack. "Get in and start the car. Follow me. We need to get out of here now!" Henri ran toward his car as Jack got in the Citroën and started the engine.

Henri knew the road ran north for about a kilometer then wound around back to the southeast. He remembered a path which ran through the large wooded area and would allow them to make it back to the barn. They needed time to think about what had happened.

Jack was right behind Henri trying hard not to destroy the transmission of the Citroën. He was thankful the steering wheel was on the left side. He glanced in the mirror.

"We're awfully glad to see you. We thought you were up the creek," he said to Keith in the backseat.

"Up the creek?"

"It seems your driver was collaborating with the Germans. We were told you'd been picked up by their police several hours ago."

"Things were rather murky I'm afraid, must have been the morphine. Not really sure what was going on for the most part."

"How's the arm doing now?"

"Hurts like a bitch. But no more morphine. I want to know what's going on around me."

"We've got codeine tablets. They'll help some."

Dicky Thompson checked the backlit clock on the instrument panel of the Lysander. He was ten miles north of Foxtrot 2 and it was 0348. *Right on time*, he thought. Pulling power, he began his descent to 500 feet. The moon was nearing the horizon and the lack of illumination was going to make the landing a challenge. Habit patterns took over as his eyes moved from gauge to gauge, checking pressures, temps and RPM. The Lysander was running in top order tonight.

Rechecking the chart, he reviewed his two key navigation checkpoints. There was a very distinctive horseshoe bend in a north south road. Two miles directly north of Foxtrot 2 was a large farm with a distinctive two-story barn.

The hills on the east side of the valley now helped to funnel him toward the road bend. He saw the north-south road and thought he could see the bend. There it was! He flew directly over the bend and turned slightly right to 170 degrees magnetic. *Should be over the farm in about 90 seconds. There it was.* Marking on top, he turned right to 180 degrees and punched his clock. At this speed, he should be over the field in one minute. He started looking for the signal lights.

The countryside was totally dark, the only illumination came from the moonlight. He saw a large field, but there were no lights visible on the ground.

Schmidt and Priller were standing next to the large truck, which was blocking the road at the southern end of the field. They'd sent Walck with Lenz and the northern group. Schmidt wanted one of his men with the Luftwaffe troops. He heard the aircraft engine to the north and was able to see it outlined against the broken cloud layer. "There it is, right on time." He turned to the Sergeant. "Tell your men to be ready."

The aircraft flew from north to south and was going to pass only 500 meters west of their position. They heard the engine RPM increase and watched the aircraft commence a shallow turn.

Nothing. Dicky added power and started a climbing right hand turn. *I'll make another run over the field. They might be late.* He strained his neck to make sure he was looking at the entire field. Not a light in sight. Without a signal, his standing orders were to abort the mission and return to base. He reached the northern edge of the field. *One more circuit.* If Jack was down there, he wasn't leaving without him.

Schmidt saw the plane begin a left hand turn when it reached the north part of the field. "Something's wrong, he's not landing. Wiegand must have warned them," he said to Priller. Schmidt turned to the soldiers. "Sergeant, open fire with your machine gun."

Sergeant Krumholz had placed the MG-34 on a mound of earth by the ditch. Watching the aircraft, Krumholz knew he couldn't elevate the gun enough to fire. Picking up the weapon with a belt of ammunition already threaded, the big Sergeant ran to the truck. He put the bipod legs on top of the hood and was able to swing the sights to the aircraft which was now climbing away from him. Squeezing the trigger, he adjusted his aim using the tracer patterns from every fifth round. He kept the trigger depressed until the belt of 50 rounds was spent.

Dicky reached the southern end of the field. Not seeing any signal, he commenced a climbing left hand turn to the north. "Bloody hell," he yelled aloud as several tracer rounds flew past his canopy. He'd seen enough tracers in Blenheims to know instantly he was in someone's gun sight. His instinct for self-preservation took over. Immediately adding full power, he reversed his turn violently rolling the aircraft to a 100 degree angle of bank and putting on a "4-G" pull.

The Lysander's flight path changed so dramatically the remaining tracer rounds flew harmlessly into the dark sky. Rolling its wings level, he put the nose down and dove for the deck. Staying low for another two minutes, he checked his gauges to make sure all was normal. *Jerry's on the ground. Did they have Jack?* He set 345 degrees magnetic in the compass indicator and set a course for Tangmere. He'd make a radio call to Tangmere Ops as soon as he got over the water.

Henri was relieved when he saw the barn they'd left less than two hours before. After pulling the cars inside, they lit a candle and discussed their options. If they could establish radio contact, a new pickup could be set up. Unfortunately the nearest radio was in Rouen, a two-hour drive on roads, which would certainly be swarming with Germans.

The SOE's default procedure was to proceed to a predetermined backup field and attempt an extraction exactly 24 hours after the original pick up. Jack explained the procedures to Henri and they pulled out the map to locate the backup field which was designated Hotel 23. It was 20 kilometers southwest of where they were now, just east of the small village of Grandcourt.

Henri wasn't familiar with the area and Louis wasn't comfortable they'd know the field well enough without checking it out firsthand.

"The other problem is Standish. If they send an Mk 4, he can only carry three passengers. We have four." Jack said quietly. "Henri, if you think we can make it for a 0400 pick up tomorrow morning, we can put three on the aircraft. I'll remain behind."

Broussard thought for a moment.

"Can't you have the plane come back and pick you up later?"

He was thinking of his very strong desire to finish this operation and find his wife.

Jack shook his head. "Not enough time. The sun'll be up by the time the pilot could get back."

Phil lit a cigarette. "I'm staying with you. That'll allow more room in the plane for Standish. Besides, you need someone to watch your backside. And don't try to say "no". You know it's the smart thing to do. We get all the radar parts and manuals on the Lysander, then we go to ground for another day."

Jack knew he was right. Their priority had to be

to get the radar information out first, the injured pilot second and the team after that. "It makes sense if Henri's willing. What do you say?"

The Frenchman was quiet. He walked over to the back of his car and brought a bottle of wine over to the bench. He pulled the cork from the top and took a drink. Putting the bottle down, he turned to Jack. "We must get someone down to look over the area during the day before we try anything at night. Now let's get some food and rest for a couple of hours."

Louis assumed lookout duties. From the cottage he could see the road in both directions, which would give them some warning if the Germans came to search the area.

The three men sitting at the table in Tangmere Operations looked tired. Dicky and Tommy both needed a shave. They were sitting with Squadron Leader Brian Woolsey, who was the Tangmere Operations Officer. He was the man who would make any decisions on future flight operations in support of the mission.

Dicky finished a full debrief of his flight to Foxtrot – 2. He had landed about 0500 and on aircraft post-flight inspection the mechanics found seven bullet holes in his Lysander. Most of the damage was cosmetic but there was one flap hinge which would need to be replaced before the aircraft was signed out as serviceable. There was a map of the area around Rouen spread on the table in front of them.

"There've been no replies to our radio calls to the resistance unit," Tommy said. "That in and of itself, may mean nothing. They may not be able to get to their radio or it may be broken."

Woolsey, a fighter pilot who had been severely injured in late 1940, was now on non-flying duty.

"So we've had no contact with them since they departed last night? There's no indication they accomplished their mission."

"That's correct, but there was never any plan to contact them. This was planned as an in and out," Hudson replied. He knew Woolsey's reputation as a solid operator. However the ambush of Thompson last night had them worried.

"So the question remains. If the team is still at large, how the hell did Jerry happen to be at the pick up field in France at the right time?

"I can't answer that question. All I can do is ask you to send an aircraft tonight to the backup field." Tommy said. He could see Woolsey's position. How could the team be free if the Germans had information on the pickup field? But he wouldn't write off Jack if there were any reasonable chance of recovery.

Woolsey stood up. "Why don't you two get some rest. I'm inclined to go along with you. I need to kick this one up to Wing Commander Toms. The final decision is his. It's 0700 now. Let's meet back here at 1400 and I'll have a decision." He turned and walked toward the door.

"Major, I'll go get them. One way or the other."

"Why don't you get some sleep?" Tommy said. "I'm going to check with our communication people for any updates. See you back here at 1400."

Priller had worked for Schmidt for almost two years, and he'd never seen him this angry. Following the failure at the airfield, they'd raided the Broussard cottage and found no one. A call to Rouen Police ordering the arrest of Marie Chapuis and Broussard's wife revealed both had gone.

Schmidt knew there was an enemy group in the immediate area with critical information, and he wasn't able to do anything to capture them. He directed the local police to set up roadblocks on all of the major roads in and out of Abbeville. Based on past experience, Schmidt had no confidence in their abilities to set up an effective search. On a positive note, the airfield commander authorized an additional twenty security troops to assist the effort. Major Lenz was conducting spot searches of both vehicles and buildings in the area northwest of Abbeville.

The two Gestapo agents were drinking coffee and eating rolls provided by Fabien's men. Checking his watch, Priller noted it was 0815. "Do you want me to check in with Paris?"

Schmidt didn't look at Priller.

"And what would you suggest we tell them. How successful our efforts have been to this point?

"No, sir. I wasn't going to tell them anything other than to make contact in case there are any messages for us." Priller's face was red. He should have kept his mouth shut.

"We could end up having the group slip completely through our fingers. Are you sure the names and descriptions of the Frenchmen have been distributed to all the search teams?"

Priller nodded.

"Go ahead, see if there're any messages," Schmidt said as he stood up and stretched. I'm going to grab an hour of sleep. Wake me in an hour. Maybe we'll have heard something by then."

Louis had spent two hours as lookout when Jack came out of the barn. The young man was sitting on a small wooden box at the corner of the cottage's porch. Jack was impressed with Louis and wondered if he had been in the French Army during the first part of the war.

"Hello, Louis. How are you?"

Jack knelt down by the young man.

Louis grinned at Jack.

"I'm well."

He stood up and rubbed his eyes.

"Haven't seen a thing. Not even a deer or rabbit in the last two hours."

"Go get some rest. Henri's awake."

Jack sat down on the box, laying his Sten on the wooden planks of the porch. He surveyed the landscape. It was a quiet morning, almost no wind and scattered clouds remaining from last night. It was a perfect summer morning in the French countryside.

He'd been able to rest and felt better although his back was still bothering him. He thought about the encounter with the German technician. *I wonder if I could have used the knife?* There was something different about using a knife.

Jack had been on watch for an hour when he heard the sound of an engine. He quickly moved to the corner and looked north. A German Kubelwagen was coming down the dirt road.

His hope the car would drive past the cottage faded as he heard the engine slow. Wheels crunched on the gravel in front of the cottage and Jack felt his stomach tighten. Slowly, he moved to look around the wall. Two German soldiers sat in the small vehicle in heated conversation. Jack could tell the driver was angry with his companion who abruptly got out of the car and slammed the door.

Jack could see under the latticework on the front of the porch. The driver was still sitting in the car, but he couldn't see the other soldier. *Where was the son of a bitch?*

Pounding came from the front door and the German was hollering in broken French to open up.

Glancing over to the barn, Jack saw no activity and knew he had to act. He slid the .45 from its holster and quietly pulled the slide back, putting a round in the chamber.

It sounded like the man was walking on the porch, probably looking in the windows. All he would see was empty rooms. Jack heard the man tell the driver the place was deserted.

Leaning his back against the wall, Jack looked around the bottom of the porch and saw the German was headed to the barn. Shit.

Without thinking, Jack stepped around corner and rushed toward the walking man, who was blocking the seated

passenger's view. Jack closed to ten feet before the soldier realized what was happening, brought the pistol up, sighted on
the man's head and pulled the trigger once. The man's head exploded in a burst of blood and bone. Moving his sight pattern
down, Jack aimed at the man's chest and pulled the trigger
again. He didn't stop running toward the vehicle, firing three
times as he closed to point blank range. The silenced handgun didn't make much noise but the damage done by the large
caliber slugs at short range was lethal. Both Germans were
dead. Jack stood with the weapon still at the ready position
checking both his victims. The door to the barn flew open.
Henri, Phil and Louis ran toward him with their own weapons
drawn.

Jack went over and sat down on the steps. His hands
were shaking slightly and his heart was still pounding. Glancing back toward the German car he looked again at the car-
nage he'd caused. His prior experience in combat, even last
night, was not the same. Although he'd caused death before
he'd never looked at the results this closely. He took a deep
breath as his pulse began to slow.

Henri took charge. They loaded the dead soldier into
the vehicle's back seat.

Louis started the vehicle and drove behind the cottage,
down the service road and into some tall bushes.

"I didn't know if you heard the Germans," Jack said, the
pistol still in his hand.

Henri put his hand on Jack's shoulder.

"We did. Now, we must get out of here."

With the Kubelwagen out of sight, the group moved
back to the barn. Henri knelt over Phillipe.

"Phillipe, you may still live through this after all. But
your survival will depend on telling us the truth. Do you
understand?"

Phillipe Wiegand was a broken man. He knew that no
matter what happened now, Charles was dead.

"Henri, you've known me for what, twenty years?" Phillipe said softly. "I've done something that no man should ever have to do. Choose between his comrades or his son. I chose my son. God forgive me, but now it makes no difference. They'll kill my boy no matter what I do. What do you want to know?"

"Do the Germans know of Louis and his part in the group? Our lives depend on this, Phillipe." Henri looked deep into his friends face and waited.

"I never gave them Louis's name. There was never any need."

"So you told them nothing about his car or where he lived or his description. Anything they might use to identify him?" Henri pressed.

"No. I swear it."

Broussard stared hard at Phillipe. "I believe you."

Henri laid out his plan. Louis would leave immediately, in his own car, with no weapons or any incriminating material and go to Rouen. He would try to contact another resistance group and to make a transmission on their radio. His next task was to reconnoiter the area around Hotel 23. He would then rendezvous with the others at a nearby farm.

Quickly the cars were loaded. The radar parts were split between the two Citroëns, which Henri and Jack would drive.

Louis checked the Peugeot to make sure there were no indications of the previous evening's activities.

They also put together an outfit for Standish, who was still in his flying coveralls. Everyone had identity papers except Brian, so they took Wiegand's papers and shoved him in the Citroën's trunk with his hands tied and mouth gagged.

Broussard looked at his watch. It would take Louis at least two hours to get to Rouen and find their contact in the other group. They couldn't stay here but he didn't want to run the risk of meeting any Germans on the main road. He knew a route which would allow them to drive to the farm using only back roads.

"Louis, be on your way. You know what to do. We'll meet you in the apple orchard behind the farm at 2200."

The young man nodded and got in the car. Jack came over and closed the door for Louis. "Good luck."

"Keep Henri out of the cafés on the way!"

Louis started the car and pulled out on the dirt road.

Henri turned to Jack. "Don't follow too close. Maybe 200 or 300 meters. I don't think we'll run into any checkpoints on this route but there could be patrols. I'll take Terry with me. You and Phil follow with the pilot."

RAF Tangmere

Dicky Thompson sat alone in the officer's mess at Tangmere. He felt rested after five hours of sleep. A quick shower and plate of corned beef hash and he was ready to go. On the attendant's desk the phone jangled.

"Flight Lieutenant Thompson, they want you in the Operations office."

He took one more swallow of tea. "On my way."

When he entered the Operations office he saw Major Hudson talking with Squadron Leader Woolsey. They had a chart on the table and Hudson was making notes.

Hudson turned and grinned. "Dicky, we got an R/T signal. They're alright and heading for an alternate pickup point. And they have Brian Standish with them. No other details right now. But we need to get them out of there. Come here and take a look."

Woolsey pointed to the chart twenty miles southwest of Abbeville. "They're going to be at Hotel 23 tonight. We sent word back that we wanted the pickup at 2330 for best illumination. They acknowledged the new time without protest, but the problem is the number of people we need to pull out of there. We only have one serviceable Mk 4. We'll need to send it, plus a Mk 3."

Lysander operations were always single ship operations. They flew low level, used no external lights and often had to make unorthodox maneuvers. None of which was conducive to successful formation flights. Woolsey continued, "I'm going to put Kelly Parker-Smythe in the Mk 4. He has plenty of experience. I want you to fly wing in the Mk 3 to pick up the last man. Your time in Blenheims flying night formation will come in handy."

"Yes, sir," he replied.

"Take some time this afternoon to go over the charts, nav check points and pictures we have of the field. Final briefing at 2100. Parker –Smythe will get the weather brief. Any questions?" Woolsey was picking up his papers, preparing to leave.

"No, sir."

It always amazed Dicky. Once you became an experienced aviator, the most challenging and demanding evolutions were so casually laid out. Prior to the final briefing he had hours of target study, a navigation route to lay out, weather pre-brief, check on the assigned aircraft, get his survival gear together, grab a bite to eat and take a nap. *Business as usual*, he thought.

Occupied France

Schmidt and Priller had spent several frustrating hours waiting at the Prefecture in Abbeville. At 0945, a call was finally received from the field. One of the search teams southwest of the town had discovered the wreckage of a British aircraft. Immediately, the two Gestapo agents were on their way to the site. Schmidt was out of ideas. Perhaps this would open up new leads.

Cresting a small knoll, Schmidt saw two civilian cars coming down the small road toward them. Perhaps it was the policeman in him, but he thought it looked suspicious. "Stop here and block the road. I want to see who these people are."

Priller pulled the large sedan across the road with the passenger side facing the oncoming cars. Schmidt reached into the back seat and grabbed an MP-40 submachine gun.

"Stay here. I'll see who they are and what they're doing." Schmidt opened the door and got out, slinging the MP-40 over his shoulder. He raised his free hand directing the car to stop.

The first car slowed to a stop. Walking up slowly, Schmidt could see two men in the front seat and no one in the back. The driver's window was open.

Schmidt looked down at the driver.

"Papers."

The second car had stopped ten paces behind the first.

Schmidt looked at the identity card of the driver, who was identified as 'Andre Moulin', age 41 from Rouen. He asked the other younger man for his papers, and saw it said 'Phillipe Vouillon', age 27, also from Rouen. "What is your business here?"

The driver replied, "We've been helping my cousin harvest apples on his farm outside of Abbeville."

"Where are your registration papers for this car?" Schmidt asked. Their clothes didn't look like they'd been working in an orchard.

"I borrowed the car from a neighbor. I don't know where the papers are."

"Get out of the car and move over to the side of the road." Schmidt pointed with the MP-40 directing the men in front of the Daimler. Looking in the passenger compartment, he saw a leather knapsack with large initials "H.B" burned into the flap. Henri Broussard! He raised the MP-40 and yelled, "Hands up!"

Jack saw the German yell and raise the machine gun. He flung the door open, pulling the .45 from his holster.

At the edge of his vision Schmidt saw movement and spun to face the other driver who was aiming a handgun at him. He squeezed the trigger of the MP-40.

Jack aimed at the man's chest and squeezed the trigger. Bright flashed came from both his gun and the dark figure he was aiming at. Before he knew it, he felt a sharp, concussive impact, and was propelled helplessly away from the car.

Henri and Terry dove for the roadside ditch and both pulled handguns from under their coats. Peering up over the edge of the ditch, they saw the driver jump from his seat and sprint back to the rear of the car. They moved down the ditch trying to get a good angle on the driver. Phil yelled in English.

"Terry, this one looks finished! Do you see the other one?"

Phil jumped from his seat and moved forward using the Citroën as cover. He saw that the enemy driver was gone from the sedan. He carefully looked over the hood of the sedan. He could see the German on the ground was not moving, the machine gun lying awkwardly on the ground under his outstretched arm.

"I think he's behind the car." Terry yelled back.

"Where's Jack?"

"He's hit. Let's get the other one first."

Phil saw the man look around the Daimler's right rear fender. He raised his pistol and fired two rounds. "He's behind the car. Watch the driver's side and work your way around."

Priller knew he was in serious trouble. He was outnumbered, outgunned, and it stood to reason these men were no slouches when it came to matters of combat. Schmidt appeared to be dead, and there was no way to summon help. His only chance was to escape into the thick bush behind him. Trying to use the large sedan as cover, he sprinted toward the bushes. He plunged into the thicket and rushed headlong away from the road.

Used to operating under the minimal cover of the North African desert, Terry quickly moved down the ditch. He ran across the road and into the bushes to outflank Priller.

Henri moved cautiously from the ditch using the large car for cover. He saw Phil crouching behind the Citroën. Henri motioned with his hand, indicating Terry was working his way around the flank.

Priller was a policeman, not a woodsman. He careened through the bushes in his haste to put distance between himself and the enemy agents. He never realized Terry Howe was kneeling behind a small bush listening as he approached.

As the German appeared from the underbrush, Terry fired two rounds and the man collapsed on the ground. Cautiously approaching the man, Terry saw he wasn't moving. A bloody exit wound in the man's back appeared to be fatal. He then pushed the German onto his back to see both rounds had impacted his chest. The man was making a wheezing sound as he gasped for breath. Terry checked him for identity papers and removed a small leather wallet from his coat pocket. He left him lying there and headed for the road.

As Terry emerged from the bushes, he saw Phil and Henri moving toward the man on the ground. "Check him," Phil told Henri. Hatcher then ran back to where Jack lay on his left side.

Kneeling down, Phil carefully rolled Jack over onto his back. There was a substantial amount of blood on his face and in his hair. In addition, a nasty furrow ran across the left side of his jaw, which was also bleeding. "Terry, get me the medical kit."

Jack could tell Phil was kneeling over him. His ears were ringing and a sharp pain seared into his head. Little sparkles and flashes of light floated in his vision. "God, my head hurts," he whispered.

Phil wiped blood away from Jack's head wound. He

was relieved. It appeared the injury to his head was a glancing wound and didn't penetrate the skull. "You're going to be fine."

Terry retrieved the canvas medical bag from the Citroën and handed it to Phil.

Henri knelt by the German who was still breathing, but not moving. The man's eyes were open and staring up at the sky. Jack's bullet had entered just below the sternum and his breath was coming in labored gasps.

Terry walked over and searched him for any identification, finding his wallet in the breast pocket. He read it to Henri, "Standartenfuhrer Gunther Schmidt." He looked closer at the document and reported his findings through gritted teeth.

"Gestapo."

Henri's eyes narrowed as he knelt down and looked at the man.   "Do you understand French?" he asked the man. No response. The man stared up at the sky, his pupils dilated. Henri turned to Terry. "We need to get out of here. Help me move him to the car."

Opening the back door to the Daimler, they manhandled the German into the back seat.

Henri and Terry walked back over to Phil and looked on as he applied a large gauze compress to the scalp wound. Next he wrapped a longer gauze bandage around Jack's head. The deep furrow in Jack's cheek was bleeding and Phil found a smaller bandage which he taped in place.

"We need to get moving," Phil said as he put his hand under Jacks armpits. Terry grabbed Jack's legs. They carried Jack to Henri's Citroën and helped him in the back seat.

Henri and Phil followed Terry down the road in the two cars and the three of them stacked bushes up to hide the German car. The entire encounter had taken less than fifteen minutes.

"Leads, down."

Dicky heard the pre-arranged radio transmission from Parker-Smythe after landing at Hotel 23.

Holding at 75 knots and 1000 feet, one mile south, he was awaiting the transmission

"Leads rolling."

Dicky would then commence his approach to the field.

The flight across the channel had been uneventful. The night formation reminded him of his missions in Blenheims. He checked his instruments and scanned the sky for any unwanted company.

The rendezvous with Louis in the orchard had gone as planned. Jack rested during the afternoon, despite a terrible headache and some nausea.

There had been one brief argument between Phil and Jack over who would be the last man to leave. Phil told Jack that with his head injury he should be on the first Lysander. As far as Jack was concerned, he was the commander and the commander left last after his men were safe. Phil realized his argument was futile. When the first Lysander took off, Terry, Brian and Phil were safely aboard with half of the radar gear.

Jack watched the second aircraft glide down in the moonlight, the power back on the engine. A slight flare and then touchdown. Jack, Henri and Louis moved out to the plane.

Louis carried the radar parts. As he got to the Lysander, Louis opened the cargo hatch placing the knapsack inside.

Jack had left all their spare ammunition, grenades and the Sten guns with the French.

They arrived at the aircraft, and watched Louis climb up the ladder and slide the cockpit canopy back.

Jack turned to Henri, "Thank you, my friend. I wish I could say more, but what's there to say?"

"Good luck, Englishman." Henri smiled in the moonlight.

Jack grinned back and said, "Luck to you as well."

Jack shook hands with Louis. "Many thanks." As he climbed up the ladder, the prop wash felt good. The smell of aviation gasoline was a comfort after the last 48 hours. He climbed into the cockpit and eased into the seat.

"It's about bloody time, Stewart."

Dicky turned round and grinned.

"You look like hell. Ready to head for home?"

"More than ready. Let's go."

CHAPTER TWELVE

10 Downing Street
London
1 July, 1943

Winston Churchill was preparing for his upcoming trip across the Atlantic for the North American "Quadrant" conference. He knew the subject of intelligence cooperation, particularly concerning the atomic issue, would come up at some point. He also knew Franklin Roosevelt wanted full integration of their efforts. Not willing to completely join with the Americans, he'd come up with a superb plan and was quite pleased with himself.

Noel Greene had debriefed the Prime Minister on the mission and its aftermath during an afternoon session in the PM's office. The material the team returned from France would allow the electronic countermeasures people to design and produce a hybrid chaff bundle. This new variation would degrade the new enemy radar regardless of the frequency selected. Greene felt this would save bomber crews in the near term and allow the British strategic bombing program to continue. Churchill was very pleased to hear the results and that Jack Stewart and Brian Standish were mending well.

"So Stewart gunned down a Gestapo colonel face to face at 15 paces," the PM commented. "Glad to hear he's the fighter I imagined."

Greene nodded. "Would've been hell to pay if we'd lost the lad."

"Colonel, Stewart has done a great service to the war effort. I think a DSO is in order. What are your thoughts?" Churchill was referring to the Distinguished Service Order, one of the most prestigious British military awards.

"Most appropriate, sir. I'll take care of it." Greene made a notation in his folder.

"I have another mission where I think Stewart would prove quite useful."

After two days in hospital at Tangmere, Jack was able to return to London. His head still throbbed on occasion, but generally he felt well. His scalp wound had been sutured, but the doctors had left the bandage off. He did have a rectangular bandage on his cheek to cover the bullet wound, but in a medically assisted bout of rare vanity, he thought it made him look tough.

At Baker Street, he finished the debrief process which had started at Tangmere. He also directed Terry and Phil to take a weeks leave. Jack saw a change in his relationship with both of the men. The events in France brought them together much like squadron mates after flying combat missions. There was still the military structure, but they were now his brothers in a way most people could not understand.

He'd been able to get a call through to Pam when he arrived at the hospital. The last time they'd talked, he had been at the Whitchurch training area and he implied he was still there. In any case he couldn't come up with a good way to explain to her where he'd been and he certainly couldn't tell her what he'd been doing.

After reading through the signal traffic of the last several days, Jack heard the yeoman telling him Major Hudson was coming down to see him. Tommy had been waiting at Tangmere when he and Dicky landed but Jack hadn't seen him since the hospital.

Tommy knocked on the doorframe as he walked

through the opened door. "All caught up by now?"

"Pretty much. I sent Hatcher and Howe on a week of well-earned leave." Jack put down the signals board. "Two good men there, Tommy. I'd trust my life with them any time."

"It's no different anywhere, old man. People make the organization. For the record I think you're right about both of them. By the way, a little time off for you makes a great deal of sense. Don't you agree?"

Jack laughed a little. "Afraid to face the music, quite frankly. I never told Pam anything about going on a mission. I'm a bit dodgy about seeing her with my new complexion," he said, motioning toward the bandage on his cheek. "I swore Dicky to secrecy when we got back to Tangmere. Still leaves me in very sticky situation."

Hudson sat down on one of the chairs, and smiled. "Jack, as your superior officer and good friend I've taken a small liberty."

"I don't know exactly what that means. But I suppose I probably need to start worrying."

"Actually, there's no reason to worry, Jack. At least not yet. I signed your leave papers. One week. A little convalescing is certainly in order. You've got a reservation at the Connaught and I also took the liberty of arranging a short leave for Pamela Thompson. I believe she's arriving at the Connaught about now."

Jack smiled and sat back in his chair. "Thanks, Tommy. I appreciate it. Does she know anything?"

"I told her you got scraped up slightly. Nothing serious. Alluded to some kind of training accident. What you tell her is up to you. Now get out of here."

The Connaught Hotel
London

Jack looked at the front entrance of the old hotel. He

couldn't wait to see her, but he still wasn't sure how to explain his injuries. As far as she knew. he'd been training. That was all he really was able to tell her, anyways, but he also knew she deserved better. Suppose the German had been a better shot? She could've gotten the call or visit without even knowing he was in any danger. On the other hand, why should he make her worry? He probably wouldn't be going on any other missions. He still didn't have an answer as he went up to the desk.

"Hello. I should have a reservation under 'Stewart'." He recognized the desk clerk Harry from his last visit.

"Good to have you with us again, sir. Mrs. Stewart is waiting for you in the lounge. If you'll just sign here, I'll get your keys." Handing Jack two room keys, he smiled. "Enjoy your stay. Please let us know if there is anything you need."

Jack turned to go to the lounge. "Thanks, Harry."

Pam was sitting at a small table next to the window staring out at the street. There was a wine glass on the table, half empty. She turned to look at him and smiled. Looking surprised, her smile faded. She watched him walk toward her and her smile reappeared.

"Hello, darling."

Leaning down, he kissed her and said quickly,

"How's my favorite flying officer?"

She reached across the table and put her hand on his chin, turning his head slightly. "Wondering what happened to you?"

"Long story. I'll tell you all about it, but first, how have you been?"

They sat chatting in the lounge, happy to be together. It was thirty minutes before Pam asked again about his injuries. He told her it would be inappropriate to discuss in the lounge. Perhaps it was time to go upstairs to their room he suggested.

Pam observed proper decorum in the lounge and lobby. But exiting the elevator to a deserted third floor hallway she slipped her arm inside his and pulled Jack close. As the door to their room swung open Pam took two steps inside, turned around and put her arms around Jack. "I missed you."

Much later, Jack lay on his back looking at the ceiling. "Have I told you today how much I love you?" he said.

"I keep pinching myself to make sure this isn't a dream. How did we find each other after so many years?" Pam took his hand and kissed the top of it. "Now, are you going to tell me what happened to you?"

Jack sighed. "I can only tell you a little. There are security issues neither of us can get around. All I can say is that I was on the continent and got in a bit of a scrape."

Pam sat up in bed and faced him directly. There was enough light coming from the curtained window for Jack to see the anger on her face.

"You were on the continent. That's all you can say?" Her voice was quiet and questioning. She sat quietly, looking at Jack, waiting for an answer.

Jack had known this was going to happen. He still didn't have any good ideas. "Pam, that's all I can say, honestly. I'm like any other person in uniform in this country. I do what I'm ordered to do. Your RAF crews go over the continent on a daily basis. This was no different."

"You said you were on the continent. There is a difference. What am I supposed to think?"

"Just know you are very much loved by a man who is simply doing his job." He sensed she knew he was telling her everything he could.

"Do I have to worry now? Never knowing where you might be?"

"You know, I really don't think so. I suspect my adventurous days are probably over. No guarantees. But I'm not going looking for ways to get in trouble. Trust me."

Pam leaned forward and put her arms around his neck. "Jack, I do love you."

When Jack arrived back at Baker Street, there was a message. Colonel Greene wanted to see him straightaway. He was glad Terry and Phil were back from leave. Terry had originally been only temporarily assigned to Section F. Because of the team expanding, Hudson had made the assignment permanent. Both of them were busy going over the latest signal traffic, which was particularly heavy with recent operational debriefs. Jack left them with piles of reports to digest and went up to see Greene.

"Come in, Jack." Noel Greene came over to shake hands with Jack. "Splendid job on Quarry. Initial indications are the material you brought back is just what the technical chaps needed. Sit down. How's the head doing? Healing well, I hope?"

Jack sat down. "Doing very well, thanks. Guess I have a hard head. Must be the aviator in me."

"I read about your back injury flaring up. Should I be concerned?" Greene's eyes were boring a hole in him.

"No problem, Colonel. Just a bit stiff after the crash, but right as rain now." Jack crossed his legs, trying to look comfortable.

"Good to hear. There's a lot on the agenda. Ah, here's Tommy now."

Jack turned to see Tommy walk in and saw he was wearing the pip and crown insignia of a lieutenant colonel.

"Tommy! Excuse me—Colonel Hudson. Congratulations!"

Hudson smiled self consciously. "Thanks, Jack."

"Close the door if you would, Tommy," Greene asked. Congratulations are in order for you too, Commander Stewart. I received word this morning that you've been awarded the Distinguished Service Order for you actions in France. Well done."

Jack looked surprised. He didn't know what to say.

"Thank you, Colonel. How about, Howe and Hatcher?"

"In the works. I'll need a write up from you, but there's no question they will be approved for awards. Now, on to other matters. Jack, your position here is unique to say the least. The path you followed to be here is also unusual. We know you've had no contact with the U.S. liaison in London. We think it's time for you to make a connection but on the other side of the Atlantic."

"What are my orders?" Jack asked Greene.

"We're moving into interesting territory here. The original agreement between President Roosevelt and the PM was that you would be privy to our efforts to crack the German atomic research effort. As you know, you've had no contact in that particular area. Not so much by design, but we wanted to use your talents for another project we felt was equally important. I think we made the right decision, but several developments have taken matters out of our hands. The PM wants you to accompany him to the Quadrant Conference scheduled for mid-August in Canada and the States. You'll be traveling as one of his aides and will have two primary missions. Without divulging the specifics, you'll be able to ensure the President and General Donovan that we have every reason to believe the German atomic research program is not as advanced as we'd originally feared. You're going to be privy to information only a very few on this side of the Atlantic possess. No one in the U.S. chain of command knows this information, nor will they in the future. This is the critical test, Jack. The PM had this in mind all along when he laid out his conditions for your intra-country move. During your time here we've come to the conclusion you'll honor your secrecy pledge to the United Kingdom. If you have any reservations, we need to know now." Greene looked at Jack, wanting his response.

"Colonel Greene, when I accepted a commission in the Royal Navy it wasn't some public relations gimmick. I know President Roosevelt and General Donovan expected me to exercise my loyalty to King and country. I intend to do exactly that. I've been proud to be a member of the Navy and MI-6. I don't take that lightly."

Greene smiled. "Tommy told me you'd say as much. But I had to ask the question. There are less than half a dozen people in the military and government who know of a project with the codename 'Bishop.' We have an operative placed at one of the most critical locations in Germany. A German by birth, he came up within their system, but something triggered a spark in him when he watched how his country was descending into Hitler's nightmare. At great personal risk, he approached one of our military attachés in 1938. Initially we suspected a plant by the Germans, but we were wrong. Since then he's consistently been able to provide us with critical information, which has time and again proved to be valid. I'm not going to tell you his name, which is close hold by only three people. However, I can tell you that this person is on Hitler's personal staff. His information is not tactically useful but he allows us to get glimpses into the strategic issues and direction of the Reich. This is so valuable and sensitive we are not willing to let that fact out to anyone, even President Roosevelt."

Jack was confused.

"I don't see how this affects me or atomic intelligence research."

Greene continued, "At his level, Bishop has been able to put together a number of pieces of the puzzle on their research effort. When those pieces are put together, they tell us the Germans are a long way, if not actually unable, to develop an atomic weapon for a number of years. Let me summarize what we know at this time. Most of this is corroborated by the information we have from both our chaps and the Americans who are working on a similar project. It appears the most likely candidate for the material to make this weapon is uranium. However it's a specific isotope of uranium, one which might be capable of producing a self-sustaining chain reaction. The isotope is very difficult to isolate. We estimate it will take millions of pounds sterling, a huge diversion of assets, and a massive industrial effort to even attempt to process the material. All of our communications from Bishop tell us Germany is unable or unwilling to commit the level of resources it would take to refine the isotope. They had one hope. A process using what they call "heavy water," but it didn't work. Everything we've used to corroborate this tells us Bishop is right. Despite the great scientific minds in Germany, they don't have the resources to mount a viable atomic effort considering the strategic bombing campaign, the Russian front, and their efforts to field other, more advanced weapons. Churchill can't tell Roosevelt what I just told you, but you can tell the President you've seen the data, and your opinion is the Germans do not have a creditable atomic threat."

Jack tried to digest what Greene was saying.

"We've put all of the Bishop communications together for you to read. We'll have our Section IX boys provide the liaison with our atomic group. In fact, Ian Thompson will be the liaison. Look at every bit of info and data. Check our corroborating material and come to your own conclusion. But if you feel as we do, you would do England a great service by assuring the Americans we are not concerned."

Tommy Hudson had been quiet since sitting down. "This is quite a departure from Lysander and Sten guns, Jack. But it will allow us to share key information with the Americans and make sure we don't endanger Bishop. Even the codeword is classified. I have a list down in my office of those cleared. A short list. You can't even use the word around anyone except the people on the list."

Jack looked at Greene.

"Colonel, let's get started."

"Thanks, Jack. Tommy will coordinate your briefings. Also there's one other matter we need to go over. More aimed at Section F's next project." Greene continued. "Although it seems we're gaining ground in our battle with the U-boats, we need to keep an eye toward the future. The convoy system has had a very positive effect, just as they did in the first war. Long-range aviation is taking a toll on inshore operations by the Germans. When the new escort carriers are available for antisubmarine work, the airborne gap which now exists in the mid-Atlantic will disappear. However there's a recent development which would significantly alter the balance in the submarine war. What we're about to discuss is classified 'Ultra'."

Greene continued. "Since 1939, we've been slowly breaking the Germans' ability to encrypt message traffic to their operating units. Our boys at Bletchley Park have finally figured out how to decode transmissions from the Enigma machine. This information is very closely held on this side of the Atlantic. Almost no one in the U.S. knows. I'm putting a large burden on you, Jack. We've been reluctant to share our capability on Enigma with the U.S. because of possible compromise. You're being read into this program because of the situation in the Atlantic. We've learned the Germans are working on a torpedo which has the ability to home in on ships. This weapon also has a significantly longer range than current German torpedoes. The end result would be submarine attacks from greater ranges with much higher hit rates. This weapon on its own would have a devastating effect on convoys. However there's also a program we are just starting to learn about using a new propulsion capability which would allow longer times submerged and give the U-boats greater range."

Jack knew the success of the war in Europe depended on the ability to get men and material across the Atlantic.

"We want Section F to focus its efforts on further discovery of these two new developments. Also, investigate any efforts to delay deployment or degrade their performance. It's pretty straight forward. Any questions?"

Greene sat back in his chair and began to light his pipe.

"None right now, sir. Give my people time to look at

this."

Over the next two days, Jack and Section F went over the mission tasking by Greene. Ian was particularly helpful directing them toward the areas of technical expertise the mission might require.

On the second day, Jack received a call from Squadron Leader Hugh Wylie. The PM wanted to meet with Jack next Friday. Jack asked Wylie if this was unusual. Wylie told him the PM was very much a details person and enjoyed getting right in the thick of events. Wylie also mentioned the travel schedule for Quadrant. The PM wanted Jack to be with him for the majority of the trip. He expected they would also work the schedule for a meeting with General Donovan at some point during the Washington stop. Jotting down all the details, he and Wylie agreed to get together the following week to go over Jack's specific duties on the trip.

True to Colonel Greene's word MI-6 put together all communications from Bishop. Jack was required to do all of his reading in the basement vault at Baker Street. Two sentries, badge checks and a cipher lock put him in the Sensitive Materials Archive. Mabel Thorncraft, the classified material custodian, ran the vault with an iron fist. It took Jack multiple visits over the next week to get through the primary source documents and supporting material. At the end of his research, Jack came to the same conclusion as Noel Greene. The chances the Germans could devote the assets that scientists theorized would be needed to produce the uranium isotope were slim at best. Simultaneously, the German war production was starting to feel the effects of the allied long range bombing campaign. The drain on manpower and material from a two-front war was slowly eating away the industrial heart of the nation. Jack was ready to carry Churchill's message to the President.

Ward 3C

German Military Hospital
Rue St. Germain
Paris

The doctors attending Gunther Schmidt were amazed at his gradual recovery. A deep chest wound such as his was normally fatal if medical aid wasn't immediately available. In addition, he hadn't received medical attention for over five hours after his injury. After regaining consciousness, he'd crawled to the road and was discovered by a German patrol. Following initial surgery in Rouen to remove the bullet and repair major damage, he was transferred to the large hospital in Paris. Another surgery had been required almost immediately on arrival in Paris to stop the internal bleeding. His condition remained critical for two weeks. A long recuperation period lay in front of him but he would return to duty sometime in the future. As he fought through the cloud of confusion and pain, he slowly remembered the events on the road. The first emotions he felt beyond his primal need for survival were fury and hate.

London

The invitation to tea at 10 Downing Street made arranging a duty swap easy for Pam. Jack had told her of his initial meeting with the Prime Minister in May. The news that he would be accompanying Churchill to America came as a shock.

She left the base Thursday afternoon so they would have some time together in London. Pam treasured any time with Jack and the train trip seemed to take forever. When she finally met Jack at the Connaught, he told her she was invited for tea at 1600 hours on Friday with the Prime Minister. Jack's meeting was scheduled for an hour earlier.

Pam was at once excited and yet at the same time dreading she might make a mistake with protocol.

Jack reassured her the tea was a very small event. It might only be the three of them.

She knew sleep that night would prove elusive for a number of reasons.

The next day Jack departed via taxi wearing his best blue service uniform, his gold wings and DFC sparkling in the mid afternoon sun. It was a beautiful, mild summer day in London. Jack was surprised to find he wasn't the least bit nervous. His previous meeting was pleasant and he felt comfortable with Mr. Churchill to a degree.

Hugh Wylie met Jack when he arrived. They shook hands and Jack sensed he had Wylie's approval. "Good to see you again. The old man is just finishing with Lord Beaverbrook. Let's go down to my office. They'll let us know when he's ready for you." They made their way down a corridor and into a small alcove office. Hugh sat at his desk and Jack took the small chair next to the desk.

"We did some checking on your service record of course. You were a fighter pilot." Wylie was friendly and relaxed.

He made Jack feel very much at home.

"I loved to fly, and fighters seemed like the best flying there was." Jack saw the wings on Wylie's chest over two ribbons, the Distinguished Service Cross and DFC.

"Felt the same way. Ended up in Hurricanes, initially. Transitioned to Spits in the spring of '40."

"We watched the news and read the reports of the air battles. The whole world was impressed with what the RAF did." As far as Jack was concerned, the British fighter pilots of 1940 defined the role of a fighter pilot.

"I'll be honest, Jack, it was a blur. It seemed all we did was fly and sleep and fly again. Lost a lot of good men. But that's the story of this war. Your chaps did a job of their own at

Midway."

"I guess we looked at it the same way you did in '40. We were out of options."

A yeoman stuck his head in the office and said, "The PM is ready for Commander Stewart."

This time they met in Churchill's office which was part of the Downing Street residence. As Jack was shown in he saw that Churchill was again in a white shirt and bow tie.

"Commander Stewart, good to see you. None the worse for wear, it appears." He looked at the bright red scar on Jack's jaw.

As they shook hands he said, "Hello, sir."

After sitting down, Churchill looked Jack hard in the eye. "I read with great interest the debrief summary of your mission into France. You did a magnificent job. We thank you for it." He paused momentarily, then continued, "I know Colonel Greene covered the situation and our intent on conveying information to the Americans at the upcoming conference. Jack, this is very important. Do you see our logic in following this rather unusual course?" Churchill's jaw was set and his eyes were boring into Jack.

"Yes, sir. I understand. Based on the information I reviewed, I strongly agree with the conclusions drawn by our experts. I'm ready to deliver that message to the President and General Donovan."

"Having an American mother gave me a special feel for the United States, but England is my heart and soul. I think you're walking down a remarkable road to become a man with two mother countries as it were. I suppose at some point Franklin will make us hand you back over. But let there be no doubt in your mind Jack, we would be happy to pick up your option permanently." Churchill gave him a warm smile and as he stood up and walked to the sidebar he patted Jack on the shoulder. "I think a short libation is in order. To toast the success of your mission and safe return."

Jack felt humbled and proud at the same time. All he could say was "Yes, sir." He rose and walked over to the bar, where the Prime Minister handed him a glass of scotch. They toasted, "To success."

"Now, we have a bit of formality laid on. A surprise, I daresay." He opened the door and in filed Colonel Greene, Tommy Hudson, Phil and Terry, Ian Thompson and Pamela. Everyone was smiling and enjoying Jack's confusion. They lined up in a semi-circle and Hugh Wylie handed Churchill a small rectangular box.

"Attention to orders...." Hugh Wylie read the citation for the Distinguished Service Order as Winston Churchill pinned on the white enameled cross, suspended from a red ribbon with blue edges.

"Well done, Commander. Your King and country are proud of you." The Prime Minister turned to the group. "I know my aide mentioned this would be tea. But I think champagne is in order. Hugh, if you would."

After making a toast to Section F, Churchill made his way over to where Pam and Ian Thompson were standing with their glasses. "This must be Flying Officer Thompson." He smiled and offered his hand.

Pamela blushed. "Mr. Prime Minister, this is my father, Professor Ian Thompson."

"Delighted to meet you, Professor. Jack mentioned the great help you provided him. My thanks." Churchill did not see the look Pamela gave her father who still had not mentioned he and Jack were working together.

"It's been my pleasure, sir. Jack was a student of mine at Oxford back in '35." Ian missed the look from his daughter but knew some explanations would be in order later tonight.

The party broke up in twenty minutes, most of the group decided that another round was a splendid idea and headed toward Mayfair and the Red Hearth Pub.

HMS Queen Mary
The North Atlantic
8 August 1943

As a Navy man, being back at sea had been a very comfortable experience for Jack. However, he'd never been involved in an experience quite like this voyage. Departing from the Clyde four days prior he was part of the Prime Minister's delegation, which totaled over 150 staff, guests and security personnel. Jack assumed the duties of Churchill's junior aide, assisting Hugh Wylie. The day-to-day contact with the Prime Minister was exhilarating. Churchill's enthusiasm, ability to work for hours and his total command of the war effort gave Jack great confidence England was in good hands. He met Mrs. Churchill and their daughter Mary, who also functioned as an aide-de-camp to her father. They were charming, friendly and completely dedicated to supporting Churchill and his efforts

On the second day out, Hugh Wylie introduced Jack to Wing Commander Guy Gibson, who'd become a legend in the RAF after leading an historic raid on the Mohne and Eder dams. Using specially developed skip bombs and perfecting a unique low altitude delivery, Gibson led the squadron, now called the "Dam Busters," on a dangerous night mission to flood the valley. For his action he'd been awarded the Victoria Cross. Jack immediately liked him. He was an aviator's aviator and they enjoyed sharing stories.

Another remarkable officer included in the official party was Brigadier Orde Wingate. A scrappy little chap, Hugh told him he was a terror in jungle fighting and expected they would hear a lot about Wingate as the war progressed.

Jack realized he had begun to forget the U.S. Navy. Instead he felt he belonged exactly where he was, serving the country he had come to love as much as his original homeland. With the exception of the still distinctive American accent, which was slowly being altered by vocabulary, Jack was indistinguishable from any of his British counterparts. To Jack it was not something in the front of this thoughts and he probably wouldn't have thought the change dramatic but he was a changed man on his way to America.

The White House
Washington D.C.
September 2, 1943

After landing in Halifax, Nova Scotia the official party traveled to Quebec for the Quadrant Conference. The agenda was crowded and the staffs took the opportunity to continue to hammer out the details of the proposed cross-channel invasion. Jack was extremely busy coordinating the myriad details of Churchill's meetings and correspondence. He was more than a little impressed with the parade of senior officers from the United Kingdom, the United States and Canada.

Churchill wanted to schedule Jack's meeting with the President after their arrival in Washington. He felt it would be better for Roosevelt to get Jack's report on home ground. General Donovan was not present in Quebec so he'd be able to see both of them in Washington.

Entry to the White House had proved much more involved and lengthy this time compared with his last visit. He was, after all, an officer of a foreign power and his credentials must be thoroughly checked.

Churchill had arrived earlier and was staying in the White House. Hugh would accompany the PM and Jack would stay at the Stratford Hotel reporting each day for duty. Today however, he was a key participant not just a "strap hanger," the not-so-kind term applied to aides the world over.

A young Marine escorted him to the executive offices. On arriving at the Oval Office, he was shown in immediately. Present for the meeting was the President, Admiral Leahy and

General Donovan. Jack had left his cover in the outer office and walked toward the desk.

The President looked tired but he had a broad smile and offered his hand. "Welcome back, Commander. Good to see you, although you look much different."

Jack firmly grasped the President's hand and smiled. "Thank you, Mr. President." He nodded to Leahy, "Admiral."

Donovan came over, shaking hands and patting him on the back. "Jack, we've been debriefed on your mission to France. Quite an adventure."

As they all sat down, Jack said, "One I shouldn't be forgetting for a long time to come, sir."

"Commander, I understand your efforts made a significant contribution toward the strategic bombing campaign?" the President asked.

Jack realized he didn't know what this group was cleared to know about his mission to France. He suspected they would have clearance, but he was circumspect just in case. "Yes, sir. The analysis was rather positive. We hope it will make a difference."

"Well done. I also understand you were wounded in a shoot out with the Germans?"

Jack wasn't sure where this was going. Were they really interested? Or was he going to get reprimanded for not attending to the primary purpose he was there. "Yes, sir. Nothing serious."

"Well, you have quite an admirer in the Prime Minister. He said they want you to remain with British intelligence. Just another version of Lend Lease, I guess." Roosevelt smiled. "Now, what can you tell us of their efforts to penetrate the German atomic research program?"

Jack was surprised that the President's use of "their" irritated him. He was part of "them" and he liked it that way. "Mr. President, I can tell you I have seen the entire file including source intelligence on the German's efforts. There is overwhelming evidence the Germans not only will not, but also cannot, field a viable weapon production effort. This is primarily due to the constraints on resources required by the primary war effort and their more conventional programs. The strategic bombing campaign is one very critical part of the equation."

Leahy leaned forward and asked, "How do you know this? What source intelligence could be that definitive?"

Jack swallowed, knowing this was going to be difficult. "Admiral, I'm unable to divulge the exact intelligence source. But I'm convinced totally of the validity of our conclusions."

Jack's use of the term "our" was not lost on any of the three. Donovan was the first to speak. "Jack, that's not good enough. We can't make strategic decision on a hunch. We need to know exactly how they know these things."

"Sir, with all due respect, I'm forbidden by the Secrets Act to divulge that information. When I started this journey I was told that I must give my loyalty to king and country. Mr. President, you told me that in this office last November. This is not a gimmick. I'm a serving officer in the Royal Navy. The only reason I was given access to that information was because of that fact. Just as this country doesn't share every piece of information with our allies, England is no different. I know this is valid intelligence. You must believe that also." Jack's heart was pounding. He had just said no to the President of the United States.

Roosevelt was the first to speak, "Gentlemen, as a wise man once said, be careful what you wish for, it may come true. Commander, I do understand your position. Quite frankly I would've been surprised if you had acted otherwise. It's difficult for us to be kept in the dark because of our sense of responsibility to this nation. But I know your sense of responsibility is no less than ours and we will put our trust in you.

"Thank you, sir."

Roosevelt turned to the other three. "Gentlemen, we need to wrap this up. I have to prepare for a meeting. Commander, thank you for coming. Please remember our trust is with you. If there is any indication of a change in your analysis, we need to know."

Jack stood up. "Sir, I understand completely." He turned and moved toward the door.

"Would you stick around for a moment, Jack?" Donovan asked.

"Yes, sir."

As Jack left the room Roosevelt smiled at the other two. "I think Winston just beat us at our own game."

Donovan came over to Jack in the outer office. "We would like to sit down with you while you're in town. Is that feasible?"

"Yes, sir. I've learned a great deal and would be happy to sit down and go over it. And I'd like to see Colonel Miller."

"He's the one who started this ball rolling. I know he would like to talk to you. How about tomorrow afternoon, 1400 at our place?"

"I'll be there, General."

Donovan and Miller found the meeting with Jack very beneficial. They were interested in Jack's impressions of the training system for agents, the operations support group and the communication systems. Although they were familiar with all of these subjects, they had not been able to get a personnel perspective from someone working all facets of espionage/intelligence.

They talked for over two hours and Jack told General Donovan he would begin an informal correspondence on any subject he thought the General might be interested. When they finished, Colonel Miller invited Jack to go out for a drink. They headed for the "Olde Stein," on Massachusetts Ave.

The two friends sat in a booth. The happy hour was in full swing. There were men in every type of uniform and lots of young ladies, from the many office buildings surrounding the bar.

"Jack, thanks for taking the time to talk to the directors this afternoon. I know they appreciated it." They sat opposite each other and thankfully were in a quiet end of the bar.

"It was the least I could do. MI-6 really does have an organization that gets the job done." Jack took a small drink of his scotch and continued, "I have a lot to thank you for, personally."

"What's that, Jack?" Miller looked genuinely puzzled.

Jack laughed. "I never mentioned it before. When I was at Oxford in '35 I developed a relationship with a lovely English girl. We thought it was something but then I left England. We just drifted away from each other. When I get back from this trip I'm going to ask her to marry me. I never would have met her again if you hadn't taken up my case. Hell, I'd still be counting F-4Fs rolling off the production line. Colonel, here's to you." Jack raised his drink and they clinked their glasses.

"Life has a funny way of always keeping you interested. I couldn't be happier for you. Best wishes for you and your bride. Which does raise an interesting question. How long do you see this assignment continuing? I know we never set any time frame, we weren't sure what we were getting into."

Jack grinned. "You've hit on the subject that keeps me awake at night. I don't know what the future will hold. Hell, if I come back to the Navy I'm a grounded aviator who spent the war out of the U.S. uniform. Don't see any of those things as being career enhancing. I get the impression my commission in the Royal Navy is open ended and they'd keep me on for the future. Same question, how do I make a career, when my active service began in 1942?"

Miller motioned to the waitress for another round. "You might do what I did after the last war. I realized I couldn't compete with the guys on the fast track and returned to a very rewarding civilian career."

"You're right. But I've always worn a uniform. I put it on at 18 when I left home for Annapolis and have never taken it off."

"Jack, you have a lot of questions. I wish I could provide some of the answers. But I think those lie somewhere on the other side of the Atlantic."

Jack stayed busy for the remainder of his time in the capitol. The visit culminated with a relaxed train trip from Washington to Halifax and a six day voyage home onboard H.M.S. Renown. His daily efforts on behalf of the Prime Minister didn't go unnoticed and the day before arriving in port Hugh told him the PM had requested that Jack join him for lunch.

Churchill was in a good mood. He felt the conference had gone well and wanted to thank Jack for his efforts in talking to the President. FDR had taken the PM aside and told him he was comfortable with the information received from Jack. The United States would alter plans accordingly. Mission accomplished with no damage to trans-Atlantic relations. Churchill was clearly delighted at the result of his strategy. Jack was not surprised when the PM brought up his future.

"Jack, I know your situation is unique. I expect when you began your journey you saw yourself returning and picking up where you left off. Am I right?" As always, the Prime Minister was direct and to the point.

Stewart paused for a moment carefully phrasing his response. "Prime Minister, I think that was in the back of my mind. But I had no idea what was waiting for me."

Churchill went on, "Do I detect a possible change in your thoughts about the future?"

"Yes, sir. I'm a fighter pilot who's missing all the major career steps of my contemporaries. I'm not sure I would have a viable career if I returned to duty with the U.S. Navy. At the same time how do I make a career as a Royal Navy type who's never served actively with a Royal Navy unit? Seems bleak on both fronts."

Churchill finished a lamb chop and put down his fork. "When we win this war, and we will, the next big war will be with the Soviets. Don't repeat that, after all they are our Allies for now. We're going to need intelligence agents who know the ropes and know how to take action. Much of our intelligence network is made up of reserves and volunteers called up for the duration. We'll need regular officers who can take on the communist intelligence apparatus and make sure we win the next war. It strikes me that you fit the bill superbly. Think it over."

Jack had never thought about remaining in intelligence, but why not?

CHAPTER THIRTEEN

64 Baker Street
London

When Jack detached from duties as Churchill's aide, the Prime Minister made a point to have the photographer take a picture of Jack with Churchill in the P.M.'s office. When the photo arrived at Baker Street, Jack saw Churchill had written a message across the bottom. It said, "Jack, thank you for a job very well done. Winston Churchill, 1943".

Jack was pleased that the program he had asked Hiram Baker to put in place was going at full speed. During Quarry, the language barrier was more of a problem than Jack had anticipated. Jack was able to pick up a foreign language very easily. That was one reason why he'd studied both French and German in high school and also at Annapolis. The agents on his team didn't have that luxury. Jack asked Hiram to get with the MI-6 training group and put together a crash course for the agents in both French and German. He didn't know how long before they might go back in action, but he wanted his operatives to be as fluent as possible when they did.

Phil Hatcher added to the cadre, bringing in four more agents to the section. The three men and one woman, Edith Moulon, were all graduates of the course at Arisaig. Two of the men were British, Jimmy Hunt and Curtis Livesy, both former commandos. The other man, Pierre Goillet had been recruited from the Free French forces in North Africa.

The cryptologists at Bletchley had succeeded in

breaking the newest version of the Kriegsmarine Enigma codes. The message traffic to the submarines based in Brest talked about field deployment of the new acoustic torpedo within the next three months.

Ian Thompson had put together a working group from Section IX to address the new weapon allowing Jack and Phil to blend their conclusions into a contingency plan, which Jack presented to Tommy Hudson in the first week of December.

In the team's view it was imperative the intelligence effort focus on getting any information on the technical capabilities of the new torpedo. There were two options, either go to the source at the German torpedo production facility in Bremerhaven or attempt to get access to a weapon in the field. Jack wrestled with the different nature of this operation compared with Quarry. An airborne radar set is slightly more portable than a 2000 pound, 18 foot long torpedo. The other issue was gaining access to the weapons. Security would be tight at Bremerhaven and the facility was almost 100 miles inside Germany. The team was in favor of trying to access the weapons during their transport to the U boat bases on the French coast. The problems didn't get much easier but at least they were closer to England and the resistance could possibly offer assistance. After looking at all options, the team decided the weapons depot at Brest was the most vulnerable to penetration. They started to put together an operational plan.

An ultra intercept noted the allocation of a small percentage of the new torpedoes to the Second Schnellboote Flotilla which was based in Oostende, Belgium. These fast motor patrol boats were nicknamed "E-boats" by the Allies. Roaming the channel and North Sea, they wreaked havoc with their torpedoes and mines. A little publicized part of the war was the vicious night time fights which took place between German fast patrol boats and Costal Command motor torpedo boats (MTB's). It became clear to Jack they had a third option and in his mind it was the best one.

"Let me get this straight. You want to steal one of the

new torpedoes off an E-boat?" Tommy Hudson didn't appear to like Jack's idea at first glance.

"Tommy, not off an E-boat, we steal the whole boat. Make sure the new 'fish' are on board. Then we drive the boat out of the harbour and across the Channel." Jack looked at the surprise on Hudson's face and laughed. "I'm not kidding. We've looked at the harbor layout, known security and think this is something we can do."

Hudson didn't say anything at first. He got up and walked over to his window. "I'd be foolish to reject something out of hand. Put together a plan and we'll take a look at it. But it has got to have a better than even chance of success, or you're done before you start."

Jack got up, and said, "Tommy, that's all I'm asking. Take a look and then make a decision."

"Now get out of here and let me get some work done!"

"Whatever you say, Colonel. I just need one bit of help. Who do we know in Costal Forces who can teach us about fast patrol boats?"

Gestapo Headquarters
Paris
September 20, 1943

Gunther Schmidt had recovered enough to be put on light duty at Gestapo Headquarters in Paris. One of his first actions on returning to duty had been to order the transport of Charles Wiegand from the prison at Romainville to the Buchenwald concentration camp outside of Weimar.

Schmidt had sworn to himself that he would hunt down Phillipe Wiegand's group and see them hung on meat hooks. But now he must focus on completing his physical recovery and making sure there were no personal repercussions from the incident at Abbeville. As the senior agent he didn't need a successful British raid affecting his chances of promotion. He would place most of the blame on Priller. Walck was another story, he could provide very embarrassing information to the regional director. Schmidt went over many scenarios before it came to him. Contact Walck and offer to bring him in as his assistant with the lure of promotion. He would become Walck's benefactor.

Schmidt was nervous when he finally received a summons from his immediate superior Hans Schenk, the director for all Gestapo operations in occupied France. But he also knew if he was being called to his office during the working day the danger was minimal. Normal Gestapo procedure for someone who is being cashiered was to 'visit' the individual in the middle of the night and take him off for interrogation. Still, Schenk was known as a particularly brutal character and a favorite of Reichsfuhrer Heinrich Himmler. Schmidt felt very uneasy.

The orderly had shown him in as soon as he arrived, also a good sign in Schmidt's mind. "Reporting as directed, Herr Director." Schmidt came to attention in front of Schenk's desk.

"Gunther, please sit down. How're you feeling?" Schenk smiled and sounded sincere.

Schmidt felt tremendous relief. He allowed his eyes to move around the room and saw an unfamiliar figure standing by the window. The man wore a dark suit and had small glasses, much like Himmler's. "Very well, thank you. I'll be fully ready for duty in a week or so the doctors tell me."

"That's good to hear, we need you back on the job. I wanted you to meet someone from headquarters in Berlin, Standartenfuhrer Manfred Kolsch. He's with Department 3A, working on our espionage effort into England. Although most of what they do is very classified, he has uncovered information which Berlin felt they needed to corroborate with you."

Schmidt was confused but attempted to maintain a cool demeanor. "Certainly, sir. At your service."

Kolsch came over and sat in the chair next to Gunther. "When you were wounded, we feel you were correct in assuming it was the same British team which penetrated the Abbeville airfield."

Schmidt's interest was growing.

"I can tell you we have an agent who has recently joined the very same team and found out who was involved in the mission. She sent a photograph via courier and we want you to verify if you recognize this man." Kolsch handed Schmidt a small photograph.

Schmidt felt like the bullet had hit his chest again. He saw the same face he'd seen on a dusty French road less than three months ago. "That's him. He's the man who shot me. But I was sure I'd hit him also."

"Apparently you did. But he survived the wounds. The man is a Lieutenant Commander in the Royal Navy. His name is Stewart."

"Stewart," he repeated. His hatred now had another name in addition to Broussard and Wiegand.

"The Reichsfuhrer has been personally briefed. He directed we arrange for Lieutenant Commander Stewart to have an accident. We'd like to take out the entire team, but we would possibly compromise our agent. We intend to use her to slowly decimate the team."

Gunther Schmidt was pleased and curious at the same time. "How will you do it? Don't they provide security to their key people?"

For the first time, Kolsch smiled. "Their security for key personnel is remarkably lax. We'll probably use a motor car, it's too simple."

The thought of that Englishman dead made Gunther Schmidt feel good.

Kolsch continued, "It also appears this same team is working on some upcoming operation. Our agent hasn't been brought into the plan yet. We may know more shortly."

Standartenfuhrer Gunther Schmidt felt excited for the first time in a long time.

Onboard H.M.S. Whitney
Depot Ship
Motor Torpedo Flotilla Seven
Harwich
October 15, 1943

Jack had briefed Phil on proper etiquette for going aboard a naval vessel in port and the former policeman thought it was amusing, but he went along with tradition for Jack's sake.

Arriving on the quarterdeck of the big patrol boat tender, they'd been escorted to the flotilla's senior officer, Commander Ian Parker. A veteran of the pre-war navy, Parker had been assigned to oversee the training and operations of a dozen fast patrol boats. These boats were manned primarily with volunteers who signed on for the duration of the war. Sprinkled amongst the crews was the occasional regular sailor who provided some balance to the wild characters of the MTB crews.

Parker welcomed them warmly, trying to find out exactly what they wanted. "Commander Stewart, I'm not sure who you know. But we were told in no uncertain terms our job was put on the dog for you."

Jack laughed. "Sir, nothing quite like that. We do need to get smart about fast patrol boat operations. And also get to know some of your people for a possible operation."

"Sounds rather hush-hush. Nothing else you can tell me at this point?"

"Plans are still in the formulation stage. We need more info from your chaps to put it all together." Jack imagined how he would've felt if he were in Parker's shoes.

"Here's what I propose. Let me assign you to a boat for as long as you have to devote to this. You can learn about the boat and go on operations with them. If you still need more information you can let me know."

Parker made perfect sense to Jack and the two MI-6 agents began two weeks as honorary members of the crew of MTB 5122 under the command of Lieutenant Lee Powers, RNVR, DSC.

Jack and Phil met the crew the next morning. The flotilla was returning to Harwich after a night in the Channel trying to intercept a German costal convoy near Calais. Jack and Phil stood on the deck of the Whitney watching the arrival of the six MTB's. In the crisp morning breeze, the line of sleek gray hulls approached their moorings in a column. Each boat had crewmembers on deck waiting to secure lines. The muffled roar of the idling engines mixed with the cries of the gulls overhead reminding Jack of Annapolis.

He looked closer and saw that there was recent battle damage to several of the boats. The third boat moved out of line and proceeded to a small pier where he saw an ambulance and medical personnel waiting.

The 5122 boat turned out to be the fifth boat in line. On the open bridge he saw the commanding officer, standing alone in a heavy duffel coat. In short order lines were passed to the pier. One by one the engines were secured. As the last boat stopped engines he saw the boat officers making their way toward the accommodation ladder.

Fifteen minutes later he and Phil sat in the back of the operations briefing room as Lieutenant Commander Jocko Smith, the senior officer, debriefed the night's mission. The group of skippers slumped in their chairs, mugs of hot tea in their hands. They were all in their early twenties, but looked old for their years.

"All in all a nice job, gentlemen. We need to compare notes with the debriefers but from my view it was Shepard's boat that hit the tanker with his torpedoes. Pat, nice shooting. By my estimate there were four E-boats as the escort. I think we traded even there. Other than the 27 boat, were there any wounded?" He looked at the group who all shook their heads.

"Right. Tommy, how bad were your two hit?"

A young Lieutenant wearily said, "My coxswain was hit in the leg with shrapnel. He'll be fine. I'm afraid it doesn't look good for my signals petty officer."

"Keep me advised. That's it for now. Be sure to get your written reports into the Ops Officer straight away. And finally, well done to all hands. Our fire discipline was superb and reaction to my signals couldn't have been better. Now, get out of here and get some sleep. Nothing slated for tonight. Lee, you'll be the duty boat. That's all. Oh Lee, would you stand by for a moment."

A tall dark haired Lieutenant, with a ruddy complexion walked up to Lieutenant Commander Smith who'd been joined by Commander Parker.

"Lee, I would like you to meet Lieutenant Commander Jack Stewart and Captain Phil Hatcher," Parker said.

"Once you've had something to eat and checked on your crew, I want you to meet us in my office. Say, in an hour?" Parker asked.

The young skipper smiled and nodded. "Aye aye, sir. I'll be there."

Lee Powers was a volunteer officer. Until the fall of 1939 he'd been a second year law student at Cambridge. At the outbreak of the war he had been commissioned a sub-lieutenant in the Royal Navy Volunteer Reserves. Called the 'wavy Navy' from the wavy rank rings on their sleeves compared to their regular Navy brethren, they made up a large percentage of those currently serving in the Navy. In the ensuing years the young officer had become an experienced combat leader, rising to command his own boat and winning the Distinguished Service Cross in the process. Known throughout the flotilla as a solid commander, he was often selected for the most hazardous missions.

Jack liked him immediately. He was easy going but at the same time there was an attitude of deadly professionalism about him. Jack told Lee they needed to get totally familiar with the capabilities of the MTB and current operations.

"How long are you available, Commander?" Powers was sitting back in his chair in the Ops office rubbing his blood-shot eyes.

Jack replied, "Two weeks at least. Although we'll let you call the shots. You let us know when you think we've seen enough."

"You may regret that," Lee said. "There are stretches where we really don't see much action. Then all hell breaks loose. We spend a lot of time patrolling convoy routes in the Channel and North Sea. If our intelligence people get the right picture we've been able to beat up the Germans. Their E-boats and trawlers do make it a nasty fight at times."

"Hopefully we can get a good appreciation of MTB capabilities and see some of the enemy coastline in the process."

"Commander, hope you don't mind me asking. Are you Canadian?"

Jack laughed. "That's a long story. I was born a Yank but managed to undergo a bit of a transformation."

The young captain looked at Jack curiously but didn't say anything.

In the next week, Jack and Phil became familiar with the capabilities of the MTB and the attitude of Costal Command. Only fourteen men and two officers, there was a spirit and comradeship that reminded Jack of a fighter squadron. Over time their sorties into hostile waters had bred a confidence, which can only come when men have faced tough, demanding challenges and triumphed. Lee was particularly proud they'd not lost any men over the last year. During that time they had been involved in a number of vicious battles in the Channel.

The crew was an interesting group. Like their Captain they were all volunteers in service for the duration. There was an easy going relationship between Powers and his men which was very different from what Jack observed as the norm in the Royal Navy. Lee's "Number One" or second in command was a young sub-lieutenant Keith Caulfield. He'd been with Lee for eight months, and seemed competent.

Late one morning, Jack and Phil were down in the engine room getting a brief on the three turbo charged Rolls Royce engines. Lee came down the ladder with a folder in his hand.

"You're in luck, gentlemen. We've been alerted for a sortie tonight. There may be a small German costal convoy in the Channel. We're going to try and intercept." He looked grim. "The weather is going to be on the nasty side. I wouldn't blame you for sitting this one out."

"Lee, we came here to see what you do," Jack said.

Phil, who had been seasick before was quick to ask, "What do you mean by nasty?"

Lee grinned. "Should have winds of 20-25 knots with six to eight foot seas. The temp will be down with mixed rain and sleet in most of the op area."

"Sounds wonderful," Phil said. He didn't look enthusiastic.

The flotilla started engines in the fading daylight. By sunset they were clearing the harbor, accelerating to 25 knots in two lines of three MTB's each. Jack stood on the bridge with Lee watching the boat in front of them crash through the rolling water. Despite wearing woolen long underwear, wool trousers, a heavy wool sweater, duffel coat and rain gear Jack was shaking with the cold and his eyes stung from the salt spray. He had to raise his voice to be heard over the roar of the engines and the wind.

"How long to transit to the convoy area?" he hollered at Lee, who was braced against a steel tube railing at the back of the bridge. Lee looked like he was totally in his element, his knees absorbing the pounding motion as the MTB slammed into the oncoming waves.

"If we can keep up this speed, about two hours."

Jack looked forward to the large Bofors 40mm cannon on the forward deck. The gun crew was below waiting to be called to action stations. Two 18 inch torpedoes were loaded in metal tubes mounted on each deck edge. The most lethal weapons on the boat, either one could sink warships or merchantmen by ripping open the side of the ship with over 1,000 pounds of torpex. Aft there were two twin Oerlikon 20mm cannons. The MTB's were capable of putting out heavy firepower when they got in close with the enemy patrol boats. The one advantage the E-boats did have was diesel fuel, much less flammable than the hi-octane gasoline, which powered the MTB's.

The sun was fully set and Lee was maintaining position on the lead boat using the boats wake and dimmed running lights. Jack felt numb as the minutes ticked by, much like the drone of a fighter in a formation on the way to a target. Why was it that these are the times that you dig up the most difficult memories? His thoughts returned to Quarry and the anxiety he felt as the Lysander headed to France. Always the question, What in the hell am I doing here? His thoughts would stray to Pam. He wondered what she was doing? He had been non-committal about the trip to Harwich. "Just gathering some info on the Navy" was how he had described it. One more time he found himself in harm's way without allowing her to know. He still wasn't sure how to approach a problem he never had to worry about it when he was on a carrier. The whole idea of fighting a war and going home at night was crazy. But these MTB guys do it day in and day out he thought. They never know if they might be home for breakfast or floating face down in the North Sea. God, this is a crazy war.

Phil came up the small ladder from the chartroom and yelled to Jack, "We're nearing the area they think the convoy may be transiting."

There was a blue filtered signal from Jocko Smith in the lead boat. Lee immediately yelled down the voice pipe, "Half ahead, both engines". There was a reduction in the noise and vibration as the boat slowed. Another light signal and Lee called, "Port 15, steer 120. All hand to action stations."

Jack understood the MTB's were spreading out into the pre-briefed attack formation, which was a wide "V." The gun and torpedo crews ran on deck and manned their weapons.

Ten minutes later another light signal winked from the lead MTB and Lee ordered, "Slow ahead, both engines." The boat maintained steerage in the rolling waves.

The rain and sleet were intermittent, blown by a bitter wind. Now it was a waiting game with everyone on deck cold and miserable looking for unknown danger in the darkness.

The wait ended an hour later when the RT crackled, "Lead's engaging. All others to follow." Jack saw the wake kick up behind the lead boat. There was a boom across the water as the leader's Bofors opened up. Criss-crossing lines of tracers began filling the dark night. Keith Caulfield was standing behind the 40mm deck gun. Lee yelled down, "Commence fire. Full ahead, both engines."

It was clear where the enemy tracers were coming from and 5122 had a shot. The smell of cordite and the concussion from the gun added to the urgency of the situation. Lee was maneuvering the 5122 aggressively and the Oerlikons opened up on the source of tracers. There was a reverberating crash as an E-boat exploded, flames leaping in the air, the sound echoing across the water. In the momentary flash a costal tanker was visible turning away from the MTB's. Lee and the boat on their left altered course toward the tanker.

"Torpedoes, stand by," Lee yelled. "Port 15." Jack watched with fascination as he saw a gunnery solution unfolding before his eyes. Lee was swinging the boat wide to get a beam on aspect shot at the tanker. The MTB accelerated through 30 knots, the tanker now off their starboard bow.

Powers yelled in the brass voice tube, "Starboard 30." The boat violently reversed back to the right, the bow now aligned at the tanker and the range closing rapidly. "Helm amidships, starboard tube, FIRE". Jack heard the whoosh of compressed air as the black shape cleared the tube and splashed into the sea. Immediately, Lee commanded, "Port 5." As soon as the bow started to move, "Port tube, FIRE". As the torpedo cleared the deck edge, Lee called, "Starboard 30!" The boat swung sharply to the right as the night was shattered by a violent explosion, erupting from the port side of the tanker, ugly orange flames visible through the smoke. Powers looked back briefly then returned to conning the boat, now racing at 30 knots through the darkness. "Half ahead both engines. Let's be on a lookout for our boats. There may still be E-Boats out here so stay sharp."

Over the next 30 minutes the flotilla rendezvoused and began the transit back to Harwich. The only casualties were on the lead boat. At least one E-boat had been destroyed plus the costal tanker, not a bad night's work. Jack and Phil went below to the small wardroom for hot cocoa.

"These are pretty impressive boats. What do you think?" Jack asked.

"Hell, I'm not crazy about any kind of boat. But these could be the key." He stared into his steaming cup. "It strikes me that in the dark all of these fast movers look alike."

"That's just what I was thinking. It sounds simple but most good plans are simple. With a little good intelligence we could take one of these into Oostende and steal one of their boats."

"Think I'd like the young gent on the bridge to be the one to take us in there."

"What do you mean us. I need you back home coordinating operations." Jack smiled.

"Screw you. Where you go, I go. You told me I get the say on all operational matters." Phil sounded indignant.

"So I did. Actually, I wouldn't even attempt it without you watching my back."

64 Baker Street
London
November 4, 1943

Colonel Noel Greene sat in his office re-reading the plan Jack and Tommy had presented to him earlier. Back from Harwich for a week, they'd formulated what looked like a superb plan with a good chance of success. Greene thought about the key elements of the plan. There must be an advance intelligence team on the ground in Oostende to survey the E-boat base. They also needed a concerted attempt to obtain, via Ultra intercepts, the Kriegsmarine recognition signals for the region. Another challenge was training a hybrid team of MI-6 personnel with Costal Command sailors who could operate an E-boat. All of these requirements were reasonable. But he'd have to call in a few favors to have Bletchley Park work the recognition signal part of the plan. All in all it gave them a fair chance to pull a tremendous intelligence coup on the Germans. On concluding the meeting he'd directed Jack to take the plan to the final stage. Now it was a matter of assigning and briefing the people involved and putting a full and detailed plan in place. There was a sense of urgency in Greene's mind. The new torpedoes were potentially going to be operational in a short time.

Jack felt much more confident in this plan compared to Quarry. There was probably no reason to feel more confident, the mission was much more complex. He thought about it and realized he felt good about his team. Phil and Terry had become a nucleus for the new agents. Eager and talented, the new group jumped into the language-training program and was also honing many of the skills they learned at Arisaig.

The next operation would be named "Vixen." He would probably use Edith Moulon and Pierre Goillet as the advance team to go into Oostende and set up surveillance on the E-boats. He thought Phil, Terry, Jimmy Hunt and Curtis Livesey would be with him as part of the group which would commandeer the E-boat. He would coordinate with Harwich for the MTB crew that would man the German boat. He wanted to have the combined team together and run several dress rehearsals at one of the piers in Harwich prior to the mission.

"I think the old man likes this one, Jack." Tommy Hudson walked into his office. "Can you have a final draft by the end of next week?"

"If I leave Phil here to work the plan and I get over to Harwich to solidify the Navy end, we'll be ready."

"Right. I have it on good authority there is a lovely young WAAF officer who's been asking for you down at the security desk. You better get going."

"I lost track of time," Jack said, irritated with himself. "Pam is down for just a night, actually on official duty. She has a conference to attend at the Ministry of Defence tomorrow morning." Jack grabbed his blouse as he headed out the door. "I'd ask you to join us for dinner but I know you're busy," he yelled as he went around the corner.

Tommy Hudson watched him go. "Love. God help the poor man."

Jack took the steps two at a time down to the ground floor. As he came out of the stairwell he saw Pam standing by the guard desk talking to the Royal Marine sentry. He smiled at her and she beamed back at him. He hadn't realized how much he had missed her. "Sorry I'm late. You look marvelous."

"You're forgiven. I'm officially off duty and ready to be treated like a lady." Pam turned her face, looking deep into Jack's eyes and smiling.

"Then, off we go. No expense to be spared. A night on the town, fit for a lady." They both laughed as they walked down the steps to the street and into the fading light of the fall afternoon. Coming toward them was Phil Hatcher.

"Phil, do you remember Pam Thompson?" Jack asked.

"Certainly, from the PM's wing ding. Pam, it's nice to see you again." He grinned like a schoolboy. "And what are you two up to? There's a war on, you know. No time for what is most certainly a social outing."

Jack laughed. "Let me share a famous saying from the colonies. 'All work and no play makes Jack a dull boy.' I believe it came from that famous revolutionary, Ben Franklin."

They all laughed.

Jack heard a vehicle coming fast up Baker Street. He turned to look for the car and felt Phil pull him toward the building. Jack couldn't see what was happening as he stumbled with Phil pulling on his arm. Landing on the pavement, Jack felt the car race by, just missing him. He rolled over and saw Pam. She was lying on her side, her cap several feet down the street. Her raincoat was disheveled and torn on one side. Jack struggled to his feet and saw a black car turn and disappear on Dorset Street. He ran to Pam and knelt down. She was still. There was a small amount of blood coming from her ear.

"Phil, call an ambulance!" He knew not to move her.

A Royal Marine guard appeared.

"Get me some blankets, now!" He took off his blouse and gently laid it over her shoulders and tried to straighten her raincoat. Jack felt totally helpless.

Royal London Hospital
November 5, 1943

Pam lay in the hospital bed with a full bandage around her head. Her eyes were closed, her breathing soft and rhythmic. An intravenous tube was inserted in her right arm, a glass bottle hanging inverted from a stainless steel holder next to the head of the bed. Ian and Jack quietly sat in chairs at the foot of her bed.

"Ian, can I get you some tea?" Jack asked softly.

"No thanks. Why don't you go stretch your legs? I'll watch her."

The older man was somber. To Jack he looked older than he had ever seen him.

Aside from bruises and contusions, Pam's injuries included a broken collarbone, several broken ribs and most seriously, a fractured skull. Last night she had undergone surgery to relieve cranial pressure. According to the doctor her condition was guarded and the next 24 to 48 hours were critical.

"Sure I can't get you anything?" Jack stood up and arched his back to get rid of some of the stiffness. He saw Ian smile and shake his head. Jack quietly opened the door and made his way to the cafeteria on the ground floor.

Sitting with a cup of hot tea Jack stared out at the falling rain. He felt empty. Christ, why did this have to happen? He started to get up after finishing his tea when he heard Phil Hatcher.

"Jack, Ian said I'd find you here. How're you doing?" Hatcher sat down at the table.

"I'm okay. Thanks for coming over. We don't know much, but Pam's surgery seems to have gone all right. Now we just have to wait." He sat looking at his empty cup.

"Jack, this is part official. If you can spare an hour Colonel Greene needs you back at Baker Street. I brought a car, so if there's any way you can break away, you need to hear what he has to say." Phil looked intense, his lips pursed.

"It's that important?" Jack sounded skeptical.

"Jack, it concerns what happened to Pam."

The attending physician assured Jack he could take a short trip. The doctor expected Pam would remain asleep for some time. Ian was anchored in the room and told Jack to go with Phil. Reluctantly Jack left for Baker Street.

When Jack entered Noel Greene's office, Tommy was there already.

"Close the door and sit down. Jack, I can't tell you how sorry we all are. How's she doing?" The older man was leaning forward, the concern evident in his eyes.

"Too early to tell," Jack sighed. "The doctors say the next 24 to 48 hours are critical. We just have to wait and see."

Greene said. "If there's anything you need, let us know."

"Thank you, sir"

Tommy, who'd been quiet to this point, spoke up. "Jack, the reason we called you here is that it appears Pam's injury was no accident."

Jack wasn't sure he'd heard Tommy correctly. "Would you say that again?"

"We found the car abandoned five blocks away. It had been stolen earlier in the day. When Scotland Yard went over the car it had been completely sanitized. We think this was a pre-planned attack. Pam simply got in the way."

"You mean someone was trying to hit me?" His voice was distant and lacked any emotion. "Pam's in a hospital because of me."

"Jack, you can't look at it that way. If what we think has happened, the Germans have moved to a new level of play," Greene said.

"I looked at everything myself, Jack," added Phil. "There're too many things that point to an intentional hit. We heard the car's engine accelerate. There were no skid marks from attempted braking and the car left the scene. Jack, I'm a cop and this was intentional."

Deep within Jack a cold and dark anger spread. The woman he loved might die. Someone had tried to kill him and missed. It would be the worst mistake they would ever make.

Greene said, "Jack, we don't want to keep you. I'm assigning Phil to conduct an investigation into what happened. This investigation is only to be known within this group of four. Someone apparently identified Jack or Phil. I've got to think there's some connection with Quarry. We need to find out how the information got out and fix the problem. Future operations could be in jeopardy. We need to immediately review our security arrangements for all senior MI-6 personnel and take measures to mask identities. Tommy, I want you to look at the bigger picture. Phil, concentrate on the current problem."

A few minutes later Tommy, Jack and Phil were in Tommy's office. "I asked our Royal Marines to issue weapons for all of us. I expect them to be carried at all times."

A Marine sergeant came in with an armory case and opened it on the table. Inside were four Webley .38 caliber pistols, ammunition and shoulder holsters. "Gentlemen, please select a weapon, a box of cartridges and a holster. I've noted the serial numbers right 'ere, if I could get you to sign for 'em."

They accepted their weapons, put on the holsters and loaded the revolvers.

Jack put on his cover and headed for the door. He turned to face the other two. "I'm headed back to the hospital. You can reach me there for the next day or so. After that I'll be back here ready to go. Phil, you find out who did it." He turned and walked out the door.

Phil and Tommy were stunned at the cold, vicious tone in Jack's voice.

Gestapo Headquarters
453 Avenue Louise
Brussels, Belgium
November 15, 1943

SS Brigadefuehrer Gunther Schmidt sat in his large office on the fourth floor and marveled at the recent turn of events. His wound and recovery seemed like a rebirth to his career. Promoted and posted to Brussels, he was in charge of all counter espionage efforts in Belgium. Not a bad accomplishment for the former policeman from Bavaria, he thought.

Walck had accompanied him as his special assistant. As a general officer in the SS, he was entitled to an assistant and he liked Walck. It was particularly nice to have someone to take care of all the little details he preferred not to worry about. The only blemish in an otherwise wonderful month was the word he received via "back channel" from Berlin that the attempt to take out his British assailant had failed. It would take a little more time to close the chapter on Abbeville. For now he had a big job in hand. The resistance in Belgium was becoming more active and it was imperative he penetrate the organization much like he done in France. It was time to get settled and on with business, he told himself.

CHAPTER FOURTEEN

Regents Park Road
London

Phil Hatcher sat next to Senior Inspector Frank Bridger in the Scotland Yard sedan. A cold breeze blew scattered leaves up the quiet street. The two had been watching the comings and goings at 24 Regents Park Road, a three-story brick apartment building. Bridger had been working counter-intelligence since 1939. Scotland Yard had a remarkable record for intercepting German agents. One of those agents, who chose collaboration over a hangman's noose, led them to this address. Phil had spent the last two weeks with Frank trying to get a lead into the attack on Pam. None of Frank's informants had any knowledge of the attack or how it had been orchestrated.

Security for MI-6 personnel had increased significantly. Armed body guards now protected key members of the organization. MI-6 had always tried to maintain a low profile, but recent events made it even more important to be as discrete as possible. Any reference to specific personnel or organizational details was now classified. All personnel were given extra training in security procedures. There'd been no subsequent attacks, but Noel Greene knew they were still in danger until they discovered the leak.

One of Frank's turned agents told him they expected a drop tonight of information to be transmitted back to Germany. They didn't know who was conducting the drop. It might not be related to the MI-6 issue. All they knew was that it would happen between 8:00 PM and 9:00 PM. The drop point was an apartment on the second floor in the back of the building. Frank had discreetly placed surveillance in a perimeter around the building. It was tough not knowing who they were looking for or exactly when they would be here.

"Reminds me of the old days in the west end waiting to raid those counterfeiters. Remember that?" Frank asked Phil.

"Yeah, I do. Damn near as cold too. Why don't we ever do these things in July?"

Phil looked at his watch. It was time to head up to the dummy apartment across the hall from the drop site. Frank's two-man team was already there. The drop apartment was wired with a microphone which led to small speaker where they could monitor activity in the apartment. The agreed upon plan was to allow the drop to take place, then follow the suspected agent to determine where he was going. The intent was to dig deeper into the network, not arrest the small fish.

"I'll follow our target out after the drop. Be ready to alert the others on the trail team." They'd be able to use the wireless transmitter in the sedan to alert the others with a description of the target.

"Right." Bridger said as Phil got out of the car.

An hour later they heard a voice from the other apartment say, "Someone's here." Phil went over to the peep hole in the apartment door to see the target. Looking into the small lens he could only see the back of a woman. She was of medium height, her dark hair under a small hat and she was wearing a raincoat. He couldn't see her face as she waited for someone to answer the door. When the apartment door opened the woman turned her head checking to see if there was anyone watching her enter the apartment. Phil's heart almost stopped, it was Edith Moulon.

Jack and Ian spent most of the first week after the accident at the hospital with Pam. On the morning of the third day she opened her eyes and turned her head but didn't saying anything. Jack raced to the nurse's station and shortly the attending physician, Dr. Roger Hanson, was at her bedside. The next several days blurred in Jack's mind. The joy at seeing her eyes open was suddenly shattered when they realized she wasn't able to talk and apparently had suffered damage to her eyesight. Jack spent hours sitting at her side and talking quietly. Pam would look at him, but without focusing. There was always a slight smile when Jack was in the room. She was getting better physically, eating solid food and her color was better, but something was missing.

Ian had been rock steady throughout the ordeal. Jack could see it was tearing him apart to see his daughter a shadow of the vibrant young woman she'd once been.

Dicky had been able to come up from Tangmere.

Dr. Hanson told them the more contact she could have with familiar people and things, the better chance she would have of making a recovery. He was trying to keep their spirits up, but at the same time told them he didn't know what the eventual resolution might be. He'd seen too many serious head injuries during the blitz and knew the prospects for a full recovery were slim. As Jack sat in the hospital he told himself no matter what happened he would take care of her for as long as necessary.

By the middle of November Pam was well enough to be transferred to Ramsgate, a military convalescent hospital in Northeast London. He was thankful he could still spend time with her. It only took him an hour to reach the hospital from Baker Street. Between Ian and Jack there was constant contact with Pam. She'd still not spoken and the doctors were unsure how bad her eyesight had been damaged. When asked any question she would simply look at the questioner.

Late one afternoon Jack was quietly telling her of the day's events. Sitting next to the bed holding her hand, he leaned over and said, "Pam, I love you." For the first time since the accident she squeezed his hand very softly. It was like an electric shock to Jack. He leaned down and kissed her forehead. As he sat back, he noticed her eyes were tearing slightly. It was a small step, but it was a step.

During Jack's time away, Hiram had kept the section on task. Phil Hatcher continued to work the operational details preparing for Vixen. But Jack knew it was time to get back. Pam was out of danger and he needed to get back into the war.

He arrived ready to get his hands back around the operation. His first priority was to visit Harwich and figure out the details for MTB participation with Commander Parker and Lieutenant Powers.

Sergeant Major McGinty was waiting for him when he arrived. A leather case was sitting on Jack's desk as the older man greeted him. "Good morning, sir. Thought I'd start your day off with a present. You might find this little darling useful."

It was good to be back he thought. "Sergeant Major, I suppose I'm forbidden to ask where this present came from?"

"Aye, sir. That was our arrangement," McGinty said. "Wouldn't do to change the rules, now would it?"

"Exactly so. Now, what have we got here?" Jack opened the clasp and lying in a felt covered cutout within the case was a small pistol. It looked familiar to Jack from his weapons course at Arisaig.

"A replacement for that immense horse pistol they have you carrying now. This is a Walther PPK, a beauty of a gun. 7 shot semi-automatic. Uses 7.65 ammo and fits nicely in a shoulder holster."

Jack picked up the sleek weapon from the case. The chrome finish gleamed in the light. The black pistol grip fit his hand perfectly. It was light and compact compared to the Webley.

"You've done it again, Sergeant Major. This is superb. Where do I sign?" Jack removed the Webley from the holster and set it on his desk.

"No need to sign, sir. I'll have one of those custom shoulder holsters later this morning. There's a box of 50 cartridges in here and an extra clip." He handed Jack a paper bag.

Jack held the weapon and rotated his wrist, looking at the sight picture. He reached into the case and grabbed the clip. Checking to see there were cartridges in the clip, he inserted the clip in the grip and slid back the receiver to chamber a round.

"Very nice indeed, Sergeant Major."

As McGinty exited the office, Phil Hatcher entered. His eyes were bloodshot and he looked like he'd slept in his clothes.

"Come on. We're wanted in the front office."

Gestapo Headquarters
Brussels
November 14, 1943

The report of the attack in Leuven had come in early. Schmidt had seen the preliminary assessment by the Wermacht officer who reported the local resistance group had attacked a patrol of four German soldiers. Two soldiers were able to escape, but the other two men, including a sergeant, had been shot and killed.

The Wermacht had asked for Gestapo assistance in responding and Schmidt and Walck were on the road in two hours with SS troops from the local barracks. The soldiers were directly under the command of Hauptmann Bernard Schroeder. But as the senior officer, Schmidt was in overall command.

"What do we know about this area, Walck?"

"According to the files there've been sporadic incidents. Shots fired at Wermacht patrols, several bombings, but so far no arrests." Walck knew Schmidt wouldn't like to hear about the lack of arrests.

"I prefer to operate quietly. But it appears to me this is one of those times a lesson must be taught."

"Yes, sir."

Arriving in Leuven, they met the commander of the battalion with responsibility for the area. Major Gerhard Heinz commanded the 3rd Battalion of the 38th Infantry Regiment. The unit had been on garrison duty in Belgium since the conclusion of the land campaign in 1940. Traditionally the unit was comprised of soldiers who were either recovering from wounds suffered in other theatres of war or young conscripts who'd never seen any combat. Most Wermacht units in Belgium were under strength, the eastern front taking all available manpower.

Gerhard Heinz was one of those officers who were comfortable with the quiet garrison life. He was furious over this incident in Leuven. Any time the SS and Gestapo got involved everything became more difficult.

The meeting between Schmidt and Heinz had been a one-way conversation. The more the senior officer asked about the regiment's efforts against the resistance, the more his anger grew. It appeared to Schmidt that, with the Gestapo concentrating on the coastal areas and Brussels, these inland areas had become uncontrollable.

"Major Heinz, your troops will cordon off the area which I've noted on this map. I want your troops in place by 1300 today. At that time my SS troops will conduct a sweep and arrest a representative number of men ages 20-40 years old. I want your people to construct a scaffold here in Prince Albert-strasse. I want it in place by 1600. At 1700 there will be ten locals hung in the square. They will be identified as resistance members. Their bodies will remain there for one week. Do I make myself clear?"

"Perfectly clear, Herr Brigadefuhrer." Heinz didn't like what he heard but this was now a Gestapo matter.

After the major left, Schmidt turned to Walck. "Once we

have the arrested people back here, select ten to be executed. I want to take ten back to Brussels and let the rest go. From the ten I suspect we can get one to talk to us about who's in the resistance."

64 Baker Street
London

The initial anger on discovering the real identity of Edith Moulon had given way to a professional discussion of what the next course of action should be for the best advantage. Although arresting her made sense initially, it would immediately telegraph her discovery to German intelligence. On the other hand they couldn't leave her in place for a host of reasons including the threat to all key MI-6 personnel and danger to ongoing operations. Was there a way to use her while protecting MI-6?

Tommy sat back and wiped his face with a handkerchief. "If we want to feed false information to the Germans we need to let her think she's undiscovered. If we try to turn her she could use the pre-arranged signal she's been co-opted." Tommy was referring to the hidden sign in each message sent by operatives, which signal they are under duress and to disregard the contents of the message. Both sides used it.

"True. But if we leave her in place God knows what she might stumble on," added Greene.

Phil leaned forward. "I don't know how we keep up appearances with her knowing what we know."

Jack didn't say anything. The others saw the anger and fury in his eyes.

Greene returned to the operational problem. "She already knows Phil and Jack have been working with the MTB boys. She must have sent that information to Germany. The language work with German must signal to them that we're up to something. But they don't know where. We've been accumulating information on Belgium recently and she knows it. Where do we go from there?"

Tommy spoke up, "How does this sound? We're preparing a team to infiltrate the Antwerp harbor area to establish data points for eventual use of the harbour by the cross channel invasion. It covers all the points and makes sense."

"We could send her into Antwerp as part of the team," Phil added.

As they talked about the different aspects of the problem a plan was beginning to form. To throw the Germans off the trail of Vixen, she'd be part of a team, which would go to Antwerp. That team would set up surveillance while supposedly waiting the arrival of a larger team with several key operatives. The follow up team would be the bait and was totally fictitious.

Greene found a partner for her, a native of Belgium who had escaped in 1940 and been used successfully several times. Herman Devold hated the Germans and had proved to be a resourceful agent in challenging situations. His ability to speak Flemish and also having contacts and relatives in Belgium made him a perfect choice. The two of them would immediately be sent to an isolated location in the country to prepare for the mission. Once on the ground in Antwerp they would send intelligence back awaiting the larger team which would be a superb catch for the Gestapo.

On completion of Vixen, Devold would eliminate Moulon and make his way back to England. The key was to maintain a feeling of normalcy within the section until Moulon left. Jack knew this would test his ability to suppress his true feelings but he had to do it.

"All right then. I'll get in touch with Devold and start the wheels in motion. Jack, you need to brief her on the plan. We'll use the farm in Whitesbridge as the holding area. It'll take two days to set up a phony mission package so business as usual until then." Greene seemed very enthusiastic. "We need to look at the timetable very carefully now. Jack, you need to get over to Harwich and finish the planning with the Navy."

Jack briefed Edith two days later. He tried not to think about Pam. Edith was very attentive during the entire meeting. She acted intensely interested when Jack connected her mission with the eventual invasion of Europe. She seemed surprised about the isolation, but Jack explained it was standard MI-6 procedures and it would be for her protection as well.

Jack also met Herman Devold in Greene's office a day later and liked the man. He was about 30, slim and quiet in manner. It was difficult to imagine he was the same man who had completed three dangerous missions into France and Belgium, including an assassination. After the meeting there was no doubt in his mind Edith Moulon was living on borrowed time.

Greene mentioned they had received information that the SS colonel they thought Jack had killed in France was alive, promoted to brigadier general and in now Brussels. He'd been involved in a reprisal against the resistance, which involved the hanging of ten Belgians in a town called Leuven.

Ramsgate Military Hospital
London

The highlight of every day was Jack's trip to see Pam. He would vary the time of day so it helped to break the routine for her. Thankfully Ian had been able to take a leave of absence from Trinity. For the time being he was doing general research for the section, which he could work on a couple of hours each day.

Pam slowly gained strength and mobility. She was able to stand with help and carefully walk across the room. It appeared there was recognition of people, particularly Jack and Ian. She still hadn't tried to speak and the doctors didn't know why.

Dr. Hanson from London Royal continued to treat her.

His specialty was neurosurgery and there were aspects of her case he felt were unique. The hard-pressed staff at Ramsgate was happy to have the help. Jack and Ian knew they had a true ally in Roger Hanson. His interest in the case went beyond the clinical aspects. He had become a friend to them as well as Pam's physician.

As the days went by and they watched her get stronger, Hanson felt there was a better and better chance for a positive resolution. Ian and Jack could sense it also. It was as if a switch was waiting to be thrown.

Ten days after Pam arrived at Ramsgate, Jack was in the room as Dr. Hanson conducted his daily evaluation. The doctor talked very slowly and directly to her. In the past he'd ask questions and she would look at him but never react. Jack watched as he ran a small light from pupil to pupil.

"Pam, do you see my fingers?" He held up three fingers on his left hand.

Jack saw her nod.

The doctor turned to make sure Jack had seen.

"Pam, do you see the man in the chair?"

Again she nodded.

"Do you know who he is?"

For just a moment there was no movement and then she looked right at Jack and nodded.

Jack moved over to the bed, tears welling up in his eyes. He put his hand on her arm. "Of course she knows me. I'm her Yank."

Three days later Pam said her first word, "Jack."

Motor Torpedo Flotilla Seven
Harwich
November 24, 1943

Within a week of arriving in Harwich, Jack assembled

a group of "cutthroats and scallywags" as he described the pickup crew which would attempt to steal an E-boat from Oostende harbour. Lee Power's crew would provide the nucleus. Consequently they needed another boat to take them into the harbour. Lee recommended and Commander Parker concurred that "Winky" Alderton was the best choice.

Lieutenant Winston Alderton, RNVR, DSC, MC was a legend among costal command. Among his exploits, he'd sunk a German destroyer off the Dutch coast, carried several raiding parties into occupied territory and infuriated almost every senior officer outside Coastal Command. Known for his wild trips ashore he looked at the staid traditions of the peacetime Navy as ludicrous. Identified by the bright yellow scarf he always wore on the bridge of his MTB he was utterly fearless when the bullets started to fly. Jack met him in the wardroom of the Whitney.

"Winky, I'd like you to meet Jack Stewart. He's got an op he'd like to talk to you about," Lee said to an average looking man with a weathered complexion and big grin. The two men shook hands.

"Buy me a gin and I'll talk to bloody Archbishop of Canterbury," Alderton replied.

Lee motioned to the mess attendant. "Three neat gins, if you please. On my tab, of course."

"Why thank you. You are indeed an officer and a gentleman." Winky had been at the bar for some time but appeared to be in complete control of his faculties.

"So what does the Fleet Air Arm want with those of us who motor about in our little speedboats?" He asked.

Jack smiled. "I'm not with the Fleet Air Arm. Actually I'm with MI-6 in London." He took a drink of his gin, the liquor burning in his throat.

"Lee, what have you got yourself involved in this time? You didn't volunteer again, did you?" Winky was having fun with Lee.

"Winky, just listen to what Jack has to say. We need

your help." Lee suddenly sounded very earnest and Alderton changed his demeanor.

" I'm listening." He took a long drink and looked at Jack.

"I need an MTB to take me and a team into Oostende Harbour and up to the E-boat piers," Jack said quietly.

Alderton didn't say anything for a moment and then turned to Lee. "I'm guessing if you need an MTB to carry this team in there, you're part of the team?"

"The team is made up of part of my crew and some of Jack's crowd," Lee answered.

He sat there looking at Jack and Lee. "And for what purpose would we be wanting to motor into Oostende? Shoot the bastards up?"

Jack leaned over and quietly said, "We're going to steal an E-boat."

Winky grinned and looked at Jack. "Are you Canadian?"

"No, I'm a Yank. Why do you ask?"

"That explains it. Only the Yanks or Canadians would be crazy enough to try something like this." He sat there for a minute. "You know I don't think I can miss this one. Count me in. But it's going to cost you another gin!"

Over the next ten days the new team worked hard to learn the mission.

The two new members of Section F had turned out to be solid and reliable. While both Curtis Livesey and Jimmy Hunt were from the commandos, they were as different as night and day. Curtis was from a farming village in Lincolnshire while Jimmy grew up in the terrace houses of Manchester. They'd become good friends since their arrival in MI-6. They brought experience in both hand-to-hand combat and use of multiple weapons.

The natural friction between the different groups, Army, Navy, MI-6, American, and British made for some interesting encounters. The personalities of the three key players, Jack,

Lee and Winky made it work better than anyone could have expected. This became evident to the leaders when they spotted a mixed group from the Vixen team out at a local pub one evening after a long day of practice.

Jack brought Sergeant Major McGinty down to Harwich as the logistics coordinator. In short order a steady stream of weapons, ammunition, explosives and material made their way to the two MTB's. Within several days the team was equipped with the latest in hand held automatic weapons, every possible grenade they might need, German pennants and uniforms, and the finest Scotch to be found in England. McGinty hit it off particularly well with Lee Power's Chief Mechanic Andy Dudley. The Sergeant Major found several parts for the engines on the two MTB's which would improve their performance and reliability. With those parts Dudley and his counterpart in Winky's boat, the 5043, had their engines running better than when they were built.

The plan required two MTBs. Winky would command the primary boat for the harbour penetration. There would be a backup boat which would sortie with the primary and remain ten miles offshore for contingencies. The backup boat, Lee's 5122, would be commanded by Lt Frank Meriweather and crewed primarily by the remainder of Lee's crew.

The crews had gone over every aspect of the mission. A practice target had been put together using a damaged motor gun boat set up in a little used part of the shipyard. The team practiced approaches and commandeering the target.

After two days of practices in daylight they moved to night ops. The next step was to go to a full dress rehearsal using "German" opponents who played the parts of sentries and the E-boat crew. Despite the different twists and variations laid on by Phil as the operational coordinator, the team had been able to deal with each situation. The additional language capability brought by the MI-6 members was proving very useful. There was a sense of urgency to get it right. They all knew their lives would depend on it.

A key aspect of the mission was the ability of Dudley to get the diesels of the E-boat running and ready to provide power quickly. His extensive experience with marine engines was a blessing. Having spent most of his adult life in an engine room, there was no doubt in his mind he could get the German engines running.

Terry Howe ran a quick German tutorial with him to allow him to recognize common engineering words and symbols. They were also able to get him some time on an engine that which very similar to the ones found in the "S-100" class of German E-boats.

At the completion of two weeks of workups, Jack felt they were ready for the mission. The big unknowns were the code words and getting the final reconnaissance from Oostende. Pierre Goillet had been in France for ten days and was making his way to Oostende. His job was to conduct a final check on the E-boat base and transmit the information back to England. The final key step was confirmation, via Ultra, when the new torpedoes were in Oostende and installed on the E-boats. Vixen was on alert.

Jack left Phil in tactical control of the combined team and returned to London. It had been two weeks since he'd last seen Pam. He had resolved to never leave her in the dark again. But now with her injury he was torn. All he could do was go see her and try to do what was best.

Gestapo Headquarters
Brussels
December 4, 1943

Schmidt listened as Manfred Kolsch briefed him on the most recent activity of the MI-6 team which he'd tangled with at Abbeville. The importance of this recent activity had risen to the level of the Reichsfuhrer SS Henrich Himmler. It appeared to SS analysts that the small team in Antwerp was probably the advance party for a much larger group to follow. This might be some of the initial steps by the Allies to successfully invade the continent. In the minds of the German intelligence experts, this was critical. If they could capture the larger team there must be significant knowledge of invasion plans they could extract from them. Himmler had ordered Schmidt to take direct control of the situation. This included taking measures to ensure Edith Moulon "escaped", allowing her to return to England to continue her activities. Personal interest by Himmler coupled with an important operation was the opportunity he'd been waiting for. He must not let this chance slip through his fingers. Success on this assignment might move him up one more notch in the Gestapo hierarchy.

Kolsch was to be attached to Schmidt's headquarters until completion of the mission. He would conduct liaison with the SS communication intercept group in Berlin. This would allow Schmidt to be aware of all communications between the British team and London. With luck they would discover the plan for the larger team. An interesting thought occurred to Schmidt. Perhaps Stewart would be part of this team.

In Antwerp the MI-6 team set up a systematic observation system. Edith and Herman were able to note the comings and going of shipping traffic, what areas of the docks were fully functional and any preparations for harbour defence. This information was transmitted to London using a code which Bletchley Park was certain Jerry had broken. Unfortunately this meant there was no secure radio link for Herman Devold to communicate with Baker Street. Greene set up a drop system with a local resistance group who then would send a message to London on their own wireless system. The requirement for them to each check out the harbour separately allowed him to make the drops and pick up replies from

London. Greene also knew this system allowed Moulon to meet her Gestapo contacts.

Herman Devold realized the dangerous game he was playing. He wondered if the woman did also.

Ramsgate Military Hospital
London

The train from the coast arrived at Paddington Station at 1115 hours. Jack immediately headed for the hospital instead of Baker Street. Greene could wait. He'd called Ian regularly during his time at Harwich to check on Pam's progress. According to her father it had been steady but slow. She was getting out of her room using a wheel chair. She had also been able to stand on her own without help. The next big physical step, relearning to walk, would start next week.

When he got to her room, it was empty. The orderly told him that her father had wheeled her down to the day room at the far end of Corridor "C". Hurrying down the hallway he saw the sign and went inside.

She was sitting near the window with her back to the door. Ian was facing her and could see Jack immediately. Ian took her hand and said something to her as Jack walked quietly across the room. Slowly her head turned to the right and she saw Jack as he knelt down next to her wheelchair.

"How's the most beautiful girl in England this morning?" He took her hand in both of his and looked into her eyes. Slowly her mouth turned into a smile.

So softly that he almost couldn't make it out she said, "I am well."

Jack could see a sparkle in her eye and gently kissed her cheek, "I missed you, Pam."

Again the soft reply, "I know."

Ian stood slowly. "I think I'll go for a cup of tea and leave you two alone. Meet you back in the room."

Taking Ian's place on the bench Jack continued to hold

Pam's hand, and now faced her. "You look wonderful, really wonderful. Your father said you were doing better each day."

She sat there for a moment as tears welled up in her eyes. "Jack," she said in a whisper. "I am trying to get better."

"And you will get better. And we'll be here to help you each step of the way. I'll always be here to take care of you."

There were tears running down her cheeks but Jack knew she'd be fine, one way or the other.

During her afternoon nap Jack and Ian walked to the cafeteria for a cup of tea. Ian had been able to get the latest medical update from Dr. Hanson who was surprised and pleased at her progress. He told Ian they knew so little about the ability of the brain to heal itself. Sometimes cases just like this never recovered and other times there was a full recovery. The doctor felt her rapid regaining of speech, recognition of people and the ability to stand was very encouraging. He was still cautious on the eventual resolution but he was going to continue as the primary attending physician going forward.

"Ian, we have another problem. I need some advice," Jack said. "You know what's on tap and you know the role I've got. Ian, for the first time in my life I'm scared about what might happen."

"What do you mean?"

"I always had a pretty fatalistic attitude toward what I did for a living. Sure I didn't want to get hurt or killed, that would be crazy. But I didn't worry about it. We used to tell ourselves, 'screw it you're dead anyway, quite worrying about it.' I know that sounds ludicrous but it was how many of us were able to deal with flying off the ship and getting shot at. It was the same attitude I felt in France. But now I have Pam depending on me. There's nothing more I want to do than take care of her, see her get better and protect her from the world. And I'm terrified that if something happens to me it'll set her back God knows how far."

Ian sat for a moment then said, "Jack, to the best of

my knowledge what you're doing now is voluntary. Go tell Greene you have to bow out for personal reasons."

"And hate myself for the rest of my life. Ian, there's nothing worse in my profession than deserting your shipmates. Hell, I'm the leader of this whole plan. It doesn't help knowing that Winston Churchill and Franklin Delano Roosevelt are paying attention to what I do either."

"Jack, I don't know what to tell you. I can't really understand the code of conduct you grew up living. Is what you are doing important for the war effort? Yes, I think it is. Are you the most important thing in Pam's life right now? Same answer, yes. This question doesn't lend itself to scientific examination. It's totally a matter of the heart. I'll be here for her until the day I die. You know that. Tell me what I can do to help you and I'll do it."

Jack sighed and sat back in his chair, "It's something I have to do. I know that and I'm just going to have to put my feelings somewhere I can't get to for right now. But you tell me, do we tell Pam when I go or do we hope for the best?"

"Jack, I've been wondering that myself. The worrying alone could hurt her for no purpose. On the other hand if something happens and it's a total surprise, I don't know. I think we better ask Hanson. This is a medical decision in my book."

Later that afternoon, Jack went to see Colonel Greene. He wanted to see if there was any update on Oostende. Greene confirmed there was still no hard information on the arrival date of the torpedoes from Germany. Greene also said the dummy reports on the Antwerp harbour were coming in regularly from Moulon and Devold. Devold hadn't seen any indication of her contact with the Gestapo but assumed there must have been some meeting. Greene was concerned the "observation" phase by that team could not go on too long without raising questions by both Moulon and her handlers. He thought they might have two more weeks before they needed to pull them out. Hopefully Vixen would take place before that was necessary. Jack briefed him on the final preps at Harwich and answered a few specific questions on tactics.

With a big part of the section still at Harwich, the offices seemed deserted. There were a few of the support staff but without Phil and Terry it seemed too quiet. Jack sat in his office later in the afternoon taking stock of where he sat right now. In less than two years he had shot down four enemy planes, been shot down himself, lost his wingman, met a President and a Prime Minister, changed countries, traveled half way around the world, conducted a raid into occupied France and fallen back in love. It was almost hard to believe but it had all happened. And now he sat in the quiet office and wondered what the future would bring. Where would he be a year from now? How would Pam be a year from now? What would he do when the war was over? Where would he go? He tried to invoke the old aviator rule, don't worry about anything after the next mission but he couldn't help himself. He guessed that's what love does to you. It takes away your ability to not give a shit.

Looking at his watch, he knew Pam would be getting ready for dinner. He opened his lower desk drawer and pulled out the bottle of scotch he kept for late night sessions with Tommy. He reached over to the shelf and grabbed a tumbler, pouring a little in the glass. I've even come to like this without ice.

"I hoped I'd find you here." Tommy walked in the door.

"Glad you stopped by. I hate to drink alone." Jack poured a drink for Tommy who sat down heavily in the chair.

"How's Pam?" He took a short drink.

"She seems much better but it'll be a slow process. I know she'll get better, I feel it."

"I know how hard this hit you, Jack. You've had an awful lot on your mind recently. I'm concerned Vixen might be too much right now." Tommy looked at him hard. "We can put it into Phil's hands. He's as good as they come and you know it."

Jack put his drink down. "Are you telling me you don't think I can cut it?"

"That's not what I'm saying. I'm responsible for the success of this mission just as much as you are. I have to know you can do the job. I'm asking you as a friend and your boss. Are you up to it? If not, I'm duty bound to remove you from the mission."

Jack stopped his immediate urge to disagree with Hudson. Here was the answer to his problem. Tommy was offering him a chance to gracefully remove himself from the mission and save face. He'd be able to stay with Pam and make sure he did everything in his power to help her recover. "Tommy, I'll be honest with you. With Pam's situation right now, I really don't want to go on this mission. But that's beside the point. We get paid to do the things other people don't want to do. The last time I checked I was still taking the King's shilling. Could Phil run the show? Yes, there's no doubt in my mind. But do we have a better chance of success if I'm there? Yes, I think we do. And I'm not willing to give that up. I'm all right."

Jack downed his drink and set his drink down, "Figured that's what you'd say. Good thing, the torpedoes are in Oostende. Word just came in from Bletchley. Vixen's on for tomorrow night. We need to get you to Harwich tonight. Our request for RAF support has come through as well for the supporting destroyers."

Gestapo Headquarters
Brussels

The rain was falling in sheets as a winter storm front buffeted the channel and low-countries. The two Gestapo officers sat in Schmidt's office going over all of the recent radio intercept traffic from Belgium. There were also several in-depth reports on resistance activity in this area. Schmidt and Kolsch had been at it for several hours.

"It doesn't seem like the Antwerp team is doing very

much. The info from our agent confirms they spend most of their time reading." Schmidt was scanning the radio transmission summary sheet.

Kolsch didn't even look up. "Perhaps they're waiting for the full team."

"But that doesn't make sense. They never leave a team partially active. It's either full speed or they go completely to ground. I don't like the smell of this."

"But we have our own agent monitoring events." Kolsch now looked up at Schmidt and saw the older man frown a bit and reach across for a briefing folder.

"And suppose the Brits have found her out somehow. She could be the deception while they're going somewhere else. Remember, she said her team leader, this Stewart, had been gone for part of the time to visit the motor torpedo boats on the coast." He continued to leaf through reports, looking for something specific.

Kolsch thought for a moment. "That's right. It was just after she joined the group. He and another agent spent some time there. But she never found out why."

Schmidt found what he was looking for and started to turn the pages. "Why would MI-6 need to use motor torpedo boats?"

Kolsch came back immediately, "Commando insertion into the coast."

"Exactly what I was thinking. I thought I read that there had been a small increase in radio traffic from the Oostende area in the last two weeks. Here it is." He began reading from the Operational Summary. "German Naval Forces have recently begun using the most advanced new torpedo system in both the submarine forces and the costal forces. These new torpedoes, with advanced guidance capability and increased range, will allow our submarines and patrol boats to engage enemy surface forces with much greater effectiveness." He put the folder down on the desk. "Where is the only operational patrol boat base in Belgium?"

"Oostende?"

"Oostende. They're trying to do it again. Steal information on our new torpedo." Schmidt looked like a great weight had been lifted off his back. He pushed the intercom box. "Walck, get in here. We're going to Oostende."

Jack and Tommy sat in the back seat of the staff car as it sped toward Harwich. Both men were lost in thought. Tommy was thinking about sitting in another staff car a year ago driving the new Yank into Baker Street from Biggin Hill. They'd come to treat each other like brothers. There was a mutual respect in addition to the bonds of friendship. Hudson was not normally an introspective person. However tonight he reflected on the events of the last year and how Jack Stewart had become part of MI-6. Deep in his heart he hoped all would go well. He didn't like to think about losing a close friend. He felt the mission was well planned, had talented operatives and stood a good chance of success. But he also knew the ops have a way of going in very different directions from the original plan and people get hurt.

Jack's thoughts kept returning to his parting from Pam. He had tried to be as bright as possible telling her he had to run back to the coast to check on some items. But he would be back the day after tomorrow and they had a date for dinner. He remembered the look in Ian's eyes. He knew Jack was lying with the tacit approval of Dr. Hanson. Pam seemed happy and she smiled when Jack kissed her good bye. The walk from her room to the car was one of the longest of his life. He wanted to run back and hold her and let the war go on without them. But he kept walking.

"Let's get together with Lee and Winky. I want to take a look at the weather situation," Tommy said.

Jack thought for a moment. "I think we go. The bad weather will make it tougher for the Krauts to tell exactly who we are. Besides, bad weather makes sentries and guards find places to hide from the weather. That's good for us."

"Let's see what the skippers think."

An hour later the two MI-6 officers sat in the Operations Office on the *Whitney*. Phil and the two MTB skippers joined them. They'd received the latest weather from the staff weather officer and gotten an update on the overall disposition of German naval forces. The inclement weather and the attrition by allied bombing had resulted in a minimal German presence at sea over the last several days. Another front was moving in from the west that would bring winds of up to 35 knots and a sea state with waves 10-12 feet. The forecast called for both rain and sleet with lowered visibility throughout the operating area. The intelligence briefer cautioned there were still significant German forces in the area to affect daily operations by Coastal Command.

Tommy waited until the briefers left. "There you go, gentlemen. What are your thoughts on launching Vixen tomorrow night? One thing we need to consider is the code boys felt each day we delay the chance increases there may be a new recognition code put in place."

"Bloody awful weather if you ask me." Winky sat back and looked at the group. "I think we can do it. But there will be some sick chaps on the boats. We'll be fighting the sea as much as Jerry."

Lee Powers added, "Winky has a point there. Even our boys get a bit green in weather like this. How are your army types going to do? Hard to be aggressive if you're throwing up."

Phil didn't say anything.

Jack knew he wasn't happy about the idea of going in this weather. "Almost all of my sea time has been on aircraft carriers so I don't have a good feel for this. But I have got to think the last thing Jerry would expect in really lousy weather is for a British MTB to run into Oostende harbour. Does the advantage of surprise and lowered defences outweigh the bad effects on our people?"

Winky thought for a moment, "I've never run into Jerry in the Channel in weather like the forecast. So that's a plus. Winky, you've looked at the harbour layout and E-boat moorings. What's a strong west wind going to do as you try to maneuver into the E-boat nest?"

"Actually it should be better with a west wind. There's a lee shelter as you get into the inner harbour." He stood up and pointed to a large scale chart of the Oostende harbour. "Once I get past this point of land it should be manageable."

A door opened and Frank Meriweather came in, water dripping off his raincoat. "Sorry I'm late, gents. Just got back from a run to the signals section to get any last minute radio traffic."

Jack stood up. "Lieutenant Frank Meriweather, this is Lieutenant Colonel Tommy Hudson, from MI-6. He's my boss in London."

The two men shook hands and Meriweather sat down next to Powers.

Tommy remained standing. "Well then, let's do what they pay us to do. Make a decision. For Coastal Command, MI-6 will defer to your call. We can go or we can delay. We will not cancel in any case even if we have to wait a month. This mission is that important to the war. We've been able to plus up our forces and will be getting some significant support from the Air Force and destroyers out of Southampton."

Thirty minutes later the decision was made.......Go.

Oostende
Belgium
December 7, 1943

From his vantage point in the third floor of an apartment near the waterfront, Pierre Goillet surveyed the windswept harbour and channel of Oostende. He could see eight German E-boats securely moored to their piers. Two sentries walked up and down the wet piers.

He had received a coded transmission telling him Vixen was on for tonight. The Frenchman thought it was crazy to be out in weather like this but he was not a sailor. They must know what they're doing, he thought.

His responsibility was to transmit any status change of the E-boats or harbour defenses. Oostende was well defended by anti-aircraft guns and shore batteries designed to thwart any sea threats. In addition there was a harbour boom near the entrance to the channel controlled by a small tug. Several minefields protected the approaches to the channel.

The E-boats were moored at the naval pier area of the harbour. A temporary wartime arrangement, there were offices and machine shops plus a barracks ship which supported the patrol boats. The area was strictly off-limits to any civilians and patrolled by local army units. Several times a week a group of the boats would sortie on missions into the North Sea, departing at dusk and returning early the next morning. Today nothing looked out of the ordinary.

Five kilometers east of the city, Gunther Schmidt was talking with the commander of the Kriegsmarine forces in Oostende, Kapitan Hugo Lenz. Arriving earlier, the Gestapo agents had immediately contacted Captain Lenz and conveyed their concerns. He did confirm the new MK 13 acoustic torpedoes were now loaded in all boats. Those weapons however could only be removed from the firing tubes by a trained team and a support boat with a gantry. He did think that the ready service weapons storage was an area to protect. There was also a torpedo maintenance building where they had several spare systems to repair any torpedo which failed system checks.

Three hours later, after an extensive inspection with Kapitan Lenz, Schmidt decided to bring more security troops in from Brussels. By putting additional security in place but out of sight, they should be able to prevent any attempt to break into the base. He remembered Abbeville and he was not going to be caught unprepared again.

HMS Whitney
Harwich

The Vixen team had spent the day making sure all of their equipment was ready. The MTB's were topped off with fuel and were ready in all respects for sea. Everyone was relieved as the winds hadn't developed as forecast, nor was the sea state as bad as predicted. The weather was still going to be a challenge, but they'd be able to focus more on the Germans and not on a stormy English Channel.

Tommy spent the morning coordinating events as they unfolded. There were multiple calls with Bomber and Fighter Commands. The weather, from the aviator's view, was not ideal but they thought the forecast ceiling and visibility were sufficient for the mission.

Departure time for the MTB's was set for 1700 hours with a time on target of 0100.

At 1600 they all gathered for a last briefing in the Operations Office on Whitney.

Tommy stood at the chart hung on one bulkhead. The weather forecasters had just given them their latest estimate. "All right, then. Are there any last minute issues we need to discuss?"

The mixed group of officers sat quietly. They had gone over all possible contingencies.

Jack turned in his seat and looked at the others. "We just received several photos a Mosquito took early this morning. If we're lucky the boats will still be moored the same way." He handed a packet of photos to Winky. To Hudson he said, "If you get any indication from our observer they might have moved or sortied, we need to know as soon as possible."

"Agreed. We'll pass any info as soon as it comes in,"

Tommy assured the group.

Winky Alderton spoke up, "It always seems like these grand plans go down the crapper as soon as it gets dark and people start shooting. Make sure we keep everyone aware of what's going on via the tactical circuit. Keep it short, but let us know what's happening. I have a date with a gorgeous WREN tomorrow and I don't want to miss it."

There were a few good-natured comments around the room.

Tommy closed the meeting, ", gentlemen. That's it. Good hunting and God speed."

Thirty minutes later the powerful engines roared to life in the MTB's. Jack stood on the bridge of 5043 and listened to the traditional commands of a vessel getting underway. Slowly the boat began to edge away from the pier where Tommy Hudson stood alone. The MTB started to surge forward, the smell of exhaust mingling with the salt air. Tommy raised his hand in farewell. Jack did the same.

The two boats began to move forward toward the harbour defense area, their wakes white in the gray water. On the pier Tommy Hudson turned and walked back toward the Whitney.

CHAPTER FIFTEEN

German Naval Facility
Oostende Harbour
Belgium
December 7, 1943

Hauptmann Reinhard Rutger arrived with twenty-five SS troopers at 0700. The call had come in from Schmidt the night before when he was desperately trying to entice a young Belgian lady into bed. He was still irritated with Schmidt. Perhaps he could find some eligible young ladies in Oostende. After all, they were used to the Navy and he would be something new.

On the senior officer's orders, he'd deployed his men on two shifts guarding the main ammunition storage area and the torpedo maintenance shed. It was a miserable day, the wind whistling off the North Sea and the rain moving horizontally. The base commander Kapitan Lenz seemed like a decent sort. However he wasn't at all comfortable with land security issues. Schmidt wanted his men to conduct their security patrols very unobtrusively. The senior agent was convinced there would be an attempt at penetrating the base. How many times had Rutger heard the same type of false warnings? He'd believe it when it happened.

From his vantage point, Pierre didn't see the arrival of the additional troops. He was more interested in the E-boats themselves. During the day he'd seen the crews doing routine maintenance. But the activity was minimal, none of the normal preparations he had observed prior to night missions.

At sunset he transmitted the codeword telling Hudson the boats were still in port. It took about forty minutes for the word to be relayed to Harwich and from there to Jack.

In the inky blackness of the North Sea the two MTB's pounded through the heavy seas, sea spray coating both vessels with a glistening sheen.

Jack Stewart returned to the bridge from the wireless room below.

"Last report from our man in Oostende says the boats are still in harbour," he yelled to Winky over the wind and roar of the engines. Alderton had been on the bridge since they'd left Harwich. Jack knew he must be numb from the cold wind and rain.

"Think we could get your chap to stay there permanently? For once it's nice to know the bastards aren't out here waiting for us." Alderton turned back forward, scanning the dark ocean as a matter of habit. "How're your lads holding up?" The seas were rough but hadn't worsened as they moved into deeper water.

"They're all right. We'll start changing shortly."

With the exception of the engine room gang, everyone on the boat would be wearing the Kriegsmarine coveralls.

Jack would be on the bridge to assist Winky during the harbour penetration. The key would be the recognition signal to get them past the boom tug at the entrance. Bletchley Park boys had assured them they would be challenged with a light signal. Jack knew they must get the reply right. Oostende's harbour entrance was very narrow with German gun emplacements on either side of the channel. The MTB's would be sitting ducks if the Germans opened up at close range.

Jack went down to the wardroom. Terry was opening up the equipment bags and starting to distribute the weapons.

Howe was already wearing his German coveralls. The two former commandos, Curtis and Jimmy, looked a little white but seemed to be doing all right. Jack checked his watch, it was 2130. "Everything in order?"

Terry nodded. "The boat's coxswain already passed out their weapons and he's starting to hand out coveralls."

"Good. We got the message the boats are still in harbour. We'll stick with our original plan. I still need to make the radio call. After that it's a waiting game." He went over to the stainless steel carafe strapped against the bulkhead and drew some hot cocoa into a mug. "Anything we're forgetting?"

Phil was sitting on one of the benches with his knees braced against the boat's movement. "If we are, it must not be important."

Jack turned to the two youngest members of the team. "Glad you signed up?"

They both smiled. Jimmy said, "Like they told us, it'd be an adventure. They weren't kidding."

Good men Jack thought, they'll do fine.

At 2200 Jack was in the small wireless room amidships. The RT operator had made sure they were on the correct tactical frequency. Keying the microphone he said slowly, "Ranger ....Ranger". Releasing the key, he found himself holding his breath hoping for the pre-briefed reply.

The RT crackled to life, "Landslide......Landslide".

He breathed a sigh of relief. That signal meant there were two "L" class destroyers moving in the same direction. They had sortied from Southampton earlier. Between the two ships, they mounted twelve 4.7inch guns, a multitude of automatic weapons, eight torpedo tubes and radar. They were acting as "big brother" in case they ran into unforeseen forces. Jack headed for the bridge to let Winky know the destroyers were on station.

RAF Biggin Hill

2330 Hours

Four Mosquito fighter-bombers sat on the ramp, their ground crews busy with mission preparations. The two-man crews were completing their pre-flight inspections and getting ready to start the twin Rolls Royce Merlin engines. The Mosquito was ideal for its roll as a fighter-bomber with unmatched speed and a lethal arsenal of four 20mm cannons. Used for pathfinder and reconnaissance missions, the aircraft had recently been brought into the world of special operations. Precisely at 2330 the first Merlin coughed to life and then roared as the start checklists were completed.

Squadron Leader Jack Whitney was the flight leader for "Bandsaw" flight. Currently with 85 Squadron at Hundon, he had been specifically requested for this mission by Colonel Greene. The four ships had flown down to Biggin Hill yesterday. Whitney's mission was to provide fire support for the Vixen team when they entered Oostende harbour. It made the mission very personal to Whitney knowing the men on the boats. The flight would be airborne at 2400 and headed for a holding point off the Belgium coast. They would be under the control of two "L" class destroyers who were equipped with both surface and air search radar.

Jack finished his post start checks and keyed his microphone. "Bandsaw flight, check in."

"Four."

"Three."

"Two."

"Lead, roger. Biggin Tower, Bandsaw leader, taxi a flight of four."

Whitney looked across the ramp and saw a great deal of activity on the Spitfire ramp. He knew the Spits were on five minute alert for Vixen but would remain on deck unless scrambled.

"Bandsaw leader, cleared to taxi to runway 09, 1013."

He pushed the throttle forward slightly to get the aircraft moving and then back to idle as he turned the Mosquito and followed his taxi director until clear of the congested line. As they made their way to the runway he and his bombardier, Glenn Farley, went over the take-off checklist. He could see his flight following on the taxiway.

"What's the call sign of the destroyer leader again?" he asked Glenn.

The crewman looked at a card on his kneeboard and replied, "Lima Able."

"Let's hope their radar controllers know their business. It's going to be a bitch to pick up those targets, especially if there's a blackout."

"I thought that was the idea. No diversion raid so they'll leave their lights on for us."

"That's the plan. But you know how well plans tend to go."

"Bloody right there."

Whitney looked at his watch. "We're ten minutes early. Let's go and we can throttle back and save some petrol. Biggin Tower, Bandsaw flight, takeoff for a flight of four."

Ninety seconds later, the fourth Mosquito lifted off runway 09 and turned to rendezvous with the other three fighters.

Combat Information Center
HMS Lancer
0045 Hours

In the darkened space the only light was from several red overheard lights and the illumination from radar screens. There were several plexi glass status boards on the bulkheads with information on call signs and radio frequencies. An atmosphere of quiet tension filled the room as the operators maintained a watch on the sea and air around the two destroyers.

Lancer had been in radio contact with the two MTB's for the last several hours. The two boats had separated about an hour ago. Currently they plotted MTB 5122, call sign "Baker Romeo," about 15 nautical miles off Oostende. The other boat, "Able Foxtrot," was approaching Oostende harbour.

Holding overhead the destroyers were four Mosquitoes, two at 1000 feet and two at 2000 feet.

Lieutenant Commander Geoffrey Lines, the ship's second in command, pushed the intercom.

"Skipper, the lead MTB is approaching Oostende."

Commander James Randolph looked into the inky black night from his chair on the bridge.

"Thank you, Number One. Keep me advised."

Winky Alderton stared through his binoculars at the faintly visible coast.

Jack was standing behind him, wearing German Kriegsmarine coveralls, a black leather sea coat and a white German peaked naval cap. His silenced Sten gun was in the wheelhouse and his Walther PPK in its shoulder holster.

"There it is, the northern channel light. I can see the boom tug at the north side of the channel." Winky kept the glasses at his eyes. "Signals, be ready with the Aldis lamp and watch for the challenge."

The MTB was making twelve knots with a quartering sea and closing the channel. Lee Powers stood on the bridge as well, but this was Winky's command and he remained in the background. Closed up at action stations with all guns manned, Phil and Terry were now down below with the raiding party. Once in the harbour they would come on deck as crewmembers.

Winky turned to Jack and Lee. "Still no challenge. I'm not sure when we should expect it. Maybe they don't see us."

Jack thought for a moment. "We didn't think about this one. We could send the recognition signal and see if it wakes them up."

Alderton shook his head. "I think we motor in closer. It's dark enough tonight, they may not see us yet. They may not be expecting any traffic tonight so maybe they aren't paying attention."

The MTB was now two miles from the tug and channel entrance. Suddenly, a light blinked from the small tug.

"There it is. "M" and "U." Sigs, send the reply," he called to the signals yeoman.

"Aye aye, sir." The signal lamp rapidly clicked out the two-letter code.

"Both engines slow ahead. Let's give him time to move the boom." As the boat slowed, the quartering sea rocked the boat with a sickening motion. The wind was now from behind them and had dropped to 10 knots. Clouds totally obscured the moon, making it as black as the bottom of a mineshaft. Slowly the tug started to move from left to right dragging the anti-submarine netting free of the harbour entrance.

"Engines, half ahead. Pass the word down below we'll be in the channel in ten minutes. Standby to man all deck stations." Winky turned to Jack and Lee. "Well, gents here we go."

Kapitan Hugo Lenz was an old school naval officer. A veteran of the Grand Fleet and Battle of Jutland, he'd spent most of this war in administrative support roles. He had never joined the Nazi Party and his loyalty was to Germany not Adolph Hitler. In command of the naval forces in Oostende for the last year, he'd developed a respect for the young German sailors who sortied out to battle the British in the Channel. He knew the tide of the war was turning and that invasion loomed on the horizon. Regardless of the future he would continue to do his duty as long as he was able.

Tonight he had invited the two Gestapo officers to dinner at his quarters, which were a mile from the piers. To Lenz, the Gestapo officers were glorified policemen. But he felt it was still correct to extend a dinner invitation to Schmidt, who did outrank him. He got along well enough with the senior man. However his assistant Kolsch had been obnoxious. It was a trait he'd observed among the younger Gestapo agents who had never known another job or different times.

Dinner had been pleasant and they talked about Belgium and what Lenz discovered in the way of good food and wine in the last year, the leisurely dinner finally wrapping up around 2300. Schmidt and Kolsch were staying at the Arnaud and after their final drinks the two left for the hotel.

Lenz was asleep when the phone by his bed rang. It was the night duty officer.

"Herr Kapitan, the harbour defence boat just reported a patrol boat entering the channel. We have no operations scheduled tonight. It must be a boat transiting."

Lenz couldn't remember any scheduled visits. Although there had been several times during the last year when E-boats transiting to or from Germany had used Oostende as a fueling stop. "I don't recall any. Check with their commanding officer when they tie up and then give me a call."

Hanging up the phone he realized he needed to use the bathroom and swung his legs down to the floor. Sitting on the edge of the bed he thought for a moment. Was there a connection between the current security alert and this strange boat? He rang the duty officer back and told him to contact Schmidt. "Tell him I'm going to go down to talk to the boat's commanding officer. This may be nothing but I wanted him to know. And send a car to pick me up. I'll be ready in ten minutes."

"Pass the word to man deck stations," Winky said down the voice tube. He could see the pier area where the E-boats where berthed but couldn't make out the individual boats themselves.

Jack stood next to him, Sten gun in hand.

Lee Powers stood beside Jack and they all strained to

see the target.   Fortunately there was no blackout and the lights on the waterfront provided some illumination. The plan called for Winky to reverse course in a wide turn pulling up to the outboard side of the target boat. Their team would then cross to the E-boat taking out any Germans on board.

The number two circuit on the bridge was tuned to the frequency used by German harbour operations. They weren't sure if the circuit would be manned tonight, but it made sense to monitor it in any case.

The channel was choppy, a steady wind blowing off the sea.

As the MTB approached the E-boat piers Jack could make out their target boat. It had hull number "S-110". There was an open berth directly behind it on the pier and another E-boat directly ahead.

The German radio frequency came to life. "Naval vessel approaching the finger piers, this is Oostende Operations. Identify yourself and say your intentions."

Jack picked up the microphone. "This is S-185, enroute to St. Malo from Bremen. I'll need fuel and berthing for my crew."

"Acknowledged, 185. You'll berth behind the 110 boat on the outboard pier. I'll get some line handlers down there to meet you. We had no notice of your arrival."

"Don't bother your men. We can take care of it."

"Jack, I see two sentries on the pier. They're right behind the target boat. I think we need to go pier side instead of alongside the target. If they see us pass up the open berth, it'll raise questions," Winky said. He was starting his wide turn bringing the bow around toward the piers.

Jack looked and could see two sentries on the pier, both had on helmets and overcoats. "I'll pass the word to the deck crews."

"Both engines, slow ahead. Stand by to come alongside the pier."

Lenz and Schmidt arrived at the Naval Operations Office within minutes of each other. They both listened as the duty officer relayed the boats identification, destination and request.

"Sorry to drag you out at this time of night, Brigadefuhrer. Looks like it was a false alarm." Lenz sighed, there would not be much sleep for him tonight.

The two Gestapo officers were drinking coffee. Schmidt put his cup down. "Kapitan, since we're up anyway let's go down and greet the boat's commanding officer. I need to stretch my legs."

Six crewmembers jumped to the pier, the MTB's engines having reversed momentarily before the boat nudged the wooden pilings. The two pier sentries now standing side by side did not notice the knives in the hands of two of those men.

Terry Howe walked over to the Germans with Jimmy Hunt at his side.

"Miserable weather tonight," Terry offered.

One of the figures answered, "Another winter night in Belgium..."

Before either of the soldiers realized what was happening both lay dead on the pier. Two crewmembers helped Terry and Jimmy drag the bodies to the edge of the wooden planking and roll them into the dark water.

On the pier the team was moving quickly toward the E-boat, which apparently was not manned by a watch or caretaker crew. Jack led the move down the pier, Sten gun at the ready. The rest of the pier was deserted. He jumped aboard the E-boat with Lee Powers in trail.

Andy Dudley and his crew sprinted for the engine room.

Petty Officer Ferguson, the Electrical Petty Officer, ran to the breaker box on the pier to turn on shore power.

Down in the engine room Dudley was going over the

arrangement when shore power kicked on flooding the room with light.

"Nice work, Fergie," he said aloud. "Now let's get these buggers up and running."

Jack and the team had checked the boat for any un- wanted passengers and found none.

Phil briefly detoured to the torpedo tubes to check they were loaded with the new version. The technical types told him how he would be able to access the torpedo through an inspection port on the launching tube. He checked and the weapons had the telltale rubber diaphragm which covered the acoustic sensors. Closing the inspection port he headed for the bridge.

Working through their pre-start sequence Dudley was glad he'd taken time to learn German labels. These engines were very similar to the ones he'd worked on before and he quickly completed the pre-start procedures. He heard Lee Powers voice in the voice tube.

"Engine room, bridge. Chief, how soon will we be able to get underway?"

"Almost done with pre-start checks, sir. Starting in about two minutes."

"Right. Standing by."

Lenz, Schmidt, Kolsch and Hauptmann Rutger walked down the darkened wharf toward the finger piers. There were two SS troopers five paces behind them. The two senior men were leading the group as they turned down Pier Two where the visitor was assigned to berth.

At first Captain Lenz thought it was the shadows cast by the angle from the pier lights that made the boat's outline unusual. But then he saw the lights and activity on S-110. He looked again and put his hand out to stop Schmidt.

"My God, that's a British MTB at the end of the pier," he blurted out to the group.

Schmidt was shocked. "What?"

"Get down." Lenz herded the group over to a darkened spot on the pier behind a large bollard. They heard the engines kick over on the German boat and then the engines start on the MTB behind her.

Lenz yelled, "They're stealing the boat!"

Schmidt turned to Rutger. "Get back to the office. Turn out your troops and notify headquarters in Brussels. Tell them we have a British MTB in the harbour trying to steal one of our torpedo boats." He gestured to the two SS troopers. "Work your way down the pier. Try to take out the bridge areas of either boat. GO....GO."

The two German officers squatted behind the bollard. Lenz spoke first. "They have to get back through the boom defence. At the harbour mouth we have gun batteries on both side of the channel. We should be able to stop them. I need to get back to my ops building to get the word to the boom defence boat and the gun batteries. I'll also get the duty patrol boat manned in case we need to go after them."

"Kapitan, we damn well better stop them or both of us will regret it," Schmidt almost hissed his words. "Kolsch, go with Kapitan Lenz. Use my authority if you run into any problems with anyone, understand?" Kolsch nodded and the two headed up the pier.

Jack stood on the port side of the German boat waiting to cast off lines. There were men on each set of lines ready to let go at Lee's word. The silence was shattered by blasts from two machine pistols at close range. Jack involuntarily ducked and he heard bullet impacts behind him on the bridge. His men dropped to the deck and began to return fire down the pier at the muzzle flashes. Jack knelt for a moment and heard the British MTB boat backing out of its berth.

Phil yelled at him from behind the bulkhead ladder going to the bridge. "Jack, Lee's been hit. Get up here!"

MTB 5043's engines rumbled in reverse as Winky backed

away from the pier, ready to lead the German boat out of the harbour. He saw the fire coming from half way down the pier directed at Jack's boat.

"Port Oerlikon, clean off the pier," he yelled. Immediately a hail of 20mm shells chewed up the pier with devastating results. Alderton picked up the microphone and transmitted, "Lima Able, Lima Able, this is Able Foxtrot. Lightening bolt, I say again, lightening bolt. Acknowledge over."

Out of the darkness he heard the RT speaker, "This is Lima Able. Acknowledge, lightening bolt."

Winky knew things were going to get nasty.

Squadron Leader Jack Whitney heard "lightening bolt" and immediately pushed the throttles forward, turning his flight toward the target area. The code signal told all units the mission had been discovered and the boats would need air support to clear the harbour. As the indicated airspeed passed 350 knots he heard the air controller aboard HMS *Lancer*.

"Bandsaw leader, steer 080 degrees, target is 12 miles. Mission urgent."

"This is lead, roger. Inbound now, estimate on target in two minutes."

Jack climbed on to the bridge and saw Lee Powers sitting on the deck. The young officer's legs were stretched out straight and with his back against the aft bridge bulkhead.

Phil was kneeling down in front of him. There was blood smeared on the gray bulkhead.

"Jack, get the boat out of here." Lee's voice was strained.

"Phil, take care of him." Jack turned and yelled across the deck, "Let go all lines." He heard gunfire coming from down the pier and heard bullets whistling by in the darkness. "Right ten degree rudder, all engines, back slow."

Schmidt remained behind the bollard and was stunned when the British Oerlikon shredded a large part of the wooden pier. The two SS troopers were ripped into bloody rags. As the German boat started to move a dozen soldiers arrived, one carrying an MP-40 machine gun.

"Fire at that boat, NOW," he yelled. Several soldiers began firing their rifles immediately. The machine gunner set up on the pier and began firing rounds at the slowly moving E-boat.

Seeing the MTB idling at the end of the pier, Jack ordered, "All engines, stop. Right 20 degrees rudder. All engines, full ahead." The E-boat began to move smartly, the bow coming around toward Winky's boat, which was now accelerating toward the channel.

Jack turned back to make sure their stern would clear the next boat forward and was knocked down violently. The bridge had exploded in splinters of wood and shards of metal. Stunned, he got on his hands and knees and looked around. Lee was laying flat on the deck, not moving. Groaning, Phil was on his back next to Lee. Jack felt a sharp pain sear through his side. He was dizzy but struggled to his feet.

"Cox'n, get someone up here to help the skipper. Follow the MTB. Stay right in her wake," he called into the voice tube.

Jack crawled over to Lee who slowly turned his head. "Are we moving?"

Before Jack could answer he saw Lee's body go slack.

The two patrol boats roared out of the Naval Pier area and headed for the main channel. They were 4000 yards from the boom and closing at 20 knots.

At the gun emplacements, located on both sides of the channel, alarm bells were ringing as the gun crews ran to man the 88mm guns. Primarily for anti-aircraft protection of the harbour, they could also be used as surface batteries. Orders had been received to open fire on any vessel trying to leave the harbour.

Kapitan Hugo Lenz was confident they would be able to capture or destroy the enemy forces within the confines of the harbor. To cover any eventuality he decided to get the duty patrol boat underway.

With the boat at action stations Winky only had to issue one order, "Torpedoes, standby starboard tube." The MTB sped toward the boom. The anti-submarine boom was a wire net supported on the surface by a series of floats, the netting extending down to impede any submarine attempting to enter the harbour.

"Starboard tube ready, sir," yelled Petty Officer White. The MTB was accelerating past 20 knots, 3000 yards from the boom.

"Starboard tube, FIRE!" There was a loud 'whoosh' as compressed air propelled the torpedo out of its tube. Accelerating to 45 knots it would impact the boom in 45 seconds.

"Torpedoes, stand by port tube," Winky yelled as the crew ran to prepare the tube. There was an ear shattering scream as an 88mm round missed the MTB and exploded in the water 50 meters behind it.

Winky knew the two Mosquitoes were inbound and grabbed his microphone. "Two friendly boats are in center of channel approaching the boom. We're taking fire from gun battery north of channel, over."

There was a huge explosion at the boom, a dark red fire followed by a vertical plume of water that went up a hundred feet.

Winky yelled at his 40mm crew, "Open fire on the gun emplacement!" The tracers started to mark a path from the MTB toward the German gun emplacement.

Jack was holding on to the bridge rail making sure the boat was following the MTB as Winky approached the boom. The violence of the torpedo explosions had surprised him. Jack saw the tracers from the 43 boat's 40mm arching toward the German gun as a second torpedo exploded on the boom.

The two Mosquitoes screamed toward the target at over

400 knots. Whitney could see tracers from the MTB arching toward the spit of land north of the channel. He rechecked the master armament switch on and that all four 20mm cannons were selected. The ammunition was a combination of armor piercing and high explosive. The reticles were illuminated in his gun sight. He pushed the nose over, the illuminated gunsight approaching the gun emplacement, pulled the trigger and all four cannons began to fire. His tracers were converging with tracers from the MTB.

Winky saw the RAF's cannon shells impacting. He knew there wasn't time for the 88 to swing around to engage the aircraft. "Cox'n, maintain this course until we are through the...."

The final round from the German 88 impacted the main fuel storage tank of the MTB. A shattering explosion tore the boat apart in a vicious orange and red flash.

The concussion threw Jack Stewart back against the bridge bulkhead, sending a searing pain into his chest. Through the pain he realized Winky's boat was gone, only a few pieces of burning wreckage marking the site.

"Cox'n, full ahead, maintain this course until we pass the tug," he yelled in the voice tube. He turned to see Terry kneeling next to Phil. "How're they doing?"

"Lee's bought it and Phil has lost a lot of blood. It looks like one round in the thigh, but it must have hit an artery."

"Cox'n, get Livesy and Hunt up here to help with the wounded."

Jack Whitney saw the MTB explode just as he released the weapons trigger and commenced his pull up He jinked hard right then left over the channel. He could see a second boat continuing out the channel. "Lima Able, Lima Able one boat has exploded in the channel. There's a second boat under way and clearing the mouth of the harbour."

Two officers heard the transmission. Lieutenant Frank Meriweather on MTB 5122 and Commander James Randolph aboard HMS *Lancer* ordered both vessels to turn toward Oostende and went to full ahead on their engines. They rapidly began to close the distance to the unknown boat.

Aboard *Lancer*, Geoffrey Lines watched the big picture on the air and surface radars. The radar target was four miles off the coast with MTB 5122 closing on it. Orbiting overheard were the two Mosquitoes awaiting orders. A quick plotting board solution put the target speed at 16 knots, but who was the unknown contact?

Having removed Lee Power's body to the main deck, the MI-6 crew carried Phil down to the wardroom, laying him on the main mess table. A tourniquet appeared to have slowed the blood loss. Phil was in and out of consciousness as Terry administered one vial of morphine.

Sub-Lieutenant Keith Caulfield, Lee's number one in 5122, joined Jack on the bridge.

"Sub, I'm sorry about Lee. There's nothing anybody could've done." Somehow the words seemed hollow. His side throbbed and each movement sent a shot of pain through his body. "Go below and try to establish radio contact with our forces."

"Aye, sir," the young man said and disappeared down the ladder.

Jack leaned over the engine room voice tube. "Any problems with the engines, Chief?" There was a lot of water between here and Harwich. The weather was slackening but he knew it could come back with a vengeance.

"No problems, Commander. I checked the fuel and oil levels. All right there. All pressures and temps are normal."

"Thanks, Chief."

Moving to the pilot house voice tube Jack said, "Cox'n, run a line from our estimated present position to Harwich and steer that course. Try to maintain 18 knots."

"Harwich it is, sir," came the reply.

Terry climbed up the ladder to the bridge. "Jack, all hands accounted for. Two of the Navy lads are wounded but not bad. Phil's in bad shape. He's lost a lot of blood and we can't stop the flow completely."

Looking ahead, Jack saw a signal light flashing in the darkness off the starboard bow. He asked the signals yeoman if he had seen it.

"Sir, it's a challenge. One of ours."

Jack said, "Get out the correct reply. We don't need anyone else shooting at us."

The signals yeoman flashed the recognition using an Aldis lamp. After a minute, more flashes came from the other vessel.

"Sir, it's our MTB. He's asking us our condition."

Jack felt relieved. They couldn't have put up much of a fight in a strange boat with a pickup crew. "Tell them one dead, three wounded, one seriously. Need urgent medical assistance."

Frank Meriweather relayed Jack's message to *Lancer*. The destroyer did have a Surgeon Lieutenant aboard, but how to get him to the E-boat? Commander Randolph weighed his options. A small boat transfer in this sea state was extremely dangerous. He needed radio contact with the E-boat to find out the exact situation.

"Bridge, combat, we have a fast moving surface target just clearing Oostende harbour. Judging by the speed it's probably an E-boat."

Randolph thought for a moment. "What's the range from the E-boat to our boys?"

After a brief pause, "Twelve thousand yards, Captain."

"Range right now to the enemy boat?"

"22 thousand yards, sir."

The Captain stood to the intercom set and started to fire orders. "Gun control, bridge, be ready with star shells for a maximum range shot in 60 seconds. Break, combat, contact our air cover and tell them their target is an E-boat clearing Oostende and we intend to provide star shell illumination.

Contact the MTB and tell him to get the MTB and E-boat headed this way at full speed and brief him on the Germans coming out of port. We'll work on his medical problem after we deal with this one. Now look lively."

Jack could see the MTB approaching. There was a furious light signal flashing and Lowery, the signals yeoman, was watching with his glasses.

"Commander, they're sending, 'E-boat in pursuit, full speed, follow me'."

Jack saw Meriweather's boat commence a sharp left hand turn.

Yelling down the voice tube, Jack called for full speed and told the helmsman to follow the MTB. He felt the hull accelerate, the rough sea throwing spray the entire length of the boat.

Jack Whitney's radio came alive, "Bandsaw leader, vector 110 degrees. Your target is an E-boat heading west in pursuit of two friendlies. Expect illumination."

He keyed his radio, "Take loose trail, two. Make sure we split our runs by 30 degrees."

As he pushed the throttle forward, Whitney looked into the blackness knowing his target was out there somewhere. There was a bright flash and then a second as two star shells illuminated the sea about four miles at 11 o'clock. *Good shooting.* There, in the circle of light under the star shells, was a fast moving E-boat.

"Master armament, on."

Gunther Schmidt was out of his element and he knew it. When Lenz offered to let him go on the pursuit craft he felt he had no way to gracefully decline. Lenz led him onto the bridge of S-195 under the command of Lieutenant Peter Weir. They'd cleared the harbour quickly and were in close trail on the stolen E-boat. He'd never imagined the violent pounding of the sea and the roaring engines. He was holding on desperately to the metal rail that ran along the bridge bulkheads. The chase was a chance. They were after a boat which had the same exceptional speed. Their torpedoes were useless against the speeding boat with its light draft and in these heavy seas. They'd have to close to within gun range and hope to inflict enough damage that he would have to slow. Schmidt knew if this boat got away he would be in terrible trouble with Himmler. He shuddered to think what would happen to him. In the Gestapo the worst punishment was reserved for those who embarrassed the Reichsfuhrer with Hitler. This would rise to that level. He was turning to ask Lenz how he thought they were doing when a bright spot of light, then a second, burst over their heads. He saw the look of concern on the boat's commander and heard him order a violent turn away from the light. Then he felt the world around him start to come apart.

There were only two firing passes by the Mosquitoes. As the number two aircraft pulled off the target, Schnellenboat 195 was coasting to a stop and wallowing in the waves with smoke pouring from bow to stern. Most of the upper deck personnel were now dead or wounded, the high explosive cannon fire ripping them apart. There was an eerie silence as the boat began to rock in synch with the waves. Flames were beginning to spread and the below deck crew appeared on deck. Hugo Lenz had died instantly, his body torn in half by a cannon shell. The young boat commander, mortally wounded, had ordered his men to get the rafts in the water and take care of the wounded.

An engine room petty officer dragged Schmidt to the life raft, pulling him aboard. The waves were brutal and the raft immediately separated from the burning hull of the E-boat. It had been less than five minutes since the first attack run by the British aircraft.

"Commander," young Caulfield called. "We have comms on the tactical frequency down in the RT shack."

Jack felt weak, his side pierced with pain. He had seen the star shells behind them, but it was hard to make out what had happened.

"Keith, take over up here. I'm going below."

Making his way down below, Jack felt his energy drain. He knew he was losing blood, but he had to find out what was happening. Turning into the wardroom, he saw Terry leaning over Phil Hatcher. Jack could see blood covering the wooden table.

Phil was conscious, his breathing shallow.

Jack put his hand on his friend's arm and smiled. "How're you doing, old man?"

"Don't think I'll be dancing for a while." He grimaced as pain came through the morphine.

"We'll have you home in no time." He turned and moved into the passageway aft toward the radio room.

Terry followed him.

"Jack, I'm worried. He's already lost a lot of blood and we still can't stop the bleeding.

Jack knew Terry didn't spook easily. "Check around and see if there's any additional medical equipment. Maybe we can arrange a transfusion."

"I'll look, but I'm no doctor." He turned and headed forward.

Petty Officer Jenkins was sitting in front of the transmitter adjusting the gain. He saw Jack and handed him the microphone. "We're talking to Lima Able. That's *Lancer,* sir. She's running the show."

Sitting down very slowly, Jack took the mic from Jenkins. "Lima Able, this is the 110 boat commander, over."

On *Lancer,* James Randolph replied, "One ten, what's your status? Over."

"Boat is seaworthy, engines good and enough fuel. I have one very seriously wounded man. I need a doctor right away."

Randolph thought for a moment. "One ten, maintain course 280, 15 knots. I have you on my gadget and will come alongside. I propose sending my doctor down on a Jacobs's ladder."

"One ten, roger."

The destroyer skipper turned to his deck officer. "Go get the doctor. He's about to earn his sea pay."

There are men who are natural ship handlers. They understand the effects of wind, waves, engines and rudders. It's a unique skill, some of which can be learned but the truly great ship handlers all have a sixth sense on the water. Randolph was one of those men. Fifteen minutes later he'd joined on the E-boat, adjusted their courses based on conditions and pulled slowly alongside the smaller boat.

Several packages went down on lines and then a lone man wearing a harness with two safety lines made his way down a metal and wood ladder hanging down the port side of the larger ship. Gauging the deck movements, he timed the waves and leaped into the darkness, the safety lines paying out behind him. The man landed in the arms of Jimmy Hunt on the E-boat's deck.

Two hours later Phil Hatcher was resting easier. A surgical procedure coupled with three pints of blood plasma pulled him out of danger.

Surgeon Lieutenant Trevor Ainsworth sat on the small bench, the sweat glistening on his brow despite the cool temperature of the E-boat's wardroom. His first year in the Navy had been spent at the large naval hospital at Portsmouth, primarily seeing daily sick parade. For the last six months onboard Lancer his medical duties had been very routine. Tonight's wild arrival on the deck of the E-boat at night in the North Sea was something he would have never imagined. The surgery was fairly routine although in this case it had been critical to the survival of the patient. The doctor was glad he'd be able to walk off the patrol boat when they arrived in Harwich. His trip down the Jacob's ladder was enough to last an entire naval career.

The young doctor sipped a hot cup of coffee the men had been able to procure from the German galley. The coffee was terrible, but it was hot and he needed to relax.

"Sorry to bother you, Doc. But you need to take a look at Commander Stewart."

Terry Howe had assisted Ainsworth while he worked on Phil. Now he was getting concerned about Jack Stewart.

"Where is he? I'll go have a look," he said, setting the mug down.

Terry stood up. "You stay here. He's up in the wheelhouse. I'll go get him."

Terry found Jack in a chair behind the helmsman, watching the sea. His eyes were closed, the signs of fatigue evident on his face.

"You need to let the doctor take a look at your side."

Jack nodded. "Get Caulfield up here, he can take the bridge."

Ainsworth was shocked when he saw the man who entered the wardroom supported by Howe. Wearing Kriegsmarine coveralls and a German sea coat, his face was drained of color.

"Commander, I'm Doctor Ainsworth. Please lay down here and let me take a look at you." They laid Jack carefully back on the table still stained with Hatcher's blood.

Jack let out a sigh as he lay fully back. "Doc, thanks for taking care of Phil. They tell me he'll be okay."

Ainsworth began to carefully cut away clothing to expose Jack's right side. "He'll be fine," he said, concentrating on cutting. "Probably won't be too mobile for a while, but he should make a full recovery."

The doctor began wiping oozing blood from a wound that ran from Jack's hip to his breast. He carefully probed the wound. It appeared that a bullet, probably on a ricochet, had tumbled, impacted his right side and damaged the ribcage.

The injury was not life threatening, but the broken and splintered ribs had the potential for doing further and possibly serious damage. His biggest challenge was to immobilize the patient until they could get to hospital.

"Commander, we need to keep you as still as possible until we get to port. You have a number of ribs that are broken. I don't want any of those damaged ribs doing any further harm. We're going to need to get in there and clean things up. But that can wait until we get to Harwich. I'm going to give you a blood transfusion which will make you feel better."

"There goes my dinner date for tonight, doctor. I'm going to be in serious trouble." He turned his head to Terry. "Go up and stay with young Caulfield. We're several hours out of Harwich. Tell him he's in command of this boat. Also tell him to let me know if anything comes up. When we get in, take care of the men. Make sure Phil is squared away. Then find Colonel Hudson and point him my way. If he's not in Harwich, let me know. If I'm not coherent make damn sure he calls London and tells Ian Thompson I'm fine. I don't want Pam to worry."

Howe reached down and grabbed Jack's left arm. "I'll take care of it, Skipper." Stewart's eyes were closed.

CHAPTER SIXTEEN

43 Duboisstraat
Antwerp, Belgium
December 8, 1943

Herman Devold had been able to get out of the apartment early by telling Edith he needed to buy cigarettes. In reality he wanted to check the drop to see if there were any messages from London. He left one outgoing message noting Edith was getting more and more anxious about the arrival of the main group. He wasn't sure how long this was going to continue, but he knew it was going to be more difficult each day.

He'd been friendly and civil despite knowing she was a double agent. He wanted to make sure there were no suspicions and they did have to share the small apartment. She was an attractive woman and in another time and another place, who knows? He did wish she wouldn't talk about her family in France. Maybe she was making it all up, but the details seemed very real. Edith told him she was from a big family and grew up in the outskirts of Paris. She'd always wanted to work for a newspaper and worked her way from local papers to one of the Paris dailies. The war drove her south to Vichy and then via Portugal to England. Herman always wondered what the real story was but knew he'd never find out.

He retrieved his message but didn't look at it until he returned to the apartment building. When he read the message he stopped and read it again. There was the codeword which signaled the conclusion of Vixen in Oostende. Now it was time for him to leave Antwerp. Before he left there was the last job.

10 Downing Street
London

Colonel Noel Greene was not used to being summoned to see the Prime Minister. He was fortunate his immediate superiors in the chain of command were staunch supporters of Winston Churchill and allowed this circumvention of normal protocols. The Prime Minister wanted a report on last night's action and Noel Greene possessed the information. In a very unusual move, the Colonel had joined Tommy Hudson in Harwich to monitor the operation. He had talked with Jack Whitney by telephone from Biggin Hill last night. On the arrival of the group this morning in Harwich he'd seen Commander Randolph and Lieutenant Meriweather to get their reports on the action. Finally he went over debriefs from the Navy crewmen and talked at length with Terry Howe.

Following a chronological run down of the mission, he summed up the key result. "Sir, we now have in our possession two of the German's most advanced acoustic torpedoes. We paid dearly for them losing an entire MTB and crew. Losing men is never easy, but what they accomplished was significant. I know this will save lives in the Atlantic."

The PM had been very quiet listening to the report, unusually so for Churchill. He was looking at the photographs of the E-boat taken that morning in Harwich. "Colonel, I am everyday heartened by the actions of our men in the most hazardous situations. I am sorry for the loss of the MTB and her gallant crew. Some day we will stop losing our young men and women. Tell me of Jack Stewart. I understand he was wounded."

Greene cleared his throat. "Prime Minister, Jack led the crew which captured the E-boat. On the death of Lieutenant Powers, Jack assumed command of the boat. He was wounded in the harbour but able to get the boat out of Oostende. He underwent surgery this morning at Harwich for a bullet wound to his side. The doctors tell me he came through with flying colors." He stopped for a moment and then quietly continued. "Sir, I know you were briefed on the incident which took place outside our headquarters on 4 November. His young lady, whom you met, is still recovering in hospital from a severe head injury. I'm very proud of Commander Stewart for doing his duty in the face of serious personal and professional challenges."

The old politician sat back and began the ritual of lighting his cigar. "Colonel, I would have expected no less, nor would you. Jack Stewart is the type of young man who will ensure we win this war and then win the next one too. I just hope Franklin Roosevelt doesn't call in his marker and want him back." He puffed several times to get the dark Havana lit. "This is the second time young Stewart has performed heroically and with distinction in service to the King. I would strongly endorse a D.S.O. for his command and execution of this operation. I tell you, Colonel, if he hadn't become so damned effective with MI-6, I'd pull him down here and put him on my staff. In fact I may still do that."

Greene couldn't tell if he was serious or not. "I'll take care of the paperwork for the D.S.O. sir."

Naval Hospital
Harwich

A few well-placed phone calls resulted in Jack and Phil assigned to the same room in the east wing of the hospital. Both had undergone surgery on their arrival at the hospital. The surgical reports for each officer were quite straight forward: Hatcher's wound, although life-threatening at the time, was relatively easy to repair. The constant loss of blood had been from the femoral artery, nicked by a bullet. With the artery was repaired the healing process should be normal. Stewart had been very lucky. A bullet of unknown caliber impacted his right side. It had done damage to the rib cage, breaking four ribs, but there was no damage to any internal organ. The surgery to remove the splinters of bone and suture the wound took over three hours.

Slowly opening his eyes, Jack felt a weariness and dull sense of discomfort. It was very quiet and he lay still enjoying the peace. He remembered the arrival in Harwich and being carried by stretcher to an ambulance. Tommy Hudson had been on the pier and they'd spoken briefly. He had assured Jack the phone call would be made to Ian Thompson. On arrival at the hospital he had received a brief from the lead surgeon prior to going into the operating room. He remembered being told Phil was also going into surgery.

The need to find out about his friend moved him from inaction. Turning his head to locate a nurse he saw another bed next to his. Phil was propped up on a double pillow. A nurse was standing on the far side of the bed taking his pulse.

Jack's mouth was dry, but he asked, "How're you feeling?"

Both the nurse and Phil turned to look at Jack. She was the first one to speak, "Lie still, Commander. I'll be there in a moment."

Phil smiled at Jack. "All things considered, I'm doing well. You were in surgery a lot longer. How're you doing?"

"Not sure yet." Jack tried to turn to face Phil.

"Commander, please lie still. I will get the surgeon to come in and explain the surgery and the recovery plan." She finished marking Phil's chart and bustled out the door.

Within a minute a white coated doctor entered the room. Jack recognized him from the pre-op briefing. His name was Roylston.

He had a rosy face and smiled as he approached Jack's bed. "Commander, good to see you awake. The surgery went very well but took a bit longer than we anticipated." He went on to describe the injuries and what they had done in the operating room.

Other than nodding Jack wasn't able to get in a word. He finally interrupted Roylston, "Doc, how long before I can get out of here?"

"I should think we could look at a discharge in a week or so." He continued to smile pleasantly.

"I need to get back to London and I can't wait a week.

"Commander, you have to give your injuries time to heal. We must restrict activity or you'll aggravate the wound." His smiling demeanor had changed to a serious look of concern.

"Can I at least make a phone call?"

"I think we can arrange that. Nurse Chapman, would you please have the phone line to the room connected?

Several hours later the Senior Surgeon at Harwich received a call from the Director Medical Services, Home Fleet. He was directed to arrange transportation for a Commander Stewart from Harwich to the Medical Rehabilitation Hospital at Ramsgate. When he questioned the authority he was told the order had come from the office of the First Lord of the Admiralty. Being a career naval officer, the Senior Surgeon knew this was a battle which made no sense to fight.

Noel Greene sat in his office at Baker Street and reflected on the events of the last two days. He felt Section F had performed superbly. The loss of life by Costal Command was regrettable but he had to look at the big picture. The weapons experts were already taking the torpedo guidance sections apart to determine how to construct countermeasures.

Tommy Hudson had called right after Stewart and Hatcher came out of surgery and both were good condition. When Hudson asked about getting Jack to London he had no qualms about calling in a few markers. There were times where you had to disregard the rules for the good of the individual. The ringing of his phone jolted him out of his thoughts. It was Tommy Hudson who was still in Harwich.

"Sir, we just got word from the Provost. They were processing the three German E-boat survivors from last night. It would seem that one of the three is Gestapo, not a sailor." He paused, which allowed Greene to interject a question.

"How did a member of the Gestapo get on the E-boat in the first place?"

"That's the amazing part of the story. I guess the two sailors don't like the SS or Gestapo. They were happy to volunteer they'd taken aboard a very senior Gestapo officer when they pulled out."

"Very senior. What does that mean?"

"SS Brigadefuhrer Gunther Schmidt."

"There was the Schmidt who tangled with Jack in France. Is this the same man?"

"It appears so. I can't wait to find out why he was in Oostende. I'll arrange for our chaps to take custody and we'll begin the debrief process. I know Jack would like to chat with him at some point." Tommy Hudson suspected Schmidt was the most senior Gestapo officer the Allies had ever captured. He would provide a unique look at the German security service.

Greene said, "Jack will have to get in line."

43 Duboisstraat
Antwerp

Devold unlocked the door and swung it open. He walked down the short hallway which opened into the kitchen. Edith was sitting at the kitchen table reading a book. She turned as he walked in and smiled at him.

"I just put on water for tea. Can I make you a cup?" She closed the book and started to get up.

He shook his head. "Thank you, but no. I'm fine."

She opened her book and said as an afterthought, "Did you see any Germans when you were out?" Both commented earlier there seemed to be many more uniformed patrols around the harbour district.

"No, not today." He was hanging up his leather coat on a wall hook and she did not see him remove a short length of rope with wooden handles at each end. Edith was focusing on her book as he walked up behind her. The tea water kettle began to whistle and she looked up instinctively. In seconds Devold had the rope around her neck and viciously pulled it tight. Her eyes went wide in horror as her hands grasped desperately at the rope cutting into her neck. Harsh gutteral sounds came from her as she struggled frantically. Devold lifted her slightly, adding her weight to the rope strangling her. She was not a large woman and in two minutes her struggle was over. He dragged her body over to a closet, covering it with a wool blanket. His mission was accomplished.

Ramsgate Military Hospital
London

The Navy ambulance arrived in late afternoon with the two patients. Jack and Phil had brow beat Phil's physician to allow him to also transfer to Ramsgate. Both men promised to take everything as easy as possible and in the end Dr. Roylston had said, "Get them out of here."

They left Harwich at mid-day, side-by-side in the ambulance with a medical orderly keeping watch on them. Propped up on pillows, they either dozed or talked during an uneventful trip.

Jack had been in his room only a few minutes when Ian Thompson pushed the door open and entered.

"A bit banged up, I understand." Ian's face showed concern.

"I'm okay, really, just a bit sore. How's Pam?"

Thompson walked over to Jack's bed.

"She's doing very well, actually. But I'm more interested in what happened to you."

"Nothing serious, honestly. Ribs torn up a bit but I'm doing fine. We were damned worried about Phil. A ballsy Navy surgeon leaped down to the boat and sewed him up. He's two rooms down." He lowered his voice, "Ian, we got the torpedoes."

"Well done. I hadn't heard anything except you'd been wounded."

"We lost an MTB and a lot of good men." Jack paused a moment remembering Alderton and his crew. "Now tell me about Pam. Did she suspect anything?"

"I don't think so. But it's going to be tough hiding your situation."

"Ian, go grab a wheelchair from the nurse's station. I want to see her."

Pamela Thompson sat in a chair by the small table in her room. She was wearing her light blue hospital robe and staring out the window. The last several days had been good for her. She was feeling steadier on her feet although she continued using a cane when she walked. Her speech was getting better every day. If her progress continued, Dr. Hanson said she would be ready to leave the hospital in two weeks. She heard the door open and turned to see a wheelchair come through the door pushed by her father. For a moment she was confused and then she heard Jack.

Putting on his biggest smile he said cheerily, "Hello, dear."

She looked confused and said, "Jack?"

"It's . I got scrapped up a bit. I'm just fine and now we get to spend everyday together." He reached out to grasp her hand. "I love you more than anything in the world."

Ian had quietly exited the room. She looked at Jack, her eyes moist and her smile happy. "Jack, I'm so glad you're here."

Other than a few cuts and scratches, Gunther Schmidt was none the worse for his survival experience. He did have hypothermia when rescued in the Channel but warm blankets and liquids soon had his temperature back to normal. The reality of his situation didn't hit until he was recovering in sick bay aboard the destroyer. All of his consciousness effort had been focused on surviving the sea. As a senior Gestapo officer he would surely be singled out for interrogation and worse. If he could convince the English he was Kriegsmarine, perhaps he could disappear into anonymity until the end of the war. This might be the best possible situation. He would be in serious trouble with Himmler because of the theft of the E-boat.

What Schmidt did not comprehend was the utter contempt the uniformed services had for the Gestapo. They certainly feared the secret police and would not take overt action against the organization but this situation was different. Both German sailors were not reluctant to tell their captors about the Gestapo officer. Once he realized his ruse would not work he admitted his real identity to the British Provost personnel.

He now sat in the back of a large military truck. The area was enclosed with a canvas cover. Seated on the wooden benches were two armed guards, both carrying weapons. Schmidt's hands were handcuffed behind his back. It seemed neither of his guards spoke German and he didn't know English. He had no idea of their destination. They'd been on the road for over two hours. A vision flashed into his mind: 1941 in Poland. As a mid-grade Gestapo officer he'd been assigned during the initial round up of Jews and gypsies. He remembered the SS troops forcing the people into truck with bayonet points. They were considered more like cargo than people. His whole purpose was to get them on the trucks and moving to the execution pits. They had no idea what lay in store for them. Now the threatening unknown was all Gunther Schmidt had to think about on his long ride.

CHAPTER
SEVENTEEN

10 Downing Street
London
February 4, 1944

The two men sitting outside the Prime Minister's office had grim looks on their faces. Despite having waited for over thirty minutes they were not impatient. They were bringing Mr. Churchill a problem and they did not have a solution. Major General Colin Gubbins was the Executive Director of the Special Operations Executive, privy to the most sensitive secrets of the British Commonwealth. He seldom brought operational issues to the level of the PM. This was a most unique situation and newly promoted Brigadier Noel Greene accompanied him with the details.

Greene had been in this office less than a month ago in response to a request from the PM to meet with Jack Stewart. As a 'former naval person' Churchill could not resist getting the details of the Vixen mission from the person responsible. Greene also suspected, in addition to the unique arrangement with FDR, he truly liked the young officer. They'd spent over an hour with Churchill and he plied Stewart with many questions as Jack went over the mission. At the conclusion of the meeting he'd informed Jack of the award of the Distinguished Service Order for Operation Vixen. In addition Churchill had recommended to the First Lord of the Admiralty that Jack be considered for immediate promotion to the rank of Commander. The request had been returned noting Commander Stewart would have a date of rank of 1 February, 1944. That meeting had been a high point for Noel Greene seeing one of his own recognized for outstanding service to the King.

This meeting didn't promise to be as uplifting. Gubbins and Greene were two of the three people who knew the actual name of the deep plant agent Bishop. Churchill was the third.

The Prime Minister was in a black mood. Setbacks on the Anzio beach head and a major Japanese offensive in Burma reinforced the long battle still ahead for the Allies. Gubbins knew this but the Bishop matter was critical for the war effort in Europe.

"Good afternoon, gentlemen. I hope you are bringing me good news. But I fear you wouldn't be here if that were the case." Churchill was gruff, but as always engaging.

Gubbins got right to the point. "Prime Minister, we have received a message from Bishop which we feel requires action. Whatever we do will have potential repercussions both good and bad. We need your decision on which course of action to pursue."

"Go on."

"Bishop passed a message saying he feels he's under suspicion and is concerned he may be arrested. He said there have been small indications of dissatisfaction among the general staff. There may be a more pointed security effort by the Gestapo. The information which he's provided to us for the last two years has been invaluable. I feel we owe it to him to attempt an extraction from Germany. An operation to pull a member of Hitler's personal staff out from under his nose would be extremely dangerous. If we could carry it off then we alert Hitler that one of his inner circle has been sharing Germany's highest secrets with the Allies. One option is to let Bishop fend for himself. Not let the cat out of the bag. Of course if he were to be arrested and interrogated they would eventually find out his connection with MI-6. Therein lies the difficult question. Do we attempt to rescue Bishop, knowing he'd bring us unique information on the German high command? Or do we leave him to his fate, not wanting them to know we've been listening at their door for years?" Gubbins finished and waited for the reply.

Churchill frowned as he rubbed his temples. "What's your estimate of the potential success of a mission such as this?"

Noel Greene spoke up, "Sir, we've looked at several scenarios. I have to be honest it's a very difficult challenge. This mission would be into the heart of the Reich. There are long distances involved. No resistance to assist us. Their internal security services are at their best."

"Can it be done?" His question was emphatic. Both of the uniformed men knew he was asking for a commitment.

Gubbins replied, "Yes, sir. We think there's a chance. We'd like to examine it further. At this point we think it can be done."

Getting up from his chair he walked over to the bookcase, turned and stood thinking. "Gentlemen, there's a fundamental difference between ourselves and the Nazis. We value the worth of each man and are willing to risk other men to save that one man. We cannot sacrifice Bishop without abandoning the very principles that differentiate us from the Hun. General, go get him out. I want to meet that man."

The two men got up to leave and Churchill walked them to the door. "When you have a plan put together. I should like a short brief."

The Reich Chancellery
Berlin
February 18, 1943

Commander Erich Von Wolner sat at his desk in the Reichsfuhrer Secretariat reading morning communiqués from each of the major headquarters of the embattled Reich. One of his many duties as director of the secretariat was to assemble the Fuhrer's morning message brief. He would select the most critical messages, write an executive summary and then deliver them to Hitler. He also controlled the production of outgoing messages to the operational forces. Normally there would be a flurry of messages transmitted following the morning strategic briefing session which occurred at 11:00 am. Wolner was Hitler's executive secretary and in one of the most unique positions in the bureaucracy. He was privy to all field reports sent to Hitler. He was able to listen to subsequent discussions and then would see the outgoing personal messages from the supreme leader of Germany. His perspective was complete.

Von Wolner's naval career began in 1930. Erich came from a family with long traditions of service in the Navy. His family background was Prussian and aristocratic. There were several members of his family in the High Seas Fleet during the last World War, serving with distinction at the battles of Dogger Bank and Jutland. His father commanded a cruiser division and held the rank of Rear Admiral. After several tours in destroyers, Erich had come to the attention of Admiral Wilhelm Canaris and was assigned to his staff in 1938. His efficiency and excellent performance opened many doors and in an effort to break down some of the walls between the services, he'd been pulled to the Fuhrer's staff in 1940.

Erich had been stunned by the events he saw occurring in Germany as the Jews were singled out for persecution. He watched the Gestapo instill a regime of fear throughout the German people. Realizing there was no longer a viable system in place to work for change he decided to try do what he could to help break the Nazi's stranglehold on Germany. In an incredible act of courage he approached the British Naval Attaché and offered his services. From that day forward he'd passed information to the British Special Intelligence Service. With the increasing level of paranoia within the senior staff, his chances of exposure were growing. Erich knew if he could get to England he could hasten the downfall of the tyrant. But it was a long way from Berlin to London.

64 Baker Street
London

Following Vixen, Section F took almost a month for physical recovery, intelligence debriefs, leave and mustering in several new members. Jack wondered if his promotion to full Commander would jeopardize his position as head of the section. Noel Greene would not make any promises but he felt the section would stay under Jack until at least the completion of the invasion of the continent. That was fine with Jack. He'd come to feel like this group was family and was in no hurry to leave.

An efficient staff resulted in a light workload for Jack during this administrative time. It was ideal, allowing him more time to be with Pam. She'd been released from Ramsgate just before Christmas and they spent the holidays in Oxford. Dicky had been able to get leave and it was a very merry time for all. Her recovery was progressing better than Dr. Hanson expected. She regained almost all balance and speech skills. Her memory, both short and long term, was fine. She did occasionally stutter but it was not a problem. The doctor felt she would be able to go back to full duty in June. Jack couldn't imagine life without Pam. If they hadn't been totally in love before she was hurt, their support of each other during the recovery connected them at a level most people never share.

One of the new members of Section F was Herman Devold who'd successfully made his way back to England via France and a Lysander flight. Jack immediately liked the quiet man who seemed more like a librarian than an accomplished operative. In a closed door meeting with Greene, Hudson and Stewart he debriefed the termination of Edith Moulon. Jack did not think twice about the sanctioned execution. He would have done it himself if given the opportunity. Officially her file folder at MI-6 simply noted: "lost on mission to Belgium, December, 1943." The matter was never spoken of again.

It was the first week of February when he received a call from Tommy Hudson. Jack sensed from the tone in his voice the meeting with Greene was not routine. His intuition turned out to be correct.

When the Brigadier had finished briefing him on the mission, a cold chill ran through Jack.

"You want us to put together a plan to get into Berlin and extract a member of Hitler's staff?

Tommy sounded a little apologetic. "Jack, what we need is an investigation to come up with the most logical plan with the best chance of succeeding. You'll have the full resources of MI-6 at your disposal. We're not asking for miracles. We only want you to look at it."

"The PM is personally involved with this one. It has that level of priority," Greene said, leaving no doubt in Jack's mind this mission was going to take place. He had better get it right.

"How much time do I have?"

Greene shook his head. "There's no hard time limit. But Bishop does feel time is getting short."

"Sounds like I'm already behind."

There were now five men in England who knew the true identity of the agent known as Bishop. It was up to them to bring him out of Germany regardless what the cost might be.

Phil Hatcher was still using a cane to get around, slowly regaining full use of his leg. He took a lot of kidding from the section that he could never go back to walking a beat in East London. According to the doctors, he'd have a clean bill of health within six weeks. Jack's side was still slightly tender but didn't prevent him from full duty.

For a second time Jack descended into the classified vault run by Mabel Thorncraft. He read all of the communications ever received from Bishop. Jack wanted to get a feel for the flow of information hoping it would give him some thoughts on an extraction plan. There were very few solid facts about the man himself. Jack knew little about his personal life or routine. It was a tough way to start a plan. He knew they were going to have to collaborate on this plan with Von Wolner. The communications came via a double drop system using a member of the Swedish embassy staff. Unfortunately it often took ten days for a message to get to Berlin and the same amount of time to get a reply. Son of a bitch he thought, how hard can this get?

On first examination it was clear to Jack that extraction by land transport was the most difficult. Many security checks coupled with the extensive distance made it almost foolish to attempt. It needed to be by air. Something like the bizarre flight from Germany to Scotland by Rudolph Hess in 1941. Hess had commandeered an aircraft and flew to England in an unusual attempt to affect a peace settlement between England and Germany. Perhaps something like that would work, steal a plane and fly to England. But he knew the chances of success would be minimal. There was no significant resistance organization within Germany, to say nothing of trying to steal an aircraft. Jack was coming up short on every idea he considered.

Some of the latest message traffic mentioned that Von Wolner was "in the east, at the Rastenburg headquarters." Maybe there was something to work with there.

35 West Bridge Street
Oxford
March 2, 1944

Following her release from Ramsgate Pam had moved in with her father at his apartment in London. Ian had been spending more and more time in the city as the invasion approached. To have Jack around every day had been wonderful for Pam. Despite the frantic work at MI-6, Jack had spent every possible moment with her.

Her recovery was ongoing. She had the occasional speech problem and more puzzling, she seemed wistful and quiet. Jack had noticed the difference in personality and asked Dr. Hanson about it. The doctor asked Jack to be patient. They didn't now, nor would they probably ever understand the inner workings of the human brain. She'd received a severe injury and there were many documented cases of a permanent personality change. It was simply too early to tell in her case. The only advice he could offer was to give her his love and attention. Jack didn't have all the answers but perhaps the extremes of experience and emotion which came from war made their relationship deeper, their love stronger.

One weekend they ventured back to Oxford to spend the weekend at the house and enjoy the slower pace.

There was still a hint of winter in the air and Jack had started a fire in the early afternoon. Their lazy afternoon consisted of reading the paper, talking and listening to the afternoon programming on the BBC.

Jack stretched his arms up and arched his back on the couch. "What sounds good for dinner, lovely lady?"

Pam was curled up, leaning against his chest. "Let's see, a gorgeous roast goose, with all the trimmings, a trifle pudding and a bottle of very expensive Madeira wine."

"Actually I was thinking about a walk down to the Castaways for a pint and some fish and chips." He leaned down and kissed her forehead.

"If it's not to be goose I guess fish and chips would be a good second. Why don't you give me half an hour to get ready."

Pam went upstairs and Jack poured himself a short

scotch in a wide tumbler. Sitting down he twirled the dark liquid in the glass as if it was a crystal ball in which he might find answers. The last two weeks had been frustrating. They had gathered as much information as possible and tried to tie it into a plan. The section planners kept running into major problems with distances, security forces, lack of in-depth knowledge on Germany. They were trying to put a puzzle together with half of the pieces missing. As he looked in the glass a series of disjointed thoughts would come and go as he rethought each of the problems. He started to imagine crazy solutions to those problems and how they might run together. There were several key issues. Maybe they had been trying to solve them each separately. Think big Jack. How do we pull this off?

Pam could tell he wasn't totally with her at dinner. Jack seemed to be off thinking in his own world. She decided to let him think, it must be important.

Later in bed she could tell he was lying there awake. When she asked if he was all right he just told her he was trying to solve a problem and for her not to worry. She didn't hear him at daybreak when he said aloud, "That's it!"

The Reich's Chancellery
Berlin
March 7, 1944

Commander Erich Von Wolner walked briskly down the wide corridor leading to Adolph Hitler's office. As he approached the door he was eyed by the two SS soldiers who stood on either side of the large wooden doors. These guards were more ceremonial than functional. At this point, any visitor had passed through four separate security checkpoints. Inside the doors the Fuhrer's outer office was manned by a full staff of receptionists, phone operators and Hitler's personal secretaries. There were also two Gestapo special security officers near the wide set of doors which opened into the massive main office of the Reich's supreme leader.

This was a daily trip for Erich carrying the priority message board for Hitler to review prior to the morning strategy session. His heels clicked on the marble floors as he opened the door to the inner sanctum.

Hitler was sitting at his massive desk looking at maps. He looked up as Erich approached the desk.

"Good morning, Commander." He returned to looking at the map.

"Good morning, my Fuhrer." Von Wolner stood at attention in front of his desk waiting for him to finish.

Hitler was looking at a map of the Ukraine. "Zhukov has opened an offensive near Tarnopol. The weather seems to be cooperating for him. What have we here?" He reached for the leather folder.

"Field Marshall Kesselring sent an update on the enemy ground offensive from the Anzio beachhead."

The Fuhrer began reading while he talked. "Tell Keitel I want a full brief tomorrow on our options to reinforce the defensive line southwest of Rome. I also want a report on the radio controlled bombing of American shipping off the coast."

"Yes, sir." This morning was no different than most. Hitler would read through the messages and would list tasks for Erich to communicate to the immediate staff.

After twenty minutes, Hitler looked at the desk clock. "Make sure you're at the meeting this morning. I want to discuss our move to the eastern headquarters.

While maintaining his detached expression, Erich's pulse increased. The last communication from London asked about the feasibility of an extraction from East Prussia. He hadn't replied because he didn't know the long range plans on returning to the "Wolf's Lair" near Rastenburg. Hitler, for some reason, which probably went back to his time in the infantry in World War One, needed to command from the field. Consequently there was a full command bunker and support structure constructed in a remote wooded section of East Prussia. Erich knew he must get a message to London as soon as possible with dates of the move to Rastenburg.

Operations Building
RAF Biggin Hill

Squadron Leader Jack Whitney slouched back on the couch in the operations briefing room. He'd just arrived in a Mosquito and been met by Jack Stewart and Phil Hatcher. The tall aviator stretched out his legs, lit a cigarette, continuing the small talk they had begun on the tarmac.

"They've been keeping us busy. Lots of raids into Northern France, bridges and marshalling yards mostly." He exhaled and eyed the two other men. "But I suspect you didn't ask me to come down here to hear about what I've been doing?"

Jack smiled. "Phil, you can never fool those RAF types. Actually, we wanted to thank you in person for saving our lives at Oostende. If you hadn't been there, we wouldn't be here."

Whitney looked serious for a moment. "Sorry about the MTB. If only we would have been earlier."

"Jack, everyone did their best. Sometimes it just doesn't make any difference. Anyway, we need to ask for your help again."

Sitting up Whitney said, "What's up?"

Jack leaned forward, his elbows on his knees and fingers intertwined. "We need to do a feasibility study on a long range Mosquito mission which includes landing in East Prussia." Framing the mission with operational requirements he didn't discuss the underlying reason.

Whitney sat and listened to Jack's full outline before he replied. "You're talking about a mission that has a one way distance of about 900 miles. With internal fuel only, a Mossie can go about 1500 miles. If we use the special bomb bay tanks we can add on another 400 miles. And if we carry external fuel tanks, another 200 miles on top of that. So in theory we can make the distance if we aren't carrying any bombs and we don't to get into any dogfights"

Phil asked, "How about landing on unprepared surfaces like open fields?"

"Not normally a problem. We're not heavy and our main wheels are wide, designed for operating off grass airfields."

"What kind of landing or takeoff distance do you need?"

"Landing distance isn't the problem. We've got great brakes. For the takeoff, if we've burned half the fuel, have no bombs and there's no wind, we can get off in about 4500 feet."

Jack thought for a moment. "It seems like it's workable from your end. I suspect you're going to find yourself loaned to MI-6 for the foreseeable future. Now, if you don't have to get back to Hundon tonight, let's find the Officer's Mess. We'll buy you a drink or two for saving our hides."

Baker Street

Major Billy McClaren had been summoned from Arisaig for a meeting with Greene and Hudson. As the officer in charge of the agent training facility he saw every candidate coming through training. He was also responsible for passing them out at completion. The purpose of the meeting was very specific. While not divulging the mission itself they asked McClaren to rank the Polish graduates of Arisaig from top to bottom. The qualities they were looking for included: ability to work alone, professional competence, survivability and loyalty. The two were surprised when he didn't hesitate.

"I don't have to think about it. There's one Pole who went through about six months ago who was without question the best we've seen in a long time. He was a Captain in the Polish Army. He escaped and was in one of the Free Polish

Brigades preparing for the invasion. Got tired of waiting for the invasion and when we were looking for agents, he volunteered. We didn't have to teach him much in the way of weapons training, hand to hand, or signaling. He was better than many of the instructors. The only area he needed instruction was in clandestine operations."

Greene interjected, "Do you feel confident we could drop him into Poland and he'd be able to operate effectively on his own?"

"No question about it, sir. He's as capable as they come. Course there's never any guarantees but if anyone can survive, he's the one."

Hudson grabbed a notepad. "What's his name?"

"Lubowisz, Captain Jerzy Lubowisz."

Greene turned to Tommy. "Find out where he is and get him over here."

Jerzy Lubowisz had been raised in Warsaw, the son of a prosperous banker. Always athletic, he'd been drawn to the life of the Polish Cavalry. Receiving his commission in the Warsaw Brigade in 1932 he loved the camaraderie and fast paced life in the Army. Unfortunately a long tradition of gallant service by the cavalry allowed the senior officers to ignore advances in war fighting. While Germany was designing and producing tanks, the Polish Army prepared for the last war. The result was a swift and vicious victory by the Germans in 1939 despite a very heroic defence by the Poles.

Jerzy fought with his brigade as they tried unsuccessfully to defend against armored columns and Stuka dive bombers. Within four days of the invasion his brigade ceased to exist as a fighting force, having suffered over 85% casualties. When Poland surrendered he made a vow he would fight for his country until the Germans were driven out. A long and difficult escape across the Czechoslovakian border resulted in his eventual arrival in France. He fought with the Free Polish

Forces, eventually escaping the continent at Dunkirk. The reconstituted Polish forces had been on garrison duty in Scotland for over two years when he saw the opportunity to get back into the active war.

Jack was reading the latest intelligence assessment of the resistance effort in Poland when his yeoman knocked on the door. "Captain Lubowisz is here, Commander."

There was something about the tall man who walked into Jack's office. He was strikingly handsome and had an air of intensity.

"Captain, good morning. It's nice to meet you. Please sit down." The men shook hands and Jerzy sat down in the chair facing Jack's desk. The yeoman closed the door and Jack poured two cups of coffee, pushing one across the table. "Major McClaren told me you were the best natural agent he ever trained. It takes a lot to impress McClaren."

Picking up the cup, he looked at Jack without drinking. "I enjoyed my time at Arisaig very much." Jerzy's command of English was superb.

"Captain, do you believe in fate?"

"I suppose I've never really thought about it." He relaxed and took a sip of coffee.

"I asked you that question because a very critical mission has come up. Success depends on finding someone who is willing to go to Poland and risk their life. I think you might be that person."

Lubowisz sat there for a moment. "I wouldn't have volunteered for the SOE if I hadn't made that decision already."

"As of now, you're assigned to Section F. I need you to lead a team to parachute into Poland. Your primary focus will be in-depth reconnaissance and possibly liaison with the local resistance." Jack paused. "Your team will consist of three others, all current members of Section F. They have commando backgrounds and operational experience with MI-6."

Jerzy nodded. "This is very important, I take it."

Jack said, "Very important."

"Good."

Jack stood up and offered Jerzy his hand. "Let's go meet your team."

Later that morning Jack received an important message from Tommy Hudson. Bishop had sent word that the Fuhrer's immediate staff would leave for Rastenburg on or about April 15. One month from today.

Croyston Dispersal Field
Southwest of London
March 23, 1944

There was a stiff wind blowing out of the west and Jack was cold as he looked across the wide grass field. Originally one of the satellite dispersal fields which were very effective in 1940, Croyston had reverted to an outlying practice field used by several of the local bases. Jack imagined a group of young Spitfire pilots sitting around waiting to rush into the air to do battle with the Luftwaffe. He knew aircraft from this field must have scrambled in reaction to orders from Pam's group. So much had changed since then.

The direction of the war had totally reversed. As forces built up in Britain in preparation for Operation Overlord, the Axis forces were being pushed back in both Europe and the Pacific. Jack wondered about his former shipmates. Many of them would be flying off the huge Essex class carriers in the new F6F Hellcat. In a way he felt he was missing something, but he wouldn't have wanted events to unfold any differently.

Phil came out of the Ops hut. He walked over to Jack, his limp barely noticeable. "Bandsaw flight checked in. They should be here in about ten minutes."

"Thanks." Jack and Phil were out to watch the short field

takeoff and landing practice of the four Mosquitoes from 85 Squadron assigned to Operation Meteor. Jack Whitney was the flight leader and the most experienced pilot. He told Stewart that three of his best pilots were with him.

Ten minutes later they saw four aircraft in echelon formation approaching the field from the east. The twin engine aircraft were approaching the field at 300 knots and 800 feet altitude. Overhead the field the leader rapidly rolled his aircraft hard to the left and pulled away from the group. The following aircraft duplicated his maneuver at five second intervals. All four were now flying downwind.

Jack could see the undercarriages swinging down and locking into place. The leader was losing altitude as he rolled onto final, touching down about 1/3 of the way across the grass field. Jack could tell he was braking hard and the aircraft quickly rolled to a stop. Each of the wingman repeated the maneuver and then followed the leader as he taxied back to the touchdown point. Jack heard the big Merlin engines go to full power and saw the leader accelerate across the grass. The takeoff roll took only 10 seconds and lead was airborne climbing to pattern altitude.

The group continued practicing for the next hour, each pilot logging eight takeoffs and landing. At the end of the training period the lead Mosquito taxied over to the Ops building as the other three took off and headed back to base.

The propellers had barely stopped turning when the hatch under the cockpit opened. The two crewmen jumped down. Jack saw that Jack Whitney was carrying a parcel under his arm.

Phil and Jack walked out to meet the two aviators. As they approached each other, Jack Whitney removed his flying cap, wiping his hand across his face. "What did you think of our little practice session?"

Jack grinned at Whitney. "Looked like your gents have it down nicely." They shook hands.

Whitney gestured to his crewman. "This is my bombardier Glenn Farley. Glenn, meet Jack Stewart and Phil Hatcher."

Jack asked, "How many more sessions before you're ready for Meteor?"

"At least four or five. I want to do some in low light conditions just to be safe. But that'll do it for us."

"Good."

Whitney tossed the parcel to Jack. "All right, Jack. It's time to get you checked out in the Mossie."

Jack recognized flying coveralls and a flying cap. "It's been awhile but I'd love to go up with you. As long as it's with Glenn."

"I thought Phil could head back to Biggin Hill with Glenn. Then pick you up when we land."

"You're on. Phil, how about meeting us at the Ops Building at Biggin Hill, in say.....an hour?" He looked at Whitney, who nodded.

Fifteen minutes later they were strapped in with both engines running at idle. Jack was impressed with the power of the two Rolls Royce engines. The last time he had been in a high performance aircraft was almost two years ago at Midway. He was enjoying the smells and the sounds.

Jack Whitney knew Stewart's aviation credentials and briefed the procedures and capabilities of the Mosquito accordingly. For his part Jack was very impressed with the jump in technology from his old Wildcat.

As they taxied out to a takeoff position Whitney ran through the checklists.

"Because we're on grass I'm going to use 15 degree flaps. We'll use our short field takeoff procedure. Full power, on the brakes, final checks and release. Accelerate to 100 knots and rotate to 10 degrees nose up, accelerating to 150 knots. Gear will come up as soon as possible. Expect a little nose down pitch. Approaching 150 knots I'll retract the flaps. You'll feel a healthy nose down pitch. We'll continue to accelerate to 250 knots staying at low altitude. At 250 I'll pull up and start a hard climb."

"Roger."

On brake release the acceleration was rapid. Jack could feel the power of the two big triple bladed props. The takeoff transition was very impressive.

Whitney stayed below 50 feet altitude until the indicated airspeed indicator read 250 knots. Rolling to 60 degrees angle of bank he pulled 4 'g's as they turned sharply left and started climbing. Scanning the sky for traffic, he said, "Let's head over to the free flying area. I'll demonstrate some of the basic handling qualities."

"Pretty impressive already if you ask me." Jack liked the way this aircraft flew.

Over the next half hour, Whitney ran Jack though a full series of acrobatics, stalls, single engine ops and slow flight. Every minute in the air reminded Jack how much he missed flying. The Mosquito was everything he was looking for in this mission: long range, redundant systems and capable of operating on unprepared surfaces. In another ten minutes they were in the circuit at Biggin Hill. Whitney's landing was flawless.

As they walked in from the aircraft Jack was delighted with everything he'd seen in the Mosquito. "I don't think they could've designed an aircraft with this mission in mind and done a better job."

"She's a once in a lifetime design. I think if any aircraft can carry it off, the Mossie will."

"Can you be down at Baker Street tomorrow afternoon? I want to have a final session with the section before we present the final plan to Greene. Say 1400?"

"Only if you're buying drinks afterwards."

The next day, Jack sat at the head of the large conference table in the third floor meeting room. He watched the team as they filed into the room and sat down around the table. There was a real sense of pride as he watched his group, veterans of hard but successful missions. They were superbly trained, highly motivated and ready to take on this mission.

"Okay, gentlemen, let's go over the plan one last time. Tomorrow the Brigadier will see it. If it's a go, we'll execute straight away. A reminder, Meteor is classified "most secret, need to know." Our target for extraction is a single male in his mid-thirties. I know his identity. You will not for his protection."

In chronological sequence they went over the two phase plan. Phase one consisted of a four man team lead by Jerzy parachuting into the designated operating area and setting up base. The team included Terry Howe, Jimmy Hunt and Curtis Livesy. They were to conduct reconnaissance to determine enemy troop presence. If possible they'd try to contact the local resistance but that would be a secondary priority. Information would be sent back via radio. Once a suitable landing field was located they would be ready for phase two.

The next step would be a long range flight by four Mosquitoes. The lead ship would be flown by Jack Whitney with Jack as navigator and mission commander. The second bomber would be flown by a pilot only leaving a seat for the passenger. The other two aircraft would serve the role as airborne spares in case either of the primary aircraft developed problems. In addition they would provide added cover in case the flight was jumped by the Luftwaffe. The aircraft would be configured with both external fuel tanks which would be jettisoned on the inbound leg and the internal bomb bay fuel tank. The ground team would transmit weather information and last minute updates on the landing field. There was a built in thirty minute loiter time to allow for weather delays or any unforeseen problems.

Getting out of the security cordon around the Wolf's Lair and to a designated rendezvous point would be the responsibility of the passenger. This was one of the critical points.

The phase one team must find a useable rendezvous point and communicate that information back to London. Because of the slow communication with Bishop, locating a suitable location must be one of the team's first priorities.

Terry Howe looked at his map. "It looks like there are plenty of prominent landmarks on this map. I hope they're as prominent when we're on the ground there."

"We don't know how he'll travel out of the compound but we have to assume by car. Try to keep that in mind when you select the rendezvous point," Jack added.

Jack Whitney leaned toward Jerzy. "When you select a landing field remember we'll be landing at dusk. Try to avoid areas ringed by tall trees. We can handle a slope in the terrain up to about ten degrees. But if there's a lot of rain I'd like it closer to five degrees."

They went over the field marking pattern, recognition codes and contingency procedures in event there were unknown or enemy troops in the area. The ability to communicate by radio with the aircraft was critical. Jimmy Hunt had experience with field radios from his time in the commandos and would be carrying extra parts for the transceivers. They set up several light signals in case the radios were totally inoperative.

Two hours later they reached a consensus. The team felt ready. If the plan received Greene's blessing, they'd schedule the team drop on the evening of the day after tomorrow.

That night Jack met Pam for dinner at her father's apartment on Windsor Street. Ian was back in Oxford for several days so they had the apartment to themselves. He was tired after the hectic pace of the last two weeks and was happy to sit in the small sitting room reading the Times. Pam was busy in the kitchen working on dinner and refused Jack's offer to help. She came in with a glass and handed it to Jack, sitting down on the couch next to him.

He put the paper down and took the glass. "Thanks. Are

you doing all right?"

"Actually, I feel very well. It's good to be in the kitchen again, if only to make my famous sausage and potato casserole." She smiled and leaned against his shoulder.

Jack turned his head to kiss her forehead, "It sounds wonderful to me. I'm starved."

"Jack, something's up isn't it?" Pam had turned to look at him. She took his hand in hers. "I'm all right, Jack. You don't have to protect me. But I think I have a right to know. That comes with loving you."

He had already made the decision to tell her about this mission. The temptation was great to just fly the mission. It would only take part of a day and he'd be back home. But there was a faith and trust between them now he couldn't betray. "There's something in the works. You know I can't tell you much but I'm involved. I'll be going into the continent."

Pam closed her eyes for a moment and then opened them slowly, still looking at his face. "I love you, Jack Stewart."

Jack didn't trust himself to say anything. He put his drink down and held her.

CHAPTER EIGHTEEN

Operations Ramp
RAF Biggin Hill
March 26, 1944
2130 Hours

The wind was cold as a small group of men walked slowly toward the big Lancaster bomber parked in a secluded part of the aerodrome. The four engined aircraft was marked with a large "P" on the vertical stabilizer signifying it as a pathfinder aircraft. Specially configured and equipped, it normally led the large night bomber raids against the continent. Tonight it was being used to drop the Meteor team into East Prussia. A large maximum effort bombing mission was also being mounted against Hamburg which would provide a distraction for the Luftwaffe. Parked next to the Lanc were two Mosquitoes from the 85 squadron. They would be flying escort for the Lancaster, call sign Rider 21.

Jack Whitney was flying the lead Mosquito. Equipped as night fighters, the four 20mm cannons of the smaller fighter-bombers would provide protection in the event the lone Lancaster was discovered. Their route of flight would take them at low altitude out over the North Sea crossing over the Danish peninsula just south of Flensburg. Back out over the Baltic they'd remain at low altitude until coasting in just east of Danzig. Climbing to two thousand feet they would make final navigation updates and drop the team about 15 miles north of the Wolf's Lair. The mission from takeoff to drop would take four hours depending on the winds.

Standing at the boarding ladder of the Lancaster Jack shook hands with each member of the team. "We'll be waiting for your radio message that you're on the ground and safe. Transmit as soon as you can."

Jerzy nodded his head. "Okay, Jack."

The RAF crewmen leaned out from the hatch. "All right, gents. Let's get aboard."

One last round of 'good lucks' and the team climbed the ladder. Phil and Jack remained standing on the tarmac as the aircraft engines were started. Brakes squealing, the aircraft taxied out with the large bomber leading the procession.

"This one's going to be a tough one if I make my guess right," said Jack.

"My feelings, exactly."

Terry Howe had never been enthusiastic about flying and tonight was no exception. The noise and vibration seemed to work its way into his head. Checking his watch he noted they'd only been airborne for two and a half hours. Another hour or more to go he thought. It had been uneventful so far. The crewman came back to tell them they were crossing over land into the Baltic. He would have never known the difference.

Hopefully the focus of the Luftwaffe was on the Hamburg raid Terry thought. He envied the others who appeared to be sleeping. They were wearing their jump coveralls, their parachutes leaning against the cold aluminum side of the Lancaster. He felt they'd done their pre-mission intelligence well. The tough part was the slim information available from Rastenburg. Maybe the Krauts selected that part of Prussia for the headquarters because it was sparsely populated. There were aerial recon photos of several good candidates for a landing field. Tonight's drop zone was near three of the sites and seemed to be uninhabited.

Terry felt good about the team. Jimmy Hunt and Curtis Livesy were solid, steady soldiers and he'd seen them under fire on the last mission. Jerzy was an interesting character in many respects. Terry had heard of the swashbuckling spirit of the Poles but Jerzy was a quiet and intense person. His friendly nature masked a burning hatred for Germans and Germany which would surface at times. During the training for Meteor they had to order him to take breaks. When they did get him out one night to a local pub he'd shown them he could enjoy himself. Terry asked about his experiences early in the war but that seemed to be a subject out of bounds for discussion.

As the next hour droned on Terry thought about how he'd felt in the desert on those long range patrols. In Africa it always seemed they could get back to their forces if they had to. This time they seemed so far from home it was unnerving. At least they wouldn't have to walk home on this one. They'd be extracted by air several days after the main mission. He had finally nodded off when the crewman came by and shook each one of them.

"Fifteen minutes to drop."

The exit sequence would be Jerzy, Jimmy, two cargo parcels, Curtis and then Terry. The drop would be from 2000 feet and the Lancaster would be slowing to 140 knots. They'd be using static lines to keep the drop dispersion as minimal as possible. Each of the men had reserve chutes on their chest and the 2000 foot drop altitude would give them time to use the reserve in the event of a main chute malfunction. Methodically they each checked their gear and then paired off to check each other's chutes. Each man was equipped with a Sten gun and a .45 pistol. The cargo parcels contained food, ammunition, sleeping bags, and the radio equipment. For redundancy there was a complete radio set with spare parts in each cargo container.

"Any last minute questions," Terry asked the group. No one answered. "Remember to rally on the cargo parcels as quickly as you can. Bring your chute with you."

"Two minutes, stand ready." The crewman had removed the belly access hatch and the noise level went up significantly. Lining up forward of the door the RAF crew men stood next to the two cargo parcels ready to move them to the hatch.

The lead crewman was standing aft of the hatch looking forward to the cockpit. He had his hand raised like a track starter.

"Standby," he said. He paused and then dropped his hand. "GO...GO...GO".

Jerzy leaped into the black night with Jimmy right behind. Terry watched the Air Force crewmen quickly shove the two canvass bags toward and then out the hatch. Curtis jumped right after the second bag and Terry followed him into the darkness.

Jack and Phil returned to Baker Street. They spent several hours looking at different scenarios for the extraction. Each one depended on the final communication from Bishop. London's last message posed the questions to Von Wolner. How easy would it be to leave the compound? What time of day? What kind of transportation? What travel route? Depending on his reply they would finalize the pickup plan and transmit a primary date and backup. It was after 0200 when they left Jack's office and went down to the Operations Center. The duty section at the OC coordinated all activities of SOE teams in the field. When they arrived they saw Tommy Hudson sitting in one of the briefing chairs.

"Looks like we're all are thinking the same way," Jack said as they walked up behind Tommy. "Any word yet?"

Tommy sighed, "Not yet. But this would've been early. We're waiting for a signal from the Lanc crew. They should be landing at Biggin Hill about sunrise."

"No indication the Germans knew they were there?" Phil

asked.

"Not that we know. We'll get a full debrief when they land. So far, so good, but this may take awhile. Anyone for tea?"

Terry hit a pine tree as he landed and found himself in a tangle of shroud lines, small branches and parachute. Other than a sore arm where he hit the main trunk of the tree he was unhurt and relieved to be on the ground. The smell of pine was strong after four hours in the aircraft. He quickly pulled his chute out of the branches and rolled it into a bundle. Grabbing his Sten he moved in an easterly direction looking for Curtis. The area around him was grassy with clumps of trees throughout. In no more than two minutes of walking he heard the rustling of a parachute being gathered up.

"Curtis?" he said in a loud whisper.

"Right here."

The two set off to find the cargo containers. They moved quietly listening for any activity or sounds but it was eerily quiet. The first container was easy to locate. There was enough moonlight that the white parachute snagged on a high bush stood out against the landscape. The container appeared to be undamaged. Putting their chutes on top they grabbed the canvass handles and kept moving east. Rounding a clump of trees they saw their comrades standing at the second cargo parcel.

"Everyone ?" Terry asked as they approached Jerzy and Jimmy. He was answered by two nods. The team began walking toward a wooded ridge about a mile north. It would start getting light in a few hours and they needed to be under cover. The ridge would also provide a better vantage point to help them decide exactly where they were.

Forty minutes later they entered a heavily forested area and began to climb a gentle slope toward the ridge top. There was light underbrush and despite slowing their progress it would provide good cover when they set up a base camp. They didn't hear a sound or see any sign of habitation until they came to the top of the ridge. In the next valley they could see a house and barn about a mile away. There were no lights visible and it was hard to tell if anyone lived there. They needed to move south on the ridge to get a better view of the surrounding area. Looking for a place to spend the first day was becoming a priority.

It wasn't ideal but in a small wooded gulley they found a secluded spot to stash their gear for the day. Jimmy broke out the primary radio and set it up for transmitting. He quickly sent by Morse four two letter groups separated by 30 seconds. The code meant: 'on deck, operational.'

In London three men breathed a collective sigh of relief.

The Reich Chancellery
Berlin
April 2, 1944

Sitting in his private office Erich Von Wolner found it difficult to concentrate on his normal correspondence. He received the message from London and the reality of making a final plan was weighing on him. During his previous times at Rastenburg he had seldom left the compound. How could he orchestrate leaving the compound without arousing the suspicion of the Gestapo and SS contingent of Hitler's personal staff?

Understanding the time delay of messages he must figure out a plan soon. He had signed the directive for the staff move which began in one week with the advance party traveling to Rastenburg. Hitler would follow on the 15th of April with a small traveling group. The majority of the staff would remain in Berlin at the Chancellery to perform the myriad of administrative tasks needed to run the government. His mind was in turmoil when he received a summons from the Fuhrer's appointment secretary. Himmler had arrived for a last minute meeting and Hitler wanted to talk to Von Wolner.

"There you are, Von Wolner. We may have to modify our plans on Rastenburg." Hitler sat at his desk with Henrich Himmler, head of the SS standing by his side.

Bringing himself to attention in front of the desk his heart was pounding as he saw his escape plan dissolving. "Yes, my Fuhrer."

"Reichsfuhrer Himmler has information there may be a splinter group trying to instigate dissent within the senior leadership. For that reason I want to start a full security investigation by his people. I want it completed before we leave for Rastenburg. I'm making you the contact point on the staff. You may have to remain in Berlin as we wrap up this investigation." Himmler stood stone faced by Hitler's side.

Von Wolner was desperately thinking how this would affect his future plans. "I understand, sir. However I'm concerned we might lose continuity in your intelligence flow if I remain behind."

Hitler looked up from the paper he was reading with a quizzical look. "Commander, it's your job to ensure that doesn't happen. Is there some other problem?"

Close to panic, Erich realized that Himmler was also looking very pointedly at him. "No, sir. I'll make all necessary arrangements for the communication transition. I'll follow you to Rastenburg when the investigation is completed."

"Very well. Send in Major Scheller on you way out." Hitler returned to examining the paper on his desk.

"Yes, my Fuhrer."

As Von Wolner walked out of the large office he didn't see Hitler raise his head and comment to Himmler, "That was a very strange reaction by Von Wolner, very strange indeed."

Henrich Himmler noted the statement. He would make sure Major Scheller was aware of this strange behaviour. Scheller was the Gestapo liaison officer for the Fuhrer's staff and would be assisting Schenke on the overall investigation. Perhaps the Fuhrer's immediate staff was a good place to begin the probe. Schenke was without question his best investigator. Totally ruthless, he possessed an above average intelligence and more importantly he had a unique sense of intuition. Schenke would find out if there was anything to these rumors, Himmler assured himself.

Erich was angry. How could he have been so stupid to try and force an issue with Hitler? It was something he'd never done and to start now was out of character. That son of a bitch Himmler would have noted it. If he was to survive this he must think through every action and comment. He felt secure there was no physical evidence which might betray him. His drop system was fool proof. The problem now might be added surveillance, which could make future drops more dangerous. If it was possible, his life just got much more complicated.

10 Downing Street
London
April 10, 1944

Hugh Wylie had called and told Jack the Prime Minister wanted an update on "your current project". Wylie wasn't cleared to know the subject, Meteor was so highly classified. Hugh asked Jack to be at the office by 1330 for a 1400 meeting. Jack made sure to let his superiors know about Churchill's small circumvention of the chain of command.

It was good to see Wylie again. They'd enjoyed their time together last summer and chatted for a few minutes until the PM was ready for Jack.

"Jack, my boy, good to see you again. Hope the ribs healed all right?" Churchill was smiling and clearly in a good mood.

"Yes, sir. Thank you for asking. I'm back to normal." Jack immediately felt comfortable, much like last year.

"How is your young lady doing? Well, I hope."

"She is doing very well, sir. In fact they might start her back on active service in a month or two."

"Outstanding. I'm very glad to hear that. Please tell her I send my best wishes."

"I will, sir. Thank you."

"Jack, this mission to retrieve Bishop is important for a number of reasons. We believe there may be an anti-Hitler faction forming within the government or the military. We have no way of knowing the extent or purpose of this movement. It's our hope that Bishop will give us some insight into the real attitude within the senior leadership. Certainly we'll do whatever is required to vanquish the Nazis. But if there's a chance to do it with less loss of life, all the better. It's important we do everything we can to bring him out of Germany." The PM shifted in his chair and went on. "As I understand it your team is on the ground in East Prussia and selecting a landing site for the Mosquitoes."

Jack nodded. "Yes, sir. They've been on the ground for two weeks. They've located a primary and secondary landing site for the aircraft."

"How do you extract one German officer from out of the midst of Hitler's entourage?"

"Our intention is to let him extract himself. We'll provide guidance for a rendezvous with our men at a specified location."

Churchill leaned forward. "Then into the Mosquitoes and back to England."

"Yes, sir. We'll have two Mosquitoes on the ground. Bishop will get in one and the flight of two will return to England. The rendezvous and flight are planned for dark to complicate any efforts by the Luftwaffe to locate us on the return flight."

"And, you'll be going on this mission?"

"Yes, sir. I'll be navigating for the lead pilot. Also I'll be on scene in case we need to make any changes to the plan."

The Prime Minister was uncharacteristically quiet. "It gets more and more difficult to send young men in harm's way, Jack. You've performed what can only be described as exceptional service to England and now you are going to the very heart of that evil empire."

"Sir, when I first started down this road an old infantry colonel told me all we could hope for was to do our jobs and hope it made a difference. I guess that's what this is all about. This can make a difference."

"Well said, Commander. Good luck to you."

Near Rastenburg
East Prussia
April 12, 1944

The team had selected a primary landing field for Meteor. Located in a valley running north and south there were no farms or houses within 3 miles of the field. The ground was relatively clear and there was a safe landing and takeoff area of almost 5000 feet. They had seen a fair amount of military activity but the vehicles and troops stayed on the main roads.

On one of their first scouting trips they'd found a large wooden bridge which spanned a small river and mud flat. It was on the main road from the airport at Rastenburg to the headquarters area. Just north of the bridge, a dirt road ran west toward their valley. It was almost seven miles from the bridge to the closest point from the dirt road to the valley. From the dirt road it was another two miles following a winding path up and over a ridge and through a wooded area to the landing area. If London was able to direct their passenger to the dirt road, they'd be able to affect a rendezvous. Not once since they'd been in the area had they seen a vehicle on that road after dark. If they were waiting for the passenger at a certain distance from the main road it should be easy to meet him.

In the event something was amiss in the primary valley they found a smaller open area as a backup. It was not as secluded but offered a reasonable landing surface. It took several days of short radio transmissions to convey all of their information to London and hope they were able to pass it to their passenger. Now it was a matter of waiting.

Terry lay on his back looking up at the tree branches overhead. He felt good about their progress on the mission but the team was getting tired. The constant stress of remaining undiscovered in hostile territory was wearing them down. The weather had been cold but thankfully there had been no snow since they arrived. The need to stay covert made their fires at night small and they always seemed to be chilled. It would be good to get back and sit in a hot shower. Their food would last for another week to ten days. Although sparsely populated, there were farms in the area and if necessary they could forage for food.

Jerzy proved to be a perfect fit for the team. He was quiet but friendly and very capable in the field. On either two or four man patrols Terry felt confident they could handle any unforeseen events.

The sun was just starting to come up when Terry heard someone approaching their campsite. He sat up expecting it would be Jimmy Hunt who had the last night watch.

"Wake up," Hunt whispered harshly as he shook each sleeping bag.

"I'm awake, Jimmy. What's up?" Terry replied.

The other two were also now awake. "There's a group of people moving across the valley toward us. There were six of them and they were carrying weapons."

"Germans?" Jerzy demanded.

"I don't think so. It looked like they were wearing civilian clothes. No helmets either."

"How soon before they could be here?" Terry asked.

"Maybe twenty minutes."

Jerzy took charge. "Put the camouflage over our gear. Get your weapons and let's move up to the top of the ridge." There was no time to pack up their gear but they'd cut pine boughs to provide quick cover in an emergency.

Ten minutes later the four commandos were on the top of the ridgeline looking down the wooded slope. Jimmy pointed out where he had seen the strangers.

Terry guessed these people were now several hundred yards below them working their way over the ridge on the way south.

Several minutes later they could see them through the trees. There were five men and a woman, all dressed in civilian work clothes. They were carrying bolt action rifles but nothing heavier. The team watched as the group stopped and started to make camp. Stacking their rifles together they began to gather wood and make a campfire. Listening carefully for a few minutes to the bits and pieces of conversation he could make out, Jerzy turned to Terry and said quietly, "Partisans."

Reich Chancellery
Berlin
April 15, 1944

There was something about SS Standartenfuhrer Heinz Schenke that scared Erich Von Wolner. He sensed Schenke suspected him and knew something. The last ten days had been hard on the staff. There were many interviews which took on the tone of interrogations. The Gestapo had conducted a total review of correspondence, visitor records, travel vouchers and telephone logs. Erich understood this effort was but one part of an investigation which the Gestapo had initiated across all major military commands and civilian ministries. It seemed to Erich that Schenke and his lap dog Scheller paid particular attention to his office as they went through records. Von Wolner felt very uneasy when Schenke ordered him to write down his schedule for the last month including all contacts. What did he suspect? Erich had never met his contact. They communicated through a drop system at the main Berlin Library. This complicated system allowed them to use a series of books in the reference section for passing coded messages. They'd used the system sparingly over the years to prevent compromise. Over the last month he used the drop three times but there had been no choice. The last message from London laid out the desired rendezvous point near the Wolf's Lair. He knew the bridge they mentioned although he'd never left the main road from the airport. All the British needed from him was a message with a primary and backup date. He must send that message before leaving Berlin. But with Schenke watching him, he was concerned it might look suspicious. Erich remembered the last session with the investigator. Schenke noted two visits to the library and questioned why a busy senior officer would not just send a subordinate to pick up or drop off a book. Erich wasn't sure his answer of "I enjoy libraries," had satisfied the man. Now he must make one more trip to the library. He was scheduled to fly to Rastenburg in six days. Somehow he had to get to his drop before then.

The opportunity came two days later in the afternoon. With the Fuhrer already in Rastenburg, Erich had more control of his schedule. He told his secretary he needed to run some errands before leaving Berlin. The coded message to London was already concealed in his library book at page 111. Once in the library he would transfer the slip to the next book on his list, Weintraub's "Communicable Diseases of the African Continent," at page 53.

Von Wolner took a street car south toward the main library on the Unter den Linden. He didn't notice he was being followed by two men in a black Porsche. Lost in thought, Erich got off at the closest stop to the library.

The car pulled over to the curb behind the stopped

streetcar. When Erich exited the streetcar both men got out of the car and walked toward the main steps of the library.

Erich climbed the marble steps leading up to large doors of the library. Knowing the library well, he turned right and went up to the second floor where the reference books were housed.

The two men followed through the main doors. Both looked around quickly but didn't see Erich. One man went into the main lobby and reading area while the second went up the stairs.

Unaware he was being followed, Erich turned down the stack where the Weintraub book was located. Looking around he pulled the book down. Quickly he transferred the slip of paper from his book to the large reference book and replaced it on the shelf. Finished with the transfer he moved down the stack and turned into the main corridor.

The Gestapo agent was looking but didn't see Erich turn right and move down the other staircase to the first floor.

Erich reached the bottom floor and stepped into the non-fiction stack. He wanted a moment to compose himself.

"Herr Commander, may I have a word with you?"

Erich turned to see a man in civilian clothes coming down the aisle. He heart started to pound in his chest. The man walked up to him holding up an identity card.

"Gestapo. May I ask you what you're doing here?"

Trying to maintain a calm expression, he said, "I'm returning a book."

The man looked down at the book in Erich's hand. "May I see it?"

Erich handed it to him without saying anything.

"Crime and Punishment, by Dostoevsky. Never read it." He was flipping through the book. "Why are you back here in the non-fiction section?"

"I like to browse. To see what's available."

"I see." He handed Erich the book back as his partner came down the aisle. "Thank you, Commander." The two walked off.

He was starting to sweat. For a moment he felt he might be sick. Erich knew Schenke suspected him and time was running out.

Biggin Hill
Operations Ramp

Over the last ten days Jack had logged over thirty flight hours in the Mosquito. It felt good to be in the air again even if he wasn't handling the controls. From the first flight with Whitney Jack felt comfortable in the cockpit. It was strange to be sitting side by side. He was used to tandem seating in trainers or flying solo in fighters. There was a unique coordination which the pilot and navigator developed as they spent more and more flight time together. Jack was impressed with Whitney's ability as an aviator. He and the Mossie seemed to be part of each other.

The original Mosquito design had been converted into many different variants: fighter, photo reconnaissance, bomber, and night fighter. The Navy even developed a folding wing Mossie for use in the Fleet Air Arm. The aircraft from 85 Squadron were the Mk. XII variant. Equipped with four 20mm cannon and airborne radar, they were long range capable and well suited for the Meteor mission.

Jack spent hours learning to work the radar for basic air to air intercepts and ground navigation. The rest of the pilots continued their work on their rough field landings, night formation flying and studying the navigation plan. Flight Lieutenant Stirling Hadley was scheduled to be Whitney's primary wingman. He would be flying solo to allow a seat for Bishop in his aircraft. Jack liked the young Londoner. "Stirls" was always ready with a wisecrack and a smile. Jack learned from Whitney the young pilot had been awarded the DFC for shooting down three German bombers on one mission over

Southern England. By all measures they were ready to go. All that remained was getting a message from Bishop with a date.

CHAPTER NINETEEN

Near Rastenburg
East Prussia
April 15, 1944

Terry turned to Jerzy and said in a whisper, "How can you tell they're partisans?"

"The pieces of conversation I can hear are Polish. They're wearing civilian clothes, carrying weapons and are out here in the forest. They must be some of the partisans who moved north from Warsaw after the city fell. Let me borrow your glasses. I'm going to slip closer and see what I can find out. Cover me."

Rolling over, Terry removed the strap of his binoculars from around his neck and handed them to Jerzy. "Be careful."

Jerzy slowly moved to the top of the ridge. Crouching low and using the brush as cover he worked his way down the slope to a point fifty yards from the small campfire. Jerzy could hear snatches of conversation talking about tomorrow and something about a farm. It was getting lighter and he was able to use the glasses to get a better look at the people. Three of the men seemed to be in their 30's and looked very rugged. He couldn't see the other two, who apparently were now lying down. The woman was fixing some food, her back turned to Jerzy as she worked over the small fire.

There were many things to consider with this new development. Should they remain out of sight and hope this group went on their way tonight? What were the loyalties of the group? He knew there were a few Polish separatists that had thrown in with the Germans. Perhaps this group was out hunting loyal partisans. But if they could ally themselves with a local group they might be able to add to their intelligence data of the area. There was also the issue of food. They didn't know when the call would come for Meteor. Their food was only going to last for another week. And additional manpower was always a plus in the event of unforeseen problems. It made sense to talk with Terry about approaching the group.

He took one last look at the camp before heading back up the slope. Two of the men moved to the fire. The woman picked up a coffee pot and turned to pour into the men's cups. Jerzy stared hard at the group of three around the fire moving to each man and then to the woman. He focused the lens on her and looked again. His eyes were playing tricks on him. He closed his eyes for a moment and then looked again through the glasses. It was Mariska.

Ten minutes later he was back on top of the ridge kneeling next to Terry. "I know one of them."

"What?" Terry asked quizzically.

"It's been five years. But it's her."

"Her! Are you sure?" Terry asked.

"We were engaged to be married when the Germans invaded. I escaped and haven't been able to locate or get word about her since." Jerzy knelt with his head down staring at the ground. "I've thought about the advantages of linking up with a local group. But I was always concerned about knowing whose side they were on."

Terry linked the thought. "This solves the problem, right?"

"I don't think there's any question. Mariska is Jewish."

They called Jimmy and Curtis in from the flanks and explained the plan. Jerzy handed his Sten to Terry and took a deep breath. "All right, here I go."

Jerzy stood totally upright as he slowly made his way down the slope. He was wearing the British Army battle dress which the rest of the team wore. His hands were up indicating his non-threatening intentions. As he got to about 75 yards he called out in Polish, "Hello in the camp. I'd like to talk with you." The group quickly grabbed their weapons and formed a defensive arc. "I'm alone. Can I approach?" He saw Mariska lower her weapon and take several steps toward him.

One of the men called out, "Come in slowly."

He continued to hold his hands up and worked his way down the slope. The group spread out, keeping him covered with their weapons. Mariska started to move toward him and he saw one man grab her arm trying to pull her back. She broke away and ran up the slope stopping five yards in front of Jerzy. He slowly lowered his hands as he saw the tears running down her cheeks.

"It is you," she cried and ran into his arms. They held each other tightly for a moment then kissed.

The men lowered their weapons and cautiously approached the two. She looked at him with wonder. "How can this be? How can you be here?"

"It's a long story. We need time to catch up. Who are your friends?"

She turned to see the men walking up the slope. "A group that's been together, off and on, for several years. They're good men and hate the Germans as much as I do."

After several minutes of introductions, the group was all smiles. For years they'd heard of Mariska's fiancé. For him to show up in the forest was beyond good fortune.

Jerzy was very circumspect on the mission only saying they were conducting reconnaissance for the allies. He told them about the rest of his team and motioned for Terry to come down the ridge. It was going to take time on both sides for the groups to get to know each other.

Templehoff Airport
Berlin
April 18, 1944

Erich had been manifested on a priority Luftwaffe transport mission from Berlin to the airfield at Rastenburg, scheduled to take off at 1100 hours. Over the last several days he tried to maintain his normal routine and act as if he would be returning to Berlin, but now he was ready to leave the city, perhaps forever.

It was hard to consider the future with the Gestapo investigation so close to him. But he couldn't ignore what might lay in store for him. Flight from Germany would leave him with no worldly assets, alone in a strange country and considered by many a traitor to his country. But he knew it was the only course he could take. When it was time to board the Ju-88 transport he walked across the parking ramp wondering where his journey would end.

He entered the cabin and moved down the aisle, his pulse quickening when he saw Schenke and Scheller sitting in the final row of seats. He nodded at them and sat down.

Erich had given London a primary date of April 28 for the escape, with 30 April as the backup. An earlier date would've been more desirable in view of Schenke's suspicion, but he couldn't trust the message to make it to London in time. The reply provided key information, which finally brought home the reality of escape.

The trip to Rastenburg would take a little over three hours. He could only sit back and read knowing it would be difficult to keep his mind on his book. Shortly the engines were started and the aircraft was taxiing out for takeoff. There were only six passengers on this flight, all headed for the Fuhrer's headquarters. Everyone seemed anxious to get on their way. The daytime air raids by the Americans had been increasing and this was not a good place to be during a raid.

The flight had been airborne for an hour when Schenke moved forward and sat in the seat next to Von Wolner. As always the agent seemed to be suspicious and secretive.

"Your staff was cooperative during our investigation." Schenke smiled slightly. "Your records contain a great deal of very interesting material."

Erich wondered what he meant. "I'm glad we were able to be of assistance. My people are very meticulous with all records."

"So we found. There were records of phone calls which were very helpful. We uncovered interesting patterns of communication within the Chancellery."

Erich tried to sound uninterested. "Did you?"

"It was unusual to see communications from subordinate military commands which seemed to bypass their immediate commanders. Those communications came directly into your secretariat."

Hiding his anger Erich said, "When information needs to get to the Fuhrer or he has a specific order, we often will circumvent the chain of command. It is more efficient for the Fuhrer."

Schenke turned his head with a smirk on his face. "Can't that be dangerous?"

"I suppose it could be in the right circumstances. But efficient communication for the secretariat outweighs the need for everyone to be aware of what the Fuhrer is doing."

"I see. Of course all I can do is present Himmler my best assessment of the situation. Have a pleasant flight." He got up and moved back.

Erich felt a wave of panic. He hoped he could last until the 28th. It wasn't unheard of for senior officers to be detained for questioning and then returned to duty. He could only hope this wasn't Schenke's plan for him when they got to Rastenburg.

The remainder of the flight turned out to be uneventful and the transport was met by two sedans for the trip to the Wolf's Lair, a twenty-five minute drive. Erich would normally have been reading correspondence on this drive, but today he was focused on the road, looking for the bridge that would be his navigational checkpoint. Ten minutes after leaving the field he saw the wooden bridge. Just prior to the bridge was the dirt road leading off to the west. His escape plan now began to seem real.

He must figure out how to leave the compound on the 28th by himself. Normally staff cars had an SS escort vehicle or several SS guards in the staff car. This was in response to the sporadic reports of local resistance activity. Erich was deep in thought as they slowed to a stop at the first ring of security checks. Glancing out the window he saw the large concrete bunker, a wooden guard shack and a dozen SS troops manning the security gate.

The car was quickly cleared through, arriving at the inner checkpoint 500 meters down the road. Similar to the outer checkpoint this one was also manned by several Gestapo agents in addition to the SS guards.

After clearing the last checkpoint the sedan pulled up to the admin building where Von Wolner's office and staff were located. Erich had never looked at the checkpoints as obstacles to overcome and was now discouraged.

64 Baker Street
London
April 21, 1944

Yeoman Fogerty stood at the door to Jack's office. "Commander, a message from the Brigadier. He would like to see you in his office, straight away."

"Thank you. Please tell him I'm on my way." Jack grabbed his coat and pulled it on as he strode out the door. He wondered if this would finally be the word on Meteor. The waiting had been difficult. He knew every day on the ground for Jerzy and the team was hard. But the extra time had allowed him to log another twenty hours with Jack Whitney in the Mossie. Some day he'd love to get in the left seat and see what he could do with her.

"Jack, come in and close the door." Greene was at his desk and Tommy was sitting on the couch.

Jack closed the door and asked, "Is this what I'm hoping it is?"

"It's on for the 28th. We'll have the 30th as a back-up if needed. Is there anything we're short on at this point? Or are we ready to go?" Greene looked at Tommy and Jack.

Tommy said, "I do want to get a long range weather forecast to see if there are any problems developing. If not, then I say we alert the ground team so they can make final plans.

"I think that's all we need right now. The Mosquito crews are ready to go. The last status report from Whitney listed all the aircraft as fully serviceable." Jack couldn't think of anything else.

"Then I'd say we're on track. Tommy, let us know what you find out from the metro chaps. Jack, I just found out an acquaintance of yours is coming into town to meet with the boss, a Brigadier General Miller, the operations director for Bill Donovan."

Jack was pleased to hear Bill Miller had been promoted to brigadier. "Any idea when he'll be here, sir?"

Looking at a typed page on his desk Greene said, "This memo from upstairs says he'll be meeting with General Gubbins the day after tomorrow. If you call Gubbins' secretary I know they'll be able to get word to his escort. I suspect you'd like to see him."

The meeting with Bill Miller was not at all what Jack expected. It started well enough with mutual congratulations on promotions. They shared their thoughts on the general situation in Europe but Jack sensed Miller wanted to talk about something more.

"Jack, we're rapidly gearing up for the final push into Europe and the follow on effort in the Pacific. The OSS has grown in size and complexity. We need more and more experienced people. We just don't have enough. Plus there are major geopolitical issues which are starting to become clear as the war winds down. We may be starting to look at the end of the shooting war, but that's just the beginning."

Jack wasn't sure where this was going. "I'm not sure I totally understand."

Miller sat forward in his chair. "The world after this war concludes is going to be an entirely different place from the world in 1939. The victors who've been united to defeat the Axis will all start to pursue their own national agendas. We need intelligence specialists who can to make sure the United State's interests are covered."

"Why do I sense this involves me personally," Jack said.

"Jack, we've maintained a strictly hands off policy when it came to you and MI-6. It was clear to General Donovan your work here was making you a skilled operative. The kind of operative we'll need in Europe as this war concludes. God knows what's going to happen as this continent transitions to peace." Miller sat back, letting his message sink in.

"I'm involved in something at the moment. You just turned my world upside down and I have to do some thinking. But I can't do anything right now." Jack was being honest. Bill Miller deserved nothing less.

"Fair enough, Jack. I'm here for the next three weeks. We're getting very busy with the invasion as I'm sure you are. Think about what I said. There's going to be a new world out there. You can be part of shaping it. Give me a call when you can discuss it some more."

Near Rastenburg
East Prussia

The last week had been a gift to Jerzy in many ways. The group's knowledge of the local area allowed him to make a better plan for the extraction. Their diet had improved considerably with the fresh food from the partisans. Despite the language barrier the desire by both sides to cooperate made for a positive atmosphere. And it appeared both sides were enjoying the reunion of the two lovers.

The partisans were from both the area north of Warsaw and the lakes district. Stefan, a former army sergeant, was the leader. He fled north from Warsaw after the surrender and had slowly gathered comrades. The group connected with Mariska who'd been in hiding in the town of Steihmen with friends. Realizing she was putting that family in danger she made the decision to join the group. She had been with them ever since. Although not as coordinated as the French underground, their organization was growing as the tide of the war turned against the Germans. Stefan's group had primarily been working northwest of Rastenburg attacking communications and transportation lines.

Jerzy and Terry felt these men could provide real help on the night of the mission.

There'd been no change in German activities. Troops were evident on the main road from the airfield. Only occasionally did they leave the road and never at night. When the message came in confirming April 28th as the primary date, Jerzy finally asked Stefan for assistance. He explained they needed to have additional men posted around the area to help with a rendezvous. Stefan readily agreed. Jerzy felt the group was excited to be doing something with commandos from England. The partisans assumed the British were commandos. Jerzy and Terry agreed they didn't need to know the team was from British Intelligence.

It was difficult to decide how the partisans would react to a German officer, even one who was on the Allies' side. Jerzy told Stefan they needed to get a man away from the area who was sympathetic to the allied cause. The explanation seemed to satisfy Stefan and his men.

Jerzy decided to not mention the aircraft mission. That would wait until the night of the 28th. He had not been totally forthcoming with Mariska either. They didn't want the mission compromised in the event any of them were captured.

Spending time with her had given Jerzy a new lease on life. He'd forgotten how he loved to sit and talk with her. They were able to spend time off by themselves trying to make sense of the last five years. After their initial kiss they both had become strangely shy about physical contact. There was a re-kindled love between the two but neither was ready for intimacy after so long. But while time built up shyness between the two there was no doubting their desire to renew their love. The two cherished their time together. Late one afternoon they sat alone near the top of a ridge.

"What of your family?" Jerzy asked.

Mariska's eyes clouded over. "In early February I was able to get a message to them in the ghetto. But we continue to hear how the Germans are emptying the ghetto and sending families east. I've heard nothing since then. And your family?"

"No messages since late '40. I tried to get letters through the Swedish embassy but they were all returned."

"What happened to the world we knew? Our families, our friends, our country – it'll never be the same."

"I wish I could tell you it would. But we'd be fooling ourselves. All we can do is take each day and do our best to make a life for ourselves." He put his arm around her.

"What happens now? The war is coming here. The Russians are advancing, we know it. How do we survive in a world that's going to come apart? How can I let you go again, knowing we might never see each other? It's not fair....... it's not fair." She buried her head in his chest.

He held her close and kissed her hair. "I know."

To prepare for the rendezvous, the team began its rehearsals. The directions which had been sent to London instructed Von Wolner to drive eight kilometers and look for a white flag on the side of the road. At that point he should stop the car and await instructions.

Jerzy and Stefan assigned their men to several key vantage points around the road. They would be able to see the approaching car and also monitor the surrounding area. Once the car was stopped Terry would approach and exchange passwords. The teams would close in and escort the passenger back to the area where the Mosquitoes would be waiting. It should take about twenty minutes to transit from the rendezvous point to the aircraft. If all went well the planes should have landed right at sunset. They simply had to put the passenger on the aircraft and get them on their way.

The combined group conducted several practice runs with each team member in their assigned places. Jerzy and Stefan visited each spot and went over contingencies with the men at that location. These practice sessions allowed the two leaders to get a feel for the fields of vision each group would have. With their commando credentials Jimmy and Curtis were put in the most critical position in the trees where the car would stop. They had a view of the entire section of the road and could also cover the first part of the route to the landing area. Dobry and Ludwik would be stationed several hundred yards down the road in the direction of Rastenburg. Their position wasn't elevated but there was very good concealment in a group of trees. Patryk and Milos were stationed on a rocky ridge overlooking the road from the side opposite the commando's position. Jerzy, Stefan and Terry would be together in the tree line on the south side of the road. Mariska would remain behind at the landing field to watch the surrounding area for any unwanted guests. On the morning of the operation they'd reposition the radios to a spot overlooking the landing area. They were ready.

The Wolf's Lair
Rastenburg, East Prussia
April 27, 1944

Von Wolner was doing his best to maintain a normal schedule. He was still worried by the actions of Schenke and his assistant Scheller. Each day they would ask for the message traffic logs to see both the incoming and outgoing messages from the headquarters. Their questions were directed at Erich in an accusatory tone demanding the rationale behind each message. Perhaps they thought there was a conspiracy throughout the armed forces and they could find a pattern in these messages. Erich was thankful they seemed to be spreading their attention around to the different directorates within the headquarters. He was still trying to find a valid reason to be out of the restricted area tomorrow evening. There wasn't any place to go in the immediate area. There was a small lake some of the staff would visit during the summer but it was too cool at this time of year.

His answer came when headquarters received word Admiral Doenitz was arriving the next day to confer with the Fuhrer. The Admiral was scheduled to arrive at the airfield in the evening around 2100. It didn't raise any attention when Von Wolner assigned himself as the welcoming officer. That duty was normally rotated among the staff officers when very senior officers arrived in Rastenburg either at the airfield or by train. Von Wolner let the protocol section know he would be heading out to the airfield early to make sure all preparations were complete. They could send the large Mercedes VIP sedan to arrive at 2000. He had a plan.

CHAPTER TWENTY

Operations Briefing Room
RAF Biggin Hill
April 28, 1944
1100 Hours

Squadron Leader Jack Whitney stood in front of the briefing room facing the mission crews assigned to the mission. Several of the men were smoking cigarettes and there were steaming cups of tea in front of some of the flyers. Whitney went through the basic information: aircraft assigned, fuel loads, call signs, radio frequencies, the litany all combat aviators recite before each mission. Following the basic briefing he called up the air intelligence officer who ran over expected enemy forces they might encounter during their mission.

The biggest threat was the Luftwaffe fighter force, which was heavily concentrated in central Germany. This afternoon the American Eighth Air Force would be conducting a series of raids on targets from Bremen to Hamburg. Whitney hoped the day fighters would be reacting to those raids and not paying attention to a small flight of low-flying Mosquitoes.

During the return trip a maximum effort strike was being conducted against Berlin by Bomber Command. Again the intent was for the major raid to overshadow any interest in what was most likely an unarmed reconnaissance flight It was assumed there was some amount of German anti-aircraft defence around the actual restricted area but if the approach and departure were north of the Wolf's Lair the threat should be negligible.

"I love it when the ground pounders say a threat is negligible. They're not going to get shot at by that negligible threat," groused Flight Lieutenant Glenn Farley who was going to be in the number three aircraft.

The RAF meteorological officer estimated about forty percent illumination from the moon and scattered to broken cloud layers beginning at 2000 feet and extending up to 12 thousand. Low altitude winds should be out of the west at 10-15 knots. Not a bad prediction for northern Europe in early spring.

Whitney resumed his briefing. "Make sure your fuel tanks are fully topped off. I want you to visually check the drop tanks and the bomb bay tank to make sure they're full. Hold starting engines until you see me start to crank. I don't want to burn extra petrol on deck." He paused looking at the group for any questions.

"This will be a maximum range trip. Pay attention to fuel transfer. If you have any problems getting the fuel out of the auxiliary tanks it will be an abort. I want you each to figure your minimum return to base fuel and if you hit that amount turn the aircraft for home. The upper level winds are strong out of the west so you'll be better off to stay on the deck. And run your engines at the max range setting assuming you have that choice. There aren't a lot of options if you get in a pinch. Sweden, if you can. If you have to ditch make sure you get a radio call out before hand. Any questions?"

The room remained silent, each crewman silently thinking over the problems and options a mission like this presented.

"Once we clear England I want the second section to take a slightly stepped up trail about a mile behind us. Your job is to make sure we aren't jumped. If we are, I want three and four to keep Jerry busy while the lead section disengages. Clear?"

There were mumbled acknowledgements along with

nods from several heads.

"Assuming we don't have any problems en route, as we cross the coast into the target area I want the second section to detach. You'll hold in the area for thirty minutes, or until you hit your return fuel limit. Your purpose will be to provide support if we get into a problem on the ground. We'll transmit 'Able' three times when we're safely on deck. If there's a problem we'll transmit 'Zebra'. If you hear 'Zebra' close the target area and be ready for anything. On your way home I want you to climb to 6000 feet and follow the coast line unless intercepted. You'll be the decoys as we stay low and remain over the water."

The number two pilot Stirling Hadley asked, "We'll be using our squadron tactical frequency for all radio comms?"

"Correct. I want everyone to monitor air distress but let's keep everything on our tactical."

Over the next twenty minutes they ironed out several last minute questions and made sure everyone was comfortable with the entire flight plan.

Whitney wrapped up the brief. "Gentlemen, let's man up and be ready to start engines at 1340."

Jack sat at the desk gathering up the cards, notes and charts he would take with him on the mission. It seemed like he'd put a foot back into his previous life, briefing for a mission. Of course he was wearing dark blue RAF coveralls and had a Walther PPK in his shoulder holster. Not quite like a hot and humid ready room on the Yorktown. It was strange to Jack how the war had come full circle for him. This was going to be a tough mission by any estimate. A long range profile, significant fighter forces along most of the route and a landing on an unprepared surface in a hostile country at night. This was one of those times where you tried not to dwell on all of the possible problems. You could only take each part of the mission in order and do your best. With the thought of worrying about only what you could control he headed for the loo. It was going to be a long flight.

Near Rastenburg
East Prussia
April 28, 1944
1400

Terry was pleased as the day unfolded. The low clouds which were present at sunrise continued to break up and there was an occasional patch of blue sky. The two teams spent the late morning moving from their main campsite to the landing area.

Jimmy Hunt broke down one radio and transported it to a spot overlooking the valley.

Jerzy and Terry positioned the signal fires which would be ignited at 1800 to outline the landing area. They also walked the area one more time making sure there were no obstacles or obstructions for the landing. Initially there'd been logs, large bushes and several depressions. Over the last month the team had cleaned up the area and there should be no problems with the landing surface.

After talking with Stefan, Jerzy decided to leave the area in company with the partisans after the aircraft departed. There was a very dense forested area to the northwest where they'd be able to go to ground awaiting extraction. One question they couldn't answer was how the Germans in the local area would react to something like this? The forests remained a refuge for the partisans. The lack of a decent road system kept the Germans away from large areas of land. He hoped the situation wouldn't change.

"Hard to believe there will be RAF bombers sitting there in four hours." Jerzy walked up and was standing next to Terry who was looking out over the field.

"I have a feeling this is going to be one of those events you'll remember for a long time. Is there anything else to do?"

"Stefan sent Patrick and Milos over to the next ridgeline to make sure things were quiet. Other than monitoring the radio and getting in position, I think we're set."

"How's Mariska doing?"

"Having a lot of trouble thinking about me leaving when it's over." Jerzy sounded depressed himself.

"Then why don't you stay here?"

"How can I do that?"

"Talk to Jack when he gets here and come up with a reason for SOE to have someone on the ground in Poland."

Jerzy didn't reply to Terry. He looked lost in thought.

Bandsaw Flight
Over Southeast England
1415

Jack's oxygen mask hung loosely from one of the attachments on his flying helmet. So far the flight had gone as briefed, taking off at 1400 hours from Biggin Hill. Looking over his right shoulder he could see Hadley, flying a loose cruise formation. If he adjusted the mirrors on the canopy rail he could see number three and four in trail about a mile behind. They were currently at 2000 feet, the Kent country side slipping by underneath them. They would descend to 1000 feet when they crossed the coast and out over the North Sea. He and Whitney were quietly monitoring the aircraft systems and their navigation track. It was important they cross over their navigation checkpoint at Ramsgate. They would be over water for the majority of the flight using one nav update on an island off the Dutch coast, Vlieland. Their next landfall would be Amrum, a small island off the Danish Peninsula. The total distance over the North Sea was almost 400 miles and they couldn't afford to miss their check points.

Whitney rotated a selector switch. "We've got good fuel transfer."

"Rog."

"Think your boys on the ground will remember the

ground priming procedure after six weeks?" In order for the Mosquito to be started a ground crewman must manually prime the engine during start until the engine driven fuel pump picked up the fuel flow. All four of the Meteor team had been given a lesson at Biggin Hill in order to start the aircraft after the passenger pickup.

"They bloody well better remember. I wish we didn't have to shut down. You know how bad things tend to happen on starts."

"Whatever it takes, Jack, we'll get them started and airborne. I have no desire to spend anymore time than needed in Prussia."

They hit their first checkpoint off Holland four minutes ahead of schedule. The winds must be stronger than forecast, Jack thought. He did several computations and adjusted the preplanned course to the next point to compensate for wind drift. So far there had been no radio transmissions from their wingmen. They assumed all was well with their aircraft systems.

Flying at 1000 feet they hadn't received any indication the German radar sites had seen them. The black box which gave off an audible tone if illuminated by radar remained silent.

While they were peacefully transiting the North Sea, 100 miles south of them a desperate battle was being fought in the air. B-17s from the U.S. Eighth Air Force were engaged with German fighter forces over Hamburg. The German air defence network was throwing almost three hundred day fighters, mostly Me-109s and Fw-190s, at the bombers. By the end of the day twenty six of the big planes would be shot down over Germany with the loss of 10 men killed or captured per aircraft. But the Germans did not see the flight of four Mosquitoes.

The Wolf's Lair

Rastenburg
East Prussia
1600

Commander Erich Von Wolner stopped by the protocol section to get the briefing sheet from Major Wiescheller. Having picked up the briefing packet, Erich was walking back to his office in the main admin building when he saw Schenke standing by the main entrance. It would look odd to change direction at this point so he kept walking toward the door. He walked up the steps and nodded an acknowledgement to Schenke.

"Standartenfuhrer."

"Commander, can I have word with you?" Schenke sounded like a policeman who had nothing better to do than harass people.

"Certainly. What may I do for you?"

"I noted you were going to be meeting Admiral Doenitz tonight at the airfield."

"That's correct. We rotate greeting duty among the senior staff officers. I'm going to take care of the Admiral tonight."

"Isn't it strange for a senior Admiral to be arriving at the Fuhrer's headquarters so late at night?"

Erich was desperately trying to figure out where Schenke was going with this. "I don't think so. I'm sure the Admiral has a very pressing schedule. He's scheduled to meet with the Fuhrer tomorrow morning."

"How many people is he bringing with him?

What the hell is he getting at? Does he think there's some coup being planned by the Navy? "According to the advance message only his aide and several assistant chiefs of staff."

"I see. Perhaps I'll accompany you to meet the Admiral."

His heart almost stopped. "If you would like. Although it's very routine stuff."

"Humor me, Commander. I'll meet you at 1800 by the

motor pool." The Gestapo agent walked away and down the stairs.

Erich stood watching the man step purposely across the courtyard.

Mariska and Jerzy sat on a log overlooking the wide valley. They could make out the four piles of wood located at each corner of the landing area. Dried wood and kerosene soaked rags would make a quick signal for the British aircraft. Preparations for tonight had dominated their activities for the past two weeks. But now there was a moment to think about what the future might bring.

"As soon as we get the aircraft out of here we need to push north." Jerzy didn't look at Mariska.

She slipped her arm through his and also looked straight ahead. "How long after they depart will you be picked up?"

"We'll wait to see what kind of reaction there is by the Germans. Once any activity dies down we'll try an extraction." He knew Jack wanted the team out within a week.

"Will you come back here to get picked up?"

"It depends on the Germans. We've got our radios and can adjust the location of the pickup with London."

"London. Oh God, how I miss the cities. I think when this is over I may never enter the forest again. But I'm afraid of what we'll find when we go home." She leaned her head on his shoulder.

"I know."

Bandsaw Flight
Over the Baltic
1715

After hitting their nav point at Amrum, Bandsaw flight crossed the Danish Peninsula south of Flensburg and headed into the Baltic. The weather was holding with the ceiling staying around 3000 feet over the water. No one had broken radio silence within the flight and they hadn't sighted any other aircraft. Whitney conducted a fuel check and they were slightly ahead of their planned amount. The tail wind allowed them to throttle back now but it would cost them fuel on the return trip. The radio came to life interrupting the fuel calculations.

"Lead, from three. Aircraft at your two o'clock high."

They both turned to try and pick up the target. It was a single aircraft traveling parallel to their course approximately 2000 feet above them and a mile and a half away. They could see two engine nacelles, much like a Mosquito. This one had a twin tail identifying it as a Me-110. The German must not have seen them. He continued flying straight and level. The 110 was one of the best German twin engine fighters and carried a lethal mix of machine guns and cannons. Flying alone off the coast it might not be on a combat mission. Perhaps it was a training or ferry flight. Whitney reduced his power and began dropping behind the German. He didn't want any rapid movements which might catch the attention of the enemy fighter. Suddenly the 110 turn rapidly to the right and dove for the water, apparently running south to get away from the Mosquitoes.

"He's seen us. Let him go." Jack Whitney didn't want to lose the guns of the second section chasing after a lone fighter that wasn't an immediate threat.

Jack keyed the ICS, "Let's hope it takes them a while to figure out where we are."

"Right. But I think the cat's out of the bag," Whitney replied.

The flight was currently ten miles off the coast. In twelve minutes they would turn into the Gulf of Danzig. They must find their coast in point. By hitting the coastal checkpoint they could verify their navigation plot. If on track they would be able to find their last checkpoints allowing them to locate the landing area. Jack checked the compass and confirmed Whitney was locked on the correct heading.

The Wolf's Lair
1720

Erich Von Wolner strode into the dispatchers office at the motor pool with the confidence of a man who has made an ultimate decision. Waiting for Schenke would destroy any chance he might have to make his escape. He'd leave early and hope he was able to get past both security checkpoints before anyone knew he was gone.

"Sergeant, I'm ready to leave for the airfield. Where's my driver?" Erich put an edge on his voice. His tone told the sergeant it was not a time to argue.

Getting up and coming to attention, the sergeant said, "Sir, we didn't think you were leaving until 1800." He looked concerned.

"There's been a change of plans. I need to leave immediately. Is that going to be a problem?" Erich's heart was pounding as he continued his bluff.

"No, sir. I'll have the duty driver take your vehicle and your driver will take over as the duty driver, no problem....Corporal Weiss." He turned to address a tall gangly corporal who was reading a magazine. "Get your cover. You'll be taking the commander to the airfield."

"Yes, sergeant."

Five minutes later Von Wolner was sitting in the back seat of a Mercedes sedan as Corporal Weiss started the engine. Everything seemed to be going in slow motion. *Come on.* If he was sitting here and Schenke showed up it would be all over. *Thank God.*

The driver put the sedan into gear and they began to move down the road toward the first security point. Because he was scheduled to depart, there should be no problem at the check points. The key was to get by the second point before Schenke showed up at the motor pool and found out Erich had already left.

At the first check point Von Wolner pretended to read a file he'd brought with him. The driver let the SS guards know his identity so they could check their schedule. Listening as closely as he could it sounded to him like it was business as usual. As the big sedan pulled ahead he sagged with relief. The inner checkpoint is staffed better, he thought, and that's where the Gestapo puts their people. The last check point should only be SS troops of the security battalion.

He checked his watch as Weiss slowed to a stop at the last barrier before the main road. It was 1745. Hoping desperately that Schenke was not early he continued reading his files.

"Herr Commander, may I see you identity card please?" A tall trooper was looking at him through the driver's open window.

"Just a minute." He tried to sound interrupted and put down his papers. Reaching into his inner breast pocket he pulled out his identity wallet. Handing it to the soldier he looked straight ahead trying to look bored.

The SS man leaned back into the driver's window, "Sir, we have you scheduled to travel to the airfield. Is that correct?"

Mother of God! "That's correct. I'm going to meet Admiral Doenitz." *Just let me go!*

"Thank you, sir," he said as he handed back the wallet and raised his hand in a stiff salute.

Erich looked straight ahead as they accelerated away from the check point. His knees were shaking.

The flight missed the inlet by less than a mile and quickly spotted the distinctive landmark east of their position. A quick course correction and they were back on track for the next checkpoint, a triangular shaped lake just north of the town of Piesen. After the lake they would follow a valley and river which should lead them to the landing area. All combat checks had been completed: external lights checked off, armament switches set, fuel checked, radios checked to correct frequencies. The sun was beginning to set and the shadows from the hills were growing longer.

Jack felt confident as the Mosquito banked gently to follow the pre-planned course. Checking the time on the instrument panel clock he noted it was 1750.

"What do you mean Commander Von Wolner has already left?" Schenke's eyes narrowed as he focused on the transportation dispatcher.

"Yes, sir. He left with our duty driver about thirty minutes ago. He said there'd been a change of plan." The sergeant was not comfortable around the Gestapo. "Is there something wrong, sir?"

"Get me a line to Security Checkpoint Four." Schenke came around the counter and stood at the sergeant's desk.

A moment later he confirmed that Von Wolner had passed. Quickly he dialed the last checkpoint and demanded to speak to the senior officer. After a terse conversation Schenke slammed the phone down.

"Get me a driver! Call Checkpoint Four and tell them I want two of my people to be ready to join me when I pass through, and I want them armed. NOW."

"There's the lake straight ahead." Whitney had seen it first.

Jack focused on the area in front of the next ridge. He saw the triangular shape. "Roger, outbound course is 126 degrees and 15 miles to the landing area. I'm gonna see if they're up."

Before Jack could transmit, Whitney keyed his radio switch. "Three and four detach. Good luck." A mile behind them, the two trailing Mosquitoes banked hard to the right and set up a holding pattern at 1000 feet.

Jack keyed the radio. "Viceroy, Viceroy, this is Bandsaw, over." He was using the pre-briefed call sign for the ground team.

Their radio came to life. He could tell it was Terry on the radio. "Bandsaw, this is Viceroy, read you five bye. Cleared to land, I say again, cleared to land."

It was good hearing Terry's voice.

Erich felt the car start to brake. Looking forward he saw a cluster of vehicles. A large truck had slid off the side of the road on the right and was stuck with its wheels in the ditch. A tank retriever had been pressed into service to pull the vehicle back on the roadway. There were troops standing around and several military police directing traffic. The road was impassable at this point. Erich felt panic rising up from within.

"Corporal, go see how long before we can get past this mess. I'm in a hurry." He hadn't planned for anything like this. He was stuck on the only road and Schenke might have discovered his departure by now.

"Tallyho." Whitney saw the valley. In the diminishing light they could make out two of the signal fires about two miles ahead. The winds appeared to be light judging by the lack of movement in the trees. Whitney slowed to 180 knots and was heading directly for the lights. Jack started to read down the landing checklist.

"Brake pressure?"

"200 psi"

"Superchargers?"

"Mod."

"Radiator flaps?"

"Open."

"Armament?"

"Switches safe"

Jack Whitney banked the Mossie left to a downwind leg, slowing to 150 knots. "Undercarriage, coming down." He moved the selector lever down. The bomber continued to slow to 130 knots. "Flaps coming full down, wheels are all down."

Turning on final, Jack could see they were below the ridge on their right. The open area between the fires looked small, like the deck of an aircraft carrier.

Rolling out on final Whitney pulled the power slowly back as they floated for just a moment then touched down.

The brakes began to slow the aircraft on the rough ground. As they slowed to taxi speed Whitney guided the aircraft to the edge of the marked area leaving Hadley as much room as possible.

"Son of a bitch, we made it," Jack said. Keying the mic he transmitted "Able.....Able" to numbers three and four.

Looking around from the cockpit Whitney replied, "That's one for the logbook. I'm going to shut down number two. Jump down and see what your folks have to say."

After securing his equipment Jack opened the hatch by his right foot and swung down to the ground. He looked to the right and saw Stirl's aircraft parked fifty feet away, his starboard engine shut down. Turning around he saw Terry approaching with a woman walking beside him. She must be with the partisan group they reported.

Terry extended his hand. "Welcome to Germany."

"Good to see you, Terry. What's the situation?"

"Jerzy's at the rendezvous site with the rest of the team and the partisans. By my watch we have time to make it there by 1850. Our boy's supposed to be there right after."

", I'm gonna shut 'em down. We need to get to the rendezvous point." Jack ran out in front of Whitney and made a slashing motion across his throat. He ran over to Stirls and repeated the signal. Both engines began winding down, running rough for a moment then stopping. The silence was eerie.

In a moment the two pilots were out of their aircraft. They joined Jack and Terry in front of the first Mosquito. There was still a little daytime illumination but it was fading fast.

"I want you to give the aircraft a good pre-flight. Be set up for starts in 45 minutes. Terry and I will head over to check on the pick up. You've got weapons with you so stay alert. We don't know who's friendly and who's not. This is one of the partisans, her name is Mariska. She'll be staying here with you. No English so you'll have to make do. Any questions?"

"Get going. The quicker you're back, the quicker we're on our way." Whitney was grinning. He turned to Hadley. "With the light winds we'll plan on taking off to the west. It'll save time on the departure."

Jack grabbed his Sten and followed Terry toward the dark woods.

Corporal Weiss ran back to the sedan and stuck his head in the window. "The military police said they can have the road clear in five minutes, Commander."

"Very well. Tell him we're ready to go as soon as they can clear a path." Von Wolner felt sweat forming on his face.

It was a little more than five minutes later when Weiss started the sedan. In response to a signal from the military policeman he began to slowly move the car forward. To make it past the accident they had to edge all of the way to the left of the roadway between the road edge and the side of the big tank retriever. Erich was thankful they were at last moving. Once past the bottleneck they'd be able to run at full speed.

Weiss switched the lights on as the last of the daylight faded. Quickly they were back up to speed and heading toward the bridge. In his relief to be moving again, Erich didn't see the new set of headlights pulling up to the accident site.

Jack and Terry moved quickly over the trail. They bantered back and forth as they walked, catching up on the small details of the last month. He almost stopped dead when Terry mentioned the girl was Jerzy's fiancée from before the war. *What a crazy war.* He pressed to keep up with Terry who was moving quickly up the tree covered ridge. In another ten minutes they'd moved up and over the ridgeline. The two men approached a tree line, which overlooked a small clearing. Out of nowhere Jerzy was standing next to him.

"Jack, it's good to see you. Welcome to my country."

They shook hands. "Hello, my friend."

"Let me introduce you to the leader of the partisans who are helping us – Stefan Zlotnik." He made a motion to Stefan who offered his hand to Jack.

"Hello."

"Yah." Stefan nodded and smiled.

"You can see the white flag on the pole by the road. That's our signal. We have our men spread around the clearing with good views of the surrounding area. Now we wait for our passenger."

Jerzy pointed out the spots where they had the teams of two waiting. Jack liked the location. There was enough open area to prevent being surprised while there was plenty of cover for their people. For the first time in several hours he felt himself relax a little. This operation was going as planned. The big question was whether or not Bishop made it out of the Wolf's Lair?

The military police Sergeant knew that he'd just encountered a very senior and very angry Gestapo officer. The Sergeant's attempt to be helpful and polite was met with a fury that scared him. Hurriedly the troops repositioned the tank retriever and the sedan tore through the small space next to the road.

"Do what you have to and catch that car," Schenke barked at the driver, and then sat back with two of his Gestapo agents. Next to the driver was an SS sergeant carrying a machine pistol.

As they came around a wide bend they could see the lights of Von Wolner's car flashing on the roadside trees. "There he is. Stay with him."

"Corporal, listen very carefully to what I'm saying." Erich had seen the headlights behind them and knew who it was. "I want you to get this car going as fast as the road will allow. Don't let that car catch us. Understand?"

"Sir, I have orders from the sergeant not to speed."

Von Wolner removed his PPK from the briefcase. "Corporal, do as I say or I'll kill you on the spot." He placed the barrel of the pistol against the back of Weiss's neck.

"Commander, I don't..."

"Shut up. There's a wooden bridge about a mile ahead. Fifty meters past the bridge there's a dirt road that turns off to the left. Slow down just enough to take that road. Then drive like your life depended on it. Because it does."

A minute later they crossed the bridge. Erich looked back at the car which was now half a mile behind. He turned to look for the dirt road. "There is it. Slow down and make that turn to the left."

Weiss cranked the wheel hard to the left as the sedan went into a four wheel slide. Careening onto the dirt road it threw a huge cloud of dust into the air. Fighting to keep the car under control Weiss over steered the turn. The sedan fishtailed back onto the dirt road barely missing several trees. The corporal jammed the accelerator to the floor.

Schenke looked across the bridge and saw a big cloud of dust. "Slow down. They've rolled the car off the side of the road. If he's not hurt he may try to escape into the woods."

Pulling up to the cloud of dust four of the men jumped out and ran to the side of the road. Two agents had drawn their pistols.

"I don't see the car."

"Look in the tree line. They may have rolled into the trees," Schenke replied.

"Herr Standartenfuhrer, there's a road running west into the forest."

Schenke thought for a moment and realized his mistake. "Bastard," he muttered to himself. "Back in the car," he yelled and began to run toward the Mercedes.

"We're looking for a white flag by the side of the road."

Erich still had the pistol near the corporal's neck as they raced down the road. Peering forward in the glare of the headlights he knew they must be getting close. It was fifteen minutes since they'd left the road. At this speed they should have covered eight kilometers. Suddenly he saw the flag. "Stop...Stop!"

Jerzy and Stefan saw the headlights bouncing on the road. Jack and Terry were near the white flag ready, to identify the passenger. This was almost going too well, Jerzy thought. He saw a second set of headlights about 100 meters behind the first car which had slid to a stop with dust flying. The second car stopped forty feet behind the first.

"Two cars means trouble." Stefan said.

Jack and Terry crouched in the tree line thirty feet from the first car. They were getting ready to move forward when they saw the headlights from the second car.

"Shit. Terry, cover the tree line and move toward the second car. I'll check this one."

The two split up, Terry moving to his right using the trees for cover. He immediately heard a shout in German from the second car. "Commander, you are under arrest. Come forward where we can see you in the headlights." He could see several men standing beside the second car. Looking back he saw Jack sprint forward into the glare of the headlights rushing directly at the first car.

As the car had slid to a stop, Erich yelled to Weiss, "Get out of here, run, run." The Corporal seemed frozen, unable to do anything.

Erich could see the lights of the second car. A feeling of panic began to overwhelm him. He knew he must do something. "Corporal, if you stay here you'll die. Now get out!"

Weiss opened his door and ran toward the trees, almost colliding with a stranger running toward the car. The German soldier continued straight ahead into the woods.

Terry saw the German soldier run past Jack and heard the Germans yell, "Stop, or we'll shoot." He cocked his Sten gun and fired a long burst at the two men standing beside the second car.

Jack jumped into the front seat, the Walther in his right hand. Seeing a man in the back seat he raised the pistol. Jack recognized the uniform was Kriegsmarine. "Von Wolner?"

"Yes, I'm Von Wolner."

"My name's Stewart. I'm here to get you out. Now let's get the hell out of this car and into the trees."

The rear door opened and Von Wolner ran toward the trees. Jack sprinted after him. He heard bullets whizzing by him as he ran. He saw the German stumble and fall, rolling another five feet toward the trees.

"Get up. RUN!" He yelled at Von Wolner who was lying face down on the ground. Jack knelt on the ground next to him, grabbed his coat and began pulling him toward the forest. Stumbling and staggering, they lunged the last few feet and took cover behind several trees.

Terry continued to fire at the car. He'd hit two of the men. They lay on the ground not moving. The car was still running and one headlight had been shot out. The remaining headlight illuminated the road. He needed to find Jack and get out of here.

Schenke and the SS sergeant had taken cover behind the sedan and were sitting on the ground, their backs against the car.

"Sergeant, what's your name?" He was breathing hard, the adrenaline from the gun fight making his heart pound.

"Mueller, Herr Standartenfuhrer."

SS Sergeant Mueller did not seem to be bothered by being in a shoot out in a forest at night. "Sergeant Mueller, do you have any combat experience?"

"Yes, sir. Eighteen months on the Eastern Front."

"Sergeant, I'm not sure what's going on here. It may be part of a plot against the Fuehrer. Commander Von Wolner knows something. We must capture him. He's trying to escape and there are locals who are helping him." Schenke's breathing had evened out now and it was quiet except for the idling Mercedes. "If we can't catch him then we'll kill him. Do you understand?"

"Yes, sir."

"Good. I want to work our way to where we saw them enter the trees. You take the lead."

Terry found Jack leaning over the German who was on his hands and knees.

"He's been hit in the back," Jack said. "I don't think it's too bad but he needs to catch his breath."

Terry was scanning around them. "I hit two of them. But there may be more of them in the car. The sooner we get moving the better."

"Commander, we need to move. Can you stand up?"

Obviously in pain the German slowly got to his feet. "I'm ready."

The three moved west through the trees.

Jack Whitney and Stirls Hadley heard gunfire coming from the east. The aircraft were ready to start, with access panels open for the engine priming pump, pre-flight checks complete and all switches ready. They looked at each other when the sound of firing ceased.

"This is a new one for me, Jack. I'm not sure what we should be doing.'

"Stirls, if I knew I'd happily tell you. But with this crew I'm just a taxi driver."

Mariska walked up to them after tending signal fires at the four corners of the landing area. She seemed nervous and concerned after hearing the sounds of the firing. Saying something in Polish, she pointed to the east.

Whitney shrugged, he had no idea what she'd said.

Schenke and Mueller were moving as quickly as they could while trying to make as little noise as possible. The underbrush wasn't thick and there was some illumination from the partial moon. They could hear voices coming from their left. They raised their weapons and waited quietly as the voices got louder. The two voices were speaking Polish and coming closer.

These must be the locals that were helping Von Wolner. "Partisans." Schenke whispered to Mueller.

"What do you want me to do?" Mueller asked quietly.

"We'll follow them."

The two partisans were moving quickly and didn't notice the Germans following them in the darkness.

In ten minutes Schenke and Mueller had crossed the road and were working their way up the slope.

Arriving back at the aircraft, Jack and Terry helped Erich remove his uniform shirt. The flesh was torn horizontally across his upper back, a bullet having glanced off his shoulder blade. Jack was thankful there wasn't much blood loss. They quickly treated the wound with sulfa powder and put on a tight bandage. The dressing would suffice for the flight to Britain.

Jerzy tried to make sense of the action at the road. No one was sure of the total number of people in the second car or what had happened to them. The German driver of Erich's had also disappeared into the forest. When Jimmy and Curtis had left their position the Mercedes was still running, apparently abandoned. Only Dobry and Ludwik weren't back yet but they had the farthest to travel.

"Let's get ready to start. I want to be out of here as quickly as we can." Jack turned to Jerzy. "I'm sure this area will be crawling with Krauts when the sun comes up and you'd better not be here."

"I'll go pack the radio." Jimmy headed up into the trees.

"All right, let's get the Commander into Stirls aircraft. Be ready to start in five minutes," Jack said.

"Here's our last two," Jerzy said. Dobry and Ludwik emerged from the trees walking in single file with their rifles slung over their shoulders.

Suddenly the night was torn apart by the sound of an automatic weapon.

Terry saw muzzle flashes. "I've got 'em. In that group of trees past the broken stump about 50 yards out." He was able to reach his Sten and fired a burst into the darkness. Jerzy translated Terry's position estimate to the Poles.

Jack saw where Terry was describing and yelled back to him, "Work your way around to the left and I'll do the same to the right."

Sporadic fire continued as they tried to outflank the Germans. "They'll probably try to move so be ready," Terry yelled.

Moving over downed logs and using the tall brush for cover Jack moved toward the flashes. Kneeling down he listened to see if he could hear any movement. There was a moment of quiet and then more firing. It appeared the Germans were still targeting the prone figures in the field.

Schenke was watching Mueller as the Sergeant calmly took aim and fired measured bursts from his machine pistol. He could see several figures on the ground, not moving. Realizing the size of the enemy force Schenke knew they could not overwhelm them. The parked aircraft told him this was a big operation. All he could hope to do was to kill as many as possible and then retreat for help.

"How's your ammunition?"

The Sergeant replied quietly, "Two clips of 15 rounds."

"We'll pull back and go for help. Save the rest of your ammunition. We may need it to get out of here."

Schenke began to move across the slope. Turning back to Mueller he said, "Let's go."

Hearing a sputtering sound Mueller reacted instinctively, throwing himself flat as a hand grenade exploded behind Schenke. The explosion knocked the agent off his feet. Mueller moved toward him but knew Schenke was dead before he reached the body. Using the tree trunks as cover he moved as fast as he could back up the slope. A burst of automatic fire chewed up the trees around him and he pitched forward. His body rolled several feet and came to rest against a large tree.

It took Jack and Terry ten minutes to check the area. Finding two bodies, they removed the identity papers and returned to the clearing.

"It's clear for now but everyone stay alert," Jack called out. "We need to get out of here so let's get busy."

"Jack, we've got a problem," Jack Whitney said. "It's Stirls."

Stewart could see the pilot lying on the ground. Jack Whitney was leaning over him. "What happened?" Jack asked.

"Hit by a round. His arm's pretty torn up."

The cold reality hit Jack, two aircraft, one pilot. *Son of a bitch.* "Can you bandage it enough for him to fly?"

"There's no way he can fly."

Jack wiped his face. "Any ideas?" he asked Whitney.

"I can take one aircraft and fly the German home. We could try for a pickup tomorrow or the next day at another location."

"If the Jerrys find a Mossie parked within 10 miles of Hitler's headquarters this place will be crawling with Krauts. Makes it tough on the ground team. If we get both aircraft out of here they have a chance."

Whitney looked at Jack and quietly asked, "Are you suggesting what I think you are?"

"You have any better ideas?" Jack replied.

"Jack, they'll either give you a medal or court martial you."

"As long as I'm there for them to do either one I'll be happy."

CHAPTER TWENTY
ONE

East Prussia
1905 Hours

Sitting in the left seat of the Mosquito felt strange to Jack, but he told himself there was no other choice. He was an experienced aviator. Over the last month he had logged almost fifty hours in the Mosquito. If he could get the aircraft airborne they had a good chance of getting home. He had to try.

Von Wolner was with Whitney, the flight lead. Stirls Hadley was sitting next to Jack with his hand tightly bandaged. Jack would be able to have Stirls talk him through the start and takeoff. The first big test was getting the port engine started.

Jack ran down the checklist items as Stirls discussed the steps. He selected the outer fuel tanks, set the throttle to ½ inch open, prop full forward, supercharger to 'mod', fuel pressure vent – on and radiator flaps open. Looking out of the cockpit he twirled his hand signaling Jimmy Hunt to begin priming the engine.

", here we go – ignition switches – on." Jack's heart was pounding. "I'm pushing the booster coil and starter buttons, NOW."

The engine fired, roughly for a moment with clouds of

exhaust coming from the ports. Slowly the engine RPMs rose to idle. Thank God. The next engine started easily. He could see Whitney had both engines running also. Jack started the take off checks, making sure elevator trim was correct, flaps were fully down and radios set. Stirls was making comments as Jack went through the checklist like a flight instructor would make to a student.

Jack heard the radio come alive. "Two, are you ready?"

He turned and looked at Stirls as he keyed the mic. "We're ready."

The aircraft were nearly aligned to the takeoff heading. Jack watched Whitney pull forward about ten feet and angle to the right twenty degrees. Jack advanced the throttle. As the bomber began to move he tapped the right brake and the nose came around aligning with Whitney's fuselage. He heard the lead run up his engines for takeoff. Holding the brakes hard, Jack checked the prop full forward and pushed the throttle full ahead. Stirls recited the correct temps and pressures as Jack looked across the instrument panel. Everything was in tolerance. Whitney's landing light came on illuminating the field ahead as he began his take off roll.

", Stirls, he we go."

"You're going to feel the tail come up at 60 knots. I'll call your rotate at 120."

The old instincts came back quickly. He kept the nose straight using the rudder and could feel the acceleration as the signal fires approached.

"110 – 115 – 120, rotate."

Jack felt the wheels break free and they began to climb.

Stirls yelled, "Wheels, up."

Reaching down he found the undercarriage select lever and flipped it to the 'up' position. They were climbing at 150 knots. He started looking for the lead.

"Get your landing light off," Stirls warned.

Shit, he'd forgotten. Accelerating past 170 knots he saw Whitney's navigation lights turning slightly left. They'd agreed to rendezvous at 200 knots. Once joined, the flight would accelerate to cruise speed. The rendezvous wasn't pretty. He overshot badly but was able to recover and position the aircraft off Whitney's starboard wingtip.

"Bloody hell, you did it. They'll never believe this."

"Had to get you home." Jack tried to sound nonchalant but his flight suit was soaking wet. He now had four hours of night flying ahead of him over water and through enemy airspace. "Stirls, when we get back the drinks are on me."

"You're on."

Flying through scattered cloud layers, the first hour was quiet. Whitney had kept his nav lights on low, which helped Jack maintain formation. It took trial and error but Jack was able to get the aircraft trimmed correctly. As they coasted out over the Baltic Jack's exhaustion began to catch up with him. Thank God, Jack thought, Stirls seemed to be holding up well despite his loss of blood.

Jack began moving his position from Whitney's right wing to left to keep alert and awake. The one bright spot was the fuel situation. With no external drag and light winds they were doing well. Biggin Hill was easily within range.

Sixty miles east northeast of Kiel the threat warning flashed a bright strobe telling them that they'd been illuminated by German radar.

The ground team gathered up their gear and put out the marker fires. It was urgent they move out of the area. They knew it was only a matter of time before the Germans would deploy troops to search for them. Stefan wanted move at least six or seven kilometers before sunrise to the large forested area south of Kilnlodz. Once there they'd be protected by a dense forest and lack of roads. There were many places a small group of people could hide for as long as needed. Taking the radios and all their weapons, the team fell in with the partisans for the march north.

Corporal Weiss, the only German survivor of the action, did not return to the main road. He was hiding in the woods, terrified there were enemy soldiers looking for him. The first indication to the Germans something was amiss was the failure of Commander Von Wolner to meet Admiral Doenitz at the Rastenburg airfield at 2100.

Bandsaw flight was at 2000 ft and cruising at 255 knots. The threat indicator flashed intermittently indicating night fighters in the area. The Mosquitoes were at the edge of the fixed Wurzburg radar systems protecting Kiel. At this altitude the ground controllers couldn't be providing much help to any night fighters. Perhaps the indication was a random signal from a patrolling fighter. In any case Jack wasn't going to take any chances.

"Stirls, back me up here. I'm going to arm the guns and adjust the gun sight." Jack systematically moved his hands down the armament panel selecting the both the machine guns and cannons, all of which were still fully loaded. He adjusted the rheostat on the gun sight so the reticles indicated the convergence point of the guns 1000 feet ahead of the Mosquito.

Watching Jack go through the steps, Stirls didn't say anything. The young pilot had been quiet for the last thirty minutes.

"Think I've got it right. Look good to you?"

"I think so, Jack." His voice was strained.

"Stay with me, Stirls. I'm gonna need your help to get this thing home."

"Do my best….."

Operations Center
RAF Biggin Hill
2100

Lieutenant Colonel Tommy Hudson had been in the Ops

Center for the entire mission. Although there wasn't much he could do it was the best place to monitor the overall air picture and what was developing. A short pre-arranged signal had been received by SOE communications at 1930 indicating Bandsaw had flight successfully departed. When he heard it he felt a great relief.

Tommy looked at the large plotting board. The large raid by Bomber Command on Berlin took off on schedule and was now over central Germany. He hoped the raid would draw the German night fighter strength toward Berlin and away from the Baltic. In addition there was a night fighter sweep being conducted over the North Sea which would further distract any German air assets. As an added safety measure MI-6 had been able to get Coastal Forces to deploy six motor torpedo boats from Felixstowe along the return flight path of the Bandsaw flight. Hudson felt they'd done everything they could. Now it was up to Jack.

"Two, this is lead, descending. Stay alert."

"Roger," Jack transmitted. Whitney must've also received the threat warnings. Descending to a lower altitude would make it more difficult for any night fighter to get a good radar signal on them. Checking the fuel again he was comfortable they'd be fine. He had to add power to stay with the lead and he figured Whitney had come to the same conclusion. The Mosquito's speed at full power allowed her to outrun every German fighter in the Luftwaffe. That speed advantage was even more pronounced against German night fighters which had extra antennas and more drag.

They leveled at 500 feet above the water and were indicating 300 knots. Jack could make out some of the coast line and several islands as they transited up the Fehmarn Strait between Denmark and Germany.

Turning his head Jack saw something off his left. He realized they were exhaust flashes from an aircraft engine – closing for a firing solution on Whitney.

Keying his mic in desperation Jack called, "Bandsaw lead, break right! Break right!"

Instantly Whitney's Mosquito rolled to the right and turned sharply as a stream of tracer fire arched across the sky.

Jack's instincts took over as he turned on the master armament switch and pulled hard left. He brought the Mosquito's nose toward the German fighter outlined in the moon light. As the reticles of his gun sight moved toward the bandit he squeezed the trigger and felt the firepower of the Mosquito unleashed. There was a brief reddish yellow flash as a portion of the wing fuel tank of the Me-110 exploded sending the aircraft spinning into the sea. Jack kept his turn in coming left looking for any more enemy aircraft. Whitney had reversed and was now behind Jack following him in the turn.

Involuntarily jerking his head Jack saw tracers floating past his cockpit and the dull thud as bullets impacted the aircraft. He remembered that sound from Midway.

"Jack, reverse, NOW." Whitney shouted over the radio.

Full right rudder, full right stick and re-applying the "G"s, Jack moved the bomber as violently as he could. Looking around he was completely disoriented and saw tracers off to his right and a bright explosion.

"Jack, come around to 265 degrees. I've got you in sight. I'll join."

Breathing hard he pulled the Mosquito around until the compass indicator bug was directly over 265. He continued to scan the sky but saw nothing. The threat indicator was silent. Checking over the instrument panel all systems looked all right. *I know we took some hits.* He checked the fuel tanks. They'd need every bit of petrol now.

Whitney reassumed the flight lead and now had the flight at full power for the dash across the Danish Peninsula. The illumination by the moon allowed Whitney to get a good navigation update as they crossed the coast and made a course correction.

For the first time Jack began to think about getting

home. He followed Whitney in the turn as they left the Danish Peninsula behind them. 245 degrees – England – home.

Fighting the urge to relax Jack keyed the mic. "Lead, how's your passenger?"

"Seems to be doing all right. Bit of a language problem you know."

Jack laughed.

"Colonel Hudson, we've received a report from Fighter Command operations. They've heard from Bandsaw. Flight of two, estimating Biggin Hill in forty minutes." The ops messenger read the telex message and handed it to Tommy.

Sitting down and lighting a cigarette Tommy allowed himself a moment to relax. He had his head back against the wall with his eyes closed when a WAAF communications supervisor called to him.

"Colonel, there's a Brigadier Greene on the phone."

I knew he'd be sniffing around pretty soon. Bet the PM is breathing down his neck. "Yes, sir. Hudson here," he said into the phone. "Yes, sir. I understand." He hung up the phone. "Bloody amazing," he said to no one in particular.

Hudson placed a phone call to the flight line. The MI-6 special security section was in place to move Von Wolner to a secure house in the countryside to begin his debrief. Special Inspector Sean O'Bannon, formerly of Scotland Yard, now with MI-6 was in charge of the detail. It took a moment for him to come to the phone.

"O'Bannon? Hudson here. Put our plan on hold. The aircraft should be here in about thirty minutes. Instead of departing immediately as we briefed, Brigadier Greene will be arriving with the Prime Minister to meet our passenger. Please arrange a secure area for a brief meeting. Full security. Use the RAF Security people to add another cordon around the building. I'm on my way down there now."

This was one of those times Jack was happy to be flying

formation. Let the lead make the decisions, do the navigation and talk on the radios. He was totally exhausted and told himself he had to focus to get this aircraft safely on deck. He felt good on the landing parameters, speeds and procedures. Biggin Hill was a familiar airfield and had a long runway.

He went over everything in his mind. It would be a straight in approach he told himself. Be sure to check brake pressure, radiator coolers open, slow to 180 and drop the gear, flaps down at 150, touch down at 110 and then keep it on the runway. I can do this, he thought.

"Bandsaw Two, lead. Do you want to go in first?"

"That's all right, lead. I'll follow you."

"Roger, Biggin Hill is on the nose at ten miles. Descending to 3000, switching Biggin Tower. Follow me."

Jack looked over at Stirls. Tough kid, he thought. The young pilot sat with his head back against the seat, his eyes closed. *, Stewart, checklist one more time.* He checked armament off and safe, prop full forward, fuel, about 30 minutes left. He heard Whitney check in with Biggin Hill Tower and heard the altimeter setting and duty runway – Zero Nine.

"Bandsaw Two, detach for a three sixty turn and follow me in. Good luck."

"Roger." Jack made a level turn for two minutes and rolled out heading east with the runway four miles ahead. ", Stirls, here we go. Biggin Hill Tower, Bandsaw Two at three miles for landing."

"Bandsaw Two, winds are light and variable. Cleared to land in order on runway zero nine."

"Bandsaw Two, roger." Jack ran down the checklist, most of which was already done. He checked his airspeed at 175 and lowered the undercarriage selector. There was immediately a loud warning horn and he could see there were no green lights indicating the wheels were down and locked. *Shit.* "Tower, this is two. I have a problem. My undercarriage won't come down."

"Roger Bandsaw Two, hold overhead the field at 2000.

Say your intentions."

"Stirls?" Jack asked.

"Try putting the selector back to neutral. You'll have to try pumping them down by hand."

Jack returned the selector to neutral and pushed the emergency selector down. Grabbing the hand pump he tried one cycle expecting to feel resistance as the pressure built up in the system. "The pump handle just flops back and forth. The system must've lost all the fluid. What now?"

"The only choice is to drop the flaps and land with the undercarriage up. The book says it's preferable to use a grass strip."

"Wonderful."

As Tommy Hudson arrived at the flight operations building he saw O'Bannon outside and a RAF ambulance waiting on the ramp. The ground crew was watching the first Mosquito taxi in from the runway.

"What's up?" he called as he walked up to the security officer.

"Apparently no one thought it important to tell us. The pilot radioed our passenger was wounded and needed immediate medical attention. Looks like any meeting with the PM is going to have to wait."

Hudson turned to see two jeeps and a large touring car pull into the flight line parking area.

"Christ." He walked over to the car as Noel Greene and the Prime Minister exited. Saluting smartly he said, "Good evening, sir. We have a bit of a problem."

Churchill preempted Greene, "What sort of a problem, Colonel?"

"Sir, we've just found out that Bishop is wounded. We don't know how bad except the pilot called for the medical team.

Thirty yards away the ambulance was rolling toward the Mosquito as its second engine wound down and stopped.

"Colonel, see if you can find out the straight story. We'll wait for you here," Churchill said.

In less than three minutes Hudson was striding back across the ramp with Jack Whitney beside him.

"Prime Minister, this is Squadron Leader Jack Whitney," Hudson said.

Shaking hands, Churchill got right to the point. "What can you tell us?"

"Sir, the German Commander took one glancing round off his back during his escape. He's lost some blood but should be fine. They're taking him to the base hospital."

"That's good, very good. Certainly would've been a bloody shame to make it this far and not survive. Well done."

"Sir, it's not over. Jack Stewart is flying the second Mossie with the wounded pilot in his right seat."

"What! Stewart's not qualified for flying duties," Greene blurted out.

"Sir, Flight Lieutenant Hadley was wounded on the ground in Prussia. The choice was to leave the aircraft and Hadley there or have Jack fly it out. He did a hell of a job. He even managed to shoot down a German night fighter."

"Bloody remarkable," Churchill said.

Whitney continued, "One more problem, sir. Jack's holding overhead. He can't get his undercarriage down. Must be battle damage. I need to get into ops and talk with him on the radio. I had to do one of these back in '42. Normally we'd land him in the grass but we don't have time to set up smudge pots. We'll use the lighted runway. As long as he can keep it on the runway he should be fine."

Churchill, his tone turning serious, looked up at the bomber that could be seen orbiting the field. "Good luck, my boy."

Ten minutes later, after a brief by Whitney, Jack had the Mosquito on a long final approach to the runway. Stirls agreed he'd call off altitudes for Jack as they descended to the runway.

Whitney had told Jack it was imperative to be just above the stall speed of 105 knots with the flaps full down at touchdown. As the aircraft settled onto the runway he should hold the nose up as long as possible and use the rudder to maintain directional control. Sounded simple – just keep it on the runway.

The light winds allowed Jack to line up on the runway well prior to touchdown with no drift. He rechecked prop pitch full forward and flaps fully down. With a half a mile to go airspeed was stable at 115 knots as Stirls called out 370 feet above the ground.

Jack checked his descent rate at 500 feet per minute. As he crossed the runway threshold he pulled the power to idle and held the nose up. The lights were going by on both sides as the props hit the runway, sparks and metal flying. Metal screamed the fuselage settled on the concrete. *Fly the airplane, Jack.* He added a little left rudder to counter the nose moving right. *All right. Come on. Stay with me, baby.* Jack could feel the aircraft slowing and finally felt all forward motion stop. Quickly he switched off the master fuel selector and magnetos. Reaching up he pulled the quick release lever on the canopy hatch. "Stirls, get the hell out of here!"

Already attacking the lap belt fastener Hadley flung the straps out of his way. "On my way."

Crouching forward and arching his back Stirls thrust his injured arm through the hatch and began to work his way through. Jack reached up grabbed him by the flying suit and pushed him up and out of the hatch. Jack pulled himself through the hatch. The smell of burned metal and petrol hit his nostrils as exited the cockpit. He slid off the side of the fuselage and ran after Stirls. Jack could see flashing lights and heard sirens.

Two trucks braked to a stop, their tires squealing. Firefighters ran forward spraying fire suppressant on the two twisted engines but there was no fire.

Several ground crewmen grabbed Jack and Stirls by each

arm and walked them to the ambulance parked behind the line of fire trucks. A medical orderly took charge of Stirls and eased him into the back of the vehicle.

"Nice job, Commander." The young officer sat with his back against the side of the ambulance and smiled at Jack.

Jack was unsteady as he climbed in and sat next to him. "Stirls, we're still going to find a bar but let's get a doctor to look at that arm."

"I think I'd rather get a drink first, if you don't mind."

During the ten minutes required to travel from the runway to the hospital's emergency entrance Jack closed his eyes and tried to relax. He was exhausted but there was enough adrenaline in his system to keep him going. Moving slowly out of the ambulance he could tell his back had stiffened up since jumping from the wrecked Mosquito. He saw Tommy Hudson standing by the side door and walked over to him.

Hudson smiled. "It seems you've had a bit of an eventful night." The two friends shook hands.

"Tommy, I'm getting too old for this stuff."

"Keep a smile on for now, we have visitors. They're in saying hello to our German friend. I'm sure they'll want to see you next."

Jack followed Hudson into the brightly lit corridor. He noticed Military Police and MI-6 security personnel. They walked down to the second door and went inside.

Von Wolner was sitting on the treatment table. His shirt had been removed and bandages were wrapped around his chest and shoulder.

While the doctors worked on him he talked with Churchill and Greene. One of the security guards had been pressed into service as an interpreter.

"......we'll work that out. The important thing right now is to get your wound healed. Here's Commander Stewart." Churchill waited a moment while it was translated to Erich who turned his head and smiled at Jack.

Jack stepped up and said in German, "Commander, it is a pleasure to meet you again in more peaceful surroundings." They shook hands exchanging understanding glances. Stewart nodded to Churchill. "Prime Minister."

Von Wolner replied, "It's hard to believe I am actually in England."

"If I can do anything to help, I'm at your service."

"Perhaps we can have a drink sometime and talk?"

"I'll look forward to that." Jack immediately liked the man. He thought he might get to know him better before this war's over.

A few minutes later Churchill, Greene, Hudson and Jack walked out to the large car. As always Churchill took the lead. "Gentlemen, I look forward to a full debrief as soon as it's convenient. We certainly pulled one off on Herr Hitler." He stopped before getting into the car, turned and looked at Jack. "Once more into the breech, Commander?"

Jack smiled and said, "Yes, sir."

"Call Wylie and make an appointment. I want to talk with you later this week."

"Aye aye, sir."

It took two more weeks to finally bring Operation Meteor to a conclusion. The combination of bad weather and the constant movement by the partisans resulted in two separate recovery missions. Hunt and Livesy came out on the first mission with Terry and Jerzy following three days later. Three weeks after he returned from Meteor Jerzy parachuted back into the area as the first MI-6 agent in what was to become Soviet occupied Poland.

CHAPTER TWENTY TWO

10 Downing Street
London
15 May, 1944

Preparations for the cross channel invasion were in high gear across England. The hectic pace delayed Jack's appointment with the Prime Minister. Section F was totally involved in the recovery of the ground team and final debrief of the mission. Churchill's office finally called and set the appointment.

Jack looked forward to the meeting. He realized how much he admired Churchill and how lucky he was to be able to know him personally.

Keith Wylie greeted him when he arrived at Downing Street congratulating Jack on his victory over the German night fighter. Jack hadn't mentioned to anyone else the significance of that event but Wylie mentioned it straight away.

"Interesting way to become an ace. Congratulations."

"Keith, I didn't think about it until the next day. Those kills in the Pacific seem so long ago, as if it was another life."

"Jack, four plus one equals five no matter where or when you shoot them down."

"The last time I tried to shoot down an aircraft and become an ace I lost my wingman. This time it didn't seem very important."

"I didn't know."

"I've never told anyone. But it's been something I've carried with me for a long time."

"Jack, this time you did what you had to do."

"Thanks, Keith." He paused for a moment. "Any idea what the PM wants to see me about?"

"My lips are sealed," he said. "Let's go see if he's ready for you."

The Prime Minister was sitting at his desk when Jack was ushered in by Keith. Getting up he came up to Jack offering his hand. "Your aviator friend pointed out your victory over the night fighter officially makes you an ace. Well done, Commander."

"Sir, there was a time when I thought achieving that distinction was the most important thing in my life." He felt a need to share that with the man who had taken an interest in his life.

"Do I detect a change in your appraisal of what's important in life?"

"A smart man once told me that this war would change many lives. I guess it didn't occur to me it might change mine also."

"But it has, Jack. And if I'm any judge it's changed your life significantly."

"Prime Minister it seems whenever I've come to this island I'm surprised. It happened back in 1936 and again in 1942." Jack had never said that to anyone.

The PM smiled his world famous grin. "And on both occasions there was a young lady involved."

"Yes, sir, the same young lady. But it's more than that. Not only have I fallen in love with a woman, but with a country as well. That sounds corny but it's true. I feel part of something special. I'm proud of the uniform and proud of my service. And that has become a problem."

Churchill's demeanor changed and he sighed. "I know, Jack. They want you back."

"Sir, I'm not ready to go back. In fact, I'm not sure I'd go back given the option of staying here permanently."

"Jack, I like to think of myself as a soldier and public servant. But I'm probably more aptly described as a politician. I don't know if you're aware but the original arrangement which brought you here was driven by my need to repay Franklin Roosevelt for several important favors. It's interesting the tables have turned as they tend to do in any political situation. I now have several marks on my side of the ledger book." He paused for a moment and walked over to pour two glasses of scotch, handing one to Jack. "I told you once when this war is over Britain will need intelligence operators to take on the communist threat. I think you'd be of great service to this country. You would be of great service to the United States also but there's no guarantee that's where you would end up."

Jack took a drink. He wasn't sure where this was going but he could sense this was going to be something significant.

"We are totally and completely committed to never being caught unprepared again. We'll do whatever may be necessary. That includes the remake of MI-6 into a new organization, one which can deal with a new world. Jack, I want you to be part of that. I'm ready to approach the President with a personal request that you remain with the Royal Navy and in service to the crown...permanently."

The thoughts of the last eighteen months raced through Jack's mind. It would be smart to ask for time to think about Churchill's proposal. But he knew it was what he wanted, totally and without reservation. "Prime Minister, I'm honored by your support and offer. I desire in strongest way possible to remain an officer in the Royal Navy and with MI-6."

As he raised his glass to toast, Winston Churchill eyes showed a fire Jack would always remember. "Jack, you honor us with your service."

Two nights later Jack was able to slip up to Oxford to see

Pam. She'd been spending more time at the house using the quiet of the college town to continue her recovery. It struck Jack as he sat on the train watching the countryside slip by that he was home. He felt more a part of this country and its people than he ever did on the other side of the Atlantic. He still felt a sense of loyalty and duty to the United States but he felt that here he could make a difference. This country, beaten up in a long war, her economy in tatters, her casualty lists growing by the day – she needed him. This war was only going to get nastier before it was over. The challenge to preserve a country and a way of life would be daunting. Perhaps this is payback to the mother country. Those Stewarts who left these shores so many years ago could never have imagined one of their own returning as a king's officer.

Pam rushed into his arms when he walked into the house on West Bridge Street. He reveled in being with her. It made him feel whole for the first time in his life. She was almost fully recovered from the accident. The only outward sign now was an occasional stutter but those instances were fewer and fewer.

He opened a bottle of wine and they went into the living room.

Jack stared at the fire and said casually, "I had an interesting meeting the day before yesterday."

She moved closer on the couch, putting her hand on his. "Tell me."

"The Prime Minister wanted to see me. I thought it would be about the last little event, but it was about me."

"You? Exactly what does that mean?"

"He offered me a job...permanently."

"What does 'permanently' mean?" Now she was sitting up.

"A permanent commission in the Navy, a career in MI-6, trade the blue passport for a red one." Jack drained the last of his wine and set the glass on the table.

"You're kidding me, aren't you?" She paused for a moment. "You're not kidding are you?"

"God's honest truth, my dear. I believe it's like being adopted by England. And I told him yes."

Pam sat there looking at him. She didn't say anything but took his hand and laid her head on his shoulder.

"I decided I didn't want to leave this quaint little island. I didn't want to leave you either." He turned his head and kissed her forehead.

EPILOGUE

Answsworth Prison
South London
February 4, 1946

The interior courtyard was dominated by wooden scaffolding. The imposing platform had been the execution site of seven men convicted of espionage or treason over the course of the war. Today's execution was different. The procedure was being conducted by a detachment from the military justice tribunal set up following the Allied victory. As German forces capitulated, the search to identify and apprehend war criminals had moved into high gear. The apparatus for trying those individuals was now in place around Europe. Nuremburg was the location of the trials of the most famous Germans. But there were many regional courts set up to deal with the lesser know war criminals. This execution came from the verdict of the regional tribunal.

There were only a handful of observers: two members of the press, an administrator from the tribunal, several staff members from the Embassy of Belgium and Jack Stewart.

Precisely at 0855 a door opened on the far side of the gallows. Two red-hatted MPs were on either side of the condemned man. His arms were strapped to his sides with a wide leather belt which had individual straps for each arm. He was wearing a drab grey prison shirt and pants with plain brown shoes. The man looked tired and scared as they walked him to the long set of steps leading up to the scaffold. Behind the man came a priest and a prison official. At the foot of the stairs the priest leaned over to say something to the man, who nodded. The two MPs led him up the steps and the official followed.

The hangman's noose was visible. The coil of rope had been tied with light string to keep it from getting in the way of the final preparations. Standing at the rear of the scaffold was the executioner. He was a large, rough looking man who stared ahead impassively. The MPs moved the condemned over the trap door and quickly bent down to strap his legs together. They then moved to each side of the trap door.

The official removed a sheet of paper from his inner coat pocket and began to read. "Gunther Schmidt, having been found guilty of crimes against humanity by the Provisional Allied Military Tribunal and sentenced to death, I have here the death warrant signed by the senior member of the tribunal directing execution of the sentence at 0900, February 4th, 1946. Do you have anything to say?" The official then read the same passage in stilted but passable German. When finished he looked at Schmidt.

The man appeared not to hear, but instead focused on the tall naval Officer standing below the scaffold. A moment of recognition jolted him out of his trance like state and he spat out in German, "It's you."

The hangman walked up behind Schmidt placing a white hood over his head. He grabbed the noose, breaking the twine and positioned it around Schmidt's neck with the large knot under his left chin. Stepping back he removed the safety pin for the trap door. The executioner looked at the official, who nodded. The large man reached over and pulled the release lever.

Twenty minutes later, after retrieving his Walther PPK, which he always carried now, Jack shoved his hands into the heavy naval overcoat. The wind was cold coming off the dark gray river. He reflected on the events of the last four years. This was one more chapter closed for him. The security man, who doubled as his driver, was standing by the sedan and opened the door for him. As he got in Jack said, "Let's head back to Baker Street."

Historical fiction adventure novels by John Schork that
are available online from Amazon.com

DESTINY IN THE PACIFIC

Set in the first desperate year of the Pacific War, "Destiny in
the Pacific" tells the story of Brian Michaels, a disgraced Naval
Aviator. A promising career in shambles, his time in the Navy
drawing to a close, Bryan is given a second chance following the
attack on Pearl harbor. Just as that day changed the course of
a nation, it did the same for Bryan. Fueled by anger at the loss
of friends and inspired by words of Chester Nimitz, Bryan finds
his destiny in the vast Pacific.

THE FLAMES OF DELIVERANCE

Terribly burned in the air war over Europe, the wealthy son of a
New York banker discovers love, friendship and redemption as
he painfully struggles to recover. Eventually returning to the
air battle in Europe and the Pacific, Hank Mitchell finds the
strength to overcome his scars and the conviction to do what
must be done regardless of the personal cost.

A JOURNEY OF HONOR

A strange series of events results in two men from opposite sides of the war being thrown together. One is a Commander in the Royal Navy, the other a Colonel in the German SS. But they join forces in an attempt to cripple Adolph Hitler's ability to launch a weapon that could change the course of the war. Parachuting into war-torn Europe, the two men not only prevent a devastating attack on England, but realize they have become friends and comrades.

THE FALKENBERG RIDDLE

As the most terrible war in history approaches its bloody conclusion, the allies and Soviet Union are already preparing for the next. But there are secrets within the collapsing capital of the Third Reich that must never become public. A senior German at the highest level possesses knowledge which could devastate the world. Jack Stewart leads his strike team deep into the cataclysmic final battle of Berlin to ensure that information never becomes public.

THE WINDS OF BATTLE
The Journey of James Addington

Sent to sea as a young midshipman, James Addington, is the son of a British Admiral following in his father's footsteps. Born in the colonies, he sails from New York City in 1770 aboard H.M.S. Andromeda. Over the next three years, battling pirates and slavers, the young man matures into a loyal officer of the Royal Navy. But the terrible events of 1776 drag James back to the land of his birth. As a lieutenant in the frigate Challenger, he is a witness to the bloody Battle of Breed's Hill, as the fledging rebel army takes on the pride of the British Army. Stunned by what he sees, he knows the colonies will be forever changed. What he doesn't realize is that he will change along with them.

Falling in love with a young lady from Massachusetts, Addington finds himself immersed in a tangled web of conflicting loyalties and passions. Does he help crush the rebellion or does he fall victim to the lure of independence? His journey takes him from north to south in the colonies and across the Atlantic as captain of his own ship. From the Battles of Saratoga to Yorktown, he learns the price of friendship and loyalty as the fight for America's independence builds to a thundering climax.

Printed in Great Britain
by Amazon

21032731R00212